The Boredom with Death

John Belica

www.belicanovels.com
ISBN: 9929778349
ISBN-13: 9789929778344

TABLE OF CONTENTS

TABLE OF CONTENTS

BOOK ONE

CHAPTER 1

"You think... she saw something? Like a bear or a wolf?"

Dan drove his father's sedan at an even steady pace up the soft winding mountainous road while his girlfriend in the passenger seat and his two best friends sitting in the back lazily gazed out their windows at the passing landscape.

The last major town had passed by about an hour back, leaving only quaint stores and forestry service stations to pepper the roadside.

With the jubilant chatter from the young adults inside the vehicle having petered out some time ago, Dan reflected about his future as he drove them all to his uncle's property. Undoubtedly, when he had been assigned to the Navy after being drafted, luck had been on his side, and he knew it. From what he had seen on TV, Vietnam looked like a pretty scary place, two of his brother's friends had already been killed over there and a third had been listed as missing. However, he couldn't shake a particular feeling of disappointment about not going into the Army, after all his father had fought in both Europe during the Second World War and then in Korea.

He let out another sigh as he took another long upward curve as he continued to ponder what lay ahead of his future.

Kim, his girlfriend, opened her eyes and turned her head to look at him.

Dan turned his head, gave her a small crooked smile, and asked, "Done sleeping?"

She shifted her weight in the seat and replied, "Yeah. And you?"

Her humor catching him off guard, Dan let out a quick laugh and commented, "That's funny."

She smiled at him and asked, "How much more?"

"It shouldn't be too long now. Once we pass the Two Pines camping grounds... we'll be basically there," he told her as he took another curve.

"Oh good... cus I'm starting to get hungry," she said while looking back at their two friends asleep in the back. The girl, Juliet, behind the driver's seat had let her head flop onto her boyfriend's shoulder.

The road continued onward and upward.

After some time, Dan felt a click in his throat as he approached the road sign he had been waiting to see. He read it out loud to Kim as she stared at it as well, "State of California Forestry Service...Two Pines Camp Grounds."

She stretched her arms towards the windshield, wiggled her fingers and said, "Almost there."

"Yup, just eight more miles and we turn off," Dan said with renewed eagerness.

Kim began to fumble for her shoes with her bare

feet.

"Help me with the road. There's a red bicycle reflector nailed to the tree where the dirt road starts. Help me look for it," he asked for her assistance.

Slipping the final shoe onto her foot, she said she would and then sat upright.

They drove in silence for the next few miles, the vacant property amongst the tall trees.

Ten minutes later, they saw the red reflector.

Dan slowed the car to a crawl then turned off the highway. The private road itself was nothing more than a five foot wide beaten path.

Feeling the crunch of bare ground underneath the car's tires, he plunged his father's old salesman car into the foliage and came to a stop fifty feet from the highway in front of a chain link fence with a large rusty padlock.

The change of driving momentum stirred the sleeping couple awake in the back seat. Julie lifted her head off her boyfriend's shoulder with a painful wince and Tommy asked in a thick sleepy voice if they had finally arrived.

Dan answered that they had and that he just need to open the gate, then asked Kim to fish out the padlock key from out of the glove box.

She opened the small compartment between her knees and began to rummage around through the assortment of articles inside it.

Dan opened his door, stepped out, stretched, then walked to the back of the car and opened the trunk. Inside, he found the can of all-purpose lubricant which had been brought along specifically for the rusty lock.

He shut the trunk, walked to Kim's side of the car, and asked, "Did you find it."

"I think so," she answered then asked as she held up a key ring with two rings, "Is it one of these?"

Smiling, he took the keys from her hand and said, "Yup. Now just give me a second and I'll open the gate."

With silent anticipation, Tommy, Julie, and Kim watched Dan spray the lock with the multi-purpose lubricate then work one of the keys against the tumblers until the lock sprang open.

Turning towards his friends with a triumphant smile, Dan held the opened lock in his hand.

In unison the three teenagers inside the battered sedan cheered.

After swinging the gate open, Dan quickly jogged back to the car, jumped in, and drove the four of them deep into the Northern California forest.

With excitement once again restored within the car, all four teenagers gasped and cheered as the vehicle made its way over the moist uneven dirt path.

They crept further and further into the dense rich forest until finally reaching the destination; a huge clearing which measured about fifty square yards.

Dan halted the car just in front of the wide open circular span, clearly marked by pine trees around its border, and shut the engine off.

The four young adults quietly stared at their new home for the next three days until Tommy, sitting behind Kim, said, "Ok. I'm ready to get out... and see what we got."

Agreeing with his best friend, Dan stepped out first and gave himself another big stretch as he took in a lungful of crisp moist mountain air.

"Hey... what about us?" Julie asked with a playful whine in her voice from the back seat.

Dan turned, exhaled, and flipped the lever on his seat.

Both Julie and Tommy literally tumbled out in their excitement.

Laughing at her friends antics, Kim opened her door and got out.

With loud groans and moans, Tommy, Juliet, and Kim stretched away the long drive as they continued to take in their new surroundings.

The cool fresh air swept around them as if greeting them to the quiet and beautiful mountain landscape.

After a few minutes, Tommy said, "We'd better get that trench done first... since it's the hardest part."

Dan gave a nod and made his way to the trunk once again, "Ok. Help me with the stuff, Tommy."

With a nod himself, Tommy went to help out his childhood friend.

Inside the ample trunk of the car were tents, poles, a portable stove, two lanterns, food, water, sodas, backpacks, toiletries, and finally a shovel next to a large bag of kitty litter.

Dan took the bag of lavender scented litter and Tommy the shovel while Julie stepped from behind them and carried away the stove.

Kim, on the other hand, continued to stare at the wall of pines trees directly in front of her. Their rich vibrant green color seemed to almost drip a multitude of different shades of green.

She slowly closed her eyes and let the tranquil sound flow into her ears.

The whole area was alive with a rustling sort of sound, almost like a whisper that seemed to come from everywhere and nowhere all at the same time.

Quietly listening, she realized it was the music of

nature all around her.

Kim opened her eyes and gave a small chuckle as she thought to herself that she was turning into one of those dirty barefoot hippies that slept in the park by her old high school.

From behind her, Kim could hear her friends going about in an almost business-like manner as they turned the vacant property into a livable environment.

She turned and saw Dan and Tommy looking around for the best place to dig the trench they would all use as a toilet while Julie extended the stove's skinny metal legs.

She rocked on her heels as she decided what she could do to help when the need to pee suddenly took her over.

Kim looked at the woods all around, saw a crease among the wall of trees, and walked to it.

Tommy was the first to see her walking away from them and called out, "Where ya going?"

With a big wave and a smile, she answered out loud, "I gotta go!"

"We haven't started the trench! Is it number one or number two?" Dan asked her from afar.

Five feet from the line of trees, Kim cupped her mouth, and shouted, "Number one! I'll be right back!" then stepped into the wall of trees and instantly disappeared from sight.

The contrast of environment was drastically instantaneous. Where the open space of grass held the noise of life, the forest of pines trees was as quiet as anything that Kim had ever experienced.

Unnerved by the deafening silence, she nervously ran her left hand through the length of her blonde hair as the sudden need to urinate intensified.

Kim cast her eyes over her shoulder and saw that the pine trees behind her had interwoven into a wall of bark and green behind her.

With the need to urgently empty her bladder, she made her way further in the lonesome forest.

Sun rays streamed through the tree growth with an angelic quality.

Half a dozen yards from the clearing, she stopped, placed a hand on a pine trunk, and closed her eyes as a feeling of euphoria suddenly swept over her.

Slowly she opened her eyes, looked up at the sky, and marveled at the golden streams of light.

A bird sang out in the distance, lonesome and majestic, while pine needles began to rustle with a voice all their own.

She closed her eyes once again and let herself become lost in the beauty all around her.

Suddenly the smell of freshly cut mint reached her nose.

She opened her eyes and saw a woman, completely nude, standing just behind a nearby tree.

Startled by the sudden appearance of someone else in the forest growth, Kim gasped and placed her hands over her budding chest.

Motionless where she stood, the naked woman neither hid nor stepped out completely from behind the tree.

Kim's eyes slowly traveled over the unknown woman's half exposed nude body. Long and lean with pale skin and a mass of fiery auburn hair that framed her oval face in delicate tangles, the woman was beautiful.

Together for a time, they stared at each other in total silence until Kim, unknowingly, began to walk towards her.

The woman, silent and unmoving, watched the teenager approached her.

Walking to her, Kim took notice of the woman's hair. It moved as if with a life of its own, softly floating effortlessly around the staring woman's beautiful face.

Without a word, the woman suddenly came from behind the tree and stepped forward, closing the remaining distance between them.

They came to a stop only mere inches from each other.

Standing directly in front of her, Kim looked directly into the woman's eyes and noticed that the irises were as green as emeralds from a ring.

Still completely silent, the woman leaned forward the slightest of bits and, to Kim's utter shock and surprise, the green emerald colored irises began to slowly swirl around the black pupils.

Kim smiled sheepishly as she stared deep into the swirling mass of vivid green.

Motionless ,the woman exhaled her warm breath across the young girl's face and the smell of freshly cut mint drifted to Kim's nose, making her nostrils flare hungrily for the sweet pungent scent.

Then, in the distance, Kim heard her name being called out, and, like a circuit being broken, the woman blinked her eyes and her irises stopped spinning.

As if abruptly awaken from a deep sleep, Kim shook her head and blinked her eyes in rapid succession.

Again her name was called out.

Without turning around, the naked woman stepped back behind the pine tree and disappeared from sight.

Kim clamped her eyes shut and slumped against the tree trunk as a feeling of nausea overtook her.

Hot acidic foam rose up in the back of her mouth.

Putting a hand to her mouth and fighting back the urge to puke, she heard her name again and realized it was Dan, his voiced laced with concern.

With her hand still over her mouth, she opened her eyes and craned her neck to see what had become of the beautiful naked woman but found only the endless forest staring back at her instead.

The woman was gone.

With her boyfriend's hurried footsteps rapidly approaching, Kim composed herself as best she could.

Finally reaching her, Dan came to a stop behind her and asked, "Kim... are you alright?"

She took a moment to answer, "Yeah. I'm... ok."

"You sure... cus you were gone a long time," Dan told her as he reached out to touch her shoulder.

Kim pondered what had just happened to her. The whole encounter with the silent staring woman had been so surreal.

Dan gently touched her right shoulder, softly turned her around, and asked her again, "You ok?"

With the smell of freshly cut mint coating the inside of her nose, Kim nodded her head in response as an image of the swirling green irises fluttered about in her mind.

Dan was about to add something further but stopped when he lowered his eyes.

She looked at his face drain itself of color.

Releasing her shoulder, Dan took three steps back and exclaimed, "Kim... my God... are you sure... you're ok?"

Hearing the concern in his voice, she followed his

line of sight and saw, to her shock, that she had wet herself.

That night, at the clearing, the two young couples sat in silence around the camp fire. Kim's state of mind after being led out of the woods by Dan had cast a dark shadow on the trip.

Sitting quietly on a sleeping bag in front of the fire, Kim refused to talk about what had occurred in the forest earlier in the day.

Later as they prepared to turn in for the night and while Tommy assembled the bear proof food container, Dan spoke to Julie, away from the fire, about Kim, "So... she didn't tell you anything when you were changing her?"

"No. She just lied in the tent and let me undress her," Julie answered.

"Weird," Dan commented out loud.

"You think... she saw something? Like a bear or a wolf?" Julie asked.

"Yeah, probably," he replied then added, "But the thing is that she didn't look scared... just confused."

With a distant stare, Julie shook her head slowly while trying to make sense to her friend's sudden change in behavior, "Well... whatever happened to her it really freaked her out... I think... we should leave and get her home."

"Yeah. I'd like to leave tonight... but I don't want to take on that road in the dark in my dad's old salesman car."

Turning to look at the car, Julie agreed, "Yeah," then said, "Let´s leave in the morning."

Dan nodded his head as he looked at Kim sitting all alone, sedately staring at the snapping camp fire.

Walking past him towards the tents, Julie told him,

"Let's go to bed and get this day over with."

With a nod of agreement, Dan went to Kim, kneeled down next to her and asked, "Wanna go to sleep?"

She looked at him and answered in a gentle voice, "Ok, sure."

He smiled and helped her up.

Together, with the sleeping bag in hand, they walked to their tent and stepped in, leaving the camp fire to die at its own speed.

Inside, Dan took off his shoes and stripped off his jeans while Kim set the sleeping bag on the flooring of the tent and laid down on top of it with her back to him.

Dan watched her a few minutes then took the sandals Julie had put on her feet. Her own shoes still wet with urine.

Feeling concerned and a bit confused, he gently rubbed her bare feet and asked, "Kim...are you...gonna be...alright?

Without turning to face him, she answered in a low voice, "Yeah. I just want to go to sleep."

He let go of her feet, laid down beside her, and spoke to her for the last time ever, "Ok. Good night."

She uttered no reply.

Later, as the evening sky gave way to the grey light of morning, Kim quietly undid the zipper of the tent as Dan, her boyfriend since Junior High, continued to sleep silently.

She stepped out, felt the dew covered grass on the soles of her bare feet, closed her eyes, and took in the pleasant sensation of the early morning air deep into her lungs.

A moment later, she opened her eyes, faced the

section of woods where she had entered the previous day and went towards.

Convinced that the naked woman had been a fairy like the ones she had read about as a little girl, Kim walked on wet grass stained feet towards the dense line of trees with an intense desire to see her once again.

Five feet from the perimeter of the camp ground, Kim stopped and stared at the wall of foliage in front of her, wondering just how she was going to find her among the vast span of forest growth.

Suddenly, to her amazement, the woman appeared at the tree line, naked, motionless, and silent.

Kim ran her eyes over the woman's flawless nude body and smiled.

Without any words being said between them, the woman stepped backwards into the darkness of the forest and Kim followed her in.

As if with an inner compass, the silent naked woman walked perfectly backwards, around trees and outcropping, her dirt stained bare feet were sure and direct across the uneven damp ground as Kim kept pace.

Deeper and deeper she plunged them into the vast cold woodlands.

Without comment or question, Kim followed the woman as she took in the nude woman's stunning features; the lush lips, the green eyes, and the rich auburn hair that seemed to swim with a life of its own around the flawless oval face.

With each step leading further and further away from the campground the more Kim closed the distance between them.

Then, after long last, the woman finally stopped and Kim came to a halt less than a foot from her.

Breathing heavily at the excitement of being in front of her again, Kim stood silently in front of her, eager to see what came next.

Only inches apart and staring at each other intently, the woman slightly leaned in and the emerald green of her irises began to swirl once again.

At the sight of the green swirling irises, Kim's jaw slacked and her eyes opened wide into perfect circles.

With a long slow exhale, the woman basted the teenager's face with the smell of mint from her breath.

Drool spilled over Kim's lower lip as her mouth watered at the smell.

Transfixed on the rolling green color and encased in the warm sweet scent from the woman's mouth, Kim felt a state of sexual arousal awaken within her unlike anything she'd ever felt before. Her nipples painfully hardened under her t-shirt and a hot slick moisture formed between her legs.

Without uttering a word or breaking eye contact, the woman gingerly placed her hand on Kim's shoulder and gently directed her to the soft damp earth.

Doing as she was told by the soft gesture, Kim laid down on the ground.

The woman stepped forward and straddled her.

Her calm beautiful face, framed by living moving hair, looked down at the staring young woman beneath her.

Kim inhaled and exhaled deep heavy lustful breaths as she stared deeper and deeper into the swirling green eyes.

The woman's irises swirled faster and faster and the smell of mint intensified from her open mouth.

Panting with sexual abandonment, Kim extended a beckoning hand and whispered her very last word,

"Come."

A lovely serene look spread across the woman's face as she took Kim's hand and softly lowered herself on top of her.

Dan and her friends would report Kim missing hours later.

Black and ballooned with decay, Kim's mangled and torn body would be located a week later during an exhaustive search.

CHAPTER 2

"Dinnertime, Mr. Poole."

With blood from the tremendous gash on his forehead stinging his left eye shut, John Poole stumbled out of the cabin he had just rented and ran to the pickup truck parked just a few yards from the front porch.

Freezing air wrapped itself around him with a strangle hold as he sprinted across the snow.

When he reached the pickup, he ripped open the driver's side door, dove in, hauled the door shut, and slammed the key into the ignition.

As blood continued to ooze, hot and thick, into his eye, he cranked the key entirely forward and then slammed his right foot down on the gas pedal.

The large V10 engine of the rented pickup truck roared into life.

Squaring himself into the driver's seat, John looked into the rearview mirror with a panicked glance as he dropped the vehicle into gear and hit the gas.

The pickup launched itself forward, kicking and skidding across the snow covered dirt road.

John yelled out in protest as he watched in horror as his cellular phone flew off the dashboard and landed somewhere in the back from whiplashing acceleration.

With his only available means of communication out of reach and with no time to search for it, John knew that driving away as quickly as possible was now his only way of saving his life.

Grabbing onto the steering wheel with stern force, he brought the slipping skidding pickup under control seconds before it tore itself off the road.

With blood still pouring into his left eye, he looked in the rearview mirror and silently preyed to see nothing in its reflection.

Suddenly, the top heavy speeding pickup truck began to dangerously fishtail on the desolate snow packed road once again.

John snapped his eyes away from the rearview mirror and back on the road just as the tires lost their traction and the pickup jerked to the left towards the embankment of the road.

He looked at the speedometer and realized he had gunned the vehicle into doing close to sixty miles per hour on a snow covered country road not built for anything over twenty-five.

Somewhere in the dark recesses of his mind reserved only for the most basic instincts of survival, he realized that he needed to slow down and regain control of the truck before he died in a snow infested death roll.

Gripping the steering wheel hard enough to pop the knuckle on his right ring finger out of place, he stomped on the brake and cranked the steering wheel to the left.

Suddenly caught between its own forward

momentum and the feverish demands from its driver, the pickup truck spun one hundred and eighty degrees in a wave of snow and frozen dirt.

Trapped inside the out of control vehicle without his seatbelt, John closed his only one good eye and braced himself for whatever was to come in the next few seconds.

Miraculously, just as all looked lost, the traction of the tires caught hold of the icy dirt road and the rented pickup truck came to a halt facing the same direction it had been going.

Slowly John opened his one good eye and saw that he was still on the road and still alive.

He slumped back against the driver's seat and said out loud, "Still alive."

Then, like a diamond bullet to the forehead a cold numbing realization struck him; the engine had quit and he was no longer moving.

Springing into action, John worked the key in the ignition as he stomped on the gas pedal in order to restart the pickup.

The engine winced once and quit.

A cold wave of panic washed over him.

He tried again as he pleaded to anyone or anything that was willing to listen.

On the fourth attempt, the engine roared into life, rich and robust.

John screamed in triumph.

Suddenly the hood of the truck buckled with a crunching boom.

John jumped in his seat, startled by the deafening sound, then looked out the windshield and saw the creature that had just attacked him in the cabin hunkered on the damaged hood.

With an innocent look of an expressionless animal, the feline looking creature with white fur and pointy ears calmly looked at him through the windshield with its dazzling emerald green eyes as it slowly curled its long clawed fingers around both windshield wipers

John stomped his foot down on the accelerator and the large pickup exploded with blinding speed once again down the winter country road.

Feeling the thrust of speed, the creature held onto the wipers with a tighter and bared the shark-like white teeth in its wide gaping mouth that extended from ear to ear.

With his view of the road obstructed by the nightmarish thing on the hood, John did his best to steer as the vehicle bounced and rattled over the uneven snow covered road with dangerously increasing speed.

Looking at the creature's diabolical face staring back at him, John suddenly remembered the center glove compartment and what it held inside.

Holding the steering wheel firm with his left hand, he reached into the compartment with his right.

Suddenly sensing danger, the creature let go of the left wiper blade and drove its fist into the windshield.

The tempered glass spider webbed under the impact.

Startled by the sound of shattering glass, John put both hands instinctively back on the steering wheel, leaving what he had attempted to get inside the compartment.

The white clad green eyed monster reared its left fist back again, the muscles under its fur coiled as it mustered up the power to plow through the glass.

Knowing that the next punch would go through the

windshield, John stomped down hard on the brake pedal with both feet.

The front end of the pickup truck plunged downward with tremendous force into the snow and frozen dirt road, tearing apart the front bumper and grill.

John, wearing no seatbelt, was thrown over the steering wheel.

His face hit the spider webbed glass and the gash on his forehead split completely open down to the skull as his right leg broke at the femur under the steering column.

The pickup dropped back down onto all four tires and came to a complete stop.

With his vision blackening at the edges and with only one good eye, John watched the hideous creature, wiper blade still clutched in its right clawed hand, soar into the distance and land on the snow hardened ground in twisted mess yards away.

Fighting back unconsciousness, John straightened himself in the driver's seat and stomped down on the accelerator with his broken leg.

Incredibly, after all it had just endured, the rental lurched forward.

Shivering in agonizing pain, John drove towards the connecting highway and the late afternoon sun...

Filtered through the tinted tempered glass of the office building and splashed across his face, warming his skin with its waning radiance.

Standing in front of the window of his small office, John ran his hand over the scar above his eyebrow. Even two years after it had happen, the memories of that day were still as vivid as ever.

As the Hollywood hills slowly swallowed the sun, he quietly shared the last of the afternoon warm light with no one else but himself until it sank away completely and the navy blue colored evening took over.

With the interior lights of the office building now brighter than the outside, John looked at his reflection in the window. With his brown hair cut short in a Front Brush style and his oval face clean shaven, his features suggested a younger person than he actually was. The best part of his appearance, he always thought, was his eyes; flaked with specks of amber, their light hazel brown color nicely rounded out the rest of his face. While his worst feature, which no one admitted, was now the scar that ran from the top of his left eyebrow to his hairline, a sharp reminder of that harrowing day in the snow.

.   .   .

He had just finished bringing in the last two plastic bags of groceries into the cabin, which he had rented for his vacation, when the bay window of the dining room had suddenly exploded in a shower of dazzling shards of glass, sending a large piece straight to his head and slicing open skin and muscle down to the skull.

Dropping both bags and putting his hands to his injured forehead, he had stared in horror and disbelief as the nightmarish creature with the fierce green eyes and gaping mouth had slowly risen from behind the dining room table after vaulting through the window.

.   .   .

John forced the horrible memory from his mind, turned away from the window, and went to his desk and the pile of work that was waiting for him.

With just two weeks into the tax season, the firm was alive with noise and movement. Clients and employees alike buzzed about with excitement and energy. In a nonstop wave of production; morning turned to afternoon, and afternoon into evening all in a sublime fluid motion.

John especially enjoyed the months from January and April; the hustle and bustle around the office was infectious and electric and the long hours distracted him from remembering that one terrible day and at times allowing him to forget it altogether.

The firm which he worked had won a state contract five years ago and now dealt primarily with low income clients who were dependent on the state.

The crushing workload would keep him busy, many times requiring twelve hour days, until the very end of the tax season.

Suddenly, a young and cheerful temp came to a stop at the threshold of his office and said, "Dinnertime, Mr. Poole," then asked the only question she ever seemed to ask, "What would you like?"

During the tax season, the firm provided breakfast, lunch, and dinner, commonly referred to by office staff as 'the feedings', to everyone on the payroll.

John answered, "Whatever pasta they have tonight and a soda, please, Margie."

Working hard to go from temp to permanent, the recent college grad smiled at the sound of her name, "Ok, sure, Mr. Poole," and then added, "Generic ok? That's the only type of soda they brought tonight."

Only thirty-one years old, John couldn't help but

feel fatherly to the bubbly young temp smiling in front of him, "Yeah... generic is ok."

With a healthy smiling nod, she turned and continued to the next office.

John stared at his empty doorway and touched the scar. Since the attack, he had trained himself to not fully smile, doing so caused the scar tissue to slightly pull the left side of his forehead downward.

He looked at the paper mountain on his desk and decided to finish one more file before eating.

Suddenly a familiar voice boomed into his small office, "Hey, Poole... what ya order?" John looked up from his computer monitor. Filling the doorway with his overweight presence was his friend and colleague, Gil.

John answered, "Pasta... like yesterday."

"Cool," Gil commented half-heartedly then said, "Listen... lets go to Gringo's tonight. It's been a while."

John thought it over.

Placing both hands on the door's frame, Gil leaned in, "Come on, bro."

With the same small smile that he had given Margie, John asked, "Will it be ok with Susan?"

Acting as if he had just been insulted, Gil dropped his hands and said, "What? Hey, I can do whatever I wanna do. Married doesn't mean prison," then added, "Gringo's bro... come on."

Relenting with a sigh, John said, "Ok."

A boyish smile spread across Gil's round face as he exclaimed, "Great!" then turned, gave a wave, and waked away.

John gave a small huff and a smile then reached for a new folder from which to work.

That evening, as John and Gil rode the elevator

down to the basement parking lot, John felt fatigued enough to simply curl up on the dirty elevator floor and go to sleep.

Gil said, "Man, I can't wait. I love their nachos," Gil said excitedly, oblivious to his or his friend's weary physical state.

Tugging at his tie and adjusting his buttoned blazer, John gave a simple smile and nodded in agreement.

Looking at his watch, Gil added, "Let's just take one car. Parking is always a bitch at that place."

John gave another nod in reply.

The elevator chimed, its doors slid opened, and both men stepped out into the cool vast space of the underground parking structure.

Apart from John and Gil's vehicles, only two other cars remained in the level.

Gil's cellular phone suddenly rang from his hip.

With a grunt, Gil reached for it and answered heavily as he veered left, away from his friend for privacy, "Hey, babe."

John knew who it was and what the conversation would consist of so he walked to his car as pieces of his friend's conversation with his wife drifted over to him, "I know...I'll be home soon, babe... dinner... please...with who?... ya know who....John...yeah... that John...soon...come on....please say yes... please."

With the pleading fading into the distance, John approached his car, reached inside his pants pocket, and he fetched out the keys.

Then, in the distance, the sound of footsteps in high heel shoes reached his ears.

Coming to a stop next to his car, keys in hand, John listened as the sound bounced off the concrete walls and pillars of the parking level.

Rhythmically the high heeled foot falls seemed to echo all around him.

Rolling his car keys in his hand, he waited curiously to see who was attached to the echoing footsteps, but no one appeared.

Their sound neither approached nor faded, only hanging in the air with an ominous touch.

Feeling suddenly uneasy as he continued listening to the footsteps, John reached up and absently touched the scar on this forehead.

Then from behind, Gil's voice boomed, "Told her!"

Startled, John spun around as his left hand slipped inside his navy blazer.

Clutching his cellular phone in his large ample hand and smiling, Gil said, "Had to do it... had to break it down to the little lady."

Realizing that he had been completely absorbed by the footsteps, John blinked as he registered his friend in front of him.

"So... ya ready?" Gil asked with a large grin.

Slowly withdrawing his hand from under his blazer, John craned his ears to pick up the sound once again but the footsteps had stopped as abruptly as they had started.

Hungry and eager not to break the curfew his wife had just set, Gil asked again, "Well... are ya ready?"

Still a bit rustled, John finally replied, "Yeah... sure. Let's go."

"Great. Hey... let's take my car," Gil rang out.
John agreed.

Walking to Gil's car at the far end of the parking level, John did his best to put the uneasy incident behind him.

Drinks and dinner with Gil had gone as expected. Gil had talked mostly about his wife and how she insistently pressed him to make Partner at the accounting firm, a topic John heard about and knew about all too well.

Afterwards, during the drive back to the parking structure for John's car, Gil jokingly said, "Man... you should have had the venison Gringo's serves. You could have taken revenge on that deer that crashed through your windshield and gave you that scar by eating one of his relatives."

Remembering the lie he had told everyone on how he had gotten hurt during his vacation, John pretended to laugh and said, "Only if it could have watched me doing it."

Gil gave a quick laugh, yawned, and said to him, "I gotta get home. Tomorrow's gonna be another long day."

John gave a nod in agreement as he watched their work building in the distance come into view as they drove closer to it. It stood dark and devoid of all life at the late hour, a stark contrast to the living energy within its walls during the day.

Turning right off La Brea Ave, Gil entered the parking ramp that lead to the underground parking levels.

They descended past two whole empty levels until finally reaching the third where John's car sat completely alone.

Pulling up next to it, Glen said, "Ok, Champ... you're all set."

John opened the passenger door and told his colleague and friend, "Thanks for driving," then stepped out, "See you... tomorrow," and closed the car door.

Glen gave a smile in returned, waved good bye, and then drove away towards the exit ramp, leaving John standing by his car.

Tired and slightly drunk from the mugs of beer he had had over dinner, John stood by his driver's side door and took in the thick silence of the empty parking lot as he rolled his right ankle around to relieve the tightness from sitting in Gil's cramped sport coupe.

Then as if on cue, the sound of high heeled shoes started once again.

This time for some inexplicable reason, John felt the hairs bristle on the back of his neck and cold goose bumps ripple across his arms.

Just as before, the sound seemed to come from everywhere and nowhere all at the same time.

With a growing unease, John undid the button on his blazer as he continued to listen.

The sound hovered all around him.

John scanned the empty level but saw no one so he stepped away from his car and began to slowly walk towards the center of the parking level.

The footsteps echoed from everywhere.

Standing in the middle of the deserted parking level, John did a full 180 degree turn, looking for the source.

The sound persisted ever closer ever further.

He ran his eyes around his surroundings, looking and searching.

The sound suddenly stopped and, at the far end of the parking level, he saw someone.

John narrowed his eyes to see who it was.

Standing in the shadow of the furthest concrete pillar was the outline of a woman looking directly at him.

John strained his eyes to get a better look at her.

She stepped out of the darkness and began to walk directly towards him.

The rhythmic high heeled footfalls began once again.

Staring at the approaching woman, John took in her appearance. Framed by long glossy black hair her face was slender and oval while her body was long and lean underneath a black spaghetti strap dress that draped delicately over the curves of her silhouette.

Watching her close the distance between them, John felt the weight of his body go to his feet as a sense of unease creep into him.

Then, with only a few feet separating them, she came to a stop in front of him and John's heart went to his throat when he looked into her eyes.

They were the color of dazzling green emeralds.

Looking at a pair of eyes that he had seen before and could never forget and had hoped to never see again, John simply remained where he stood, shocked beyond words.

With the smallest of smiles from her lush red painted lips, the irises of her stunning green eyes suddenly began to swirl around a set of onyx black pupils.

Instantly caught by the power and allure of the spinning irises, John looked deep into the swirling enchantment.

She took a step closer and exhaled her warm breath across his face.

The smell of freshly cut mint filled his nostrils in a thick coat.

Hopelessly trapped within her stare and engulfed in the sweet pungent smell of her mouth, John felt himself begin to drift away to some unknown tranquil place in his mind.

Then, with blurring speed, her left hand struck him across the chest, and white hot burning pain exploded across his ribcage as he was sent off his feet and onto his back against the cold concrete floor.

With an emotionless expression, she watched him sail into the air and land on his back some ten feet away.

On the floor and in shattering pain, John's eyes bulged in their sockets as he looked down and saw blood bloom out onto his shirt and turn it crimson red.

With her left arm covered in white fur and her hand clawed into a grotesque mass of knuckles and long spiked fingernails, she calmly began to walk to him.

Stifling the pain through clenched teeth, he looked up at her and saw that the corners of her mouth had split from ear to ear turning her soft smile into a gaping monstrous grimace filled with razor sharp shark-like teeth.

Above them, the very last car from an upper level drove out of the parking structure.

Looking at the gaping hideous face, John began to feel the warm comforting sensation of shock begin to take hold of him.

Blood from the four slashes to his chest spilled around his ribcage and soaked through the back of his blazer onto the concrete floor.

Half-conscious, he watched her stop in front of him and looked at him with her large green eyes.

She straddled his waist, lowered herself onto him, and sat on his pelvis.

John grunted in discomfort as she pressed herself onto his pubic bone.

She grabbed his lapels of his navy blazer and raised his face towards hers.

Crying out in pain, the edges of his eyesight darkened as he was yanked upright.

The smell of mint bathed his face again in a warm sweet cloud.

She put his left shoulder into her gaping mouth and bit down.

Searing pain bore into his shoulder.

Stifling the scream that had rolled into his mouth, John gritted his teeth.

Blood poured into her sinister looking mouth as her green eyes rolled over to their whites like a shark as her razor sharp teeth gently scrapped back and forth at his collar bone.

With only a few heartbeats away from passing out, John suddenly felt a furious polarizing light explode deep within him and his eyes blinked back into focus.

She bit deeper into his tattered flesh.

Suddenly completely alert, he turned his head and saw her face buried in his shoulder while holding him by the lapels of his navy blazer.

A thunderous boom exploded between them.

Startled by the tremendous sound and a searing wrenching pain in her abdomen, she released him, leaped high into the air, and landed on her feet some twenty feet away.

Holding a snubnose .38 Special in his left hand (the very same gun that he had tried to fetch from the center console in the rental truck two years ago) and blinking back the pain from his wounds, he stared at her as he readied himself for whatever was to come next.

Standing on unsteady feet with an expression of total surprise, she placed her right hand on the bleeding blackened hole just below her navel.

Bloodied and ravaged, John slowly raised himself up on one elbow and pointed the handgun at her.

Knowing full well that another shot would undoubtedly kill her, she backed away from him as quickly as she could. Like a film projector in reverse, she took the same path she had come from and at the same pace until she disappeared into the shadows of the parking structure once again.

Alone once again in the parking structure, John lowered his gun, laid back down on his own blood, and closed his eyes.

The wounds to his chest and shoulder had already stopped bleeding.

CHAPTER 3

"It's the Bostwick girl. Paul Bostwick's daughter."

On the top floor of the homeless shelter that she ran, she closed the door of the small office softly behind her so as not to disturb those sleeping quietly below her. In her present state and appearance the very last thing she needed was any unneeded attention.

Though the bleeding had stopped some time ago, the bullet itself was still inside her.

Leaning against the door, she took a deep breath to steady herself from the pain as she reflected on how lucky she'd been tonight; although her healing abilities were unnaturally rapid, a second gunshot would have almost certainly had killed her.

She closed her eyes and worked past the pain as she did her best to concentrate on an even more immediate concern; restoring her appearance before she was seen.

With the bullet still lodged against her spine, she swallowed against a dry throat and focused with all her will.

Slowly, her appearance began to shapeshift. Her long hair shortened to shoulder length as it went from jet black to a rich Irish red. Her cheekbones rose slightly, elongating her facial structure. Her lips thinned and narrowed, her bust swelled by one full size as her hips filled out and the white of her skin warmed to a glowing tan thus completing the metamorphosis.

With her appearance back to how those of the shelter recognized her by, she opened her eyes and painfully stepped away from the door.

She shuffled to her desk at the far side of the small office and slumped into the high-backed leather chair behind it, causing the bullet to scrap against a lumbar vertebra and making her grunt in pain through even white teeth.

Sweating, she closed her eyes again and focused once more, though this time, on removing the bothersome hunk of jacketed lead and repairing extensive internal damaged it had caused.

Slowly as the night crawled towards dawn, her body and mind fell into a meditated stupor while her organs repaired themselves and the bullet inched outward.

Drifting aimlessly in the vast dell of her mind, she wandered into the memories of her long life. Scattered like stardust on a clear midnight horizon, they lay in front of her for her to relive in detail.

Floating in the tranquil stupor between pain and peace, she went to one of the oldest and grasped it...

Trudging her way through the soft bellowing New England snow, Abigail glanced over her shoulder and saw her family's small house in the distant valley below.

With her deer skin boots just waterproofed by her father her young feet were dry and warm as she continued further towards the vast forest just beyond a meadow of freshly fallen snow

Eager to explore the surrounding winter countryside since her father had moved them from Boston to the Borridge farming community the previous summer. In the city the snow always got mixed with the garbage on the streets. However, in the wide open fields of the valley it dazzled like a billion diamonds in the clear afternoon sun.

Stopping to catch her breath, she threw back the hood of her cloak to allow the cold air to blow through her blonde hair and cool her young face.

Proud of her trek, she scanned the environment around her. An endless perfect blanket of whiteness spread across the landscape. Never in her life had she seen such untouched beauty spread out to her so willingly and openly.

With the winter's cold delightfully stinging her cheeks, she lifted her blue eyes upwards towards the deep blue sky. White clouds drifted slowly while the sun offered the faintest hint of warmth on her head.

Filled with the innocence of youthful excitement, she pushed forward towards the forest.

The crisp freezing air filled her lungs as she made her way across the open field of frozen whiteness while smiling at her progress across the meadow.

With her cheeks glowing red on her twelve year old face, she saw the start of the forest just in front of her.

Her packed lunch in the pocket of her cloak thumped heavily against her left thigh.

Then the unmistakable sound of black powder rifle fire echoed and rolled to her ears.

She stopped in her tracks and noted how close it had sounded.

Another shot rang out, this one even closer than the last.

Feeling suddenly exposed in the open, she stood motionless as if rooted to the undergrowth below the snow.

A third shot boomed in front of her just within the forest cover.

Whatever was happening inside the forest was coming directly towards her, she realized with a cold certain fear as she quickly looked around for a place to conceal herself but the vast open space had surrounded her in its white nothingness.

More shots rang out followed by the sound of shouting men.

Then, to her horror, she saw a tall long limbed creature with dazzling white fur and stained with its own blood come staggering from out of the tree line.

Breathing heavily from its wide gaping mouth, it scanned the open frozen meadow with its large green emerald colored eyes.

Frozen in shock, she stared at it in disbelief.

It quickly glanced over its shoulder as the sound of shouting men grew closer and closer to where it was.

Completely transfixed on the bizarre creature standing about twenty-five yards in front of her, she watched it continue to desperately look about the snow covered meadow.

Then it looked at her.

She felt her breath leave her in a gasp.

Despite being wounded and bleeding from several rifle shots, it ran at her with stunning speed.

Motionless with fright, Abigail watched the

creature cross the distance between them and pounce on her, driving her into the soft plush snow.

A second later three uniformed militia men from the region's Colonial Guards appear from the woods, black powder long rifles in hand.

The creature, with its long clawed hands, lifted her up, placed her over its shoulder, and dashed across the snow covered meadow, away from the men and their rifles, all in one fluid motion.

Bouncing against the creature's fur lined back, she looked up and saw the militia men dumbly stared at the white monster and her as they reached the end of the meadow and darted over the side.

Descending down the hillside, she lowered her head to pray for her safety and noticed four bleeding shot holes in the creature's red soaked back, and remembered a time, back in Boston, when she had stumbled upon a slaughter house and watched a pig slip away from its killer's grasp after being slashed across the neck. It had run in circles desperately looking for an escape but a few seconds later it had fallen dead in midstride from the blood loss.

Looking at the creature's gunshot wounds, she knew it didn't have long to live.

Then as if almost prophetically timed, the creature gave two more running steps and then then crumpled as it long legs gave out from under it.

Together, they went into the virgin snow and tumbled down the final length of the hillside until they came to a stop in a clump of thin barren trees.

With the wind knocked out of her from the fall, she laid next to the wheezing dying creature.

Dizzy from the fall, she wiped the snow from her face with an unsteady hand as she struggled to catch her bearings.

On its back in the blood stained snow, the creature struggled for air with shallow snatching gasps as death continued to slowly take it.

Freed from its clutches, she slowly stood up, looked about, turned to run, and broke into a wild dash but was stopped short

With an amazing speed that had served it so well for so long, the creature's long fingered hand shot out and seized her by the ankle of her right booted foot.

Her eyes bulged in terror as she looked down and saw the creature's hand securely wrapped around her limb.

Slowly, bleeding and whizzing for breath, the white clad creature stood up right, wrapped both of its hands around her soft neck, and lifted her off her feet up to its eye level.

Feeling the vertebrates in her neck coming apart, she grabbed onto its wrist for support.

The creature's wide demonic mouth spread from ear to ear, revealing even rows of razor sharp shark-like teeth as it stared at her with its amazingly large emerald green eyes.

The smell of mint covered her face with every frosty exhaled breath that came from its horrific gaping mouth.

With their faces just inches apart, it spoke to her, in a low rumbling unsteady voice, "Finally...the end... has...arrived."

Never more afraid in her young life than she was at that moment, she stared into its green eyes as she listened to it speak to her.

It coughed up blood with a sickening gurgle and then added, "You shall...be...my last...victim."

Half-conscious from the creature's crushing grip, she reached up and touched its white shoulder with her tiny hand in a feeble attempt to push away.

Then, with the last of its strength, the monster leaned in and bit down into her neck, instantly puncturing the young flesh.

A rifle fired and the top half of the creature's head exploded in a cloud of fur, skull, and brains.

Together, they crumpled into the snow.

Lost in the peace and tranquility of shock from the wound to her neck, she watched, through half opened eyes, as the three militia men made their way down the hillside to where she and the dead creature were.

Snow and blood meddled all around her.

When they finally reached her, the older of the men spoke first as he went to check on her, "Mr. Wilson, see to that thing, please."

The youngest of the three replied, "Right away, Mr. Shaw," then leveled his rifle squarely at the dead monster's chest and pulled the trigger.

Inside the creature's chest cavity, its heart exploded into a thousand pieces.

The third militia man walked up to the Captain and looked down at the young girl's blood stained face as he reloaded his rifle by touch.

Gingerly the older man touched the horrid wound on her neck and asked as he looked up, "Do you know who this child might be, Mr. Brooks?"

Her eyes glazed over, giving her a dreamy tranquil expression, as the blood loss from the bite reached a critical level.

"I believe I do, Mr. Shaw," replied the man, "It's the Bostwick girl. Paul Bostwick's daughter."

The militia Captain looked back at the girl once

more and applied pressure with a cloth from his knapsack to her wound.

Feeling herself drifting away to a place of calm and serenity, somewhere deep in her being, she knew she was about to.

Mr. Wilson, a devout Catholic, slung his rifle, knelt down on her right, and began to recite the Lord's Prayer in an effort to comfort the girl who he knew was only moments away from death.

Suddenly a burst of dazzling light ignited within her and the men all around her came into focus.

"Will she live, Mr. Shaw?" Mr. Brooks inquired.

Running his large hand over the girl's blonde head again, the Captain checked the wound from under the cloth and replied as he narrowed his eyebrows, "Yes, Mr. Brooks. It appears that this child will live. The bleeding has already stopped. So, I suggest that we…"

Someone knocked on the office door.

She opened her eyes and the memory of her distant past disappeared.

Another knock.

With her dress soaked in her own blood and her green eyes still not covered by colored contacts that she wore to disguise them, she knew she couldn't be seen.

One final knock rapped at the door then a man's voice said through the thin wooden door, "Susan?"

She instantly knew who it was; her fattening little piglet for the slaughter.

"Susan, you ok?" the man on the other side asked with genuine concern.

Mustering up her patience, she answered in a soothing pleasing voice, "Yes…I'm fine."

"May… I come in?" the man's voice asked.

With a deep breath, she gathered herself and replied, "Sure. Come in."

The door opened and a tall man in his thirties stepped in. Though his features had been weathered by years of blue collar work and alcoholism, his eyes shined with hope and life.

She stopped him from touching the light switch, "Don't. I'm too tired to have any lights on right now."

He dropped his hand away from the light switch and stood in the darkness trying to look at her through the blackness of the room. After about a minute of silence between them, he asked, "Everything ok?"

Looking at the silhouette of the man in front of her whom she planned to murder, "Yeah. Just couldn't sleep... so I took a drive."

"Oh. Well...do you need anything?"

"No. I'm finally sleepy now. I'm good."

Fighting back the desire to approach her, he said, "Ok, then. I'll see you in the morning."

"Good night," she told him then added as he turned to leave, "Alex?"

Smiling in the darkness at the sound of her voice calling his name, he stopped at the doorway and looked back.

"That shipment of canned food we've been waiting for arrives tomorrow. Can you go to San Pedro and pick it up... for me?"

Beaming to himself at the prospect of doing something, anything, for her, he replied eagerly that he could.

Continuing to sit motionless and unseen in the dark, she added, "It'll make things easier for you if you take the van with the name of the shelter on it."

"Ok, sure," he responded with swelling of pride

then excused himself, "Good night... Susan."

"Good night," she replied as she watched him leave her office, closing the door softly behind him.

Alone once again, she opened her hand.

In her palm was the bullet that had been in her body.

CHAPTER 4

"I'll run."

John stepped into the darkened threshold of his condo and slowly closed the door behind him.

Fatigued beyond words from what had just happened to him in the parking structure, he slumped against the door, closed his eyes, and allowed the feel and smell of his home to slowly welcome him in.

Feeling too exhausted to even step away from the door, John let his knees go limp and slowly slid down onto the hardwood floor until he sat against the front door with his knees drawn up close to his face.

Sitting there on the floor, deep dark penetrating sleep slowly crept up on him.

Turning himself over to the tranquil blackness of slumber, John took a deep relaxing breath and the rich pungent odor of his dried blood wafted up and filled his nostrils.

Overcome by the stink of his wounds, he opened his eyes, rubbed his face vigorously with his dirty hands, and told himself out loud "You need to think... not sleep" then he picked himself up off the floor and stepped away from the door.

He pulled the revolver that had just saved his life less than an hour ago, dropped it on the sofa, stripped out of his bloodied clothing, and then went to the bathroom.

Naked and encrusted with dried blood from his shoulder down to his pubic hair, he stepped into his bathroom, the linoleum flooring instantly cooling his hot bare feet, and flipped on the light with a knowing hand.

Bright fluorescent light instantly filled the small tiled room.

He stepped in front of the mirror and what he saw staring back at him was shocking. Four long gashes had ripped open his entire chest from nipple to nipple. The skin had peeled back exposing dark red muscle as well as the yellowish bone of his sternum and on his shoulder was the bite wound, ragged and torn.

Staring at the damage to his body, John knew he should be dead. However, he was no longer bleeding nor was he in any pain.

He dropped his eyes away from the mirror and slowly shook his head at how something like that could even be possible.

Standing over the sink, he looked down the drain hole and said in a quiet voice to himself, "Get a grip, John. You're alive," then turned away from the mirror and went to the shower.

Eager to get the horrible smell of blood off of him, he stepped into the shower stall and turned both knobs at the same time.

Hot clean water erupted from the showerhead and

sprayed him down.

Instantly lost in the pleasurable sensation, John closed his eyes and inhaled the hot stream as dried blood and dead tissue slid down the length of his body and down the drain.

With his body soothing and his mind relaxing under the steady stream of encapsulating hot water, John assessed his situation. Within the span of two years, he had been attacked twice, once in the mountains by some insidious monster and just now in a parking structure in Los Angeles by some unknown woman who could somehow change into the same monster with the white fur and green eyes.

He ran his fingers through his wet hair as he realized just how crazy that sounded.

In the snow, he had survived only because of a broken windshield wiper and tonight he had managed to escape death due to a fortunate shot from his gun. Nevertheless, whoever she was and what her reasons were for wanting to kill him, he was certain, she wouldn't fail a third time.

With a knowing hand he took hold of the shampoo bottle on the tiled ledge, dispensed a small of amount of product into his palm and rubbed it into his hair.

He had lied to everyone about how he had come by the scar on his forehead, waiting for the day for that lie, if repeated enough times, to become the truth for him as well. But in reality, as it turned out, the truth had just taken its time to find him and finish what it had failed to accomplish the first time in the snow.

Hot water washed away the fragrant lather from his head.

If she had found him where he parked his car, he assessed, so then she certainly knew where he lived.

Next, John took the bottle of body wash, squeezed out a generous amount, and gingerly massaged it over his wounds, fully expecting to feel a dose of burning pain. However, to his surprise, he felt nothing other than the tingling sensation of the body wash's cleansing agents on his tired skin.

Tonight, she had proved that she could come for him anywhere and at any time.

Washing away the cleansing lather, he weighed his options on what to do next. 'I could go to the police or perhaps even to the press' he thought to himself but with such a fantastic story to tell, he figured, he would either be laughed right out onto the street or committed to some state run psyche ward.

He inhaled hot scented air, exhaled, and slowly shook his head at his meager options.

Then suddenly, the solution that he couldn't find found him between a heartbeat and a blink of his eye.

John turned the water off, pressed his hands on the tiled wall, and said out loud, "I'll run."

Later, dressed in fresh clothing, a duffle bag slung over his right shoulder, and the revolver tucked once again in his waistband, John walked about his condo, the only placed he had ever called home since moving to Los Angeles, one final time as he shook his head in dismay at what he was about to do.

Fleeing seemed so drastic but under the circumstances he saw no other option if he wanted to stay alive until he figured out something else.

He went to the front door and opened it.

At the threshold, he looked at a framed photograph that hung on the wall of his family (his mother, father, and younger brother kneeling in front of a fireplace), then flipped off the lights, and closed the door behind him.

John Poole would never return to his condo. It would be seized by the bank months later and everything in it would be sold at auction to cover delinquent accounts.

CHAPTER 5

"All it requires is time."

With the morning sun casting its radiate warmth on the new day, Susan, as she was presently being called, stood on the roof of the homeless shelter and stared at the garment district of the city below.

Dressed in simple clothing to downplay her figure, she contemplated the man she had tracked for two years. He had escaped from her not just once but twice, with the second encounter almost getting her killed. No one in all her years since being bitten had ever escaped from her, much less twice.

She whispered, "He has... turned out to be..."

"Now what's this for again, Susan?" Alex Clark the same man from last night asked, cutting into her train of thought.

Slightly annoyed at his intrusion into her thoughts, she turned away from the building's three story view, looked at him through her brown colored contacts, and asked, "What?"

Kneeling next to one of three 150 gallon reservoir tanks, Alex pointed to the large black plastic containers, "These. What do we need them for?"

Stepping away from the edge, she looked at the man who was the shelter's crowning achievement. Since her arrival, the Gulf War veteran had quit drinking, had gained twenty pounds of healthy fat and muscle, and had taken an interest in his appearance once again.

Staring at him, she fought down the sudden desire to tell him the truth then rip out his throat but she settled for a lie instead, "I want a secondary sprinkler system. This building is very old and I don't trust the current one very much."

Lifting his ball cap up to the hairline, Alex stared into the distance, thought about it for a few seconds, then looked up at the soft beautiful face above him, "Yeah, sounds like a good idea," then added, "How you going to get the water up here, though?"

Touching his shoulder, she answered with a smile, "We'll get it up," hitting the innuendo precisely at the last syllable.

Feeling his penis thicken at the feel of her touch and the sound of her voice, he replied, "Yeah. Ok," then quickly looked away, embarrassed by the wave of lust that had unexpectedly washed over him.

Savoring the day she'd kill him and everyone in the building, she left him to his chores and walked towards the stairwell, calling out to him over her shoulder, "I'm going inside... finish up...we can talk later over coffee."

Smiling at the prospect of having her all to himself if just for a few minutes, he looked her way and said, "Sure... sounds great."

She gave him a nod and a simple smile then, with

the sun on her back, walked across the rooftop and past the wooden door that led back into the old tired building.

Feeling the cool shade of the darkened stairwell, she made her way downward as her large glossy green emerald eyes adjusted to the lowlight and basted her sight in a luminous green glow.

From below, the bustling noise from the shelter's kitchen echoed up to her.

She stopped and listened to the happy commotion coming from the women assigned to the breakfast detail.

A smile crept across her lips as she thought once again about her vicious plan; instead of tearing her victims apart one by one, she was going to kill hundreds with just a flip of the switch.

She closed her eyes and slowly whispered, "It... is going... to be...," then snapped her eyes out and said out loud, "Special."

In the lightless corridor of stairs, she gripped the wooden banister and realized that was the word she was going to say right before Alex had interrupted her. 'Special'. That's what he was. That's what John Poole was.

"Special," she mouthed the singular word again and swallowed through a tightened throat as the banister groaned under the strength of her hand.

The thought to intentionally infecting someone else had never once crossed her mind, not once. However, now, after over two centuries, someone else besides herself was infected. In time, he would become just like her in every way, which was something she simply couldn't allow. The creature belonged to her and she belonged to it.

The wooden banister groaned louder still as she tightened her grip even more.

She had tracked him down once before and knew she could again even though, she surmised, he was, in all likelihood, now on the run.

The sound of cracking wood echoed within the stairwell.

"All it requires is time," she assured herself with a smile then let go of the banister and continued down the stairs, leaving behind the wooden railing splintered and broken.

CHAPTER 6

"Where are you?"

After leaving his condo, John Poole had gone to the first motel he could find, had checked himself in, and had collapsed onto the stiff tight bed fully dressed.

Now, with the morning sun looming high in the sky, he stared at himself in the mirror of the dresser in stunned silence.

The wounds from last night's attack were all but completely healed.

He lowered his eyes from the mirror to his body and ran a hand over his bare chest.

The jagged open wounds of exposed bone and muscle were now covered over in fresh shiny pink skin.

With what little he knew of medicine and human anatomy, he was certain that wounds such as the ones he had had simply didn't heal that fast.

He leaned in a bit forward to the mirror to examine the bite wound on his shoulder when suddenly his cellular phone on the nightstand behind him began to ring, breaking his train of thought.

He quickly went to it and looked at the number on the tiny screen.

Gil's extension number at the firm was displayed on the LCD.

John took the small phone, pressed the green button, and answered the called, "Yeah."

With a voice mixed with surprise and relief, his friend and colleague, spoke from the other end, "John?"

"Yeah, Gil, what's up?"

"What's up?" Gil retorted then asked, "Where are you?"

"I'm not at work," he replied with an attempt at humor.

"Dude… no shit. You ok?" Gil pressed.

Realizing there was more to the call then just not coming to work, John asked, "Why… you ask?"

"Dude… the old man's wondering where the hell you're at," Gil returned and then added, "Plus, this morning I found some shit that kinda looked like blood by your parking spot.

John touched the scar on this forehead as his stomach sank.

Gil asked with genuine concern, "Bro… are you sure you're alright?"

John answered with a lie as best he could, "Yeah… Gil… I'm fine."

The accountant and father of three lowered his voice and said, "Dude… I just thought…you know…since we were the last ones down there last night."

Doing what he could to sound uninvolved, John asked, "Anything exciting because of it?"

"Na, " Gil answered, "I just kinda freaked out when I saw all that thick dark goo… so grabbed that two liter

of water that I keep in the car for my lousy radiator...
and washed it away."

John removed his hand from the scar and touched
his bare chest again, "Oh... ok."

"I probably shouldn't have done that but like I
said... I kinda freaked out," Gil spoke over the phone
then asked again, "But you're ok, right?"

John answered, "Yeah. I'm fine. I'm ok."

Accepting his friends answer, Gil moved on, "So
where are you? Ya coming in?"

John realized that the moment of truth had
arrived. His next answer would truly mark the
beginning of the end of his old life and the start to
whatever was to come.

Gil asked again, "John. Are you coming in or not,
bro? I gotta tell the old man something."

Like ink poured into water, the memory of the
creature staring at him through the windshield slowly
materialized inside his head.

"John?" Gil pressed.

Then the image of the woman walking towards him
in the parking structure appeared next.

"John."

Lost in thought, he neither heard nor answered his
friend.

"John!" Gil yelled into the phone.

The loud and urgent sound of his name, coming
from the tiny phone, pulled him back to the present,
"What?"

"Fuck, dude! I'm asking you if you're coming in
today or not!" Gil exclaimed.

Realizing how simple the answer was, John said,
"No, I'm not," and then added "Good bye, Gil."

Gil returned in a torrid, "What!"

John pressed the red button ending the call and then broke the phone in half.

Using the phone in his room, for the next two hours, John closed out the life he had spent years creating. He resigned over the phone to his boss, lying about a dire family emergency. He repeated the same story to Human Resources whose only chief concern was a formal letter of resignation sent to them as quickly as possible so that his 401k, stocks, final paycheck, vacation and severance pay could be finalized with the company's payroll department.

Later, after what seemed like an eternity on the phone, he went over his total liquid assets. He had always been good with his money and his credit. He had saved well, and invested wisely and safely. His saving account and credit cards added up to a sizable sum. Plus, inside the duffle bag was the large amount of cash he had kept stored away in his condo, his father's luxury brand Swiss made watch, and a binder of gold coins his grandfather had given him as a graduation present from college, all of which assured him enough combustible funds to properly plan his next best course of action though what that necessarily was he still didn't really know.

CHAPTER 7

"I need your help in the basement."

As John Poole slept in his motel room for a second night, she stared out the second floor window of her darkened office to the street below with her emerald glossy eyes.

Even with the shelter filled to capacity, all was quiet inside during the late hours, giving her a chance to focus on the kill of the night.

The silence of the night always felt comforting to her; it was one of the few things in life that had never really ever changed regardless of what part of the world she was in or during what period in time.

With a patience perfected long ago, she waited for her prey to arrive. Anticipating the murder to come was at times just as exciting as actually committing the act.

A tingle at the corners of her mouth was the only hint of emotion expressed on her flawless features.

Finally, during the two o'clock hour of the morning, she saw her victim.

A sweat stained overweight derelict emerged from around the corner across the street.

With a slow feline blink of her green eyes, she smiled as she watched him come closer.

On uneasy feet, the fat drunkard crossed the barren street and wobbled up the homeless shelter's front steps.

She stepped out of her black high heels.

The worn rug greeted the soles of her feet with its shabby polyester fibers.

She slipped out of the tiny office with the stealth of a shadow.

Carrying his overweight bulk up the shelter's concrete steps, Mitch Bale grunted under his barreled chest.

In complete silence and with the aid of the night vision from her emerald colored eyes, she moved effortlessly down the lightless stairwell towards the first floor.

The shelter's security guard, another homeless man simply known as Maxie, shook his head in amusement at the drunken man's present condition and said as he let him in, "You're gonna get your ass thrown out of here when Rodger finds out, my man."

With a daffy smile and a dismissive wave, Mitch walked past him and entered the shelter.

Reaching the ground floor in a matter of seconds, she peered through the stairwell door's wire glass window, saw no one lurking about, and silently slipped into the main hallway.

Slowly and methodically, Mitch made his way towards the men's dormitory at the far end of the shelter.

Waiting for him to reach her, she pulled the

colored contacts from her eyes and slipped them in her jeans pocket. Though her eyes had turned their emerald green color shortly after being bitten, their power to seduce had been one of the last of her abilities to develop. Some victims needed only to be in front of her while others required a deep stare close up. The key to success was to never break eye contact.

He continued walking unknowingly towards her.

Her hair began to move with a life of its own as his footsteps echoed closer and closer to her.

He turned the corner at the end of the hallway and came face to face with the woman everyone called Miss Susan and their eyes locked, sealing his fate.

The swirling green of her irises bore into alcohol bloodshot eyeballs in the dimly lit hallway.

Instantly a sense of wellbeing overtook him.

Bathing his unshaven face with the smell of freshly cut mint, she quietly told him, "I need your help in the basement."

Staring deep into her eyes, the once former car manufacturer nodded sheepishly at her words.

Smiling, she ran the tip of her tongue across her even white teeth further enhancing the seductive lure of her voice, "Good. Come with me, Mitch," and then began walking backwards to the door that led to the basement.

Locked into the power of her eyes, he followed without question.

With perfect accuracy, she walked backwards down the hallway, never once looking over her shoulder or breaking eye contact.

With each passing second that he stared into her ensnaring eyes, the long forgotten sensations of lust awoke within him.

With the basement door only a few feet away, she opened her mouth wide and moved her tongue all around, allowing the thick wet noise to reach his ears, enticing him further.

He reached down the front of his jeans and grabbed his swollen penis with a dirty pudgy hand.

At the basement door, Susan reached out behind her, grabbed the door knob, and turned it.

The old wooden door swung open inward, exposing a dimly lit set of stairs leading downward.

Without taking her eyes off his, she gently took his large roughened hands into hers and proceeded down the staircase backwards.

Together, they descended downward, hand in hand.

At the bottom of the stairs, they came to the basement, which was nothing more than a large concrete bunker.

One bare light bulb hung in the middle of the ceiling, illuminating the both of them in a sour milk colored light.

A garden hose, a bag of lime, and a manhole cover were the only items in the otherwise empty room.

She came to a stop beside the manhole cover.

Hopelessly locked to her swirling green eyes, Mitch's heart hammered in his chest with lust.

Without breaking eye contact, she let go his hands, undid the buttons of her black cardigan, let it fell to the floor behind her, and then slowly tore open her simple white t-shirt down the front of her chest, exposing her heavy breasts.

Mitch remained where he stood, simply smiling and rubbing himself.

"Drop your pants." she commanded in a mint

scented whisper while cupping her bare breasts with her exquisitely manicured hands.

Dulled eyed and under her complete control, he unfastened the tattered belt around his gut, popped the button of his jeans, and slid the zipper down.

His denim pants, worn and dirty, collapsed around his ankles. He wore no underwear.

The smell of sweat and piss cut through the mint's aroma almost instantly.

"Lay down," she told him as she gestured with a hand to his chest to the damp concrete floor.

He complied without comment or hesitation.

Standing over him, she slowly stripped off the rest of her clothing.

Silently, he watched her with insane anticipation.

Stripped completely naked, she stepped forward on bare feet and straddled him.

Feeling the delicate touch of her bare ankles against his waist, Mitch exhaled in rapture.

Smiling wide down at him, she took a relaxing breath and then emptied her bladder on him.

Hot thick urine splashed and spilled all over the drunkard between her legs.

Feeling the hot liquid waste cover him in a tide of warmth, Mitch grabbed his penis and whimpered with sexual abandonment.

Still smiling and relishing the moments before the kill, she hawked her throat clear, bent forward, and spat the contents from her mouth across his face.

Hungrily he searched for the runny fluid with his tongue.

Next, she hunkered down on his fat belly, took hold of his engrossed member, and slid down onto it, filling her entire vaginal cavity.

Feeling the requisite sensation of penetrating into her, a grotesque mask of sexual bless enveloped his face.

Rolling up to the balls of her bare feet, she slid up and down the entire length of his cock as he stiffened and jerk with every thrust.

Watching him loose himself in the moment, her smiled began to spread wider.

Feeling the mounting sensation of his impending orgasm, Mitch dragged his dirty fingernails across the cold concrete floor, breaking two of them at the wick.

Working her body over his in a rhythmic wave of pleasure, the corners of her mouth began to tear.

His hands, one bloodied at the fingertips, shot to her naked thighs, gripping them hard as his face pulled tight in a deranged grimace of sexual delight.

Inside her, she felt his penis swell to bursting.

Mitch opened his mouth to scream out the ecstasy.

Denying him a final pleasure before dying, she turned into the creature a split second before he spilled his seed inside her. The corners of her mouth tore open to her ears as her lips turned black and her teeth sharpened to razor edged shark teeth. Her naked sweating flesh erupted with flawless white fur across her body while her hands lengthened into spiked claws as her arms and legs elongated into grotesque muscular limbs and her ears pointed upwards like that of a jackal.

Seeing the transformation happen right on top of him, Mitch pulled his hands away in shock as his penis limped and fell out of the white monster above him.

The creature, still sitting on top of him, emotionlessly stared down at him with its large green emerald eyes and its huge gaping mouth.

Looking up at the creature's sinister face, Mitch

opened his mouth to scream out in terror.

With blurring speed, the creature clamped its mouth around his face and sank its razor sharp teeth into the sweaty unshaven flesh before the scream could roll out.

Flopping his arms and legs about on the barren concrete floor, Mitch desperately tried to get away from the searing pain to his face.

Relieving in the man's harrowing and hopeless struggle to survive, the creature crunched down on facial bone.

Lost in pain and terror, Mitch slipped into shock and lost control of his bowels. Hot liquid shit spilled out of his rectum.

Triumphantly, the creature lifted its head up and then spat the contents from its mouth.

Mitch's cheekbones, nose, and upper jaw landed a few feet away in a bloody mess.

Horribly disfigured and bleeding profusely, Mitch wiggled his tongue within the bloody hole that once had been his face as he tried to scream as he slowly drowned in his own blood.

Smiling through its large gaping mouth, the creature watched in silence as the boy from Detroit who grew up to build Corvettes died in a puddle of his own blood and shit in the basement of a homeless shelter.

CHAPTER 8

After speaking to Gil and closing out his former life, John busied himself with purchasing as many firearms as he could discreetly carry in his duffle bag.

Having absolutely no clue on how to obtain guns other than legally, he went to the nearest gun store to the motel and started the paperwork and the fifteen day waiting period on an assortment of weapons.

On the fifth day after checking into the motel, what had begun as a minor muscle ache across the length of his shoulder blades turned into a full-fledged bout of crippling fever, rendering him completely bedridden in agonizing pain.

CHAPTER 9

"New memories are waiting."

As John struggled to overcome the gripping fever that had suddenly taken hold of him, she watched, from the rooftop of the building, both yellow school buses which she had rented drive slowly away from the shelter, taking Alex and the majority of the residents of the shelter to the city's largest baseball stadium to pass out flyers for the annual toy drive sponsored by the city. The arrangement for the excursion had turned a tidy profit for her from the city, but most of all; it had left her almost completely all alone to continue fulfilling her plan in privacy. Whoever was still in the building was either asleep, drunk, or both.

With the three tanks already connected to the sprinkler system and the manual switch already installed, all that remained to be done was fill them up with gasoline.

Along the low wall of the roof were five large red containers filled with the flammable fluid, which she had lugged up herself during the middle of the previous night. The amount she had today would only fill one tank. The other two she planned to fill in the next couple of days.

As the sun continued to shine and the clouds rolled along the Los Angeles basin, she went to the red containers, picked one up, and uncapped it as she walked back the water tanks.

Gasoline fumes bellowed lazily outward from the container in her hands.

She poured the combustible liquid into the large black plastic water tank and smiled as she thought about the fate that awaited everyone.

Watching the gasoline sparkle in the bright afternoon sunlight as it went into the depths of the large tank, she remembered...

The moonlight danced and flickered off the surface of the clear running river where she stopped to wash the blood off her small hands.

Hunkered down and naked along the snow covered riverbank, her young bare feet felt neither the wind's bitter chill nor the stinging bite of the snow covered ground. Since fully recovering from the nightmarish fever that had followed after being bitten her tolerance to pain and the ability to rapidly recover from injuries was astonishing.

With her new dazzling green emerald eyes, she watched through a green colored hue the clear freezing water glided over her hands and arms and wash away the thick coating of blood that covered them.

In the moon lit darkness of the night, a slow sinister smile spread across her face, as she whispered to herself, "No more claims from thee."

After handing over their eldest daughter to her shock laden parents the Colonial Guards had returned to the creature's corpse only to find the naked body of a shot riddled unknown man where the monster had once been.

That evening, as the ragged bite wound continued to rapidly heal, the town's Mayor sat by her bedside and gently inquired on what had occurred earlier in the day.

Like a soft whisper from somewhere inside her head, something cold and menacing told her not to say what had truly occurred.

The Mayor, a portly, rosy faced man, listened, while gently patting her hand, to her spin a fictitious tale about some unknown man snatching her in the woods and being saved in the nick of time by the Colonial Guards.

With her side of the event in stark contrast to the one from the Guards, the Mayor, all too happy to avoid any type of scandal during an election year, smiled warmly at the injured girl and closed the inquest as nothing more than a poor unfortunate derelict suffering from a strange dose of cabin fever.

Later, insisting that their version was in fact the true and only accurate account, all three uniformed men fervently protested the official findings upon hearing it from the town's official.

She ran her freezing wet hands through her hair and stood up.

Before she could retrieve her hidden night gown from the bushes and slip back unnoticed to her upstairs bed chamber, the rest of the blood had to be washed off her nude body so she plunged into the mind numbingly cold flowing water.

Under the water, which was cold enough to stop most men's hearts, she ran her hands about her naked body, releasing the dried blood that had caked onto her.

Once cleansed of the gore, she crawled out of the water and stood up.

The freezing midnight air turned the water in her hair and on her skin into a crust of ice.

She turned back one last time and watched the soft warm glow coming from the Colonial Guards' cabin as the fire, she had started to mask the murders, burned it and the three shredded bodies inside into ashes.

In the distance the shouts of the townsfolk reacting to the fire drifted to her ears as she dressed herself in the dark.

Satisfied that the secret to the origin of what she was turning into was now secure, she casually walked along the snowy bank towards her home, listening to the lush wet babble of the cold rushing water flowing beside her.

She set the empty red container slowly down beside her and looked at her forearms. The memory of that night had returned in such vivid detail that her flesh had rippled with icy goose bumps under the bright California sun.

She was always amazed on how clear and vibrant her memories could be at times, regardless of how long ago they had happened.

She looked at the remaining gas containers and said out loud, "New memories are waiting."

Later that night after everyone had returned from the stadium, she steered her car, a cream colored super charged sedan, out of the shelter's parking lot and into traffic.

Looking back in the rearview mirror, she saw Alex standing by the delivery entrance watching her leave. She had told him about a city representative dinner and social gathering she needed to attend to further the welfare of the shelter; a lie.

At the end of the block, she took a right and headed east towards the onramp of the 10 freeway.

Driving away from the center of the city, she watched the Los Angeles skyline slowly go from hardened skyscrapers to weathered suburbs.

Forty minutes later she exited the freeway and drove into a darkened neighborhood.

Two houses down from the main street, she made a left down the alley and came to a stop in front of the rear-entry garage of a foreclosed home. With thousands of such homes littering the county; they provided convenient temporary storage space.

Dressed in her black high heels again, fishnet nylons, black leather skirt, black tank top, and a mariachi inspired black leather jacket that concealed the shoulder holster for her Italian 9mm and two extra magazines firmly beneath her underarms, she stepped out of her car.

Illuminated only by a distant street light and the night vision of her eyes, she hunkered down in front of the garage door, unlocked the padlock, and rolled it open.

Inside, the forgotten garage was lined with thick dust.

Making haste, she jumped back into her sedan,

steered it inside, and parked it next to an older model grey Japanese import, which she had stolen two days earlier.

Grabbing a leather briefcase from the passenger seat, she slipped out of her car, climbed into the other, pulled it out, locked the garage door, and drove away.

Back on the freeway, she changed her appearance to match the description the men who were waiting for her expected to see. She removed the colored contacts from her emerald eyes as her hair shortened to a bob and the color went from red to blonde. Her nose slimmed out to a graceful point and her mouth opened slightly as she gave herself a delicate overbite. Her thighs narrowed while her breasts cupped to a smaller firmer size.

An hour later, she exited the freeway.

On the street, she was met by large darkened buildings and factories.

Using the directions texted to her cellular phone earlier in the day, she wove her way through the city with ease to her destination; an old house tucked between a junkyard and an abandoned instant soup processing plant.

A few minutes later, she stopped the car in front of the single story home and turned off the car.

She quickly looked into the rearview mirror, gave herself a nod, and stepped out of the car, briefcase in hand.

Inhaling deeply through her nostrils, she calmly and slowly turned a full 180 degrees as the cool brisk wind of the night swept across the nape of her neck and under her skirt, chilling her skin.

The scent of the surrounding air told her that there were no snipers lurking about.

The lights within the dilapidated house switched on, signaling they were inside and everything was ready to begin.

She turned towards the light, rolled her shoulders to adjust the holster a bit higher, and walked to the old house.

The porch's weathered wooden planks groaned under her weight when she stepped up to the door.

Before she could reach out and touch the doorknob, the paint chipped door swung opened on protesting hinges, revealing nothing but an empty living room.

The corners of her mouth tingled as she stepped into the house. She needed to be careful; judging by the smell trapped within the small house, she was outnumbered and out gunned.

The door closed softly behind her.

She turned to face the person who had opened and closed the door.

Still holding the knob in his large hand was a clean shaven Middle-Easterner with piercing black eyes set beneath thick brows.

She stood motionlessly in front of him.

Looking her over, he digested her figure greedily, giving validity to her knowledge of an Arab's lust for luxurious looking blondes.

He spoke first, "My dear, I see you've come to settle our business arrangement," and then gestured to the briefcase at her side.

She wet her lips nonchalantly and told him in a perfect Northern Irish accent, "I've come to get... what I've come to get," then dropped the briefcase on the battered wooden floor.

All around her, footsteps creaked on the wooden

flooring in response to the sudden noise.

She counted three sets, which meant at least four men were inside the house with her.

The man at the door, gave a chuckle (a signal, she figured, to the others that all was well) and said, "My dear, life is in the details," then added as he picked up the case, "One must always handle matters with grace."

Putting her hands on her slender hips to show off the semi-automatic handgun under the leather jacket, she said, "Details are for obituaries... not for me."

He smiled at her words then he waved his left hand towards the kitchen area.

A young man, sporting the beginnings of a moustache, appeared.

He handed the boy the briefcase with a few words to him in Farsi.

With her legs slightly apart and her hands still on her hips, she calmly stared at the large smiling man blocking the front door as the boy disappeared back into the kitchen with the briefcase.

He said as his eyes continued to breathe in her figure, "A mere formality... I assure you... my dear. After all... trust is the key to success for our two organizations."

The fatal flaw to most terrorist splinter cells was an under-funded war chest and which made them all too willing to deal with anyone who could provide them with a quick dose of money. Though her connection to the IRA was now just cosmetic (unlike before) a few well-placed names here and there still provided her with enough access to just about any black marketer. Tonight's purchase was the conclusion to months of work and planning.

"Do me a favor... never mention my organization

and yours in the same breath again," she told him flatly.

Listening to her speak to him in such a manner, the man smiled back, "My dear… you are a very brave girl to speak to me as you are right now."

She replied, "Brave isn't the word," then dropped the leather jacket on the floor behind her feet, exposing the shoulder holster and the majesty of her body's beauty.

Enjoying the dangerous banter with the gorgeous blonde, his smile widen, exposing even dazzling white teeth.

Just then, the young peach fuzzed boy returned from the kitchen carrying a glass mason jar filled with what looked like regular table salt. He handed it to the cell leader, received another instruction, again in Farsi, and then walked towards the left bedroom, snatching a glance at the blonde woman's breasts as he passed her.

Holding the jar up to her but not handing it over, he said, "As promised, my dear."

Looking at the glass container hovering just in front of her, she fought back the desire to turn into the creature and rip him to shreds but instead she licked her glossy lips and asked, "How about a taste?

He shook the jar slightly, the white granules clicked inside the glass, and replied, "But of course my dear. In fact, we have it all ready," then gestured towards the bedroom.

She waited for him to go first then followed him.

Walking through the small house, she assessed it was nothing more than a two bedroom, one bath post-World War 2 housing shortage unit.

Upon entering the bedroom on the left, decorated with nothing more than a single antique framed mirror on the wall to her right, she saw four other men, besides the cell leader waiting for her to come in. Two more Middle Easterners, one of whom was holding a power drill with a large bit attached to it, the young boy, and a Hispanic male who was tied to a chair with a BDSM red ball gag in his mouth and utter panic dancing insanely in his eyes.

All of them, except the horrified man strapped to the chair, ran their eyes over her black clad body.

As if to signal the beginning of the demonstration, the leader shook the jar again and said, "A derivative of Succinylcholine... this product offers all the benefits of the famous anesthetic but with the bonus of...", he paused for effect, "...giving the user the ability to administer it orally through food or drink," he paused again, this time staring directly at her breasts while he geared himself up for the best part of his speech, "... Also eye movement will remain unhindered, providing you with visible proof that your subjects are aware of what's being done to them."

"Show me," she told him, eager to see pain and violence.

He lowered the jar to his side, gave a small bow at her request then spoke in his native tongue to the one with the drill and to the boy.

With their orders given, the boy rushed out of the bedroom, towards the kitchen, and the other kneeled in front the sweating, muffled captive, whose baseball cap on his head was now entirely soaked through with frightened sweat.

The leader walked over to the panic stricken man, bent down, and said to him, in thick Spanish, "If you scream...when I take off the gag... my associate will drill into your knee...do you understand?"

Eyes bulging in terror, the man nodded in

understanding.

With a fatherly smile, the cell leader straightened, reached around the back of the man's head and unfastened the leather straps.

The red rubber ball, damp with sweat and drool, fell away.

Motionless she ingested every single second of the wretched man's fear. It had been days since her last kill and the creature within her was crying out for blood to be spilled.

The boy quickly returned with a small glass of water and a teaspoon. He bypassed everyone in the room, handed the two articles to the cell leader, and then stepped back away from everyone.

To show the absence of any slight-of-hand, the cell leader kneeled down on one knee, placed the jar, glass of water and spoon in a neat row on the floor, and said, "We found our good friend here waiting for work in front of a local home repair store," then added with a mischievous tone and a fiendish smile, "He has agreed to help us tonight with our little demonstration."

Staring back at him, she raised an eye brow and said, "Go on."

He continue, "Now...," unscrewing the jar, "...a full dose will provide the same effect as the parent drug," then scooped out a leveled serving of the white salt-like substance with the teaspoon, "Immediate paralysis of body with full consciousness from the subject."

He dropped the granule drug into the glass of water and began to stir, "Remember the ratio is one part for every ten parts of food or drink," he tapped the spoon on the rim of the glass and stood up.

Without having understood a single word that had been spoken, the terror stricken test subject knew that the glass and its murky white content were meant for him. He bucked and struggled within his restraints as he pleaded loudly in Spanish to be let go.

Smiling, the cell leader readjusted the sweat darkened cap squarely on the Mexican's head as he spoke to him in Spanish once again, "You agreed... to remain quiet... this isn't going to kill you...but that drill...will make you beg us to kill you...once it goes into your knee...NOW SHUT UP!" and then with blinding speed struck him across the left cheek bone.

The illegal immigrant, who had crossed over the previous summer with the hope of earning enough money to save his grandfather's lime farm in the state of Michoacán from foreclosure, tipped over from the heavy blow to his face and landed on the wooden floor, chair and all.

She watched a collective gasp radiate from the four other cell members as they witnessed their leader's hidden ability for violence reveal itself.

Like a light switch, he instantly shot back to his former smiling self, turned to her, and said, "My dear, please forgive the delay in our demonstration. I assure you...," he motioned for his men to pick up the wounded man off the floor, "... there will be no further interruptions."

She told him as the stunned victim was reset to his former sitting position, "Quite alright. I'm enjoying myself."

Hearing her approval to his violent act, he smiled warmly at her as an image of her nude body standing in the middle of a corn field flashed in his mind.

With his human guinea pig upright once again, he continued, "Now... in order to demonstrate the full effect of our product... I'll have our good friend here take a full dose."

The frightened and injured man shook his head in quiet protest.

Speaking once more in heavy laden Spanish, the cell leader said, "You'll be fine… just drink this…and tomorrow…when you…wake up… we'll let you go," then without any further speech or fanfare, he put the glass to the man's mouth, tilted it, and watched the contents disappear down his captive's throat.

Watching in silence, her heart pounded with anticipation as to what came next.

"Notice that the effect at full strength is just about instantaneously," he told her then snapped his fingers twice beside the Mexican's face.

The man's eyes moved towards the sound of the Arab's voice snapping fingers while his body sat limp and motionless in the chair.

"He is neither dead nor unconscious, simply fully awake and aware of everything around him with his ability to move subtracted," he informed her.

She silently observed what he was telling her.

"And now the best part, my dear. Observe our friend's eyes as the drill tunnels into his knee. You'll see that he is able to register pain to its fullest degree during his induced state by the expression on his eyes.

The cell member holding the drill pressed the trigger of the tool and the drill bit spun into life.

The Mexican's eyes watched in horror at what was happening right in front of him.

Holding the drill with both hands, the Lieutenant to the terror cell knelt down just off to the right of the doomed Mexican, put the tip of the bit against the man's knee, and looked up at the cell leader for the order to commence.

Smiling, the cell leader gave the nod and the Lieutenant pressed trigger of the drill.

With effortless ease the drill bit slipped past the man's jeans and into his knee.

The motor of the tool whirred and hummed as the bit bore into the limb.

Blood, bone, and meat splattered from the hole in the man's denim.

Watching the carnage unfold, she felt the corners of her mouth ache to split open while the captive's eyes bulged in their sockets like hard boiled eggs as he watched what was being done to his right leg and the maddening pain seared throughout his drug imprisoned body.

With a sickening crunch, the drill bit erupted out the back of the wrecked limb and hit the wooden chair leg.

Her plan had been simple; leave the money, take the drug, and walk away but the brutal display of torture was driving the lust for death to the surface.

She took a deep breath and swallowed through a tightened throat in an effort to calm herself.

The Lieutenant reversed the spin of the bit and pulled it out of the Mexican's ruined leg.

Ever smiling, the cell leader told her, "And now for the pelvis."

Listening to his final words on earth, the last of her endurance to withhold the need to kill within her fell away. Her mouth split wide open across her face in a demonic shark teeth filled snarl as she hissed furiously out loud.

At the sudden terrifying sound, all the cell members turned in unison towards her.

With blinding speed, she drew her handgun from

its holster and shot the one holding the drill first.

His face imploded just above the upper lip and chunks of his brains landed on the Mexican's lap.

Next, she swung the 9mm at the cell leader, who still held the glass and spoon in his large hands, and squeezed off two rounds into his chest.

With nothing more than a whimper, he dropped to the floor and died.

Quick and precise, she followed up by firing on the peach fuzzed errand boy.

The first bullet tore into his face below the right eye and the second bore into his neck.

With his spinal cord shattered and his right eye dangling from its optic nerve, the youngest member of the cell hit the ground face first and died a second later.

The fourth Arab in the room realizing what was happening, drew his weapon from its holster, raised the handgun to fire then suddenly felt his legs crumple beneath him as three hollow-point bullets slammed into his chest. He died before hitting the ground.

Then without warning, the mirror on the right wall exploded, sending jagged shards of mirror and double-ought-buck ripped into her face, breasts, and right arm.

Suddenly caked in numbing pain, she turned and saw a hole in the wall within the mirror's antique frame and a fifth man jacking another round into his shotgun from the other room.

The fired cartridge's deadly power and velocity had been drastically lost from breaking through the reflective glass. Nevertheless, the shotgun blast at almost point blank range had severely wounded her; the right side of her face was completely torn open from jaw to cheek bone, her right arm was mangled and bloodied, and her breasts had been shredded into bags of bloodied flesh.

Realizing the old frame had been used to disguise a two-way mirror; she smiled at the innovative concept and promised herself to use the same idea one day herself.

With a fresh shell in the shotgun's chamber, he aimed and fired.

The sound from the weapon's discharge thundered inside the small wooden house.

Using instincts refined to a laser's edge from over two centuries of living and killing, she dove out of the way a fraction of a second ahead of the deadly buckshot.

The spot where she had been standing a split second prior disintegrated in a thunder of shot pellets and wood.

Using the momentum of her leap, she rolled to the far side of bedroom and came up shooting, empting the rest of the magazine in a single volley.

The man in the other room stepped back from the hole in order to keep from being hit by her incoming rounds.

With nausea and unconsciousness from her wounds threatening to overtake her, she pressed the magazine release button on her gun, pulled a fresh clip from the shoulder holster, and reloaded just as the final remaining cell member in the adjacent room jacked yet another shell into the chamber of his shotgun and stepped forward to fire.

Knowing that her only defense against the superior weapon and position was offense, she took a running start and leaped into the air, arms extended out in front of her, towards the hole in the shattered mirror.

The man on the other room leveled the shotgun

and took aim.

Flying through the air, her tattered face contoured with rage and wanton survival.

Stunned with disbelief at what he was looking, the last of the cell members hesitated in firing and lost the advantage.

Tearing her breasts further with the jagged edges of the shattered mirror, she sailed into the other room, pushed the shotgun barrel up and away with her mangled right hand, sank the muzzle of the 9mm deep into his gut, and emptied the magazine in rapid succession into his body.

They landed in a heap on the floor.

Lethally wounded, cell member gasped once and died with his finger still on the trigger of the shotgun.

With her strength all but depilated, she rolled off the dead body, slowly stood up, and reloaded her weapon with the last of her magazines.

Hindered by the overwhelming pain from the shotgun blast, she labored to the other bedroom as her face shifted back to human form underneath the savage wound.

Still tied to the chair, Carlos Mynor Lopez Fuentes, whose wife and children would wonder forever to his whereabouts, followed her with staring pain-stricken eyes when she entered the room.

Without any fanfare or second thought, she shot him three times in the face, killing him instantly.

Wounded and tired, she knelt down in front of the mason jar and said out loud in a house filled with dead men, "A plan is only a plan...until the fire is lit."

CHAPTER 10

A week after falling ill with the hardest fever he had ever experienced, John rose out of bed and slowly stood on his feet for the first time in a week. The fever that had gripped him in a vice of gut wrenching pain had simply vanished as quickly as it had appeared.

With the mattress soaked in sweat down to the box spring and his skin ashy white with the powdery residue of his own body salt, he placed his hands on his hips, leaned back, and stretched out the muscles in his abdomen.

Like a caterpillar morphing into a butterfly, a sense of restoration was swelling inside him, filling his body with a feeling of wellbeing.

The rug under his feet felt alien and new as he began to pace about the room with returning vigor.

His stomach rumbled for food.

He stopped and smiled at the sensation; he was actually hungry for the first time in what felt like an eternity.

Standing at the foot of the bed, John lifted up an

arm and smelled himself; the stench of sweat and sick seemed to cover him in a film as much as the salt on his body did. He needed a shower before food, before daylight, before anything so he went to the bathroom and flipped the light switch.

Virtually untouched since the last time it had been cleaned so many days ago, the small cream tiled room filled with light.

The mirror above the sink reflected his naked body back to him.

He looked at the reflection of his face and what he saw staring back at him buckled his knees, dropping him to the linoleum floor.

His eyes had turned emerald green.

CHAPTER 11

Earlier in the evening, she had slipped out of the shelter undetected and shifted her appearance to look like a better than average prostitute; filling out her lips and ass, blackening her hair, tanning her skin and then applying black contacts to her emerald eyes. Later, after trolling a number of hotel lounges, she had allowed herself to be picked up and to be driven to a secluded hilltop in Echo Park.

The driver's had been quick yet rewarding. While smiling at her savagely and stroking his hardened penis with his hand, she had gone into her purse, under the pretense of reaching for a condom, and had produced a hooker's weapon instead, a cheap kitchen knife. His smile had melted from his face and his penis had weathered in his hand when the point of the blade had come to rest just below his Adam's apple. Then, as he had begged for his life, she had slowly slid the serrated knife into his throat.

Now, still sitting in the passenger seat of the dead

man's German import, she contently stared at the Los Angeles skyline through the fogged windshield. Born during a time of candles and kerosene lamps, she enjoyed looking at the massive buildings that seemed to literally scrape the sky above and illuminate the night with floating squares of light.

Having been so busy filling the water tanks with gasoline and dealing with the terror cell, she simply hadn't had the time to think of anything else. However, now, in the warmth of the car's interior and the smell of fresh blood filling her with a sense of tranquil wellbeing, she collected her thoughts and thought about John Poole once again.

Remembering her own transformation so long ago, she figured his eyes had probably turned green by now. And just as she had, he would continue to slowly change until finally becoming something far sinister than he could ever have imagined.

She ran the side of her palm across the car's inner windshield and swiped away the collected moisture.

The L.A. skyline reappeared once again in front of her, bright and detailed.

Looking at the vast cityscape, she thought it odd how, in some strange way, she could almost sense him slowly becoming exactly like her somewhere out there.

CHAPTER 12

"What the hell is wrong with me tonight?"

The following day.

Standing in front of the mirror, John Poole looked at himself in the new outfit he had purchased earlier in the day; grey gabardine slacks, black button down shirt open at the throat, and new leather belt. The clothes he had carried out with him the night he had left his condo no longer fit him. Since recovering from the maddening fever that had bedridden him, his body had taken on a whole new appearance; most of his body fat was gone, his limbs had stretched out, and his muscles had coiled with definition.

He leaned closer to the mirror, touched his scar, and looked at his eyes; crystalline emerald green irises surrounded deep black pupils set against amazingly white sclera. To him, they looked like orbs of hand blown glass that had been inserted into his skull.

He turned away from the mirror and sat down on the edge of the bed as he told that there was no denying the obvious point; he was turning into whatever she was.

John put his head in his hands and closed his new eyes.

An image of the creature staring at him flashed in his mind.

He lifted his head out of his hands and stood up.

He walked to the other side of the bed and sat down again, saddened and depressed by what was happening to him, John put his hands on his hips and looked up at the stucco ceiling. His life, he measured, had become a nightmare straight out of a horror movie.

John closed his eyes and lowered his head, resting his chin on his chest.

Then, without warning, an abrupt sensation in the center of his chest made him lift his head and open his eyes wide.

Confounded by the sudden feeling, he stood up and touched his scar.

The sensation pulsed a second time in his chest.

Standing completely still, John took a deep breath as he assessed what he was feeling.

Suddenly the little Hindu woman who manned the front desk of the motel came to mind and, to his utter surprise, an unexpected desire to harm her. He knew that she had already started her work day and by nine tonight she'd be all alone until she was relieved by the graveyard shift manager.

John quickly stepped to the left and leaned his back against the wall, and whispered out loud, breaking the disturbing train of thought, "Jesus… John… what the fuck!"

The desire for violence, a single melodic hum, continued deep in his chest.

A wave of claustrophobia suddenly washed over him.

John looked around the interior of the motel room as an unbearable need to be outside took hold of him.

Unable to bear being inside one second longer, he pushed off the wall, snatched his keys, and made for the door.

Outside, on the third story walkway, the cool night air soothed the sickening feeling of confinement that had inexplicably overwhelmed him a moment ago.

An image of the motel clerk's face beaten into a bloody pulp flashed across his mind.

Taken aback by another vivid thought of violence against the simple woman just three floors down, John clenched his fists and dashed down the stairs towards his car.

An hour after speeding away from the motel, John found himself driving aimlessly about the Los Angeles basin without direction or destination.

The hum in his chest had subsided some time ago to a tolerable level.

Driving through lit streets, he looked at the people walking along the sidewalk, noticed how they smiled at nothing in particular with a glazed stupidity, and felt a touch of envy ripple through his heart as he compared their seemingly vacant lives to the one he was currently living.

A few blocks later, he turned left off Wilshire Blvd and drove into a middle-class neighborhood in Korea Town.

Driving at a low speed, John looked at the stucco walled apartment buildings that lined both sides of the street.

Not sure as to why he was even there or what he hoped to find, he found an empty spot behind an SUV, parked, and shut the engine off.

Seated in the confines of his vehicle, he pushed himself into the backrest of his seat and closed his eyes.

The still of the night and the comfortable interior of his car surrounded him with a sense of well-being as he took deep relaxing breaths.

Then, to his surprise, an image of blood splashed against a white wall flashed across his mind and the sensation in the center of his chest picked up once again.

He opened his eyes and rubbed his face as he whispered, "What the hell... is wrong with me... tonight?"

The same claustrophobia as before rolled over him again.

He opened the door and stepped out into the cool darkened air of the night.

Taking the night into his lungs, John casually looked around the neighborhood he was in.

Parked cars and quiet apartment buildings surrounded him.

He scanned the desolate street and decided that perhaps a good long walk would soothe him better than aimlessly driving so he closed the door to his car and started down the dark and lonesome street.

Walking past apartment building after apartment building, he realized there were two worlds that coexisted side by side; one with monsters and the other without.

Touching the scar on his forehead, he figured that he had spent the first part of his life in one and now it seemed that he was bound to spend the rest of his life in the other.

At the end of the block, he stopped at the edge of the curb, saw a dimly lit alley and went to it without much forethought, a decision that would haunt him for years to come.

The alley itself was typical of what one would find in most L.A. neighborhoods; metal dumpsters and tiny oil stained carports with vehicles between worn white lines.

Walking along the right side, he peered into the courtyards of the apartment buildings.

When he reached the center of the alley, he heard a pair of voices coming from further down.

John stopped and listened.

The voices were of two distinct men chatting happily about something.

He started to walk slowly to them.

With every step that he took, the louder his heartbeat resounded in his chest.

Stopping only a few feet away, John hunkered down beside a dark green dumpster.

Finally able to make out exactly they were saying, he realized both men were talking about cars.

Listening to them, the sensation in the center of his chest returned.

John closed his eyes. Like lust, the sensation for violence swelled in his chest and spread out like warm oil throughout his entire body.

Beside a few school yard fights in high school, he had never felt the need to hurt someone else. However, for some unbeknownst reason, all he wanted to suddenly do was lash out at the pair of total strangers just a few feet from him.

John slowly shook his head in dismay.

One of the two men laughed out loud.

The image of blood splashed across a white wall flashed again in his mind.

John opened his eyes, and before he knew it, stood up, and stepped around the concrete wall.

Just ten feet directly in front of him, he saw two men hunkered under the raised hood of an old pickup truck.

A worker's lamp hung from a hook on the front edge of the hood. Tools littered about and a few empty beer bottles sat along the right front tire. A cooler chest rested along the wall with an oily rag crumpled on top.

The rubber soles of his leather shoes made his approach silent and sinister as he drew closer to them.

Finally, something caught their eye and they noticed him walking slowly in their direction. At first, they considered him with a just a sideways glance and dismissed him as just another neighbor entering the building but as he continued to advance straight at them, their conversation abruptly stopped and they turned to him with a confused and concerned look in their eyes.

Unsure what he planned to do, John stopped by the side of the passenger door of the pickup and stared at the two men who were now looking at him in silent apprehension. His mouth tingled furiously at the corners as the sensation in his chest hummed with a life of its own.

The one closest to him, a pudgy bellied Bobcat operator by day in an under shirt and a tattoo of a winning hand of cards on his left arm was the first to understand the quiet reverence of danger standing in front of them so he stepped around the pickup and squared his shoulders in a defensive stance.

Staring calmly at the larger man, John made no movement.

With his chest rising and falling as adrenaline filled his system, he spoke out to the well-dressed stranger standing silently in front of him for the last time using his original teeth, "What the fuck, bro?"

Then, even before he could calculate what to do, John closed the distance between them both and drove his fist into the bottom part of the man's unshaven chin, breaking the jaw cleanly in half and shattering most the man's teeth.

The devastating blow lifted the heavyset man a whole inch off the ground.

Severely injured and instantly slipping into shock, he fell flat on his back on to the pavement, bleeding and unconscious.

Later, the hospital would extract a broken tooth from his lung.

Standing over the beaten and incapacitated man, John heard the other one rush forward.

Sick with rage at what he had just witnessed, the newspaper deliverer and father of two small boys, bellowed out, "Motherfucker!" as he rounded the front end of his work truck, screwdriver in hand.

John watched the deadly tool raced towards his sternum as the enraged man thrust it at him with blinding speed.

Then, at the last second before the flat head screwdriver plunged into his body, John sidestepped the strike and sunk his fist deep into his attacker's midsection.

A tremendous rush of air escaped from the man's face and a loud wet fart erupted from out his backside as his spleen ruptured.

Freed from the man's hand, the screwdriver twisted in the air, hints of light danced off the metal before hitting the ground in a clatter.

As if stranded in a sort of suspended animation, the wounded man doubled over next to his unknown assailant, gasping for air.

Then, as the injured man continued to struggle for breath, John zeroed in and smashed his fist into the man's contorted pain filled express, shattering the maxilla and nasal bone like egg shells.

With the front part of his skull completely destroyed, the Fresno native crumpled to the ground and passed out.

Standing over the men he had just beaten half to death, a euphoric sensation, calming and gentle, washed over him as the humming in his chest completely stopped.

Suddenly, coming from somewhere in the apartment complex, John heard a woman scream out loud then yell out for someone to call the police, turned on his heels, and dashed into the darkness of the night.

Weeks later, the police would officially close the case and file it under attempted robbery with no arrests.

CHAPTER 13

"We shall walk together, side by side"

With her T-strap platform heels in her hand and the smell of blood from the dead driver still in her nostrils, she stepped into her office in the early morning of the following day.

From below the aroma of breakfast being made filled the upper halls and stairs.

Feeling the worn carpet under her bare soles, she walked over to her desk and fell into the welcoming leather executive's chair behind it with a slump, tired and sedate from the evening's kill.

After stepping out of the German sedan, she had walked in her bare feet to the edge of Echo Park and then took a cab ride to the hotel where she had parked her car, ducking into the ladies room first to quickly change her clothes and appearance. On her way back to the shelter, she had detoured to the rear of a plastics factory and disposed of the clothes she had worn during the murder into one of the company's three large garbage bins.

Feeling the chair's supple leather warm to her back, she closed her emerald green eyes and let the stillness of the new found morning slowly take her over.

The gentle hum of the streetlight just outside her window and the smell of her office gently soothed her into a stupor.

Ready to retire to her small bedroom that was Jack and Jilled to the office, she opened her eyes and caught sight of a manila folder sitting by the phone on her desk with a neon green sticky note attached to it.

She leaned forward and took it into her hands.

The sticky note, written in Alex's sweeping longhand, simply read 'For you, from the kids'.

She placed the folder in her lap, leaned back, and opened it.

Inside were half a dozen drawings, each done in a child's hand; bold and abstract in crayon.

She looked at the heading of the first one, it read; Miss Susan in gold crayon above a child's rendition of a meadow on a sunny day with a female stick figure in the center.

Captivated by the pure innocence of the drawing, her large green eyes stared deep into drawing's rolling meadow and...

The vast deep blue sky hung over her head as she lay prone against the rich rolling grass of the American mid-west.

The summer sun warmed her back underneath the worn cornflower blue dress she wore.

From her vantage point, she could make out an

Indian hunting party gathering to advance on the grazing buffalo that strolled lazily about the sweeping landscape.

Since leaving her family home decades ago, many events had passed in front of her dazzling emerald green eyes. The colonies of the New World had become a nation united, wars and conflicts had come and gone, order and stability had been established, and the push to claim for rest of the Continent had spread like wild fire, driving many immigrant families westward across endless miles of unspoiled land. For the last four years, she had been living and killing in the growing city of St. Louis, praying upon lonely men, hopeful families, and destitute women until finally opting for the solitude of the wilderness instead of the grim and dirt of the city. While living wildly in the forests, she had come to rely upon the westward trails leading out of Missouri to provide her with victims. Whether they were adventurers or whole groups of families when darkness fell, they were hers for the choosing.

Now, flat on her belly, she watched the young Indian braves, as she had been doing since stumbling upon their buffalo hunting grounds weeks ago, go about their final steps before they commenced with the hunt.

She had come to understand, from watching at a distance, their methods of selecting their target; they only ran down young male buffalos of weak character, ones that would never dominate the herd enough to mate and spread their inferior genes while the females and Alpha males were always spared thus ensuring the continuous growth of a healthy and abundant hunting stock.

With the hunt only minutes from beginning, she turned her gaze upon the leader of the hunting party ride up on a beautiful Palomino. A young man in his twenties whose rich brown skin covered a body structure alive with muscle and youthful vigor. A long mane of onyx black hair bounced off his chiseled back as he rode in a trotting gallop towards the rest of his men.

She picked herself up to her elbows to gather a better view.

The other Indians fell into a loose formation behind him, bringing their rifles to bear in the process.

She watched him review his men with a backwards glance and then produce a single arrow from his waist band, break it in half over his head, and then let the broken halves fall from his hands to either side of his spotted horse and thus signaling the hunt to get underway.

From her position on the hill, she watched the hunting party descend upon the slow moving current of grazing buffalo.

Leading the charge, the leader, who carried no rifle, raised a mahogany handle tomahawk high above his head as he steered his hard driving horse alongside the massive three mile long column of migrating animals.

Suddenly, with a communication all their own, the signal of danger went out among the herd. A wave of sound and vibration shook the earth as the buffalos sprang all at once into a thunderous run for their lives. With their eyes wild with fear and their brains pierced with the insanity to survive, the free range buffalos flowed blindly across the vast open plain with gathering speed until they were nothing more than a stampeding horde of fur, meat, and hoofs.

Riding dangerously close to the deadly swift flowing current of panicked beasts, the leader surveyed what the spirit gods had to offer his tribe today.

Alpha males bracketed pregnant females between them and the young calves hid among the adults as a blanket of dust bellowed upward from thousands of pounding hoofs.

Then, with the eye of an experienced buffalo hunter, the young Indian chief spotted their kill; a young adolescent male that was doing his best to keep within the middle of the flow yet was slowly being push out towards the edge by the stronger ones of his kind.

Signaling to the others that the offering had been found, the leader raised his tomahawk again and pointed it at the young buffalo that was now at the outer edge of the stampede.

He pulled the reins of his horse to slow it down as the other Indians sped past him towards the chosen animal.

Knowing that the kill was only moments away, she stood up on her knees to watch the action unfold.

While holding onto their hard charging horses with nothing more than their feet inside the stirrups of the saddle, the group of hunters raised their rifles to their shoulders and fired down upon the young buffalo.

All five bullets slammed into the running beast at once.

Mortally wounded, the young buffalo rolled head over hoof once and then crumpled in a heap onto the earth in a cloud of dust and dirt while the stampeding mass continued onward in their thundering escape.

Seeing the mortally wounded animal down on the ground, the leader slid his Palomino to a halt as the others steered their horses back to the fallen beast.

He swung a leg over the saddle and dropped down next to the fallen animal, tomahawk in hand.

In silence, the men hovered over both their leader and the day's catch. They watched as he gently placed a hand over the snorting animal's terror stricken looping eye and spoke to it in his native tongue, "Thank you, brother. You ran well today. The strength in your blood will always be remembered as a blessing from the spirit gods," lifted the tomahawk above his head and said, "Go in peace to the promised pasture of the gods," and then with one swift arching swing he plunged the axe deep into the thick pulsating artery in the animal's neck.

The moment she had been waiting for had arrived. With the clear blue sky and soft clouds as her backdrop, she stood up, unfastened her dress and let it fall down around her bare feet.

With his sun drenched chest covered in fresh blood from the dead animal's arterial spray, he turned towards his men, raised the blood soaked weapon high in celebration, and saw her standing in the distance.

As quietly as she could, she gathered the multicolored blanket about her naked body and slid out of the tepee.

The cool breezy comfort of the night greeted her warm exposed skin in a caressing chill.

Walking lightly across the silent sleeping Indian village, she made her way to the river bank at its western edge.

Once there, she padded her bare feet into the water and watched the glittering moonlight dance against the crystalline flowing current as the memory of washing off the Colonial militia men's blood in the freezing river returned with vivid clarity.

Suddenly, from behind, the sound of someone walking up to her reached her ear.

Knowing instantly who it was by the sound of the footsteps, she remained as she was, untroubled by the unseen figure.

The footsteps came to a stop just behind her and a deep robust voice spoke to her with a tenderness that one would find in a comforting hug, "Rolling Cloud, what awakes you tonight?"

She smiled at the sound of the voice and slowly turned around to face the man who had been the first to see her on the hill top five years ago, the hunt leader. She answered in his native language she had come to learn with the same caring tone, "The past beckoned me to remember it tonight."

He reached out, placed a tanned hand on her white delicate shoulder, and asked, "And what do the spirit gods of the past ask of you to remember, Rolling Cloud?"

She touched his out stretched forearm and answered with a small sad smile, "Death is the only element that lives in my past, Broken Arrow. And death is the only thing I am asked to remember."

Looking down at the sad smile on her face, he cupped the side of her neck, ran his right thumb softly over her left ear, and said, "You are also a spirit god, Rolling Cloud. A spirit god who has shown us many great things. My only wish is that you allow me to continue to show you the love found in the time we call the present."

"I'd like that, Broken Arrow," she said to him then turned once more towards the river bank.

He stepped forward, placing his nude body against

the contours of her back, and wrapped his grey woolen blanket, marked with the letters US in the center, around the both of them.

Feeling the heat from his body and the touch of his flaccid penis on the small of her back, she looked out across the wide open landscape on the other side of the river. She had never seen anyone from the tribe cross the river so she asked, "Broken Arrow, why is it that no one crosses the river? After five harvest cycles, I have never seen anyone go across it."

He placed his right cheek on her left temple and answered, "There is nothing we need from over there that we are not able to find on this side. Crossing would mean that we would be taking more than we need."

She turned her head slightly to catch a sight of him in her peripheral vision, "Has no one ever crossed the river?"

"No one, Rolling Cloud," he answered her question flatly.

His innocence pierced her heart like a mortal stab wound. She turned to face him again and asked, "And the white man, Broken Arrow? What about them and their hungered ways? They have no debate about crossing the river or any river."

.   .   .

He had become chief of the tribe, his father willing stepping down, the day he had taken her, the shape shifting spirit god, as his wife, and during that time he had turned to tradition and the teachings from the spirit world for guidance.

.   .   .

Broken Arrow replied, "The white man is a part of the earth, just like us, Rolling Cloud. His purpose is to bring confusion and disorder to the land. Because there can be no wisdom without confusion, and no peace without disorder."

"Are you not afraid of them?" she asked him.

"The spirit world sent you to us as protection against them and all the other Indian nations," he quietly answered.

She touched his high cheeked boned face, "Is that what you truly believe in, Broken Arrow?"

He grabbed his small tender white hand in his and answered, "I believe it with every bone in my body, Rolling Cloud. I have believed in it the moment I first saw you standing naked on the hill top then change over to your spirit form in front of us all. I will always believe it... forever."

She gave no response to what he had just said but only stared deep into his obsidian black eyes with her glossy emerald colored ones and wished for nothing more than for everything he so valiantly believed in to be true. Since becoming part of the tribe, peace had been restored once again in her life and the creature's constant need for murder had gone silent within her.

Broken Arrow took her silence and the expression in her eyes as a sign of understanding and added, "Tomorrow the buffalo return, Rolling Cloud. Though their numbers continue to decrease with every harvest cycle, the spirit world will honor us with many offerings nonetheless. Will you join us, as before, with your presence in tomorrow's hunt as a spirit god?"

She pressed her naked skin against his and answered, "I will."

As buffalo herds continued to decrease in numbers with every passing year, the hunters traveled further out of their accustomed stalking grounds. This season had taken them further south than ever before.

Clothed only in a dress, decorated in the tribe's traditional colors of orange and black with buffalo leather trim at the sleeves and neck line, she stood on a knoll, in her bare feet, a short distance away from Broken Arrow and his men.

Considered to be a spirit god annotated in flesh, it was now her duty to signal the start of the hunt. So, as she had done for the last four years, she scanned the slow moving mass of sweating buffalo grazing in the distance to her left.

Waiting calmly on horseback with the rest of his trusted men behind a cluster of isolated trees and downwind from the vigilant beasts, Broken Arrow, holding an arrow in his sun leathered hands, watched for her signal.

With one final long sweeping look across the river of living moving muscle, sweat, and hoof, she gave the signal for the hunt to begin; pulling the ties at the shoulders of her dress and letting it slip off her body onto the grass around her feet.

The sun bathed her smooth lean body in a rich radiant light of warmth as the cool wind licked at her creamy white skin.

.   .   .

On the day he was born, both Broken Arrow and his dead mother lay covered in her blood on the dirt floor of his parent's tepee. The spirit world, he would later be told on his thirteenth birthday, had reclaimed one soul for another. His father, Black Horse, about to start the first buffalo hunt of the new season, was informed of his son's birth and his wife's death minutes before beginning. Black Horse whose devotion to the spirit world was legendary lifted up a signal arrow above his head and snapped it in two, telling the gods above that enough death had occurred for one day. Thus, the tradition was created and his son was named.

.   .   .

Broken Arrow saw her signal, raised the arrow above his head, snapped it in two, and let the broken pieces fall to the ground in memory of his mother and father.

She watched the two halves of the arrow fell from his hands and sprang into a full sprint across the soft rolling knoll and towards the grazing buffalo below.

At the sight of her racing off towards the gigantic herd, Broken Arrow, tomahawk now in hand, kicked off to join in the hunt with his men following behind him.

Running at full tilt, her limbs elongated and her fingers clawed into spikes. Her mouth split at the corners to her ears as her teeth sharpened to shark-like teeth while dazzling snow white fur rippled throughout her figure.

Galloping, they stayed in pace with her as they watched her changed into her spirit self; a god of beautiful white running across the landscape like a rolling cloud.

Completely transformed, the emerald green eyed creature ran alongside the wall of buffalos.

At the sight of the monster next to them, the massive herd of American bison quickened to a nervous trot.

Broken Arrow and his men closed the distance from the rear.

The herd began to move even faster as the mounted horses closed in.

The creature's large glossy emerald eyes scanned the herd for its mark; a male runt.

Suddenly, all at once and without warning, the wild buffaloes bolted into a rumbling earth pounding run towards nowhere.

Hissing through its wide grotesque mouth, the creature kept pace and waited for the runt to be slowly pushed out to the side of the swift moving current of thundering beasts.

Dust rose upwards in thick plumes around the panicked running herd.

Then, within the stampeding mass, a young inferior male buffalo began to emerge at the outer edge.

Spotting it, the creature quickened its pace.

The adolescent buffalo emerged completely from out of the running horde.

The creature leaped high into the air, crawls extended and mouth gaping.

Broken Arrow and his men cheered.

The white furred creature landed alongside the young buffalo and instantly took hold of its small horns in its long clawed hands.

The animal bucked and struggled against the imposing strength of the creature's grip.

Knowing it could very well be trampled to death under the current of beating hoofs at any moment; the creature dug its heels down hard into the thundering ground and cranked the animal's large head sharply to the right in one swift downward motion.

Caught between its own momentum and the creature vice-like hold, the buffalo's rear legs went up and over its head and then came crashing down into the earth in a tremendous violent spectacle.

Capitalizing on the moment its prey laid head over hoof, the creature stabbed the animal in the neck with its spiked fingernails.

Blood, dark red with life, jetted out in hot streams from the buffalo's ravaged neck as it thrashed about against the lethal assault.

The creature, eager not to be hit by wounded beast's dangerous kicking hoofs, rolled away to the right.

A second later, Broken Arrow and his men unleashed a lethal volley rifle fire into the dying animal, killing it instantly.

The creature came out of its roll in a standing position beside the thundering herd.

Broken Arrow dismounted his horse, went to the dead animal, and knelt down beside it while his men tended to his horse.

With an instinct all their own, the massive herd slowed as if knowing that the danger was over for the time being.

As tribe tradition dictated, Broken Arrow gently stroked the dead animal's coat once, thanked the spirit gods above, plunged the tomahawk into the beast, and then lifted the bloodstained ceremonial weapon high above his head.

A few yards away, the creature, breathing hard through it wide gaping mouth, slowly returned to human form.

Later that night, as the buffalo hide dried on

wooden braces off in the distance, Broken Arrow and she sat together and watched the tribe's offering performance flicker among the large fire in the village center.

The old women huffed their rhythmic tune in perfect unison while the elderly men hooted methodically alongside them creating a haunting chilling sound for the dancers to move around the orange glowing fire that pierced the darkness of the night. Hence, the tribal colors; orange for fire and black for night.

Draped in a white wolf pelt, which had cost the tribe a considerable sum in trade with another Indian nation, a young Indian brave danced slowly around the roaring flickering fire while young girls followed behind him mimicking his every move perfectly in a dance created five years ago when the spirit world had declared them worthy to have a spirit god live amongst them.

Clothed once again in her Indian dress of orange and black, she marveled at the beauty of the performance dedicated to her. She stared lazily at the stomping, swaying, sweating bodies as they told of her arrival in the silent language of dance.

Broken Arrow placed a drinking vessel in her hands and stared at her face as she drank the grass and butter flavored beverage in one deep draught. He revered her as a spirit god and as the woman he deeply loved.

She set the empty vessel down between her bare knees then turned and looked at the face of the man who had given her years of peace and love. She smiled softly at him as she reflected on the fact that she hadn't killed another human since baring herself that day on the hill top. His fierce love for her and the buffalo hunt, it seemed, had waned the creature's appetite for killing senselessly.

She reached out with her left hand and softly grasped his warm flaccid penis under his loin cloth as she turned to watch the dancers once again.

In front of the roaring fire, the young brave lowered his head, hiding his face underneath the wolf's face pelt and scratched the hot air with his fingers while the young girls who had been following his every step around the roaring fire dropped to the beaten ground and curled up into tight little balls. The elderly men and women switched tempo from a rhythmic drone to a rising cascade of sharp breaths through bared teeth and when the rising sound hit its crest, they let out a roar from their throats and the white fur covered brave extended his arms upward in a symbolic display of the spirit god's power over the land while the girls leaped up from their fetal positions and waved their hands high in the air.

Feeling the hot blood pumping now in throbbing bursts into the swollen cock in her hand and the hypnotic performance beating against her large green eyes, she felt herself being drawn into the moment of the glowing night as never before.

Filled suddenly with the overwhelming need to be amongst the dancers, she stood up and slipped the dress off her shoulders and let it drop around her feet just as she had done earlier in the day.

A hush clamped down on the entire tribe gathered around the fire as they watched their spirit god, in human form, stand naked in front of them all.

With the orange glow slithering on her flawless skin, she stepped into the wide ring of dirt that encircled the snapping cracking fire.

Her vaginal area warmed seductively with every step she took towards it.

She slowly made her way to the crowd of dancers.

Not a single person spoke nor moved as they watched their spirit god make her way to the center place for the first time.

When she reached the dancers, she stopped and looked at their silent staring faces.

The flickering orange color from the roaring fire reflected off their eyes, giving their dark and dirty faces a demonic look.

She saw neither fear nor confusion just a quiet reverence to a being greater than themselves.

Then, after what felt like an eternity of silence, a low steady huff started up from the ring of spectators and slowly increased in volume.

Acting on improvisation, the girl performers surrounded her naked body and reached out to her, covering her lean body with dozens of little hands and the young brave, still wearing the wolf's pelt, stretched out his clawed hands above his head as he walked slowly around her.

When the raising methodical huffing sound reached its apex, the women broke off into a steady loud breathing through bared teeth and the men accompanied them with a deep hooting, creating a moving yet chilling rhythmic beat.

She looked down at the girls below her, their tanned hands hovering just above her warm skin as their eyes continued to reflect the orange flickering light of the roaring fire.

She smiled down at them and then looked at the teenage boy in the white wolf pelt swaying his hands high in the air as he lost himself in the rhythmic wall of sound.

She closed her eyes and allowed herself to be fully swallowed up by the moment, because tonight, at long last, she felt in control of her life again.

Later, as the celebration continued, Broken Arrow and she slipped away and fell into each other's arms in their tepee.

Locked at the mouth, they feverishly struggled to rid the small amount of clothes from his tanned and chiseled body.

The passion that had taken hold of them both was as electric as a thunder storm rolling across the plains during a summer night.

Once free of any clothing and resting in a nest of fox and beaver pelts, she grabbed his hot erect penis and placed it just at the welcoming entrance of her wetness.

She pulled away from his mouth and said, "Take me!" in his native tongue.

Staring directly into her beautiful large green eyes, he dropped deep into her with one succulent plunge, causing both of them to cry out as a wave of bliss splashed over them.

Together, they surrendered themselves completely to the depths of love and passion as never before. Lost in the heat of their bodies, they wept, laughed, and promised a thousand promises of their undying love for each other that only the passion of sexual abandonment could bring about.

Afterwards, as they fell into the darkness of sleep, she felt that tonight had been more than just a night of exquisite lovemaking. It had been a cleansing of the soul and the dawning of the rest of her life.

She was to be proven wrong.

Hours later, as her mind floated about in a tranquil dreamless sleep, a searing pain suddenly gripped her lower spine waking her in an instant.

Her eyes sprang open and bulged like cooked eggs and sweat erupted across her naked skin in an oily film under the unexpected tense pain at her lower back.

She tried to sit up but the sickening pain prevented her from moving a single inch from her sleeping position.

Through the open porthole at the top of the tepee, she saw the moon hovering in the night time sky. It loomed like an oasis, cool and peaceful as it illuminated the inside of the tepee with a soft silver glow.

Then, to her terror, the embracing agony began to spread to the rest of her body. Like acid, the pain slithered in every direction inside her.

She tried to open her mouth and scream but the muscles in her jaw refused to move.

Frightened and in unbelievable agony, she lay motionless as the saturating torment continued to spread within her.

When the pain reached her chest, her lungs felt as if they had been set on fire.

Paralyzed and helpless, she felt the black tide of unconsciousness begin the consume her.

With every fiber of her being, she mustered up the strength to turn her eyes slightly to her right to look at Broken Arrow who lay in deep sex exhausted slumber next to her.

The pain crawled up to her neck as it reached the tips of her toes.

Realizing he couldn't help her, she forced her eyes back to the porthole above her and stared at the moon in the night sky as she resigned herself to the unknown agony that had taken hold of her..

The pain reached her face.

She exhaled hard and long, and readied herself for whatever was to come next.

Finally, the burning horrific pain entered her brain and pulled her into a black abyss inside her mind.

She felt herself plummet into a lightless void of anything resembling time or form.

In darkness so complete, she twisted and turned to and fro endlessly and without meaning.

Then, after what felt like an eternity, she began to slow until she stopped and simply just hovered in a fathomless ocean of black.

Floating in her mind, in that realm reserved only for the moment when the body and soul join as one and explode in a dazzling shower of energy that is called life, she heard a deathly laughter echo from somewhere off in the black distance.

Aimlessly afloat in the void, she turned every which way to find the source of the harrowing laugh but only found complete darkness at every turn.

Suddenly, as if whispering next to her ear, a voice, dark and laced with malice, spoke to her, "My vessel."

Hearing the voice next to her, something, deep inside her, told her it was the creature.

"Abigail," it whispered gently next to her.

Listening to her name being spoken for the first time in generations, she felt the creature's age, its power, and the evil within it radiating from its voice.

"You are my instrument... and I am your guide," it

told her.

The smell of freshly cut mint leaves filled her nostrils.

"I crawled out from the depths of the earth during a time of chaos, havoc, and fire," it whispered gently and soulfully.

Listening to it, she felt its fur brush lightly against her left shoulder.

"I roamed the world's landscape for centuries upon centuries, hunting, killing, and mutilating whatever I could find," it quietly told her, "Then at some point... well before the understanding of what was or what could be by any other living thing on Earth, I discovered the ability to live within a host body... thus making myself... immortal."

She worked her throat to find her voice.

It took a deep long breath and continued, "During that time, I came to understand my purpose for being, my reason for existing."

Working her neck and facial muscles, she finally found her voice and asked, "What do you want?"

It chuckled wickedly at her question, "I have brought you here... to your black of nothingness... to tell you...your purpose. That is what I want... for you to know... your purpose."

"My purpose?" she said a bit louder.

"Yes," it chuckled again, "Your purpose for existing... became the very same as mine on that fateful day we interlaced," it took a deep breath and whispered delicately into her ear, "To kill."

She felt a chill spill across her naked floating body.

"Killing is all I have done, all you will do, and all we shall ever do together," it informed her with a chilling matter of fact tone.

She turned her head, caught sight of its large green eyes staring at her, and said to it, "I've murdered without question, without remorse for years, littering my wake with the bodies of the dead. I even killed my own parents, my family."

Suddenly its cold laughter boomed next to her.

Frightened out of her skin by the sudden demonic sound of its sadistic laugh, she tumbled forward and cartwheeled endlessly about in the black void.

Watching her spinning helplessly in the blackness of her own mind, the creature laughed even harder.

Slowly, after a long while, she came to a stop only to float in total blackness once again.

Off in the distance, the creature's laughter died out.

With her arms and legs dangling uselessly, she snapped her head in every direction, looking for any sign of the monster.

Then as out of nowhere, its voice appeared once again just behind her left shoulder, "Abigail."

With a yelp, she motioned to move away from it but this time the creature reached out with its long clawed hands and grabbed her bare arms, holding her in place.

She winced in pain under its grasp.

"Your sacrifices are but ants in the afterbirth compared to the acts of subservience and survival that I have seen over the eons," it gripped her arms tighter, "I've watched kings willingly hand over their reigns to me in order to survive until day break. I have witnessed pregnant mothers plead for me to tear out their unborn in exchange for survival."

Unable to move, she craned her head back over her shoulder and asked again as she stared into its large green eye, "What more do you want from me that I haven't given you already?"

It answered, "Time."

She closed her eyes at the sound of the word.

"Time is all I require from you, Abigail. Time to kill. Time to destroy. Time to bask in the blood of those that will fall under my... our grasp," it told her.

She repeated the word slowly under her breath, "Time."

"Yes, my vessel. Time," it softened its grip on her arms, "One day in the far future we shall walk together, side by side, on a planet devoid of all life... just as it was when I came to be... but a thing such as that requires... time."

She lowered her head.

It caressed her arms as it said, "There is a... beauty... in what we have done and... shall do. Let us commence once more and reap death, sorrow, and the splendor of pain from this world all over again."

An image of an elegant table setting for five covered in blood flashed in her mind's eye.

Then without warning the creature tightened its grip on her arms once again.

The sudden pain caused her to scream into the black vast void.

With vice-like strength, it continued to squeeze her arms.

Unable to move, she screamed louder than she ever had.

Finally, under that suppressive pressure, the humerus bones of both her arms cracked in half.

Her face contorted into a mask of pure abandonment as her screams soared to a blood curdling crescendo.

Squeezing ever harder, it calmly spoke as she continued to bellow hysterically from the pain, "The reprieve I gave you these last five years has come to an end."

The jagged ends of her bones began to protrude through her skin.

"From this time forward you will kill mercilessly, without reserve, and without remorse… forever," it whispered gently into her ear under her high pitched screams, "Contentment and peace will cradle you… as the blood of the dead covers you."

Blood poured from out of her arms.

"I shall return you here… to this black nothingness… and kill you over and over until eternity says otherwise… if the bodies of your victims should fail to reach the precipice of death that I seek," it warned her then tore off her arms just above the elbow.

Screaming, she watched it cast her severed limbs into the black emptiness.

The creature laughed out loud at her pain and torment.

Waving her bleeding stumps all around, blood from the ragged wounds sprayed across her face.

The creature spoke one last time as it recessed back into the darkness, "Go. Abigail. Go. My vessel. Kill forever… or die in the depth of your own mind forever."

She exhaled hot stale air out of her lungs and the interior of the tepee came back into focus in the moon's soft silver glow.

Still in the same position that she had been in when the creature had pulled her in, she turned her head fully to her right and saw Broken Arrow still asleep the same way she had last seen him.

Turning her head, she looked down the length of her naked body and noticed that the only physical evidence of what had just happened to her was the film of cooling salty sweat all over her bare skin.

She extended her arms out in front of her and saw that they were still intact.

Feeling oddly calmed, she mulled over what she had just experienced. The whole thing had been so bizarre yet all together as real as everything else that had occurred to her since being bitten so many years ago.

As odd as the whole thing had been, she understood the meaning of experience; she belonged to it and it belonged to her, and together they would kill until the end of time ended and … "'We shall walk together, side by side," she quoted the creature with a faint whisper.

She looked around the small cluttered tepee and then at Broken Arrow again, and reminded herself that the black void of her mind and the infinite torture and brutality of the creature awaited her if she didn't kill forever.

With a sad brief smile of resolve, she quietly picked herself up, gathered her faded cornflower blue dress, the tribe's ceremonial tomahawk, and slipped out the tepee through its leather flap.

Outside, a full moon illuminated the world around her in a basking silver light while the evening breeze cooled the drying sweat on her nude body to a chill.

The entire village, she noted, was completely asleep. It seemed, she gathered, that the powwow and the lovemaking which had followed had rendered everyone into a deep exhausted slumber.

She glanced around her immediate area and quickly found what she needed; a quiver of arrows resting alongside a saddle on the ground next to her tepee.

She reached into the tall slender leather holster, drew out a single arrow, rolled it and the tomahawk in her old tattered dress, and then silently made her way towards the river.

Walking in her bare feet, she put the village behind her as the soft flowing river, alive with the moon light dancing off its rippling current, came into view.

Even though no one in the village bothered to cross to the other side, she had been doing so for years, witnessing from a distance as farms, settlements, and army forts sprang about the once desolate landscape.

When the sound of the rolling water reached her ears, she tucked her dress and its contents tight under her arm and then broke into a full sprint, naked and bare foot, towards the river bank of black and silver colored water.

With dazzling speed, she raced down the embankment, eager to gather as much momentum as possible.

When the toes of her right foot hit the edge of the water, she leaped high into the air over the river itself, turned into the creature in mid-air, and landed on the other side of the river in a crouching stance.

Under the cover of sleep, William Connors thought he heard someone banging on the front door of the cabin but the weariness of a hard day's work on his farm begged him to dismiss the sound so he rolled onto his left side, shifted his weight on the straw mattress beneath him, and sought to regain the serene sleep of a few minutes ago.

Then, his wife's voice, slightly frantic, tore into his sleeping mind, "William! William, there's someone out front!"

Instantly awake, he turned to face the black figure standing over him in the darkness of the small cabin. Blinking away the threads of his succulent slumber, he asked, "Outside?"

"Yes," Martha, his wife of 12 years, replied as she turned away from his bed side, "Whoever it is just started knocking about a minute ago," she told him as she walked towards the oil lamp sitting on the large table in the center of their one room cabin.

A burst of banging on the thick wooden door cut into the room.

He swung his feet onto the dirt floor and instinctively reached for the double barrel shotgun next to the bed. Since their meager savings had bought them a small spread of land to farm on miles away from any other settlers and Calvary forts, any unknown persons on their property, especially in the middle of the night, most likely meant danger.

The oil lamp glowed into life and the small wooden dwelling filled with a dull yellow hue.

Standing next to the lamp, Martha stared at him with large worried eyes.

William stood up, shotgun in hand.

The dirt flooring shifted under his weight.

He looked at his spouse and at his two young children, daughter and son, who were sitting upright on the bed they shared, and told them, "Everything will be fine. Trust the Lord."

Another round of banging came through the door.

In his night clothes and socks, he turned to face the

locked door, shotgun at port arms, and asked in a near shout, "Who are you? And what's your business here... tonight?"

It seemed to him that the answer took an eternity to come, but finally a woman's pleading voice replied, "Oh, thank God! Please, you have to help me!"

He shot a confused glance over to his wife, who only stared back at him with a blank worried expression.

He turned back to the door and asked, "What do you want from us?"

The female voice on the other side responded, "Please help me! I'm all alone. I'm very frightened. Please...let me in!"

Sensing something odd, he gripped the shotgun tighter in his hands and told the unknown woman, "I have two young children in here... now, tell me who are you?"

"Please, help me!" she said as she banged twice more, "I'm so scared."

He turned once more to look at his wife, who was now staring directly at the locked door, then at his children; young Nathaniel was clutching his younger sister so as to comfort her.

The woman outside banged again and cried out, "Please help me! Please!"

A woman all alone in this part of the country at night; it just didn't seem possible, he thought to himself.

Once more the woman cried out, "Please let me in!"

The whole situation felt wrong to him.

"Please let me in!"

Unable to shake the odd feeling that something was terribly amiss with the whole situation, he said sternly, "Miss... I have my family here. I can't let you in. I'm sorry... but you have to leave."

"No! You can't mean that!" the woman outside cried out as she banged harder than ever before, "Please! I have no one! I'm all alone! Please!"

Rising the double barrel shotgun to his shoulder, he shouted out, "I want you to leave, NOW!"

Then, from behind him, his wife's voice pierced his soul, "My God, William Connors, what kind of a Christian are you? There's a woman outside that door begging for our help."

Never before had his wife used his entire name when addressing him. He was utterly dumbstruck at hearing her do so, so he slowly lowered the weapon from his shoulder, turned to face his wife, and looked straight into her eyes for the last time in his life.

"Open the door, William," she told him using her finals words.

He turned towards the door once more, placed the shotgun on the dining table and walked to the locked door.

He slid the thick iron rod out of its secured position, grabbed the rope that served as a door handle, and pulled the thick wooden door open.

Standing in front of him, illuminated only by the weak light of the oil lamp, stood a blonde white woman of stunning beauty with the greenest and largest eyes he had ever seen, wearing nothing but a tattered dirty blue dress.

He ran his eyes over her face and down the length of her fit toned body all the way down to her feet and noticed that they were bare and filthy with mud, dirt, and bits of grass.

While staring at her feet and wondering why a

woman would be all alone in the middle of the night bare foot, the tomahawk buried itself down the middle of his face.

With half his face split in half from forehead to upper lip, he looked up with a questioning expression as his heart stopped.

She pulled the ceremonial weapon free from his shattered face as he crumpled to the floor and then hurled it across the room with pin point precision at the staring woman at the far side of the small cramped cabin.

The tomahawk sharpened edge plowed itself deep between Martha's left collar bone and neckline.

Dark rich solid blood shot out from the horrid wound.

Mortally wound, Martha dropped to her knees with the Indian axe still in her.

Stepping over the dead man's body, she slipped out of the old cornflower blue dress, placed it on the tabletop next to the shotgun, and calmly walked over to the dying woman.

Speechless and motionless with terror, the boy and girl clutched at each other as they watched the murder of both their parents unfold in front of them.

Naked, she stopped in front of the nearly dead woman and looked down at her.

Begging for her life and the life of her young children, Martha Connors mouthed silent pleas of mercy to her killer.

Standing with her dirty bare feet in the pool of woman's blood, she yanked the tomahawk loose from the savage wound.

The mother of two, who once had dreamed of becoming a field nurse, gurgled and sputtered blood and bile out of her mouth as the axe was torn out of her body.

Absorbing the violence she had created, she brought the blood drenched axe down with lightning speed onto the other side of the woman's neck.

The ceremonial weapon bore into meat, tendon, and muscle.

Nearly decapitated, Martha fell to her side and died in a thick rich pool of her own blood.

Inhaling the violence with deep breaths, she turned her attention to the two cowering children still seated on the bed against the cabin's right wall.

Overwhelmed by the swift and brutal death of their parents, the two minors simply stared at the naked and bloodied woman in numbed silence.

Slowly she walked over to their bedside, smiled sweetly, and then gathered them up in her arms.

Later, as the rising morning sun bid farewell to the cold darkness of the night, she stepped out onto the cabin's small front porch, completely covered in blood, shit, vomit, and piss.

Taking in the breathtaking vista of the vast landscape of the American west from the porch's vantage point, she picked up the arrow that she had brought along with her.

Under the bright radiant rays of dawn, she whispered to the creature living within her, "Thank you for the reprieve," then snapped the arrow in half and let the two broken pieces fall from her hands.

After crossing the river and bathing a few miles upstream, she returned to the village that same morning. She gave no reasoning for her disappearance and no one asked; she was after all a spirit god living amongst them.

As the sun crested over its noon peak, she slipped into the tepee that she shared with Broken Arrow, stripped off her cornflower blue dress, laid down on top of the cool nest of fox and beaver hides, and fell asleep.

Later, during the evening meal's clatter and bustle, Broken Arrow entered the tepee and stretched himself out next to her naked body.

Though completely still but not asleep, she could feel his hot moist flesh beating with life next to her while his scent, a mixture of fresh sweat, grass, and leather, filled her nostrils and the interior of the small conical shaped dwelling.

She opened her eyes and was met by his, staring at her softly.

Her heart sank a bit at what she had set in motion.

Finally, after minutes of heavy silence, she mouthed the question, "What?" in his native tongue.

His features softened at the quiet whisper of her voice and answered, "I'm always so honored when you return to us."

She shifted her weight slightly, rolled onto her side, and said, "I shall never leave you."

"The spirit world is so far away, Rolling Cloud, that at times..." he left the statement hang in the air.

Then after taking a moment to collect his thoughts more precisely, he closed it out, "...at times I wonder if one day you'll forsake us."

She looked deep into his eyes, remembered floating aimlessly in the blackness of her mind while the creature's ancient voice whispered its hatred towards the world and its control over her, and lied, "I'll always be here for all of you... no matter what occurs."

He reached out and lightly touched her cheek.

She calmly stared at him under his delicate touch.

Suddenly, remembering, he pulled his hand away from her face, sat up, and stated in a bewildered tone, "The tomahawk. It is nowhere to be found. I am at a loss to its whereabouts."

Words such as 'steal' or 'theft' didn't exist in their language nor the concept of robbery since everything belonged to everyone and no one was the owner anything.

He turned to her, his eyes hoping for an answer from the one being he trusted most.

She rolled back onto her back and answered with the truth, "It is no longer here, Broken Arrow. It has been used to achieve an outcome set in motion long ago."

On the second day, after murdering the entire Connors family, a U.S. Calvary patrol came upon the scene. On the third day, the connection was made regarding the mahogany handle tomahawk, the broken arrow, and the Indian village they belonged to. And on the fourth day, a well-disciplined and battle hardened garrison of Calvary troops from Fort George Washington, north of the farm and west of the river, set out towards the village.

With the morning sun hours away from rising, and Calvary soldiers just over the last ridge, she opened her eyes. Some deep dark instinct told her that the end had come.

Without a final glance over her shoulder at the peacefully sleeping man beside her, she grabbed her old blue dress and exited the tepee for the final time.

She dressed and then quietly and carefully made her way out of the village in the cool moist air of the silent waning darkness.

At the top of the highest hilltop, a quarter mile from the slumbering village, she laid down on her belly to wait.   After years of crossing the river and watching the soldiers perform their combat tactics on other unsuspecting and meddlesome Indian tribes, she knew what was about to occur.

A few moments later, with the morning light just below the horizon, she spotted the Calvary's forward scouts, Indians from other tribes and white scalp hunters, lurking and dashing amongst the brush and trees around the perimeter of the silent village, no doubt figuring out the best place to situate the cannons and guns.

By the time the early light of dawn erupted upward into the sky in a blazing orb of light and heat, everything was ready to commence.

She turned her head and saw the officer in charge, off in the distance, give the signal to start the military operation on the doomed and sleeping people.

In unison, the row of cannons that had been set up on the eastern side of the village, fired into the cluster of tepees.

Spinning and skipping across the ground, the iron cannon balls crushed and tore through the buffalo skin dwellings and everyone inside it with colossal effectiveness.

The earth shattering sound of cannon fire and the ear piercing screams of the injured and dying sent everyone running from their tepees in a panic.

On queue the crank operated machine guns, in a crisscrossing field of fire, opened up.

The hand cranks turned, the barrels spun, and the bullets poured out.

Many of the confused and frightened Indians in their haste to survive ran into the flying bullets while others were simply chased and cut down by the two deadly guns.

The cannons were reloaded with fragment shells and a generous helping of spent cartridge cases poured down their snouts, and fired once again.

Like a downpour of horizontal rain; hot jagged metals pieces in the thousands swept through dozens of Indian villagers. Some were lifted off their feet in bloody tangles of ripped flesh and others were literally stripped to the bone were they stood.

Finally wrapping their heads around at what was happening, a group of young braves, under the cover of smoke, screams, and panic, made their way to their horses quarreled in a circumference of bushes at the foot of the village.

With the agility of youth and adrenaline pumping through their veins, each young Indian brave leaped onto a visibly shaken and unsaddled horse.

The horses, frightened by the bedlam all around them, stammered and paced about as the five young men struggled to get them under control.

Then, from their hiding places, six soldiers emerged from out of the bushes, each carrying a double barrel shotgun.

Still fighting for control of his horse, Flying Hawk, the youngest of the Indian braves, caught sight of the blue uniformed men a second before he died.

With years of cold harsh discipline, the six soldiers aimed their shotguns and pulled the triggers.

All twelve barrels roared into life in a blaze of fire,

lifting the five young men off their mounts in a twisting carnage of blood, flesh, and organs.

Another barrage of cannon fire ripped into the village.

Completely beside themselves with fright and horror, many of the doomed villagers dashed for the river, which they had never considered crossing before, only to be met by an ambush of entrenched soldiers.

From under the tall grass on the western bank, a Calvary Captain stood, raised his sword, and yelled, "Ready!"

At the sound of his command, a row of soldiers rose to a kneeling position in front of him, rifles in hand.

"Aim!" he commanded and his men zeroed in on the water trapped men, women, and children.

Some, in a futile attempt to save themselves, turned and started back to the village river bank while others pushed the pace and did what they could to reach the other side in order to get under the coming rifle volley.

The Massachusetts born Captain dropped his sword with ceremonial speed and yelled, "Fire!"

The bodies of the dead would float downstream for days.

Lost in the brilliance of the massacre, she raised herself up to her elbows and watched as mounted Calvary thundered across the open field, directly in front of her, and cut down fleeing Indians with their curved swords and revolvers.

She looked back at the besieged village as another volley of cannon fire rained down death on whoever was still left alive and then, to her shock, she saw Broken Arrow emerge from the smoke and chaos, bloodied and wounded, with a small knife in his hand.

With most of the left side of his face gone and his intestines held in by his right hand and forearm, Broken Arrow stumbled vacantly around his devastated village and the torn broken bodies that were once his people, swinging the knife through the acidic smoke of gunpowder at an enemy who hadn't even entered his village to kill everyone inside it.

Tripping on a large piece of meat, which had once been a person, he fell to his knees, spilling his guts over his hand and forearm onto his lap.

Bellowing out in agony, he looked down at his own intestines in dismay and humiliation.

Off in the distance, the cannons were readied.

Under the canopy of bewildering pain, Broken Arrow shouted up at the sky, "Rolling Cloud! Where are you? Where are you?"

Fresh magazines were fitted into the wells of the machine guns.

Broken Arrow screamed again into the sky, "Rolling Cloud!"

A calm cold staring Lieutenant stepped between the machine guns and looked down at the last living inhabitant and instantly recognized him as Broken Arrow, the village chief, who he had personally delivered woolen blankets to the previous winter.

Looking at the shattered man below him, the Lieutenant thought about the Connors family and the brutal way they had been slaughtered.

From behind him, a Sargent with piercing grey eyes informed him, "Lt. Bradford, sir. The guns are reloaded and the men and I await your orders, sir."

With the smallest of sighs and a slight shake of his head, the Lieutenant stepped back behind the guns and gave the command, "You have your target boys. Now, do your job."

Broken Arrow yelled one final time, "Rolling Clo-!"

Both guns cranked into life.

From her vantage point, she looked away as he dissolved in a hail of bullets while calling out the name he had given to her years ago and had whispered a thousand times at night.

The gunfire finally stopped and the proud Indian tribe was now no longer.

With nothing left to see, she carefully made her way down the hillside and disappeared into the rolling meadows and the...

Blue crayon colored sky above the stick figure was dotted by a single tear drop.

Taken aback by the tear, she touched her cheek and felt the warm wet path it had taken down her face.

Clutching the drawing in her hand, she stood up, walked to the window, and quietly said out loud, "Kill... forever."

CHAPTER 14

"Then we better get to it."

Carrying four plastic bags and a long crush proof case, John opened the door of his motel room, stepped in, and let the door swing shut behind him as he made his way to a freshly made bed.

He placed his parcels on the pastel bedspread and slumped down beside them.

Sitting quietly on the bed, John looked around the small motel room and thought it funny how in just two weeks the rented room had begun to look more like a home to him then a motel-chain accommodation.

He let himself fall back onto the stiff mattress and looked at the red digital clock on the nightstand

It read half past one.

John turned his head and stared at the ceiling and replayed previous evening again in his mind; the sudden and overwhelming sensation to hurt someone, the beckoning hum in his chest, and the two men he had violently assaulted in the alley.

With a sigh, he realized that after last night he

needed to flee the city more than ever before. It simply wasn't just about her anymore but also about what he was becoming.

Bewildered by the whole thing, John shook his head and absently touched his scar.

After a while, he got up, went to his packages, pulled everything out, and neatly arranged them on the bed.

Standing over them, John placed his hands on his hips and looked at what he had waited 15 days to receive from the gun shop; an Israeli 1911 clone in .45 caliber, an Argentinian .380, and a pump action shotgun, one box of bullets for each of his new guns and one for the snub nose tucked in his waistband, magazines, and shells for the shotgun.

Though it had taken over two weeks to obtain them, now that they were finally in his possession, John felt he had what he needed to handle whatever came his way.

Feeling a little better after looking at his new firearms, he went to the mirrored closet and began to pack. He was leaving tonight.

While he had no clear idea as to where he was going, oddly, for some strange and inexplicable reason, the solitude of the forest appealed to him, regardless of the fact that two years ago he had almost been killed in a forest by the very thing he was running away from.

Later, as darkness fell over the city, John checked himself out by phone with the front desk and gathered his belongings.

With a duffle bag in each had, one filled with weapons and the other with everything else, he took one last look at the small pastel room, gave it a small nod, and walked out.

Once in the parking lot, John filled the trunk of his car with both bags, and then climbed into the driver's seat.

Sitting behind the wheel, he reached up and adjusted the rearview mirror.

His eyes, dazzling and radiant in emerald green, reflected back at him from the small rectangle mirror.

Unexpectedly transfixed by their unnatural quality, John realized that all the changes to his body meant, in time, he would become just like her, a freak of nature, and instead of killing him, she had unwittingly sentenced him to a life of uncertainty and violence.

John removed his hand from the rearview mirror, dropped his gaze, and spoke out loud to no one other than himself, "Then we better get to it."

He turned the ignition and his trusted car roared to life.

Driving slowly out the motel's parking lot, he stopped at the driveway, leaned forward and pondered what direction to take. To the left, off in the distance, he could see the freeway onramp that would take him north and as far away from her as possible while the right lead back to the city that he had come to love and call his home ever since moving to it right after graduating from the University of Illinois.

Before he knew it, his hand had set the car's blinker clicking right.

'One last pass through the city' he thought to himself as he merged into traffic.

A fate changing decision he would ponder about the rest of his life.

CHAPTER 15

"Yes, there is one other thing you can do for me."

On the second floor of the shelter, pots and pans rattled as the smell of cooking filled the restaurant grade kitchen.

In the dining hall, on the other side of the double swinging doors, the happy banter of people filled the large dining hall with a joyful rumble as they waited for the much anticipated dinner.

Helping out in the kitchen, she stood chopping vegetables that were about to be added to the meal that would never be eaten. All around her, her staff moved with a hurried paced as they prepared the near banquet sized menu for the evening's special dinner.

As she slid the evenly chopped carrots from the cutting board to a metal bowl, Alice a former Naval cook, former Alcoholic, and former homeless vagrant, approached her and said, "Miss Susan, I think celebrating the one year anniversary of the reopening of the shelter with this dinner is such a good idea."

Placing a stalk of celery on the cutting board, Susan

turned to her and said, "Thank you, Alice. It seemed like the right thing to do, especially after all the hard work everyone's put into this place and all the wonderful strides everyone's done for themselves."

Pushing her paper hat higher on her forehead, Alice smiled and added, "Miss Susan, all of it was only possible because of you. I hope you know that... and take some credit for it tonight."

With a smile of her own, she answered, "That's not my style."

"Well it certainly should-" then from the other end of the kitchen the sound of a metal bowl striking the tiled floor rang out cutting the woman off in midsentence.

Everyone in the kitchen area screeched and hooted in united good cheer at the unsuspected racket.

Alice snapped her head over to the turmoil at the salad station, saw the trouble, and dashed towards it, "I'll talk with you later."

Susan watched her beeline to the cluster of people cleaning up the mess that had just been made and then looked around at her surroundings. Every face that she saw looked happy and glowing. The children ran about smiling and laughing. The women talked in their little groups, while the men stood along the walls joking and laughing amongst themselves.

She set the knife down next to the celery stalk and remembered the day the city had handed over the building to her and all of the walking hopeless that had come with it. Now after one whole year of killing in the dark one victim at a time since coming to Los Angeles, she was finally going to commit the mass murder she had planned on doing from the very first day she had set foot inside the building.

From behind her, Alex's familiar voice suddenly spoke to her, "Susan?"

'He always waits for my acknowledgement before he speaks to me' she thought to herself as she turned and said, "Yes, Alex?"

Looking like a bird of paradise in his best attire for the evening's celebration, he smiled boyishly under his crisp goatee, tie, and V-neck sweater vest, and told her, "Every single window in the building has been opened and all the doors at the ground floor have been locked, just like you asked."

She looked directly into his eyes and said, "Thank you, Alex."

Smiling a bit wider, he replied, "No prob."

She smiled back.

Then the slightest of shadows cast across his brow.

She watched him patiently as he struggled to ask some looming question.

Finally, he ventured and asked, "With the shelter closed for the night... where will someone looking to spend the night go?"

She cocked her smile and answered, "Don't worry. I've taken care of that with the other shelters in the area. They know about our dinner tonight and they've agreed to handle the overflow."

"I guess that explains why you had me drive our extra mattresses to St. Jude's and The Bradley, yesterday."

"Yup. So relax," she told him with a casual tone.

The shadow that had darkened his expression disappeared and his Hindu cow smile reserved solely for her returned. "Well... is there anything else I can do... to help out?"

Susan smiled at him and answered "Yes, there is

one other thing you can do for me."

"Ok, sure, no problem," he said to her.

"I want you to go up to my office and wait for me while I give the toast," she said as she took a step closer to him.

"Wha? Miss your toast?" he gasped.

In the midst of the continuing chaos in the busy kitchen, she told him, "The toast is for everyone else... but for you I have something else in mind," then cupped his groin with her hand and licked her lips inches from his face.

He stared at her silently as his heart felt as if had just fallen to the bottoms of his feet.

"Go upstairs and wait for me. I'll be up shortly." she told him with a dismissive tone and turned around.

In utter shock at what he had just heard and felt, Alex swallowed hard through a thoroughly clenched throat.

Without even a sidelong glance, she returned to her chopping.

He left the kitchen almost in a run towards her office.

Chopping, she smiled at how the whole evening was turning out.

Minutes later, a young teenage girl, a former pimpless street hooker, approached the island counter. "Miss Susan, the punch is ready."

She looked up at the girl and smiled.

CHAPTER 16

As he drove aimlessly around the vacant streets of the civic center of Los Angeles, enjoying the night air and the tranquil drive, John Poole looked at the LCD clock in the center of the dashboard.

It read 8:43 in the evening.

Making the most of his last drive through the city, he made a left and continued down another main avenue.

Neon lights and billboard signs reflected off the windshield in slick oblong shapes and contours as he sped down the smooth and ample streets.

Whether by chance or fate, a red light stopped him less than a mile from the homeless shelter.

Gazing at the towering city in front of him, a sad and simple smile crept upon his face. He was going to miss the city and everything that had come along with it including the life he had created within it.

The traffic light turned green when suddenly a tugging sensation struck him in the chest.

Stunned, John stiffened in his seat and looked around, unsure of what it was.

Unlike the humming feeling of the other night, the tugging in the center of his chest felt like a beckoning of sorts.

A car drove up behind his, noticed he wasn't moving, and drove around.

Silent and motionless in his car, John focused on the feeling inexplicably pulling at his sternum and closed his large green eyes.

An image of the white creature standing beside the woman from the parking lot flashed across his mind.

Spooked, John opened his eyes and looked up at the green traffic light glowing methodically above him.

Staring at the green traffic light, a realization slowly formed in some deep dark pit of his mind; the tugging sensation in the center of his chest lead to her.

CHAPTER 17

"Yes… I love you."

At her insistence, a large stainless steel cauldron of fruit punch had been wheeled over to her so that she could personally finish preparing it for the evening's grand toast.

She had poured the white deadly powder into the bright red liquid, dismissing it simply as imported sugar to the few that had asked.

Plastic champagne saucers had been assembled, filled, and handed out to everyone in attendance with specific instructions from Miss Susan herself not to drink until after the toast.

Now, after more than a year of planning, she stood on a wooden chair with a plastic champagne saucer of her own and looked across the room of smiling attentive faces.

Doing as they had been told to do, no one drank but instead waited with bated breath for the speech that was about to come from the woman who they all considered the spearhead to the better life that lay just ahead of them.

Fighting back the creature's fierce death lust, she found it difficult to keep her mouth from slipping open at the sides in front of everyone staring at her so she focused at the task at hand, raised her saucer high into the air, and confessed the truth to everyone in attendance, "Tonight marks the pinnacle of devotion to something greater than I. After all the hard work, the time invested, and planning that went into making tonight happen... I can tell you all with complete honesty that I was always thinking of every single one of you the entire time."

A cheer ripped into life from the smiling faces looking up at her.

"I've seen many things in my life and done just as many. However, tonight, I am very proud of what is about to occur."

Another cheer, this one louder than the first, rolled over her like a wave.

"All of you came to me for one reason or another and allowed me to make you better. So tonight, I ask only one thing from each and every one of you in lieu of payment... let me take you to the end."

The tremendous roaring cheer that followed reminded her of the vibrant parades and gatherings of Nazi Germany so many years ago.

She gave the crowd one final look and cried out with joy, "Drink!"

A half hour later, she walked up the flight of stairs to the fourth floor and then entered her office.

Inside, standing in almost military attention, Alex nervously watched her walk over to the front of the desk and rest up against it. He had waited and dreamed of this moment from the very first time he had walked into the shelter while looking for help to rid himself of a life dowsed in liquor and self-worthlessness. And from that heart stopping moment on, he had done everything possible to be near her and prove to her that he was a man worthy of her.

Resting her backside against the edge of the desk, she stared at him with a smile.

As if rooted to the floor, he smiled back at her, not sure what to do amidst the seductive silence that now seemed to envelope the room like a warm fog.

She gave him a slow blink as she exhaled long and deep, heaving her ample chest.

Feeling overwhelmed to say something, he asked, "How...did the toast go?"

She placed her hands at her sides and replied, "The toast went just as I thought it would."

"That's...great. Great," he said then added as he suddenly noticed the lack of noise coming from below, "It's so quiet...now."

She blinked her contact brown eyes, cocked her smiled, and beckoned, "Come over here, Alex... close to me," and gestured slightly with her head.

What felt to him like pulling his feet out of mud, he detached himself from where he stood and slowly walked over to her.

Enjoying the calm moment before the kill, she watched him close the distance between them.

He came to a stop in front of her and looked down at her smiling face.

The smell of mint flowed out of her mouth, strong and pungent.

He breathed in the sweet intoxicating scent as he

looked into her beautiful face.

"Do you like me, Alex?" she quietly asked him.

His throat clicked loudly from hearing that question come from her.

He answered as his heart melted inside his chest, "Yes, I do. I really do."

"Do you love me, Alex?" she asked through a widening smile.

He felt his vision swim for a briefest of seconds.

"Do you love me?" she asked again.

He answered with a mouth that felt filled with cotton, "Yes... I love you."

She nodded her head slowly. "I know. I've always known. From the very first second you walked into the building... I knew."

The desire to touch her was on the verge of becoming maddening but he didn't dare out of fear of ruining everything because of a misstep.

"Do you know... how I was able to tell, Alex?" she asked sweetly.

"How?" he managed to utter.

"It was your eyes, Alex. Your eyes have always told me how you feel about me."

Feeling like he would die if he waited one second longer to feel her touch, he reached out and took her small perfect hands into his own.

"Can I show you something, Alex?" she asked as she gingerly held his large roughened hands in hers.

Feeling the unbelievable softens of her skin against his, he simply nodded.

"It's a surprise," she told him as she released his hands.

Tingling from her touch, his hands fell to his sides as he watched her reach up to her face.

"These are the eyes... I was given many years ago," she told him as she removed the brown colored contacts, "And I want you to see them".

Alex gave the smallest of gasps as he stared into the largest most beautiful green eyes he had ever seen.

"Do you like them?" she asked.

Thinking that she was quite simply the single most perfect woman, he answered, "Yes."

The irises began to spin around the black pupils.

"Do you love them, Alex? Do you... love... them?" she asked as her smiled faded from her face.

Overcome by the dark and cursed power of her eyes, he fell to his knees in front of her, transfixed.

"Do you?" she asked again with a low voice.

He whispered the word, "Yes," and then unknowingly began to cry as he stared deeper into the swirling green.

Keeping eye contact with him, she asked sweetly, "Why are you crying?"

Under a stream of tears, he answered, "Because... you're...so beautiful...and I... love...you."

"How much do you love me, Alex? How much?" she asked with a stern and serious expression on her face.

Blubbering his confession, he told her, "I love you so much! I love...you...with all my...heart. I've always loved you... and...I always...will!"

"I like it when you say things like that," she told him.

His eyes felt glued to hers as he listened to her talk.

"And since you love me so much, I know you'll do what I ask... right?"

He raised his hands to her and babbled, "Sure. Anything. Anything you ask. I'll do it. I love you.

Whatever you want. Anything."

She rose off the desk and commanded, "Strip me naked."

Alex's mouth fell open.

She repeated the words, "Strip... me... naked, Alex."

He began to stand.

Without warning, she screamed into his face, "NO! Stay on your KNEES!"

The swirling green of her eyes blazed into a fierce rolling storm around the onyx black pupils.

Alex fell back down onto his hunkers, shocked at the sudden ferocity of her voice.

Back in her normal voice, she directed, "Start with my feet," and lifted her left foot to him.

He dropped his gazed down to her feet.

"Look at ME!" she screamed down at him. Losing eye contact meant losing the hold the power of her eyes afforded her.

Physically shaken by her scream, Alex looked up at her and spread his hands wide in a gesture of confusion.

Once again in her normal sweet voice, she told him, "Just keep looking at me as you do it, my darling."

With a slightest of nods, he trained his eyes into hers, blindly reached out and took her foot into his hands, then slipped off the loafer and then the sock.

She pulled her barefoot away from him. "Good. Now the other one," then placed the other one in his hands.

Continuing to stare deep into the green eyes above him, he did the same to her right one and released it.

Standing in her bare feet, Susan inched closer to him. "Now stand up slowly and take the rest of my clothes off."

Doing as he was commanded, Alex stood and slowly stripped her nude, piece by piece, while never once breaking eye contact, until the woman he had dreamed about for so long stood completely naked in front of him.

Hands on her bare hips, eyes fixed, she told him, "Now... back down onto your knees... my sweet."

Caught helplessly in her powerful stare, Alex lowered himself back down onto the floor.

Looking directly into his eyes, she raised herself onto her bare toes, arched her pelvis forward and said, "A toast to us," then sprayed him down with hot fragrant urine.

Held by the power of her green eyes, he took the humiliation in silence.

When her bladder finally emptied, she asked him, "Do you still love me?"

Soaked in her waste, Alex simply nodded.

"Good... because I have one more surprise for you, tonight," she told him with an easy smile as she lightly slapped the moist shaven skin around her vagina.

Wet and obedient, Alex simply waited for the coming surprise.

"I need you to close your eyes... and when I tell you... I want you to open them," she said to him.

Alex nodded his understanding as he planned their wedding in his head.

"Ok, good. Now close your eyes," she spoke to him for the final time, gesturing with her hand.

He closed his eyes.

Waiting, images of the perfect life with her and their children in the countryside danced about in his head.

"Now open them." a strange voice said.

A single scream echoed throughout the silent building.

CHAPTER 18

"So why not start with her?"

Allowing the overwhelming sensation that had taken hold of him, John Poole drove into the garment district of Los Angeles.

Closed storefronts and textile factories loomed everywhere in the night time air.

He drove around down main avenues and secondary streets as the tugging at his chest propelled him ever forward.

Twenty minutes after nine, he passed in front of the shelter, and the sensation changed from an insistent beckoning to a deep methodical one.

He hit the brakes in front of the Art Deco inspired building and knew, somehow he just knew, that she was inside.

Its large double doors were closed and not a single person milled about. The place looked desolate.

He steered his car around the back of the homeless shelter and rolled to a stopped in the damp alley alongside an overflowing dumpster.

John cut the engine and suddenly realized that he wasn't even sure what he planned to do now that he was here.

He turned and looked at the building; the building was as dark as it was silent. However, somewhere deep within him something persisted that she was in there.

He looked at his large glossy emerald eyes in the rearview mirror and spoke out loud, "I could always just knock on the front door and blow her fucking head clean off."

The sensation in his chest tugged even harder at the mere mention of violence towards her.

Taking a deep breath, John pondered if he could actually kill her or if it was nothing but tough talk on his part. He was, after all, nothing more than a simple accountant and not a killer.

Then, he remembered; the parking garage, the fever, his eyes, and the two men in the alley.

"Well... I guess... I'm going to become one whether I want to or not," he whispered, "So why not start with her?" then stepped out of his car, went to the rear, and popped the trunk where his duffle bag full of weapons was.

He pulled the shotgun out, doused it with a generous amount of lubricant, and then loaded it with shells; seven in the tube underneath the barrel, and one in the chamber.

He slipped another seven shells into his pants pocket, shut the trunk, and looked up at the four story structure.

The building loomed over him without a single light on and completely devoid of any sound.

By all accounts John figured it was abandoned. Nevertheless, if she was in there somewhere, he was going to find her and kill her for turning his life upside down.

The tugging in his chest continued to pull at him.

John walked to a side door along the building's right side, tried it, and found it locked. He thought about walking around to the front and trying the large double doors facing the street but decided against it for fear of being spotted with a shotgun in his hands so he walked down the alley to look for another way in.

The sodium glare of the street lights filled the alleyway with harsh yellowish light.

Standing next to a pile of wilted and mold covered cardboard boxes, he studied the back of the building for a point of entry and saw that every single window was open to its fullest measure, something he found strange judging by the seedy locale.

Intent on finding her, John grabbed the shotgun at the breach and hoisted himself up and over into the open window above a second trash bin.

A tattered alley cat hustled out from under the metal container from the sudden commotion.

Inside, he was met with a suffocating darkness and an eerie silence. He placed the stock of the weapon into his shoulder as he steadied himself for whatever might come.

Looking around in order to give his eyes a moment to adjust to the darkness, the building's interior slowly came into focus in a dim green glow.

Crouched in a shooting stance, shotgun at the ready, John scanned the first floor. The building, at least to him, didn't look at all vacant or deserted; notices were tacked on bulletin boards, children's drawings peppered the walls, and worn yet clean furniture sat neatly arranged in what looked like a reception area.

Slowly coming to a stand, he put the shotgun's stock even deeper into his shoulder and set off down the hallway to his left.

He looked through every room and in every corner of the ground floor but found no one so he climbed the stairs at the other end of the building.

The sensation in his chest continued to tug at him.

On the second floor, more silence and more empty rooms greeted him.

Under the weird green dim lighting, which he couldn't pinpoint its source, he continued upward to the next floor.

When he reached the third floor, he was met by the smell of freshly cooked food and the moist warmth of people packed together in a confide space that reminded him of a summer he had spent in New York where he had ridden the subways from Manhattan to Coney Island with his cousin.

With the shotgun still tightly tucked into his shoulder, he entered the silent and dimly green lit dining hall and saw what he instantly knew he'd carry with him for the rest of his life.

Dozens upon dozens of people lay scattered amongst neatly arranged picnic tables.

At first, John assumed every single person was dead but when he walked up to a woman who was flat on her back on the bare floor, he noticed her eyes moving franticly in their sockets. Under the green glow, he also saw plastic toasting saucers next to every single person.

He went over to a man, who was face down on a picnic table, and looked into his eyes; they too were the same as the woman's eyes; desperately darting from left to right in anguished terror.

John stood up and realized that everyone in the room was probably awake and alert but unable to move. Unable to put it all together in his head on how something like this was possible, he knew however with all certainty that she was responsible.

With his hands now sweating against metal and wood of the shotgun, he made his way across the surreal scene to a narrower staircase at the far end of the dining hall.

At the base of the narrow flight of stairs, he looked up at the overhead lighting and saw that all the light bulbs were off.

He waved his hand inches from his face and noted how the greenish glow seemed to be coming from all around him yet at the same time from nowhere at all.

Staring at his hand bathed in the low green light, its source slowly dawned on him with one horrific realization; the eerie green illumination was coming from his eyes. The physical change in their appearance wasn't only cosmetic but biological as well. He could now see in the dark just like some wild animal in the jungle.

He leaned up against the banister of the stairs as a sickening feeling, hot and acidic, rolled into the pit of his stomach over this new bit of information.

A few minutes later and more determined than ever to get even with the person who had done this to him; John pushed off the wooden rail and made his way up to the fourth and final floor.

On the fourth floor landing, the tugging in his chest literally began to yank him forward.

Every fiber of his being told him that she was just ahead.

Standing at the top of the stairs, he saw a single door open at the left far side of the hallway and went to it.

At the threshold, he pushed the door open the rest of the way with the barrel of the 12 gauge and saw that it was a small lightless office, cluttered with files and decorated with old functional furniture.

He peered in just a bit and saw the body of a dead man, mauled and doused in his own blood, face down in front of an old tattered desk.

He stepped into the nightmarish room.

The horrific odor of blood and shit coming from the dead body assaulted his nostrils savagely.

Turning his head away sharply in disgust, John backed out slowly.

Back in the hallway, John leaned up against the wall to catch his breath and noticed at the far end; one final staircase.

Figuring that it led to the rooftop and in desperate need of some fresh air, he pushed off the wall and made his way down the hallway, searching every room along the way, finding no one in the process.

At the foot of the stairs, the driving force at his chest which had guided him the entire night inexplicably stopped as suddenly as it had started.

Noting the sudden change in his chest and unable to decipher why it had just stopped, John focused on the rooftop, the last place she could possibly be.

With his fully loaded weapon leading the way, he started up the final set of stairs. With each step upwards the corners of his mouth began to itch more and more.

At the top of the stairs, a door stood wide open, showcasing the night sky through its rectangle opening.

The cool night time air reached down into the stairwell and stroked his face as he continued to slowly ascend.

Suddenly, a loud fizzing sound erupted from within the building, followed by the noise of spraying water.

Recognizing the sound as overhead fire sprinklers, John turned to see why they had come on.

Suddenly the sweet sickening smell of gasoline lanced his nostrils.

Smelling the intoxicating fumes and listening to the fire sprinklers, he realized that the building and everyone in it was being sprayed down with gasoline.

John turned to run up the stairs but stopped in his tracks when he looked up at the open doorway at the top of the stairwell once again.

Standing at the top of stairs and pointing an orange handgun with the biggest barrel he had ever seen was the demonic-looking white creature that had attacked him at the cabin over two years ago.

Trapped within the narrow stairwell, John knew he had lost the fight even before it had begun. With no other choice than to die fighting, he brought the shotgun up to fire.

Already aiming its weapon, the creature pulled the trigger first, and a blast of light and sound exploded outward from the wide barrel of the large orange handgun in its clawed hand.

Believing that he had just been shot and that the sudden whiteness was nothing other than the fabled tunnel of light, he lowered the shotgun from his shoulder, closed his eyes and suddenly remembered the trip to his uncle's farm and regretted being too shy to play "doctor" under the elm tree with his older cousin, Jenna Lynn.

A white blinding orb of light and heat whistled past him, singeing his left ear.

Feeling the pain to his ear, John opened his eyes, realized he was still alive, and put it all together in one horrifying conclusion; the creature had just fired a signal flare into the building that was filling with gasoline.

Half blind from the intense light and filled with a primordial fear of burning to death, John began racing up the stairs, blinking furiously in an effort to overcome the effects of the blinding light.

Then, with only a dozen stairs between him and the open night sky, a tremendous blistering heat slammed into his back.

John glanced over his shoulder and saw a churning licking fireball rolling up the stairwell towards him as it greedily sought out fresh oxygen to keep alive.

John reached the top of the stairs and launched himself into the air a split second before the rolling ball of fire overtook him.

Finding all the oxygen it needed, the fire ball expanded, the stairwell blew to hell in a shuddering explosion, and the entire building ignited in a dazzling display of light and heat, sealing the fate of everyone in the shelter to a burning blistering doom.

Landing on his face and elbows yards away from the blast, John felt the shotgun fly out of his hands.

With his vision returning, he got up to his knees, looked around for the weapon, and found it resting against one of three black plastic water containers.

On slightly unsteady feet, he went to it, picked it up, and scanned the roof top with the barrel of the shotgun, only to find himself alone on top of the burning building.

He turned to the stairwell and saw it being consumed in flames so he ran to the side of the building, looked over the edge, and saw flames licking at the night air from every open window.

Then, in the corner of his eye, John caught movement on the roof of the neighboring building.

He looked up and saw the creature observing him off in the distance.

Instantly, without thinking, he raised the shotgun at it and pulled the trigger.

The weapon kicked into his shoulder as a dose of double-aught buck roared across the open space between buildings towards their target.

Casually the white furred creature ducked behind a large air-conditioning unit an instant before the deadly metal balls struck it.

The side panel of the industrial sized cooling unit shuddered under the force when the buckshot struck its metal siding.

Amazed that he had missed, John pumped and fired two more rounds into the ruined air-conditioning unit, only to see the creature emerge from behind it unhurt.

Determined to kill it and wondering what to do next, John looked across the twenty foot distance between buildings.

Filled with a choking amount of adrenaline and an almost euphoric thrill at being in a fight to the death, a deep overwhelming sense of self confidence within his being beckoned for him to jump across the gap between both buildings just like the creature had obviously had been able to do.

With the roof under his feet hot from the oxygen rich fire burning feverishly inside the building underneath, John raced to the other end in order to give himself as much distance as possible.

Purposely giving himself no time to think about what he was about to do, he grasped the shotgun at the breach, braced himself in a runner's stance, took a deep breath, and then sprinted across the roof top towards the twenty foot gap and, in all likelihood, a plummeting death to the pavement below.

When he reached the other side, he jumped with all his might and the hamstring of his right leg tore in half from the force of his leap.

With his leg lost in agony and screaming in pain, he soared through the air over the open space between both structures.

Landing on the neighboring roof top in a twisting rolling mess and vomiting from the pain of his ruined leg while at the same time fighting to keep the weapon from flying out of his hands a second time, he crashed to a stop against the air-conditioning unit he had shot at only a few minutes before.

Noticing the glow of the burning homeless shelter in the night sky, a janitor of a textile factory from down the street dialed 911.

Unable to get to his feet from the searing pain in his leg, John slowly and painfully righted himself to a sitting position against the air-conditioning unit, put the weapon to his shoulder, and readied himself for the creature to show itself.

Suddenly and without warning, the shotgun was snatched out his hands from above and he was hoisted by the right bicep up into the air then slammed down tremendously hard onto the top of the large air-conditioning unit.

Shocked by the sheer speed and bone jarring force,

John stared in disbelief as he was tussled about then straddled by the creature.

Pinned at the chest and arms by the creature's long muscular legs, he looked up and saw the creature's demonic gaping face inches from his own.

Under the hot crackling glow coming from the roaring fire next to them, the creature calmly stared into his emerald colored eyes.

Then, in three stunning thundering booms, the water storage tanks that held the gasoline exploded in quick succession one after the other, sending heat filled shock waves across the surrounding rooftops.

The creature turned and watched the destruction. The glow from the fire and explosions reflected wickedly off its intense green eyes.

Feeling the press of its weight heavy on his chest, John watched it grin wide with satisfaction at the destruction and death it had just caused.

Slowly, it turned its attention back to him.

Beaten, injured, and unable to move under the vice-like grip of the creature's muscular legs, John simply stared at the horrid monster and waited for whatever came next.

The creature leaned closer and stared deep into his large glossy green eyes.

The smell of freshly cut mint drifted from the creature breath and laced John's face.

Smelling the sweet scent, John stared back at it in silence and wondered just how painful being killed by such a monster was going to be.

The creature sniffed the air between them, hissed, then jumped off of him, and disappeared into the darkness of the night, leaving him splayed on the air conditioning unit, battered and bruised but alive.

Staring up at the night sky, John lay where he had been left as he soaked in what had just happened; after trying to kill him twice before, tonight it had let him live.

The sound of sirens in the distance reached his ears.

Listening, he quickly assessed his situation; there was no reasonable explanation as to why he was on a rooftop with a loaded shotgun next to a burning building filled with murdered people inside. He realized, if he was found and arrested, he would most likely spent the next couple of years explaining himself without his freedom.

Not wanting to be caught, he rolled onto his left side in order to climb down off the air-conditioning unit when suddenly an itching sensation took hold of his wounded leg.

Surprised by the unexpected and intense itching, John bared his teeth and squeezed his wounded leg hard with both hands.

The itching increased in intensity to a maddening level around the severed hamstring.

Then, as quickly as it started, the itching stopped all together.

Overcome with relief, he let go of his leg, and rolled off the cooling unit, landing gingerly on his feet.

Standing upright and pain free, he realized that the injury to his leg had completely healed. Stunned at such a revelation, he simply shook his head and shelved it along with all the other new oddities that were taking hold of him.

The sirens were nearly upon him.

Pushing aside all other thoughts except escape and self-preservation, John picked up his shotgun and scampered around the rooftop looking for a way down.

At the far corner of the building, he saw a metal ladder, anchored to the wall; a fire escape.

He went to it, stopped in front of the metal rungs and looked down. A series of zigzagging metal stairs lead down the full length of the building to the street below.

With weapon in hand, he swung himself on the ladder and began the climb down.

First responders would reach the burning building in vain. There would be no survivors.

CHAPTER 19

"We don't know that yet. We don't."

Standing a short distance away so as not to have his shoes soaked in the filthy water flowing from out the building, Lt. Douglas "Husky" Mosley watched the firemen go about their duties in putting out the last pockets of fire and shook his head, knowing it was only a matter of time before the bodies would start being hauled out.

From the clatter and hustle of the firemen and their equipment to the quacking excited voices of bystanders, the sound of collective chaos loomed all around him during the early morning hour of the up and coming new day.

He shook his head again and wondered how bad his clothes were going to smell of smoke.

Then, like a ray of light, the familiar voice of his partner reached his ear, "What do we have, Husky?"

Like everybody else on the force, she called him by his nickname given to him during his time as a Linebacker at San Diego State and one season in the

NFL for Houston until a knee injury had brought it all to an end.

He turned to his left and saw her standing beside him, calmly looking at him, as if she had always been there.

He gave her a quick smile, turned back to the fire, and said, "Just a simple fire. You know how these old buildings are… in this part of town. They've passed their freshness date by some twenty years."

Lt. Mildred Tanner looked at the fire herself and asked, "Simple? Then what the hell are we doing here?"

"I'm here cus some cab driver told the first responders that he heard gunshots right after the fire started."

"Gunshots?" she questioned.

"That's why I'm here. You could've stayed in bed. There was no reason for both of us to be up at this God awful hour over a reported gunshot," he told her as he turned and faced her.

"Well… I'm here now… so there," she returned with a smile and a lift of an eyebrow.

"I'm serious. There's nothing here. Go home, Millie," he told her, using the nickname he had given her after that night in Sacramento last year.

Using her version of 'taking no for answer', she asked, "So, what now?"

Knowing her well enough to know she was going to stay, even against her own good, he looked at her slender face, and replied, "Well… I…we… are going to wait for that donut shop to open… then we are going to get a fresh cup of coffee and then after that… we are going to do some more waiting."

"Standard operating procedure then?" she

playfully asked.

"Yeah, standard operating procedures," he repeated and then started to walk down the street towards the closed donut shop and away from the heat and smoke.

She stopped him as she exclaimed, "Holy shit, Husky! I know this place!"

He turned to her with a sigh and said, "Yes... you do."

Taking in the devastated building with fresh eyes, she said, "This is the shelter where our last CI* was staying at. Fuck, we even dropped him off right in front of those double doors once," and then pointed at the charred and water soaked remnants of the hand carved double doors that had been the hallmark of the building when it had first opened back in the 1940s.

"Yup," he acknowledged as he watched the magnitude of the destruction dawn on her beautiful brown eyes, which he still secretly cherished since their first and only night together.

Still looking at the building, she said, "This wasn't an abandoned building, this...was that...shelter... that was doing so good."

With a sober tone, he replied, "That's right."

She turned with a horrified look on her face that rendered his heart, "Husky... all those people."

Mosley took a deep breath of thick smelling air, let it out, and said, "We don't know that yet. We don't."

She looked at the once proud shelter again, then back at him, and asked, "What about the CI, what was his name? Carver...Cager?"

He touched her arm and told her, "Granger. Dodson at Rampart put him on a plane to Wyoming, where his parents live... last week."

Tanner nodded and said, "Ok... that's good to know," then turned and sadly stared at the building that was now simply just a smoldering concrete box.

Touching her arm again, he told her, "Come on. Let's go to work on that cup of coffee."

She nodded again and allowed him to take her.

As they walked away, they heard a voice calling out for them to stop.

They turned and watched a young fireman running up to them waving his arm. When he finally reached them he said, "Sir, Ma'am, we were able to get up on the roof about twenty minutes ago," Then put out his clenched hand and added, "The Captain wanted you to have these."

Tanner extended her palm out.

The young fireman placed three spent shotgun shells in her hand.

Looking at the red plastic cartridges in his partner's palm, Husky said to her, "Well... I guess the coffee is going to have to do the waiting."

Standing amongst the crowd of onlookers, an Asian looking woman with startling green eyes stared intently at the two detectives.

* confidential informant

CHAPTER 20

She closed the door of her small apartment softly behind her and looked at the clock on the far wall.

It read half past one in the morning.

She leaned up against the door and rubbed her face. She was utterly exhausted. Even after everything that had occurred, she had stayed to watch the bodies of her victims be removed one by one from the ruined building.

Picking her face up from her hands, she glanced around the apartment, which she had procured months ago using one of her many false identities, and wondered when exactly she had been inside it last. The one bedroom unit was drab with very little furniture and the stale smell of unventilated air hung heavy within it.

Pushing off the door, she kicked off her shoes and walked towards the bedroom.

Feeling the dusty carpet on the soles of her bare feet, she looked down at them and noticed that even hours after running across roof tops and alleyways they were still black and filthy.

She entered the bedroom and stripped herself naked, piling the clothing in the corner.

The smell of smoke, brash and musky, clung to her skin in a thick film.

Nude, tired and dirty, she fell onto the bed in a heavy slump.

The sheets, untouched and unwashed for months, felt clammy and uncomfortable against her skin yet fatigue induced weariness prevented her from doing anything more than laying on them in a motionless state of surrender.

As sleep slowly and seductively crept over her, she rolled onto her back, placed her hands under her head, and turned her thoughts to him as she stared at the stucco ceiling. His unexpected appearance at the homeless shelter had eclipsed everything she had thought he was capable of. How exactly he had found her was a complete mystery to her. Her only guess; the tugging sensation she had felt in the center of her chest moments after killing Alex.

She inhaled and slowly exhaled the stale air of the room as she thought to herself that by not killing him on the rooftop she had extended to him the one thing which she had never been given; a choice.

With a tired smile, she let her thoughts drift away from his commendable attempt to kill her and flowed to an image of the happy and trustful faces of her victims as they drank to their own deaths, Alex's whimpers as she ripped him open, and the exquisite smell of burning living flesh, sweet and pungent in its aroma.

Content with the way her plans had turned out, she took her hands from the back of her head and ran them over her breasts down to her hips as her eyelids finally closed.

As slumber slowly overtook her, her last awaking thoughts were of the two LAPD detectives she had watched for hours. She had seen something in them, a certain kind of chemistry, a bond of sorts linking them to one another of which she found most intriguing.

She fell asleep planning their murder.

CHAPTER 21

"What was her name?"

Mosley steered into a parking space in front of the famed Los Angeles County Coroner's office. Sitting in the passenger seat, Tanner looked over the top of her sunglasses at the unassuming building and then slumped back into the seat.

He slipped the police sedan into Park and said out loud as he cut the engine, "Look, I know it's early in the morning and really early into the investigation but I was informed that Mike was going to handle the bodies himself... and knowing him... he probably worked through the night and, chances are... he's already come up with something."

Tanner turned to face him, lifted her sunglasses up onto her forehead, and said with playful sarcasm, "The only thing he's going to come up with right now is that I look just as dead from the lack of sleep as all those victims. I didn't get home until well past two in the morning."

With a cocked smile, he replied, "You know you're

right, I shouldn't have picked you up. You're grumpy as all hell when you don't get enough sleep," then added as he opened his door, "But you're here now... so come on."

Following his lead, she opened her own door and stepped out, "Buy me a cup of coffee."

"A large one." he said to her over his shoulder and he walked to the entrance.

With a cup of coffee in their hands, they quietly strolled the white 70s looking hallways towards the office of the coroner who was presiding over their case, which the media had already dubbed 'The Deadliest Fire in Los Angeles History'.

After a series of left turns and rights, they came to a door that stood slightly ajar.

Inside, a man dressed in a lab coat and scrubs sat behind his desk and typed away with lightning speed on a laptop.

Mosley gently knocked on the door and said, "Mike."

Dr. Michael Harmon, slim and pale under his mint green scrubs and crisp lab coat, looked up from this typing and said with a tired smile, "Husky, Mildred! Come in from out outta the rain."

Tired as they both were, Mosley and Tanner found his upbeat manner welcoming and uplifting. They each took a seat at the front of his large mahogany desk and watched him slowly shut the laptop.

Looking at his pleasant and tired face, Mosley asked, "What do you have so far, Mike?"

Interlocking his fingers on the desk blotter in front of him, the doctor answered, "A whole lot of dead people...actually a whole lot of charred dead people."

Rubbing her sleepy puffy eyes, Tanner jokingly told him, "You're overpaid. A fifth grader could have surmised that as they pulled body after body from out of that building."

He chuckled at her jab at him, "Overpaid for sure," and then said in a more serious tone, "But overworked too. The official count was one hundred and seventeen victims that came out of that hell hole."

Working past the stunning number of victims, Mosley asked, "What else?"

Dr. Harmon pursed his lips for a second and replied, "Not much right now but I can tell you that everyone in that building was evenly and thoroughly cooked alive."

"Alive," Mosely exclaimed.

"Jesus," Tanner said looking down at her coffee.

"Any gunshot or shotgun wounds?" Mosley asked.

Harmon shook his head and said, "Still early but I don't think so," then exhaled long and slow and added, "However, I can tell you this for sure... before I put it on my official report... that every single body has the same amount of burn trauma... not one body is partially burned... all of them were thoroughly set ablaze."

"Mike. You said... 'alive'," Mosley said as he gripped his coffee cup tighter in his large hands.

"I did, Husky. You see, I've found signs of smoke inhalation on the few bodies that I have gone through completely. Plus the smell of gasoline and evenly spaced burn patterns are all over the bodies."

Tanner leaned forward in her chair, and asked, "Meaning?"

"Meaning... no one inside that building tried to escape before, during, or after they were doused with the accelerant then set ablaze," Harmon answered in a flat tone.

Smiles and humor disappeared as the two detectives ingested what they had just heard.

"How's that possible?" Mosley asked more to himself then to anyone else in the room, finally breaking the silence.

Harmon leaned back into his leather executive chair and said, "Like I said 'the few bodies I've gone through.'"

Tanner took another sip of her coffee.

The taste barely registered in her mouth.

The doctor took another deep breath, let it out, and told the pair sitting across from him, "Listen... in life as in death... a person always has a story to tell. These poor devils are waiting a just few doors down to tell the story of their demise... to me. We owe them that much. When I hear it... you'll hear it."

As if obeying a hidden signal that the conversation had come to an end, both Tanner and Mosley stood up at the same time.

Tanner said her parting words before heading out the door, "Thanks, Mike. We want to hear their story when you have it," then left as the doctor, who would run for mayor a few years later, gave her a soft nod with a small smile.

Making his way past the guest chairs, Mosley said to the doctor, "Yeah, thanks, Mike. Call us the second you..."

"Husky," Dr. Harmon cut him off and said with a seriousness Mosley had never heard come from him before, "We've worked a lot of cases together over the years and I consider you a friend... so I just want to tell you... this case... from what I've been able to gather... you either make Chief... or you retire from it. This is the big one."

Standing at the door, Mosley looked down at the floor then back up, and replied, "Yeah... I was afraid... that was going to be part of their story," then walked away.

Mosley found Tanner in the employee lounge filling her cup with fresh black coffee. Taking a few seconds before making his appearance known, he watched her at the doorway.

Not quite petite but considerably smaller than him, he always marveled at the way she kept up with him, never backing down or falling behind, always ready with the next question, and the first to pull her gun.

Without turning her head as she poured sugar into the cup, she told him, "You better not be staring at my ass."

"No. Just staring at just how much of that shit you're putting in your coffee," he replied as he walked in.

"Only until the spoon stands up on its own," she turned to him and smiled.

Refilling his own cup, he told her, "Hell, Millie... I shouldn't have brought you along. I'm sorry."

"Forget it. I'm here now. Anyways, I'll sleep when I'm dead," she told him as she slumped down on the worn and ragged leather sofa next to the soda machine.

Putting nothing but powdered creamer in his, he thought about what Mike had said about the victims and quietly exclaimed, "Jesus... that's a lot of people."

Tanner shook her head in stunned dismay at the official count Mike had told them and said nothing.

Mosley took a chair for himself and sipped the hot fresh coffee.

She took a long draught from her cup, leaned her head back onto the backrest of the sofa, and asked in a nonchalant tone, "What was her name?"

"Who?" Mosley asked.

"The director. The woman who ran that shelter. What was her name?"

"I don't know...I can't remember," he replied opening his hands in a gesture.

"Suzette. Suzanne. Miss something or other," Tanner recited as she did her best to recall the woman's name as she stared up at the ceiling.

"We could always call Granger at his parent's house and get the name from him." Mosely jokingly suggested.

Tanner screwed her lips at his lame joke.

Mosley looked down at the floor suddenly trying to remember as well, "Miss... Miss... something or other."

"Granger always talked about her... all the time. He always referred to her by 'Miss' and her first name," Tanner said as she strained to remember that name that was hanging on the tip of her tongue.

Suddenly, Mosely remembered and boomed out loud, "Miss Susan!"

Tanner turned and looked at him with wide eyes, and said, "Miss Susan. That's right. Miss Susan. He talked about her... all the God damn time. Miss Susan this, Miss Susan that."

Smiling at the rediscovered memory, Mosley added, "Yeah, that's right. He did always talk about her."

"Yeah. He fucking really liked her... that was for sure," she said while staring up at the ceiling once again.

He took another sip and asked, "Why you thinking

of her? She's probably mixed in with all the other bodies."

Still looking up, she replied, "I don't know why I'm thinking of her. I just am." then added," You know, after helping us with that San Pedro bust, he had enough money to get his own place but all he wanted to do was go back to that shelter. I always assumed he was just being cheap but now that I think about it... he fuck'n loved that place."

"Meaning?" Mosley asked, feeling the conversation taking a serious turn.

"Meaning... everybody just like Granger... probably loved being there," she looked at him and continued, "And Mike said... from what he could tell so far...no one tried to escape."

"Meaning?" he asked again, knowing full well that her mind had grasped onto to something.

Her eyes took on a distant stare, "Meaning that..."

Suddenly Mosley's cellular phone rang, cutting her off in mid-sentence and her train of thought.

An hour later.

Standing at the same spot as the night before, both Tanner and Mosely looked at the ruined building looming over them as police officers, onlookers, and a multitude of news personal hustled and bustled in and around the perimeter.

Doing what they could so as not to attract the attention of the media to themselves, they assessed the magnitude of the damage in the morning daylight a few yards away.

Then, from out of the building's main entrance, the arson investigator of the LAFD emerged, covered in soot and wet below his knees.

They watched him walked up to them, looking tired and worn.

Wearing the traditional fireman's helmet high on his head, which gave him an elfin look to his face, he stopped in front of them, the patch on his shirt read Banks, and said, "Lt. Mosley and Tanner? Am I correct?"

Tanner spoke first to the man who without his helmet was actually shorter than she, "I'm Lt. Tanner and this is Lt. Mosley."

Smiling, yet professional, he said, "You arrived faster than I expected. I'm Captain Edwin Banks... good to meet you both... under the circumstances."

Mosley spoke, "Good to meet you. We were close by... North Mission road. Thanks for calling so soon," then asked, "What have you got?"

"Right now, all we have for you are pictures of what we've found so far. However, with the investigation being as high profile as it has suddenly become... we thought it best to show them to you straight away. We'd let you see what we've turned up first hand but, as it is, the building isn't safe for anyone other than fire personal at this moment." Banks told them then handed over a small digital camera over to Tanner, and then added, "You're going to need a drink afterwards... I guarantee it."

Tanner took the camera and looked at the display screen.

Banks continued as they skimmed through the pictures on the display screen, "Most of the roof fell in. We were very lucky... and I mean real lucky to have found those shotgun shells last night and even luckier to have found that," then pointed at the last picture.

Looking at the image, she asked, "And what is that,

necessarily?"

Shifting the large red helmet on his head, Banks answered, "It was connected to the three water storage tanks that were on the roof, which were blown clean off the building during the fire. We found one a block and a half from here just an hour ago."

Looking at what looked like nothing more than twisted metal with a few electrical wires jutting out, Mosley asked, "What is it? I can't make it out."

Looking up at him, Banks replied, "It's the remains of a simple light switch."

Knowing they were missing what he wanted them to see, they said nothing as they continued to study the image.

With a sigh at the words that were about to come out of his mouth, Captain Banks said, "The tanks were filled... as it turns out... with gasoline... and that switch emptied them into the building through the sprinkler system."

Tanner slipped her sunglasses back onto her face and Mosley felt his heart drop to his stomach.

"You have yourselves a mass murder on your hands," Banks proclaimed as he took the camera back.

CHAPTER 22

"My God, man, tell us the name!"

Being careful not to be seen at such a late hour by anyone in the bedroom community of Sherman Oaks, she quietly crept up alongside the house between the wooden fence and its east wall.

With deliberate steps and with the night vision of her eyes, she walked around an old bicycle and an unrolled garden hose before silently reaching the back bedroom window.

Standing to the right of the window with her back flat against the pale yellow stucco wall, underneath the narrow shadow offered by the awning of the roof, she glanced in and saw a teenage boy typing with his left hand on a computer keyboard while holding an energy drink in the other.

Except for the monitor's glowing blue screen, the small tidy bedroom was devoid of any light, giving it a gloomy eerie appearance.

Doing her best not to be seen entering the bedroom, she slowly and quietly raised the unlatched window until she felt it come to a stop with the smallest of thuds, and then, in one fluid motion, she took a step forward, turned, and noiselessly slithered herself through the open window into the dark warm bedroom.

With his back to the room, the teenager at the far end neither turned nor stopped typing as she entered his bedroom.

She stood up, gently shut the window, and then began walking towards him as the soft tan carpeting muffled her approach.

Then, in an easy casual manner he spoke to her without turning around or breaking the stride in his typing, "A pretty big comic book convention is happening in a few weeks. You wanna go? In the right costume, you would be the best looking cosplay there."

She stopped directly behind him, placed her hand on his shoulder, and replied, "What the hell is a 'cosplay'?"

He stopped typing at the sound of her question, craned his neck to look up at her, and asked with a curl in his lip, "You really have no idea what I'm talking about, do you?"

She slid her hand off his shoulder, walked to the teenager's small bed, sat down at its foot, and said with a sigh, "None whatsoever, Glen."

Using his feet, he turned himself around in his desk chair to face her, "Regardless, would you like to go. I'm telling you... all my chatroom friends who are going to be there would just die if they saw you with me."

Unbuttoning her blouse, she said, "You commit cyber-crimes for me in exchange for sex. Do you actually think I'm going to go with you to some convention in the middle of the day?"

He smiled, shrugged his shoulders, and replied,

"Worth a shot."

With her blouse and bra on the floor and her breasts bare, she stood up and stepped on her jeans, "You get to fuck me in your mother's house, believe me that's better than any convention can offer.

Staring at her while she undressed, Glen asked, "Ok. So, what do you need this time?"

Pulling back a matching comforter and sheet set on his bed, she asked, "You heard about that fire in Los Angeles?"

"Yeah. The one with all the dead people," he replied as he shifted in his chair.

"I want everything on the two LAPD lead investigators assigned to the case," she told him as she climbed into the narrow bed, fully naked.

"Is that all? Shoot, I've been able to log into the LAPD d-base since last spring. Some hacker in Montreal traded me the access codes for three mint condition baseball cards I had stored away in a drawer," he told her and then added proudly, "I'm making about three thousand a month just by deleting traffic violations for people."

Sitting up in his bed with the comforter drawn up just below her bare breasts, she asked, "Can you have it ready for me tonight?"

Enjoying the sight of her naked form in his bed, he wickedly smiled at her and answered, "This is going to be the easiest hack you've asked of me since I met you. I'll have it ready for you in no time."

"Good," she told him then added, "I feel like a night of sex... so hurry."

Listening to her enticing words, he spun himself back towards his computer and began.

To survive as long as she had while doing what she did required the help of others from time to time and over the years she had developed a roving clandestine network that provided her with whatever she needed. Referred to her by a hacker that she had used to create Susan Lang's identity and then had killed later, she had met Glen two days after arriving in Los Angeles. Awkward and shy, and with no obvious need for money, she had won him over with sex for his services and his silence.

Sitting up against the headboard and watching him type away at his computer, she decided that, when the time came to kill him, she was going to cut off his head and leaving it sitting on his keyboard.

After a while, the serene darkness, the soft comfort of the bed, and the methodical sound of typing relaxed her into a warm stupor.

She closed her eyes as the smoothing wave of sleep washed over her and a memory; one of thousands, from her distant past crept in...

The sound of shouting men and running feet erupted without warning.

Hidden from sight behind crates and barrels of goods being shipped to Europe, the creature suddenly realized it had been duped into the ship's cargo hold, lured with the promise of an easy kill of a succulent victim, the ship's cabin boy.

Clutching the frightened stricken child to its chest, it looked around for an escape route but found none. The only way in or out was suddenly and thoroughly blocked by armed merchant sailors.

The running and shouting stopped as the crew of

The Radiant Star jockeyed for position amongst the wooden boxes and barrels.

Cornered and trapped, the creature pressed the boy's head tighter to its chest and moved further back into the darkness, its eyes bathing the cluttered and confined surrounding in a green glowing hue.

At the other end, blocking the stairs, the crew trained their weapons at the cargo hold as the captain of the ship came down the stairs, gun in hand and addressed the ship's first mate, "Mr. Skinner, I gather you have the culprit that has cursed our fair ship?"

Turning to face his captain of ten years, First Mate Andrew Skinner replied, "That would be correct, Captain Wilkes. When we heard the boy scream in terror, we sprang into action."

Slipping his greatcoat off his broad shoulders, Captain Luke Wilkes cast his trademark piercing stare at his first mate and asked, "You used the boy as bait?"

Mr. Skinner answered, "I figured young Bradley to be the most appealing candidate for the task, being so young and small. Plus, if this killer did claim him as a victim... then we wouldn't be out any more useable deck hands."

The captain grunted under his breath and said, "You're a calculating man, Mr. Skinner. Yet, whether I commend your decision or condemn it for using young Bradley will be determined by the outcome of tonight's affair."

Weighing the heft of his short barrel rifle in his calloused hands, Mr. Skinner said, "I stand behind my decision, Captain Wilkes... come what may."

Putting the fate of the young cabin boy aside for the moment, Captain Wilkes asked, "Do we know who it is, Mr. Skinner?"

As he strained to see further into the darkened cargo hold, Mr. Skinner answered, "All of our men are accounted for... so the killer, in turn, is one of our passengers, Captain Wilkes."

Searching with narrowed eyes for a glimpse of the murderer who had already claimed a quarter of the crew and passengers, Captain Wilkes asked, "And do you know who this passenger is, Mr. Skinner?"

"Not at the moment, sir. This person, whoever it may be, possesses quite a bit cunning and stealth. Young Bradley's horrific scream was all that alerted us," Mr. Skinner told his captain then added, "I have a crew member taking a head count, as we speak, of all the passengers. After which, he'll compare that count to the passenger roster... thus giving us the identity of whom it is."

"Very good, Mr. Skinner. Are all the men in place?" the good captain asked.

"Yes, Captain Wilkes," Mr. Skinner answered.

"Good. I'd like to address our killer, now," Captain Wilkes told his first mate.

"As you wish, sir," Mr. Skinner said then scooted over to his left to make room for the captain to step forward.

Gripping his large revolver in both hands, Captain Wilkes raised his voice and spoke in his most commanding tone, "This is your Captain speaking. Whoever you are, I want to inform you that you're completely surrounded by my brave and trusted crew. Your killing ways on The Radiant Star are now over so I command you to release my cabin boy and step out from behind those shipping crates."

With the boy, whose bladder had gone loose minutes earlier, still firmly clutched in its hands, the creature remained motionless and silent as it listened.

Captain Wilkes pressed forward, "As a captain and as a man of honor, I assure you that no harm will come to you if you surrender with the boy unharmed."

Wanting a nonviolent end, he continued, "I promise you a fair trial once we reach Great Britain. You have my word as an officer and a gentleman that I will speak on your behalf to the compassion and humanity you showed that poor boy."

Slowly a plan began to develop in the creature's head as it realized how utterly dark it was inside the cargo hold and that no one, except the comatose boy in its arms, had seen what it looked like.

Mr. Skinner stood up and spoke in a whisper, "Captain Wilkes, should I have the sails lowered? We're so very close to making port."

Turning to look at him, Captain Wilkes replied, "No, Mr. Skinner. If we drop our sails now, we shall leave ourselves vulnerable to the currents," then adding, loud enough for the rest of his men to hear as well, "I assure you, Mr. Skinner, that this killer will not set foot on Liverpool soil alive unless it be in my custody."

Recalling the torn murdered bodies of both crew and passengers, Mr. Skinner said, "But, Captain, if, by chance, the culprit does escape once we reach port..."

Stopping him with a hand on his shoulder, Captain Wilkes told his first mate, "Mr. Skinner, the man at the helm stays the course. This is our ship and our situation and when we finally do reach port... our situation on our ship will be resolved. Do you understand me, Mr. Skinner?"

With a stern look of a professional seaman, Mr. Skinner answered, "Aye, Captain."

With a nod and a pat on the shoulder, Captain

Wilkes replied in turn, "Aye," then turned once more to address the hidden killer but was stopped short by the sound of frantic running footsteps coming down the stairs.

Holding a large piece of parchment, Dudley Webster, a short stocky man wearing a bowtie and vest, stopped in front of the towering captain. His face was ashen white and a look of shock hovered around his eyes.

Mr. Skinner spook to the clearly shaken man, "Mr. Webster, I gather you've found the name of our culprit?"

Looking from the captain to the first mate, the man struggled to reply, "That...that I... did... Mr. Skinner."

Wanting the name very badly, Captain Wilkes spoke in a rushed tone, "My God, man, tell us the name!"

Turning to look up at the captain once again, Mr. Webster said as every ear in the tight dark cargo hold strained to hear, "I...did the head... count and... matched it with the... passenger roster."

Captain Wilkes pressed him, "Mr. Webster...the name!"

Speaking with a disconnected tone, the pale and sweating man continued, "All the passengers were accounted for, except..."

Deciding on a fatherly approached to extract the name from the ruffled man, the captain touched Mr. Webster's shoulder and said, "Go on son... tell us."

Taking comfort in his captain's touch, he said, "Except... the passenger in cabin twelve."

A collected gasp of disbelief escaped from everyone.

Mr. Webster swallowed and gave the name,

"Elizabeth Saunders."

Shocked by what he had just heard, the captain snatched the roster from the man's hand, examined it, looked up, and said, "My God, Mr. Skinner... the woman with... the...green eyes."

Mr. Skinner exclaimed, "I can't believe it."

From within the mass of armed crewmen, Captain Wilkes heard someone say the word 'Siren'.

Knowing how superstitious career seamen were, he quickly addressed his men, "There'll be none of that kind of talk on my ship, gentlemen. The next man I hear who does will personally answer to me. Is that understood?"

Reluctant and wavering 'ayes' drifted over to him.

From behind a large crate, the creature stole a glance and saw Mr. Skinner take the roster from the captain's hand and tuck it away in his trousers pocket.

'I'll lose this ship to fairytales and superstitions if I don't end this now!' Captain Wilkes thought to himself as he turned to Dudley Webster and said, "Good job, Mr. Webster. Now, kindly arm yourself and fall in with the rest of the men."

Nodding, Mr. Webster kneeled down behind the nearest crate and took a gun from the man next to him.

"This ends now," Captain Wilkes said to his first mate then turned once more towards the darkened hold, and said out loud, "Miss Saunders, you have been identified. Your crimes aboard The Radiant Star now bear your name and face. Surrender."

The creature sat the boy down onto the wooden plank flooring in front of it and took the boy's lolling head into its clawed hands.

Feeling shock slowly turning into rage at the idea that a woman was responsible for the acts of cruelty witnessed by his ship, Captain Wilkes called out, almost yelling, "Surrender, now! Or by God, woman or not, I'll run you through then hang you by your feet on my highest mast for all of Great Britain to witness when we reach port."

Knowing they were only minutes away from rushing its position, the creature readied itself for the right opportunity to strike.

Mr. Skinner said, "This mad woman doesn't appear to be coming out under her own volition, Captain Wilkes."

Staring into the dark confines in front of him, he replied, "It appears that you're right, old friend."

Mr. Skinner took a deep breath as the coming battle tinged the tip of his tongue.

Captain Wilkes turned to him and said in a hush, "Go up top with some men and have them open the loading hatch to the hold. It is much too dark in here. We have been blessed with a full moon this night which should give us plenty of light to seek her out without our men shooting each other by mistake."

Mr. Skinner nodded then turned to leave but stopped and spoke to his captain like the friends they had become over the years, "I found Johnny Evans... I did. He had his throat ripped out and his tongue pulled through the wound. He was only nineteen years old, Luke."

"And I pushed his body into the sea and wrote the letter to his family, Andrew," Captain Wilkes said to his first mate and Godfather to his third child, "This woman dies tonight... or walks off our ship in shackles to the gallows."

With nothing further needed to be said between two men of the sea, Mr. Skinner dashed up the stairs, taking two crewmen along with him.

Hearing the running feet of men rushing top side, the creature knew it had to time everything perfectly if it wanted to live to see dry land. The element of surprise and its abnormal agility was all it had against the armed and determined men who planned to kill it. Being only able to take two to three direct gunshot wounds before its healing ability was rendered useless; the room for error in its effort to survive was marginal.

Captain Wilkes checked his six shot revolver one last time, cocked the hammer back, and said just loud enough for his men to hear, "Gentlemen... when the hatch is pulled open, I order you to gun down the killer of your fellow crewmen and of the passengers who put their trust in us for a safe voyage across the Atlantic. I command you to ignore the fact that a woman will be at the other end of your gun sights and to keep in mind that she is nothing more than a mad dog killer who has systematically murdered on our ship ever since we set sail from New York."

A flurry of 'Ayes' came over to him.

He added, "And be mindful of young Horton Bradley, who still might be alive.", then concluded, "May the Lord our God, all the angels and saints preserve all of us this night against this wicked evil that has befallen our humble ship... The Radiant Star."

The sound of cocking hammers clicked all around him.

Up top, Mr. Skinner and the two other men with him exited the stairwell, closed the door behind them, and ran across the ship's large wooden deck towards the loading hatch at its center as the full moon illuminated their way.

When they reached it, Mr. Skinner planted the

stock of his short rifle into his shoulder, pointed the barrel directly at the closed hatch, and said, "Mr. Jeffery, Mr. Clarkson, the hatch, please."

Nodding, both men tucked their pistols in their waistbands and set upon opening the large wooden hatch; first the restraining locks and then the safety catches.

Cocking his weapon, Mr. Skinner looked up at the helm and shouted out loud, "Mr. Carrington, no matter what, and I do mean 'no matter what', do not leave your post at the wheel... Captain's orders. Is that understood?"

A man of the sea as long as he could remember, a salt water weathered Mr. Carrington shouted back, "Aye, Mr. Skinner. Straight and steady."

The safety catches thudded against the wooden deck.

Mr. Jeffery looked up and said, "The hatch is now unlocked, Mr. Skinner. Awaiting your instructions, sir."

Andrew Skinner gave one final steadying exhale, slipped his finger onto the trigger of his rifle, and said, "Mr. Jeffery, Mr. Clarkson, open it, please."

Together, both men slid the hatch along its greased tracks and rich silver moonlight filled the interior of the cargo hold.

The creature bared its razor sharp teeth.

With his men armed and spread out in an even firing line safely behind wooden crates, Captain Wilkes called out to them, "Gentlemen, you're field of fire is now illuminated... commence at..." then abruptly stopped.

From the depths of the cargo hold, an object flew into the air, twisting and spinning.

The captain watched it sail through the air directly

towards him.

A second later, the matted spherical shape hit him in the middle of the chest, warm and wet.

Stunned, Captain Wilkes took a step back and looked down at what had just struck him.

Aided by the light of the moon, he realized what it was and felt his legs momentarily lose their strength.

A crew member to his left was the first to scream in horror as he pointed at Horton Bradley's small decapitated head, a grimace of pain frozen on his young face.

Terror stricken by such an act of brutality, many opened fire, without so much as aiming, into the light and shadow angled cargo hold while others reeled back in fear and disgust from the dead boy's head, collapsing the firing line.

Seizing the brief moment of utter chaos, the creature jumped up from its hiding place onto a wooden crate, bared it razor sharp teeth with a demonic hiss at the already terrified men and launched itself, using its unnatural strength and agility, out the open hatch above, just as it had planned.

Topside, Mr. Skinner watched the creature leaped out from below into the night sky above him.

Not wasting a moment of the pandemonium it had created, the creature landed on top of him, breaking most of his ribs in the process, and drove its long clawed fingers into his throat, tearing both the jugular and carotid at the same time.

Jetting blood from both sides of his neck, Mr. Skinner died on the deck without firing a shot.

Still standing at the other end of the open hatch, Mr. Jeffery and Mr. Clarkson watched in numbed horror as the first mate of The Radiant Star was struck down.

Mr. Clarkson turned and ran as a primal fear to live burst inside him.

Rolling off its second victim of the night, the creature leap to where a shock frozen Mr. Jeffery stood.

Landing right in front of him, the creature drove a clenched fist deep into man's midsection and stripped him of the revolver tucked in his waistband all in one fluid motion.

Mr. Jeffery doubled over and crumpled down onto the deck, gasping for air.

Swift, sure, and precise, the creature turned and fired at the escaping Mr. Clarkson.

Inches from reaching the door that lead to the Captain's quarters, Mr. Clarkson's head exploded in a shower of blood, brains, and skull.

He hit the deck face first, farted once, and died.

Next, the creature cocked the hammer of the single action weapon and put the helmsman in its sights.

Though terrified beyond measure by the surreal violence playing out in front of his eyes, Blake Carrington, a man of his word, had remained at the wheel.

The first bullet struck him in the left lung.

Bubbling blood and mortally wounded, Mr. Carrington yelled into the night, "Straight and ste-"

The second hit him just above the mouth.

Dead, Mr. Carrington's hands stayed on the wheel for a moment then slowly slipped off the handles.

Down in the hold, men shouted and fired out the open hatch.

The creature let the half used weapon fall from its clawed hand onto the deck as it set its attention on Mr. Jeffery who was still on his knees coughing and gasping for air.

It grabbed a hold of him by the scruff of his neck and trousers, lifted him high above its head, and then slammed him down hard onto the bloodied deck.

The tremendous impact knocked him half unconscious and ruptured his bladder.

Deep in the hold, Captain Wilkes, desperate to get control of his men, wrapped the dead boy's head in his greatcoat, tucked it in beneath the wooden staircase out of view, and then yelled, "Gentlemen. Gentlemen! This is your captain speaking. I order you to regain control of yourselves and stop shooting! Now!"

Trained in the ways of seafarers, the frightened men settled down at the authoritative sound of their captain.

He pressed on, "All of you, who have fired your weapons, please reload them now... thank you, " then, knowing he could no longer ignore the issue at hand, he acknowledged what they all had just seen and heard, and said, "What we just witnessed was no Siren or vengeful albatross but a being that is both violent and savage."

From somewhere off to his right, someone spoke, "From the dark continent, no doubt. A fitting reprimand for all the evil we've all done there."

"There'll be none of that kind of talk on this ship!" Captain Wilkes bellowed.

Another nameless voice spoke and asked, "Then, if you could be so kind, my captain... please tell us all... what that thing is."

He answered what he honestly believed, "Gentlemen, I do not know what has come aboard The Radiant Star but, just like all of you, I have sailed the vast oceans of this world and seen many creatures that have defied logic as well as understanding."

His crew, career men of the vast seas, nodded in agreement at his words.

Grateful to have struck a common cord with his men, the captain continued, "From what we have seen this night... is that this thing not only hides from us but flees as well. It is afraid to die... and if something is afraid to die... then it can be killed."

To his growing relief, a resounding cascade of agreement was heard.

With order close at hand, he hammered in his point, "It is one against all of us. We will be triumphant over this wicked savage animal," then feeling the comfort of his own words, he added , "I can tell by the gunshots just a minute ago... from up top that Mr. Skinner, your dear and trusted first mate, has in all likelihood resolved the matter already."

Then, as if on cue, the creature began to fillet Mr. Jeffery's back down to the red muscle fiber with its razor sharp claws.

Feeling as if his back had sudden been set on fire, Mr. Jeffery screamed out in sheer pain and torment like no other time in his life.

The creature, eager to create as much turmoil as possible and tip the odds in its favor, ripped into the man's back again, and Mr. Jeffery's searing piercing screams tore into the night air once more and washed away from the minds of the crew below just about everything their captain had just said.

Engulfed in the man's hysterical cries of pain, the crewmen began to shoot wildly out the open hatch again.

Determined to win the battle, Captain Wilkes called out over the sounds of howling pain and the gun fire, "Mr. Thomas! Mr. Thomas... are you here, sir?"

Sidestepping men, a dark haired man of lanky build emerged, signs of stress from enduring so much in so short a time were clearly visible in his brow, and replied, "Aye, Captain Wilkes, sir."

Putting his mouth close to the man's ear, Captain Wilkes told him, "Mr. Thomas, judging by those horrific screams up top… it is safe to conclude that Mr. Skinner and the men who went with him have fallen victim to that horrid beast."

Fresh screams from Mr. Jeffery erupted.

"Aye, Captain," Mr. Thomas concurred and then added, "May the Lord have mercy on their souls."

Keeping to the heart of the subject, Wilkes pressed on, "This now makes you first mate, Mr. Thomas. And whether you're ready for it or not, I and the crew of The Radiant Star need you to begin acting as one… right now."

Mr. Thomas gave the captain a blank stare.

"Mr. Thomas, duty calls. Are you ready, sir?" he asked, grabbing the man by both shoulders.

Hearing the words and feeling the captain's strong powerful grip on his body, Mr. Thomas gathered himself and answered with posture, "Aye, Captain Wilkes! Ready, willing, and able, sir."

With a wave of relief, Captain Wilkes let him go and said, "That's a good lad. Now divide the men into two groups. One group will go with me while the others stay here with you… in case that thing decides to jump back down."

Mr. Thomas looked at the fourteen remaining men, huddled and crouched, then back at the captain and asked, "Where are you going, sir?"

Looking straight into the face of his newly appointed first mate, Captain Wilkes replied, "I'm going to rush the upper deck and take back our ship."

Set on driving the rest of the crew completely mad with fear, the creature dug its claws into Mr. Jeffery's hairline, just above the forehead, and peeled back his scalp, revealing the yellowish skull bone from underneath.

Another wave of unearthly screams reached the terrified men below and a fresh volley of gunshots from down in the cargo hold rang out into the night air in response.

Doing his best to put aside the horrific screams coming from Mr. Jeffery above, Mr. Thomas instructed the crew to stop shooting into nothing, reload their weapons, and split into two groups.

Scared and filled with confusion, the crew, eager for the solace and comfort of leadership, did as they were told.

Mr. Thomas turned and address the captain, "The men are ready and waiting, Captain Wilkes."

Determined as never before to win back his ship at all cost, Captain Wilkes called out to his men, "The group on the left fall in behind me... the rest of you cover down beside Mr. Thomas and ready yourselves."

Without a single word being uttered, the crewmen of The Radiant Star moved into their new positions.

Captain Wilkes told Mr. Thomas in a low voice, "These men and I will storm the top deck and kill that filth," he touched the younger man's shoulder again, "If by chance we fail in our endeavor... gather the men and passengers and make for the lifeboats. Ships can be restored... murdered lives cannot."

"Aye, Captain," Mr. Thomas replied.

"These may very well be my final orders. See to it that they are followed, your captain and the good name of The Radiant Star demand it," Captain Wilkes told him then turned and started up the stairs with his part of the crew following closely behind.

With its large jackal-like ears, the creature heard them coming up the stairs.

Lost in the frenzy of violence, it took the tattered and bleeding Mr. Jeffery, his scalp flapping pathetically against the back of his neck, and drove two of its long spiked fingers into his eyes, bursting them like ripe fruit.

Half dead from blood loss, blinded, and almost completely insane from the torturous pain, Mr. Jeffery shook himself free from the monster's grip and ran about deck screaming incoherently, while holding his ruined face in his hands, before plunging headlong into the cargo hold below.

At the sight of a figure landing on a wooden crate, Mr. Thomas yelled, "Fire!"

The seven crew members crouched behind crates emptied their weapons in a fiery volley of bullets.

Screaming and disfigured, Mr. Jeffrey died in a hail of bullets on top of a crate filled with ceramic dolls.

At the top of the stairs, Captain Wilkes heard the gunfire coming from below and stopped his column of men.

In the cargo hold, Mr. Thomas gave the command as he looked at the lifeless body, "Gentlemen... reload your weapons."

A crewman by the name of Mr. Biddings curiously craned his neck to see what they had just riddled with bullets, saw whom it was, and exclaimed to the new first mate, "Saints preserve us. I do believe that was Mr. Jeffrey we just shot to pieces, Mr. Thomas."

Looking through the dissipating cloud of gun smoke himself, Mr. Thomas assessed the corpse on the crate.

"I do believe your right, Mr. Biddings," then turned and yelled up to the last man climbing the stairs, "Tell the captain to continue... it was poor Mr. Jeffery... God rest his soul."

With a nod, the crewman passed the word upwards until it reached the captain at the lead, who said, over his shoulder, "Gentlemen, this wild beast is as fierce as it is quick and cunning... so be at the ready."

Standing in single file on the narrow staircase, the seven crewmen nodded at the words from their captain.

"Now... when I open the door, I want all of you to keep in a tight formation behind me as we systemically hunt down this beast and put an end to this night of bedlam."

"Aye, captain!" the men said in unison.

"Very good, gentlemen," he replied in response to their courage under fire and then kicked opened the locked door.

A split second before he died, Captain Wilkes saw the demonic grinning face of the creature staring back at him from behind the barrel of Mr. Skinner's beloved short barreled rifle.

The creature pulled the trigger at point blank range.

Captain Wilkes' entire face imploded into his skull and then exploded out the back, showering everyone behind him with carnage and gore.

Stunned by the deafening sound of the rifle's report and the warm wetness of the captain's head splashing over them, the crewmen trapped in the stairwell in single file screamed out in terror and disgust.

The creature took a step forward, emptied the

John Belica

lever action rifle down into the confide space, and then dove headlong, claws extended out in front, into the narrow stairwell.

Listening to the gun fire and screams coming from above, Mr. Thomas turned towards the stairwell, raised his firearm to the ready, and called out, "Gentleman... hold your positions!"

Suddenly, like a rogue wave, his fellow crewmen and captain came spilling out from the stairwell in a tangled bloody mass.

Stunned by such death and violence, Mr. Thomas stared in awe at the twisted disfigured mess of torn and bullet riddled bodies in front of him as the white furred beast slowly emerged from the stairwell, its large shiny green eyes alive with a wicked kind of ferocity.

Mr. Thomas looked up at the creature who was holding a gun in each hand and yelled, "Fir-!" but was struck down by a bullet to the head before he could finish.

Knowing what he had meant to say, the last seven surviving crewmen raised their weapons to fire.

Knowing it was all or nothing, the creature threw itself at them, guns forward, and the cargo hold erupted into chaos as everyone began shooting.

Leaderless and without order, the crewmen fired their weapons wildly inside the ill lit cargo hold as the creature rolled, ducked, and shimmered in and around them.

With pinpoint precision, the creature gunned down two from the shadows.

Firing desperately at nothing, one crewman accidently blew Mr. Webster's head clean open a second before Mr. Biddings shot himself in the leg, severing the femoral artery, as he tried to reload.

206

Rolling across the wooden flooring and popping up behind them, the creature cut down the last three in a hail of bullets.

Then, as suddenly as it had started, the shooting stopped.

Twisted and bent in a kind of grotesque homage to the violence of their deaths, the bodies of the crewmen littered the cargo hold in cooling pools of blood.

The creature, wounded yet victorious, let the empty revolvers drop from its hands as it filled its lungs with a succulent smell of blood and gunpowder.

As the adrenaline gradually subsided, the pain from the gunshot wounds it had sustained came alive with a burning intensity.

Stepping over Mr. Thomas' dead body, it assessed the wounds to its body. The bullet to the right thigh had gone clean through while another had shredded flesh and fur off a left rib, but nothing more.

Knowing it had to tend to them before it went into shock and bled out, the creature sat down on the crate and slowly began to turn back into human form, making the healing process work faster.

Little by little, the long lanky demonic figure materialized back to the shape of the woman everyone onboard had come to know as Elizabeth Saunders; the voluptuous and striking passenger with long ringlets of curly dishwater blonde hair and a pair of stunningly beautiful green eyes.

A few minutes later, completely back to human form and fully healed, she stood up, naked, and barefoot, and walked over to the clutter of dead men gathered at the foot of the stairwell.

She knelt down in front of the tangle of dead bodies, found the captain's faceless corpse, and took the military grade revolver still clutched in his hand.

She checked the cartridges in the cylinder of the weapon, stood up, and then made her way towards the passenger quarters, located at the rear of the ship one level beneath the captain's chamber.

Dirtying the soles of her bare feet with their blood, she stepped over the clutter of dead men and ascended the stairs.

With the use of the night vision of her green eyes, she made her way to her final batch of victims of the evening.

Down a dimly lit narrow hallway, she walked passed the passenger mess hall before coming to a carpeted corridor lined with eight slender doors on either side.

Having already killed three during the course of the voyage, only five of the original nine travelers bound for Liverpool, England remained.

"No claims from thee," she whispered to herself in a low voice as she came to a stop in front of the first door.

Wanting to see the surprise on her victims' faces right before murdering them, she squared herself in front of the door and then kicked it hard just below the lock with her blackened right bare foot.

The door, made of solid oak, blew open and slammed against the wallpapered bulkhead with a tremendous crash.

The occupant, a sewing thread manufacturer from Delaware, shot up from his sitting position on the bed with a startled expression on his face.

With the gun hidden from his sight behind her bare thigh, she stood at the threshold, silent and expressionless, enjoying the man's fright and confusion.

Looking at the naked woman standing in front of him, the man said to her, "Good heavens! What has occurred? I heard a terrible amount of gunfire just a few minutes ago," then finally taking a real account of the woman's nakedness as well as the blood stains on her bare flesh, he asked, "Miss Saunders... are you... have you been injured?"

With a slow sinister smile, she calmly raised the large revolver, allowing him to see it coming.

Raising his hands up instinctively, he cried out, alarmed, "Miss Saunders... what are you... doing?"

Enjoying the purity of the moment, she ceremoniously cocked the gun ever so slowly.

His eyes went as big as saucers as he registered what was about to happen.

Deliberately over exaggerating the movement, she slowly put her finger on the trigger.

The man who had provided free picnic lunches to all his employees every Sunday for the last decade, yelled, "Wait! Wait! Miss Saunders, wait!"

She pulled the trigger.

The bullet entered his mouth, shattering his front teeth, and the back of his head splattered the room with its contents.

His legs gave out from under him and he fell dead beside the bed.

She lowered the weapon and walked away.

Her dirty and blood stained bare feet moved noiselessly across the floral print carpet as she made her way to the next cabin door.

She kicked in the locked door and found the two missionaries who had been assigned to Wales, cowering naked side by side on the bed, covered by only a sheet.

Petrified by the sounds of death all around them

and having been found in their forbidden homosexual embrace, the young men simply stared at her like sables in a cage.

She shot them once each, killing them almost instantly.

Dead, one fell off the small narrow bed, taking the bed sheet with him, leaving the other in the fetal position, nude and exposed.

Feeling the ship begin to sway from the lack of a helmsman to keep it in control and on course, she walked to the third and final cabin containing the last two other living people onboard.

She found the door slightly ajar and all the candle lights blown out.

Using her emerald green eyes' ability to see in the dark, she slowly pushed open the wooden door and stepped in, the smell of witch hazel and rosewater softly filled her nostrils.

Then, without warning, something hit her straight in the face, shattering her nose and shooting exploding stars across her field of vision.

Her eyes filled up with water from the stunning pain as she covered her ruined face with her free hand and backed away from the open door.

She was hit a second time, breaking all the bones between the knuckles and wrist of the hand that was covering her battered face.

Fighting through the pain, she forced herself to see who was hitting her. She blinked the tears away that had swelled up in her eyes and saw, to her amazement, a little old man in silk pajamas with an Irish walking stick held high over his head.

Remembering to laugh about it later, she aimed and fired.

The metal tipped cane spun in the air as the old man was lifted out of his leather and cashmere lined slippers and sent crashing to the floor.

With a handle on the unexpected pain to her face and hand, she noticed the old man's elderly wife, in shock by the death of her husband of over forty years, standing in the corner, between the nightstand and dresser, blankly staring into nothingness.

She fired the final round and sent the old woman to find her husband in the hereafter.

She dropped the empty revolver onto the carpeted floor.

Helmsmanless, the large merchant passenger ship pitched to the right a full measure as it took a swell broadside.

To steady herself from falling, she reached out instinctively with her broken hand and grabbed the frame of the door.

White hot pain lanced at her ruined hand.

She cried out in pain as the ship rolled again in the open sea.

She tumbled onto the carpeted corridor, got up, and dashed back towards the cargo hold, passing her cabin on the way.

With the ship now completely in the merciless control of the elements, she knew the time to abandon The Radiant Star had come.

Passing the litter of dead men that lay scattered about on the wooden floor, she made her way to the area in the cargo hold where she had first took hold of the cabin boy. There, neatly folded, near the headless body, was her favorite outfit she had been wearing earlier in the evening.

Careful not to dirty her bare feet further in the

boy's dark congealed blood and mindful of her broken hand, she dressed herself slowly off to one side.

The Radiant Star rolled again as a current of wind caught the large bellowing sails unexpectedly.

Balancing herself against the deep swaying movements of the unmanned ship, she laced up her ankle boots, working through her damaged hand as best she could.

Fully dressed, she walked passed her victims one final time, climbed up the blood splashed stairs, and stepped out into the clear night sky.

Off the ship's starboard side, under the full moon light, she could make out the English coastline looming off in the distance.

Though too cold to swim, even with the creature's pain tolerance and healing ability, she knew that her only chance in making it to shore was through the use of a lifeboat.

As the abnormal healing process finally began to take hold on her broken nose and hand, she knelt down besides Mr. Skinner's dead body, and, using her good hand, retrieved the passenger roster which had been used to match her name to her crimes onboard The Radiant Star.

Standing, she tucked the roster between her dress and leather belt and then walked to the door where the recently deceased Mr. Clarkson had tried to find refuge in.

Finding it unlocked, she pushed it and stepped into the short hallway with the first mate's quarters on one side, a multipurpose room on the other, and the captain's quarters at the far end.

She walked past the first two rooms and stopped in front of a heavy wooden door that had a scene depicting a large shining star illuminating the path of a lonesome ship over a stormy ocean carved deep into the wood.

She tried the door, found it also unlocked, and stepped in.

Inside, she found the captain's lodging to be simple and functional with very little fanfare or luxury.

She glanced around and quickly found the ship's logbook, sitting in the center of the only table in the room.

She went to it, picked it up, quickly leafed through the pages, and then tucked it under her arm.

Then, as she started to leave, a faint curious smell caught her attention, stopping her dead in her tracks.

With her nose now almost completely healed, she drew in a long slow breath of air and realized what it was.

Knowing she couldn't leave the ship without it, she paced the room while taking in short bursts of air in an effort to locate where exactly the distinct smell was coming from.

Finally, after minutes of sniffing and walking back and forth, she found it.

Nudged between a short bookcase and a battered footlocker was a small five liter barrel.

She knelt down, put her face next to it, and inhaled.

The strong pungent stench made her slightly recoil and smile all at the same time; it was Ambergris, and its value was higher than that of gold.

She gathered up the little wooden barrel...

Feeling a presence close to her, she opened her eyes and found Glen standing over her.

He smiled at her and asked, "What were you thinking about?"

"Thinking?" she asked.

"Yeah, thinking. What were you thinking about? You kept smiling."

Rising up slightly in the bed, she answered, "About the past."

"The past, huh. What about?" he asked, enjoying the rare moments such as this one where it felt like he actually had a girlfriend and not just someone who fucked him in secret.

Putting her arms over her head and stretching seductively, her breasts heaving ever so slightly above the comforter, she answered, "Oh... about a cruise I took once, you could say."

Trying to keep the conversation going for as long as possible, Glen asked, "Did you go to Cancun or someplace like that?"

Dropping her arms to her sides, she replied, "Not quite."

Looking down at her beauty and catching a whiff of mint that always seemed to come from her mouth, he continued, "Where did you go?"

Smiling up at him, she decided to tell him the truth, "I rowed away on a lifeboat with a barrel full of whale vomit."

He smiled at her and exclaimed. "Ok... fine... don't tell me then."

She watched him for a few seconds in silence and then asked, pointing to his right hand, "Is that for me?"

He raised his hand, waved the USB stick he held, and replied, "Yeah, everything you wanted on a Lt. Douglas Eugene Mosley and a Lt. Mildred Judith Tanner is in here." and then set it down on the nightstand.

She looked at the small storage device and then back at the awkward teenager in front of her, and said, "Good boy."

Proud at her words, he smiled.

"Want to claim your reward?" she asked as she threw the blankets back, exposing the nakedness of her body to him.

Knowing the time for talking was over, his eyes lapped over the flowing curves of her body and answered, "Yeah, I want my reward," then added as he began to struggle out of his clothes, "I saw something on a porn site today that I want to try out."

Enjoying the control she had over him, she slowly parted her legs.

CHAPTER 23

"Your license reads brown eyes but you have green eyes."

By the time he had scaled down the fire escape and had reached his car, the passenger side mirror had begun to melt and the injury to his leg had completely healed.

Not sure why the creature had let him live and grateful just to be alive, John realized that his original plan had undoubtedly been his best one; simply drive away and fall off the map.

Now, as she slipped out of the teen hacker's bedroom window with the USB stick in her hand, John opened his sleeping eyes to the sound of metal tapping glass.

Sudden and sharp, the sound filled his head with an intruding annoyance.

Blinking the stickiness of sleep from his eyes, he looked out his driver's side window to see who it was, and saw, obscured by the layer of dew, the outline of a man in uniform, Smoky Bear hat and all.

As he continued to tap the glass with his large black flashlight, the CHP officer, said with a stern commanding voice, "Sir, I need you to roll down your window, please."

Still heavy with sleep, John numbly complied by pushing the button on the door handle to lower the window.

The window didn't lower.

"Sir, your window... now," the faceless officer repeated his command.

Realizing the car was in the off position, John shifted his weight in the seat, rubbed the scar on his forehead, and said out loud, his voice thick with sleep, "I need a second... the car is off. I'm going to need to turn the key... is that ok?"

The officer stopped tapping and replied, "Go ahead. Put the car in its auxiliary position and then lower the window," and then took one step back putting his right hand on the heel of his service weapon.

Feeling like a goldfish in a brandy glass under the trooper's cautious stare, John turned the key over to the auxiliary position and then pressed the button on the door handle again.

The window lowered.

Keeping his hand pressed on his service piece, the CHP officer took a step forward and eyed the man he had caught sleeping in the Rest Stop.

John chose to speak first, "Morning, sir," and glanced at the name tag on the man's crisp khaki uniform, it read Richards.

Straight to the point, Officer Richards asked, "Good morning, sir. May I ask why you're sleeping here?"

Caught off guard by the bare boned question, John

blinked as he tried to formulate a quick answer.

The CHP veteran of nine years tapped the leather of his holster with his trigger finger, waiting for his answer.

John rubbed his scar again and replied with the truth, "I got tired and decided to pull over."

Looking down at him with suspicion, the officer said, "Sir, this is a rest stop not a sleep stop. You can't sleep here."

John glanced at the clock on the dashboard, saw that it read four thirty-six in the morning, and said, "Well, it's basically morning. I can leave, if you'd like?"

Stepping forward, the officer replied, "Actually, I'd like to see your driver's license, please."

Eager to get through the unexpected situation, John nodded. "Sure, of course," then he fished out his driver's license from his wallet.

The CHP officer took it from him and began to examine it carefully.

Waiting in awkward silence, John wondered how, if pushed to do so, he could ever explain all that had recently happened to him; the creature, the woman, everything.

Suddenly the officer spoke to him, "Your license reads brown eyes but you have green eyes."

John felt the air leave his body as his organs chilled to ice.

"Sir?" Officer Richards pressed with a lift of his brow.

An instantaneous thought flashed in John's mind, 'I could kill him and be five hundred miles away before they found him'.

Waiting for a reply, the officer stared at him.

"A typo," John answered with a lie this time, "I've

been trying to have it corrected for a while now but the DMV is impossible to deal with."

Though not completely convinced, the officer nodded slowly and replied, "Alright," then tapped the small radio on his shoulder and called in the license information.

As they waited for a response on the status of the driver's license, the CHP officer asked, "What are you doing so far north of Los Angeles?"

John answered with another lie, "Got some vacation time so I thought I'd drive up and see Napa Valley."

Nodding again, Officer Richards commented, "Well... doing it on the 'cheap' like sleeping in Rest Stops is no way of doing it."

Working past the indirect insult, John simply answered, "Ok."

The radio on the officer's shoulder suddenly squawked and a nest of jumbled words, distinguishable only to the uniformed trooper, blurted out.

Richards touched the Send button, confirmed the information he had just received, and said, "You're good," then added as he slowly handed back the driver's license, "But you're done sleeping in rest stops... do you understand, sir?"

Sensing that the worst was over, John replied, "Yes, I understand, officer."

"Good. Now, if you want to get some real rest then I suggest you turn around and head back a few miles... they have some good motels there with decent enough prices."

John reached out to take his license and said, "Or... I could simply keep driving."

CHAPTER 24

"The absence of evidence is the presence of evidence."

Driving away from the convention center in Sacramento, California, Tanner spoke as she looked out the darkened landscape, "You know... when I was at Fresno State-"

"Go Bulldogs!" Mosley playfully interrupted her as he steered the sedan northward towards the city.

"When I was at Fresno State.", she pressed on, giving him a fake scornful look, "I thought The Central Valley was hot... but after today... man... I tell ya... Sacramento is way hotter."

Though tired as they were from the long drive from Los Angeles to the FBI conference in the capital of the state, Mosley, for some reason, felt vibrant and energetic as he jokingly said to his partner beside him, "We're coming up on the 99... which takes us directly to Reno... wanna go?"

"Not on your life! I can't believe we didn't have enough time to even check into a hotel room before attending that massive waste of time. My feet are practically floating in sweat in my nylons."

Looking down at her feet, he made an ugly face and with sarcasm said, "Nice."

Smiling at the banter between them, she replied, "Nice my ass! You won't think so the second I take these shoes off."

Narrowing his eyes over at her, Mosley said, "Then I suggest that you don't."

Shrugging herself deep into the leather seat, she crossed her arms under her breasts, closed her eyes, and said, "Then I suggest that you get us a hotel... pronto."

They drove in silence, taking in the quiet interior of the vehicle.

After a while, Mosley said, "Could you believe that traffic on the way up here. Christ!"

She opened her eyes, looked over at him, and said, "I couldn't believe it either."

"We barely made it on time to the conference." he added.

Looking out the window again, she said, "After all that driving, then not being able to at least freshen up... man, it sucked today... sitting there... listening to all that bullshit."

"How many of us were there today representing LAPD?" Mosley asked.

Touching her chin, Tanner answered as best she could, "Us, and about half a dozen other detectives."

Thinking back, Mosley said, "What does the FBI hope to gain by holding these conferences?

"Stopping global terrorism from happening on the corner of Wilshire and Fairfax." she jokingly answered his question.

Chuckling, Mosley took the off ramp.

Knowing that the hotel section of the city was near, Tanner straightened and scanned the buildings along the Sacramento city streets.

Dropping his speed, he said, "I hope something is available."

"Well, we're about to find out... cus there it is," Tanner said as she pointed to the largest hotel in the area.

A few minutes later, rolling luggage in tow, they found themselves in the lobby of a chain hotel and staring at a young acne faced front desk attendant typing away on a computer keyboard for what felt like an eternity.

After a while, he looked up, "Well... with two other conventions in the area... it would have been best to have checked in earlier."

Wanting to strangle the attendant hard enough to pop all his acne, Tanner said through gritted teeth, "Just tell us what you have."

Enjoying the moment of control, the attendant said with relish, "Not much."

"What... do... you have?" Mosley said in a flat tone, suddenly feeling very tired.

Clearing his throat for effect, the attendant replied, "All I have is two executive Jack and Jill rooms," and then, saving the best for last, added, "At double the normal price."

Allowed only a certain amount to be charged to the precinct's credit card, Mosley shook his head in dismay.

Tanner asked, "What the hell is an executive room?"

Smiling, the acne machine said, "Free internet, alarm clock with USB dock, and a fully stocked mini bar."

Before Tanner could ask anything else, Mosley's large hand slapped down their precinct's credit card, and said, "We'll take both."

Standing inside his tiny room that looked right out of pages of a Dutch furniture catalog, Mosley shook his head at the entire day he had just endured.

Then, cutting into his lamenting train of thought, a knock came at the door.

He turned, hoping it was the front desk clerk so he could wring his neck for his conduct downstairs, and realized that the knocking was not coming from the main door but from the second door along the wall, between the mirrored closet and T.V. console.

He went to it and asked even though he knew who it was, "Who is it?"

"Jill," Tanner replied from the other side.

"Whata ya want?" he asked.

"Open the door, you moose," she commanded and knocked again.

Mosley turned the knob, felt the little button in the middle pop out, and pulled the door open.

Reminding him of the Westchester mansion that he had visited once as a kid, he found himself facing a second closed door, inches from the one he had just opened.

A second later the door opened and Tanner, shorter out of her shoes, said, "Hey Jack... it's Jill."

Acting gruff for no reason, he looked down at her bare nylon feet and said, "I don't smell anything."

Tanner looked down, then up, and said, "Well, aren't you the charmer."

Without another word, Mosley turned and walked back to his luggage resting on the narrow bed.

Stepping into his room, she told him, "Listen, they're going to workshop us to death tomorrow, I just know it. And if you think I'm going to go through all this stuff they gave us to look over by myself then you're crazy," and then held up a manila folder with a United States flag printed on the cover.

He unzipped his luggage, pulled out a wrinkled suit, and said, "No... they're crazy for giving us that stuff to go look over... and you're crazy for actually trying to make an attempt to look it over... I'm just tired."

"We gotta at least look it over once," she exclaimed as she took a chair and placed the folder on the small circular table.

Walking past her, grey wrinkled suit in hand, he went to the small closet, and said, without looking at her, "I don't want to 'look it over'... nor do I want to go back tomorrow and listen to more of their bullshit regarding preemptive counterterrorism procedures."

Knowing him well enough, she opened the folder, and began to read out loud, "Page one, chapter one."

Mosley closed the mirrored door of the closet, walked over to her, and said, "Fine...but just remember... my bad mood tomorrow is on your head."

Taking her eyes away from the manila folder, she repeated, "Fine."

"Fine.", he repeated the word as well, stepped to the mini bar located under the flat panel television, and said to her, "And since we're already in trouble for going over on the hotel charge... we might as well go down in flames with a bit of style."

She looked up at him and twisted her lip in a small smile.

Mosley opened the tiny refrigerator door and grabbed a handful of airplane liquor bottles.

Hours later, Tanner pushed the paperwork aside, knocking over the empty little bottles that littered the table top, and said, "I think it's safe to say that we're both ready for tomorrow. What da ya think?"

Arranging his assortment of empty bottles according to color, Mosley replied, "I think I'm ready for just one more drink... then sleep."

Shifting her weight, Tanner looked over at the mini bar, saw its door hanging open, and asked, "Any gin left?"

Lifting a small empty green bottle up at her, he answered, "This was the last one."

She pushed her chair back and got up. "Well, we haven't even touched my mini bar... I'll go get some," then turned and made for the connecting doors of their rooms.

Mosley watched her walk out of his hotel room.

Pushed to drink heavily during his college years, he had learned how to hold his liquor well enough not to lose control, and now, as he stood up and walked to the small black fridge to close it, he felt warm and relaxed.

From the other room, he heard her speaking to him, "I've always liked gin."

Closing the empty fridge, Mosley watched her reenter, carrying a tiny green bottle in each hand.

Smiling contently, she walked to him.

Then it happened, their eyes fell onto each other and the small distance between them suddenly became charged with an intense energy like a thunder storm in the dry desert air.

As she continued to walk towards him, her smile melted away and her face softened to a sensuous radiance.

Watching her come towards him, he extended his

hands out to her.

The green little bottles of Gin fell from her hands and their bodies collided into each other.

Locked in a crushing embrace, they hungrily kissed each other with passion and abandonment. Together, they sought the depths of their warm, wet, and welcoming feeding mouths.

Mosley lifted her high off the carpeted floor, turned, and gently lowered her onto the bed.

Greedily feasting on his deep kisses, she sucked the flavor from his mouth as she felt his solid weight press down on her body.

Drowning in the wetness of her passionate open mouth, Mosley ran his hands down the length of her body, feeling every curve of her figure under her clothes.

Staying connected at their mouths, and without a word being said, they struggled, as best they could, out of their clothes. Tanner undid the buttons of her white blouse and then the front latch of her bra while Mosley yanked the tie from his neck and tore open his shirt, peppering her heaving abdomen with its buttons.

She slid her hot wet lips across his face to his ear, and breathed, "Help me," as her hands went to her skirt

Mosley glanced down at her hands and followed them, running his saliva glistened face down the middle of her bare chest.

Together, they removed her skirt, pantyhose, and panties.

Looking intently at him, she placed her bare feet on his shoulders, exposing herself fully to him as he undid his belt and trousers.

Naked except for his socks and pants around his ankles, he buried his face between her legs and lost himself with rapture in the heat, moisture, and flavor he found there.

Feeling him pleasuring her, her bare toes curled to the breaking point as she covered her face with her hands in an effort to stifle the scream of passion that was building up deep in the inner core of her being.

Mosley ran his hands all over her body, breasts, stomach, legs as he explored her succulence to its greatest depth with his mouth.

Then, like a weakened levy succumbing to the magnificent strength of the ocean, she screamed through her fingers and climaxed.

Hot fluid sprayed across his face as he heard her scream out in delight.

Thinking she would die if she waited a second longer for him to be inside her, Tanner, with both hands, grabbed two handfuls of his hair and yanked him up towards her.

Lead by her hands in his hair, Mosley's hot drenched face traveled over her sweating deep breathing body and then collided once again onto her wanting pleading lips.

With their mouths locked and their eyes staring into each other, he plunged inside her in one smooth movement.

Together as one, they yelled out loud at the overwhelming sensation of passion and desire they felt.

With long deep slow powerful thrusts his penis explored the beauty inside her.

Loosing herself to the unbelievable feeling of sexual surrender, she wrapped her feet around his broad sweating back.

He interlocked his fingers in her sweat matted hair, pulled her head back gently, and whispered the words,

"Let me finish."

Looking up at his soft pleading eyes, she answered in a whisper of her own, "Finish... inside me," and then gripped the back of his head and brought his mouth back down to hers.

With their open mouths locked and feeding, they stared into each other's eyes once again as Mosley slowly worked himself to his climax, taking long plunging thrusts deep within her giving body.

She felt his body begin to tense.

Mosley fisted her wet hair tightly in his hands and cried out loud, "My God, I'm going..."

"Jesus... don't stop!" she yelled into his mouth over strings of thick drool as a second unexpected orgasm sprang to life inside her.

And then, as only exploding stars in the vast serenity of space can testify, their mutual orgasm struck them with stunning shuddering force...

"You ok?" Tanner said to him from the living room sofa.

Standing in the middle of his kitchen, Mosley answered, "Uh... yeah... sorry."

Wrinkling her nose in a playful gesture of concern, she asked, "You sure, cus it looked like your engine stalled there for a minute."

Picking up a pair of glasses filled with soda, he replied, "Yeah... I was just...thinking, is all," and walked out of the small kitchen, wondering if she ever thought about the night they had shared, like he always seem to do.

Taking a glass from his right hand, she told him with a smile, "Thinking... are you...well, in that case, don't let me stop you... since it doesn't happen too often."

Forcing the memory back into the corner of his mind, Mosley said as he stood over her, "If it were only so."

Moving past his odd remark, she turned back to their case notes scattered about the coffee table. "Sit down, will ya... and help me with this."

Mosley took a deep drink from his own glass, nodded, and sat himself across from her.

"We're about to hit the forty-eight hour mark on this fire and we've got more questions than answers," she told him as she shuffled the scores of paper around for the hundredth time.

He told her, "Questions lead to answers, Millie," and then took another drink.

Playing annoyed, she countered, "No... not with this case. All I see is questions leading to more questions and then more questions after that."

Mosley leaned forward and said to her, "Then lets find those answers."

Slumping back into the sofa's soft leather backrest, Tanner said, "Alright then. Question, how do you take control of well over a hundred people before setting them all on fire?"

Looking down at his hands, then up at her, he replied, "You incapacitate them."

"Which leads to another question. How do you incapacitate well over a hundred people before setting them all on fire? Or, more importantly, how do you incapacitate well over a hundred people... all... at... once... before setting them all on fire?"

Thinking about it, Mosley picked up his glass of soda, drank from it, and said, "The bodies that Mike has autopsied so far... chemically... what keeps coming up?

Tanner smiled at him. "Well look it here, another question."

Smiling back, he pressed, "Tell me... what keeps coming up?

Pursing her lips and raising her eyebrows, she answered, "Chemically... if you mean some type of sedative, poison, or illegal narcotic... then the answer is 'nothing'."

Raising his glass to her in gesture, he exclaimed, "Ex-fuck'n-actly! And what was it they taught us in the academy about 'nothing'?"

She leaned forward and answered his question, quoting a passage from the academy, "'The absence of evidence is the presence of evidence'."

"Correct," Mosley replied in a congratulatory tone and then took a slow draught of his drink for effect.

Absently touching the papers on the coffee table, Tanner asked, "Question, what do you use to incapacitate over a hundred people all at once before setting them on fire... that doesn't show up on an autopsy?"

The doorbell rang.

Caught off guard by the sound, Mosley set his empty glass down, stood up, and proclaimed, "If we can answer that then we'll have something."

Looking back down at the litter of papers in front of her, she mumbled, "No shit."

Wondering who it could possibly be, since no one ever came to see him at his apartment, Mosley stepped around his leather love seat and went to the door.

He placed his hands against the door, peered through the peephole to see who it was, and saw a green eye, pressed up against the peephole, staring back at him.

Suddenly, the eye's emerald green iris began to slowly spin around the pupil.

Mosley's body stiffened as he caught a full dose of the eye's suggestive power through the small magnified concave lens imbedded in the door.

A woman's voice bled through the door just loud enough for him to hear, "Open it!"

Mosley opened the door.

With her appearance shapeshifted to look like one of his female neighbors, she stood at his front door, dressed in a black knee length dress, patent leather high heels, and her 9mm fitted with a silencer in her left hand.

Still holding the doorknob, Mosley numbly stared at her eyes.

With full control over the towering man, she softly gestured for him to move back away from the doorway.

Mosley let go of the doorknob and took a step back.

In her peripheral vision, she caught sight of the shoulder holster strapped under his arm and quickly switched her plans for an even better one.

She dropped the silenced 9mm she had been concealing behind her thigh onto the carpeted floor and stopped the spinning of her irises.

Removed so suddenly from the hypnotic power of her eyes, Mosley felt his vision swim as if in a drunken stupor.

Taken by the woman's sudden presence, Tanner stood up to see what was going on.

She stepped into the apartment and then kicked the door shut with the heel of her foot.

Doing his best to recover his senses, Mosley took another step backwards.

In need of his weapon, she hissed out loud and tore the corners of her mouth all the way to her ears, giving her face a demonic menacing look.

Shocked at the sight of the horrific face suddenly in front of him, Mosely snapped completely out of the ensnarement of her eyes and drew his service weapon.

With lightning fast reflexes, she ducked under the barrel of the .40 caliber polymer semiautomatic before he could fire, clasped onto his gun hand, and spun around, placing her back to his chest and propping his outstretched arms over the top of her right shoulder.

Mosley stared in disbelief at what was happening.

Using the flow of her forward momentum and superior strength, she turned them both a full ninety degrees towards the living room as she simultaneously placed her index finger over his trigger finger.

Essentially, trapped between the coffee table and sofa, Tanner watched in stunned silence as her partner's weapon spun around over to her.

With her finger over his, she pulled the trigger.

Mosley watched in horror as the gunshot hit Tanner in the chest.

The force of the impact blew apart her heart and spinal cord and dropped her back down onto the sofa, where she died a few seconds later in the sitting position.

Mosley opened his mouth to scream out in rage.

Without skipping a beat, she bent his elbows with her left hand, slipped the barrel under his chin, and pulled the trigger with his finger one last time.

The bullet exploded out the top of his head in a geyser of blood, brains, and skull.

She let him go and Mosley crumpled to the floor with the murder weapon still in his hand and died.

With her ears ringing loudly from the gunfire, she stepped around the dead body and retrieved her own weapon as the grotesque gaping smile slowly receded away.

She picked up her trusted handgun, carefully decocked it, and then detached the silencer before tucking it and the handgun away in the small purse slung across her chest.

Knowing that gunfire always attracted unwarranted attention, she quickly walked through the small living room to the sliding glass balcony doors, undid the latch, and slid the large glass door open.

The night's cool coastal air flowed in and mixed with the thick smell of spent gunpowder and human gore.

Feeling the invigorating night air sliding up her dress, she turned to the silent livingroom, smiled, and spoke out loud to the bodies of her victims, "You intrigued me... thus I thank you."

A siren cried in the distance.

She turned, faced the balcony, and jumped, hitting the building's swimming pool below with a thunderous splash.

The murder-suicide of Detectives Douglas Mosley and Mildred Tanner would remain filled with speculations and theories indefinitely.

The mass murder of one hundred and twenty-eight people at a Los Angeles homeless shelter and the mysterious disappearance of its director would go unsolved forever.

CHAPTER 25

"I love it when you show up."

With her hair still damp with pool water, she carefully and quietly slid the bedroom window up to its full height and slipped in.

The computer screen glowed at the far end.

She closed the window, pulled off her shoes, unzipped her purse, and slipped her hand inside it.

Without turning to look at her, Glen said, "I love it when you show up."

Slowly and methodically she walked up behind him.

Continuing to type, he spoke his last words, "There's this website tha..."

She grabbed him by the chin with her right hand and jerked his head back, exposing his long thin neck.

With his head pressed against her abdomen, just below her breasts, he looked up and saw her, upside down from his angle, smiling sweetly down at him.

Slowly, taking her time, enjoying the moment, she placed the sharpened edge of a butcher's knife on the right side of his neck. With the homeless shelter in ashes, the time had come to tie up all loose ends connected to her.

Feeling the cold edge of the knife against his skin, Glen's eyes bulged with terror in their sockets.

Then, with a single even fluid motion, she pressed the razor sharp blade all the way down to his spinal column and then dragged it across his neck from one side to the other.

Thick dark blood erupted out of him in a torrid gush, splashing onto the glowing computer screen and keyboard.

Ravaged by the lethal wound to his neck, he thrashed his legs and arms wildly in a feeble attempt to escape.

She pinned him harder to her body to keep him seated in the desk chair.

Glen began to slacken against her grip as his last heart beats fluttered in his chest.

Smiling contently, she looked down at his eyes and watched the life drain out of him.

He died staring up at her.

She let go of his nearly severed head and his limp body slumped forward onto his bloodied computer desk.

She exhaled with satisfaction, taking a brief moment to enjoy the fruits of her labor.

The smell of death filled the dead teenager's bedroom.

Relaxed and content, she placed her right hand on the back of his head and the left against on his chin, and then gave one quick forceful twist.

The vertebrates in the neck snapped loose with a sickening sound and his head came clean off.

The headless body slipped off the desk chair and fell onto the floor with a soft thud.

True to her own words; she placed the decapitated head squarely on the keyboard.

The glow of the computer screen gave out a pinkish hue through the coating of drying blood.

She took a step back to admire her macabre handy work.

Glenn's dead face vacantly stared into nothingness.

With the crimson stained knife still in her hand, she stepped to the bedroom door that lead to the rest of the house and slowly opened it slightly.

A darkened hallway greeted her through the small open sliver.

Peering with the night vision her green eyes afforded her, she caught the bluish glow of a TV bleeding through the door frame of the second bedroom.

She stepped out into the hallway and walked to the other bedroom where Glen's alcoholic mother slept in.

She grasped the doorknob and slowly turned it until the latch gently clicked open.

Carefully she pushed the door open and peeked in.

Lying on a rumpled and disheveled bed, next to an empty bottle of charcoal filtered vodka, was Glen's mother, passed out from an evening bout of marathon drinking.

Large and unkempt, the snoring drunk of a woman neither stirred nor moved as the murderer of her only son stepped into her room.

Illuminated by the glow of the television, she walked up in silent bare feet to the slumbering drunk and stared down at her.

Suppressing the sudden urge to bury the bloodied

butcher's knife into the sleeping woman's face, she stuck to her plan and placed the murder weapon under the bed.

Before the kill, she had removed her fingerprints with the use of the creature's shape shifting ability thus making the bloodied knife the prime piece of evidence that would be used against Glen's mother for his murder.

Smiling, she slowly stepped out of the bedroom and closed the door softly behind her.

On her way back out the window, she went to Glen's desk and grabbed a red USB which held an illicit type of software that would enable her to track any person anywhere.

Emma Phillips would spend the rest of her life, until dying from cirrhosis in prison, fighting to clear her name for the murder of her son, Glen.

John Belica

BOOK TWO

John Belica

CHAPTER 26

"To be the only one."

Holding a bag of groceries in each arm, John slipped the keycard into the narrow slot, saw the little green light flick on, and then, with his right butt cheek, pushed down on the door handle and pushed open the door to his hotel room.

Dry cool air greeted him as he stepped into the vintage modern furnished executive suite.

The door, as most hotel doors seemed to do, swung closed, separating him from the late morning sun.

He placed the filled paper bags on the tiny kitchen counter, walked over to the large ample desk, and dropped his keys, sunglasses, handgun, and keycard on the blotter.

Quiet, except for the subdued clicking of the air conditioner, John looked around the hotel stylishly-furnished room and realized tomorrow marked a full week since he had checked in.

With a soft sigh, he went to the tightly made bed and sat down.

Feeling the hard mattress under him, he closed his eyes and put his face in his hands. Lucky not to be in jail and even luckier to be alive, he knew that he needed to keep moving, he simply couldn't stay here forever.

John lifted his face out of his hands, looked up at the stucco ceiling, and promised himself that tomorrow he'd get back on the road.

Suddenly feeling tired, he rubbed his scar on his forehead, swung his feet onto the bed, dropped his head into the plush goose feather pillow, and closed his eyes.

John opened his eyes.

The tugging sensation, exactly like the one that had caused him to enter the doomed homeless shelter, had started up once again in his chest, startling him awake.

Lying motionless, he looked around the hotel room and found it darkened by the late afternoon gloom coming through the open blinds.

The digital clock, sitting on the nightstand, read twenty-three past four.

Realizing, as his gaze fell upon the bags of groceries still on the counter, that he had fallen asleep unexpectedly, he swung his feet down off the bed and stood up.

He walked to the center of the room and tried to make sense of the unexpected feeling. Only miles from the Canadian border, he had felt certain that he had put enough distance between Los Angeles, her, and himself.

Touching his chest with his left hand, a horrid realization dawned on him; the sensation in his chest could only mean one thing; she was somewhere close.

Suddenly the phone, next to the digital clock, rang.

Startled by the loud unsuspected noise, John flinched with a yelp.

The phone rang again.

He looked over at it.

It rang once again.

Staring at the brown hotel phone, something deep within him said that she was on the other end.

The phone continued to ring.

He walked over to the nightstand and answered.

"Hello, John," her voice reached him and the tugging in his chest instantly ceased.

Realizing it was the very first time he had actually heard her voice, he stared with a blank expression at the papered wall in front of him.

"John," she repeated his name as if they were old friends.

Hearing her speak his name, his tongue seemed to glue itself to the roof of his mouth.

"John, I know you can hear me... because... I see you standing there... holding the phone," she said to him.

Numbing terror washed over him as he slowly turned towards the open curtains and looked across the street at the self-storage building's rooftop that was flush with his third floor hotel suite.

"That's right, John, I'm on the rooftop," she affirmed and then casually asked, "Can you see me?"

John neither moved nor replied.

"Here, I'll make it easy," she continued.

Suddenly, a red fluttering light struck him in the eyes.

Wincing, he jerked his head away from the unexpected red neon light and rubbed his eyes with his free hands as the residual effect from the strange light continued to burn brightly inside his closed eyelids.

"Look down at your chest," she told him.

Blinking, he slowly looked down at his chest and saw a bright red dot of light resting over his sternum.

"That's right, John. It's exactly what you think it is. A laser sight," her calm voice proclaimed.

He dropped to the floor behind the bed.

Absently still holding the phone to his ear, he heard her say, "Relax, John, relax. If I wanted you dead... I would have filled that plush little executive suite of yours full of rounds already."

From the floor, he franticly watched the red little dot slowly move about the wall above him.

Adding, she told him, "Nonetheless, if you try to leave that room... I will kill you before you make it to the door. So I suggest that you stay where you are and listen to what I have to say."

Crouched low on the carpeted floor, he finally spoke to her for the very first time, "What do you want?"

"Right now... I just want to talk to you," she answered nonchalantly.

"What the fuck about?" he asked suddenly angry at the control she seemed to always have over him.

"Us," she responded with a simple tone.

"What about us, God damn it!" he said angrily as he continued to watch the red dot hover above him.

"That's what I want to talk to you about... which is the reason I didn't kill you on the roof top back in Los Angeles and why I haven't killed you now."

John rolled onto his back and said, "Ok. So talk.

"No... not like this," she told him.

Bewildered, he asked, "What do you mean?"

"I mean, let's talk in person," she replied.

"What?" he erupted into the phone.

"You heard me right. Let's talk face to face."

John put his hand over his eyes and slowly shook his head.

Still using the same casual tone, she continued, "You can say yes or you can say no but only one answer will keep me from shooting you dead where you lay."

The red dot began to move slowly down the wall.

Watching it come to him, John, admitting defeat, asked, "Where?"

The red dot of light stopped.

She answered, "There's a Tea and Sympathy dance at the Pioneers' lodge tonight. We can meet there... out in the open with lots of people"

It all sounded like lunacy to him but he knew what she was capable of, "Fine... I'll go."

"Good," she replied.

The red dot disappeared.

John gave a sigh of relief.

"You can get up now," she told him and then added, "But if you try anything else besides just showing up for a bit of conversation, you'll be dead before the sun comes up tomorrow morning."

John stood up and said into the phone, "I said I'd go, didn't I?"

"Yes, you did," she replied.

John walked up to the large window and said into the phone, "Anything else... your majesty?"

Staring at him through the scope of the rifle from her sniper's nest underneath the storage building's satellite dish, she replied, "Just be sure to wear something nice," then flipped her cellular phone closed.

Hastily, John showered, dressed (stone khakis, blue dress shirt, and grey sport coat), and then drove himself to the Pioneers' lodge after finding its address in the phone book in his room.

Standing in the main hall of the lodge less than an hour after speaking with her, John absorbed his surroundings as the fragrant and pungent aroma from dozens of brewed teas filled his nostrils. Designed specifically for hosting large events, the main hall of the Pioneers' lodge was wide as it was long, complete with a wooden dance floor, modular walls, a stage at its west end, and a restaurant quality kitchen at its east. People, dressed in pastels, laughing and talking, milled about while others gently danced in pairs to the orchestra's flowing soothing rhythm.

John looked up and observed the pride and joy of the lodge; the ceiling of the hall; entirely made of stained glass, spanning across the full length of the hall with scenes depicting the journey of American pioneers into the western United States in a mosaic collage of color and shapes.

Not wanting to stick out by just standing still and gawking, John walked to the refreshment table nearest to him.

There, splayed out in front of him was a vast assortment of tea kettles and urns, in all shapes and sizes, holding teas from every corner of the world as well as delicate finger food from water crest sandwiches to fruit dappled pastries.

Feeling terribly ill at ease for his exact reason for being there, John busied himself with a cup of tea from a Turkish looking urn in an attempt to blend as best he could amongst the happily bustling crowd of people all around him.

With his cup of tea finally prepared, he turned around, put the rim of the eggshell white teacup to his lips, and tasted the hot amber colored liquid.

The flavor of rich vanilla beans and the sweetness of honey spread across his taste buds in a warm succulent flow of comfort.

Peacefully smacking his lips at the wonderful taste from the tiny cup, he realized that the forty dollars he had paid at the door had indeed been a bargain.

Standing against the long serving table, John watched the activity all around him, the smiles and happy demeanor of the party guests, the easy chatter that emanated from them, and the lay back way they laughed.

Slowly the first bites of envy nipped at his liver as he recalled that only weeks earlier his life had been as normal as everyone's in the room.

He shook his head and sighed at what his life was now, unemployed, on-the-run, and slowly becoming something else entirely.

The middle aged orchestra concluded the coda of the song they had been playing and swiftly slipped into a vintage standard, vocals and all.

Listening intently to catch the name of the piece, John raised the delicate little cup to his lips when suddenly his chest gave a sharp tug.

Knowing what that certain sensation meant by now, he lowered the tea cup down onto its saucer and trawled his eyes across the ocean of happy smiling faces.

His chest began to tug rhythmically.

Motionless, he searched for a face he might

recognize as hers.

Suddenly, the sensation in his chest stopped as quickly as it started, which he now also knew meant that she was very close.

Wanting to see her first before she saw him, he narrowed his newly green eyes and peered at every face in front of him.

Something caught his eye, off to his right.

He turned his head to get a better look.

Standing just inside the hall was a woman keenly staring at him.

Without taking his eyes off her, he gently placed the cup and saucer on the table behind him and then unfastened the buttons of his sport coat, making the .380 handgun in his waist band more accessible.

Their eyes locked onto each other.

Staring directly into her face, John could see that her eyes held the same emerald green color as his own.

She began to walk straight towards him.

As he watched her approach, he felt his eyes deceive him. Among the tangle of people, her appearance slightly changed every time someone crossed her path.

Her hair went from a mass of brown loose curls to a black and straight bob as she gracefully walked around an unknowing couple, then, stepping through a cluster of friends joyfully chatting to each other, the angles of her face softened to an oval frame as her lips slightly pursed.

Watching her slowly transform right before his very eyes as she weaved through the crowd of partygoers, John came to sudden and heartbreaking understanding; the .380 wasn't going to be enough.

Like a vintage movie reel, her appearance changed

and changed until the woman who had nearly killed him in the parking structure weeks ago came to a stop in front of him.

Amazed at what he had just seen, John stared at her dumbfounded and speechless.

She looked up at him with her own big green eyes and professed, "I knew you'd come."

Hearing the sound of her voice, his mind snapped free and his hand went for the Argentinian .380.

With lightning speed, her right hand grabbed the wrist of his gun hand. "How 'bout a truce... just for tonight?"

John winced in pain, her grip felt like a machinist's vice.

Watching him hold back the expression of pain on his face, she smiled and let go.

With a sigh of relief, John moved his hand away from the gun at his waist.

"Believe me... there's plenty of killing in store for you... so... I think you can wait... until I've fixed myself a cup of tea," she told him with the same best-of-friends tone she had used earlier on the phone.

Rubbing his wrist, he followed her with his eyes to the banquet table and took in her appearance; carrying nothing but a small black cell phone in her left hand and dressed in a powder blue and cream colored dress, her lean muscular shape moved with confidence and ease.

With cup and saucer in hand, she turned to him and asked as she stirred the contents of her tiny cup with a small silver spoon, "Have you had one yet?"

The sound of her casual tone gnawed at his brain just behind his eyes.

Smiling up at him, she continued, "I am glad you came, John."

With the flattest of tones, he asked, "What do you want?"

As if she hadn't heard his question, she raised the cup to her lips, took a delicate sip and said, "This event started back in the late eighteen hundreds between Chinese immigrants and French fur trappers. Its original name was Boomtown Follies."

He stared at her, amazed at how bizarre standing next to her was.

Looking at him, she smiled again and continued, "Later the event was given the name Tea and Sympathy to suggest a more upper class appeal."

Listening to her banter, the corners of his mouth unexpectedly began to itch.

She took another sip, closed her eyes, and let the warm liquid slide down her throat.

John asked again, "What... do you... want?"

She set the tiny cup back down on the saucer, set them both down on the long serving table, and sweetly answered, "A dance."

"What?" John exclaimed.

She repeated, "A dance," then added, "We can kill each other later... but right now I think we should dance."

"Lady... are you fuck'n kidding?" John exclaimed a second time

Her smile unwavering, she said, "Where else... but a crowded dance floor... can two people talk without being disturbed."

He stared at her without replying.

"Come on," she beckoned, "If you really wanted to kill me... you would've already gone for that gun... a second time."

Completely shocked at the conversation he was

having, he closed his eyes and shook his head.

She shifted her cell phone from one hand to the other and said, "Here. I'll make it easy for you," then reached out and gently took his hand.

Feeling her touch on his hand, his skin rippled and the hairs on his arm bristled.

"Come... on," she gestured with a toss of her sleek black hair. "I won't bite... not this time."

John blinked his eyes and shook his head again as he pulled his hand away and said, "Fine. Lead on."

She gave him a big smile, "Come on."

Together, they walked through the crowd of people to the dance floor.

Uneasy about giving his back to her, John stayed abreast to her on her left side.

When they reached the Spanish cedar dance floor, they found it filled with dozens of couples slowly waltzing to the soft flowing sound from the orchestra.

They stopped for a brief moment, side by side, and then, without a word being said between them, they plunged into the revolving mass of people.

Together, they reached the middle of the dance floor and faced each other.

Under etiquette, John slipped his left hand around her slender waist and motioned for her hand.

She held up the cell phone and said, "Careful." then tucked it between her breasts.

With her hand now free, he took it into his, let out a steadying breath, caught the tempo of the music, and then sent them both into a long gliding waltz.

Being lead perfectly to the sway of the music, she looked up at him and said, "You've done this before."

Uncomfortable by being so close to her, John moved his head to the right and replied, "Yeah. I took a dance class as an elective in college."

"Interesting," she said out loud.

Keeping in time with the live music coming from the stage, he looked directly at her and said, "You got me to come and now you got me on this dance floor... so tell me... what do you want?"

She replied, "To be the only one."

Hearing her response, he stopped dancing.

She smiled at his reaction.

His emerald green eyes looked directly at her calm face as he retorted, "What?"

She squeezed his left arm with the same vice-like grip as before. "Keep dancing and don't stop again."

Feeling his arm going cold below the elbow, he quickly focused back on the music, caught the tempo once again and dropped them back into the flow.

Being lead perfectly as before, she released her crushing grip. "You heard me right, John. 'To be the only one'."

Looking out into the distance, bewildered by the whole thing, John said nothing.

She continued, "No one else should have what I have. It belongs to me... as I belong to it."

Catching something in the tone of her voice, he looked down at her and asked, "What do you mean by that?"

With her big green eyes, she looked directly into his and said, "It means... that I can't let you live."

John felt his knees go weak for a second.

She continued, "Trust me, John... it's for the best. I've... seen things and done things... you simply couldn't believe... all for a hatred of life that was thrust upon me centuries ago. You don't want any part of such a life. "

"I don't understand," he confessed as he suddenly

caught the smell of mint from her breath.

"This thing that lives inside me...is slowly growing inside you," she took a deep breath, "In time you too will stop aging and kill for no reason... forever," she looked directly into his eyes and added, "You don't want that... trust me... you don't."

"That thing that I saw the other night on the rooftop is now inside me... thanks to you," he said to her angrily.

She said to him, "That was never my intention. What happened in the parking garage should never have happened."

He said nothing as he kept them dancing.

"But it did happen... and it can't be taken back," she said, "It just has to be dealt with."

"By killing me?" John frankly asked.

Bypassing his question, she told him, "I've killed, beaten, burned, drowned, shot, dismembered, and tortured just about everything that walks or crawls at one point or another."

John listened with a sinking feeling in the pit of his stomach.

"The creature that is growing inside you... will demand the same acts of evil from you," she said to him as she continued to stare into his eyes.

"I don't believe you," the words slipped from his mouth before he could stop them.

"You will...you will," she told him.

Then, from a distant corner of his mind, the memory of the two men he had assaulted back in Los Angeles flashed within his head like an exploding star.

He dropped his gaze and turned his head.

She gently rolled the muscle of his bicep under her fingers, smiled, and asked, "You have already... am I right?"

He swallowed through his tightened throat and nodded as he looked back at her.

She gave his leading hand a gentle squeeze and asked, "Did you kill?"

He let out a deep sigh and answered with a shake of his head.

"But you did hurt someone?"

He answered, "Yes. Two men."

The music stopped.

They came to halt in the middle of the dance floor.

"The creature will not let you kill yourself... trust me... I tried to do so... on several occasions... and every time... it stopped me. However I can help you. I can end it," she said in a soft quiet voice.

John asked, "Why me?"

She gave no reply.

He asked again, "Why me? Why did you attack me... in the cabin?"

With a nostalgic snort, she answered, "I had been living in the woods for over five years... killing hunters, campers, vagrants, anyone who I could find... when I came across you and that cabin. You were just another random kill... nothing else."

"Nothing else," he repeated with contempt and asked, "And the night at the parking structure?"

"After centuries of killing, you have been the only one to ever escape. I tracked you down just to finish what I had been started that day in the snow," she answered with her standard casual tone.

On the stage, the musicians prepared themselves for their next set.

John pondered everything he was hearing. He let go of her hand and touched his scar for the first time that evening.

She watched him do so and told him, "All these questions have answers. Come away with me and I'll help you find them... then set you free."

He lowered his eyes.

"I've had to find the answers to my questions... all on my own... during a time of very few comforts. Consider yourself lucky, " she told him.

The last word speared him like a hot poker through butter. He looked up and said, "Lucky? Lucky? From what you just told me, I've been condemned to kill whoever I can get my hands on while spending the rest of my life alone... periodically living in the woods for years. How am I lucky?"

Thinking back on her entire life, the countless endless decades of living alone, watching the world evolve into what is was today while she stood in the distance hidden from sight, she replied, "Lucky... because you still have time to end it. The one who bit me meant to infect me. That's the creature's immortality... it passes itself from a damaged host to a fresh one."

John only stared at her.

"I never meant to infect you. Believe me," she told him candidly.

John asked, "How is something such as that even possible?"

"Many years ago... the creature came to me in a dream and revealed itself," she replied.

An image of Broken Arrow flashed across her mind for a split second.

"What is the creature?" he inquired.

She looked into his eyes and answered, "Evil."

John felt his vision swim for the briefest of seconds.

"I was condemned to this life over two hundred years ago," she confessed, "My name is Abigail Brandt... and I was born when this country was nothing more than just a colony," then realized she hadn't spoken her real name in over a century.

John knew he couldn't take any more, he felt as if he was going to vomit.

The musicians on stage cued up their instruments.

She reached out and touched his arm. "Come with me. I'll answer all your questions... and end a life of death and loneliness that awaits you... quickly and painlessly"

Doing his best to gather himself over the tidal wave of stunning information, he looked away.

"I've been all over the world... and I have never found any one else like me. I let you live the other night on the rooftop so that I could give you... what I was never offered... a choice."

John lowered his eyes with the corners of his mouth itching even more so.

She watched him without any further word.

Then, slowly he looked up at her and said, "If what's in you... is now in me then you know... I can't go with you."

She dropped her hand from his arm, took a step back, and nodded slightly.

He stared at her, and, for the first time, he saw her as she truly was; nothing more than a lonesome killer lost among her victims.

Suddenly, a sinister smile spread like oil across her lips as she reached between her breasts and retrieved the small cellular phone snuggly tucked between her flesh.

The orchestra's conductor raised his arms, wand in

his right hand.

Looking directly at him, she raised the cellular phone up at him and asked, "Do you like C4?" then gestured upwards with her eyes.

John followed them up with his towards the decorative stained glass above them.

On stage, the conductor gave a flourish with both hands.

She pressed the green talk button on the phone and the vaulted wooden rafters exploded on cue, shattering the stained glass ceiling.

Over one hundred smiling people look up at the sudden unexpected sound above them, exposing their faces to the onslaught of razor sharp broken glass racing down towards them.

With the same speed and strength that had propelled him from the rooftop of the homeless shelter to the other factory rooftop, John dove to his left across the dance floor and tumbled to a stop under a banquet table a split second before the wave of deadly broken glass crashed down on top of everyone.

Screams of pain and disbelief instantly filled the hall.

From underneath the table, John peered out and saw the aftermath from what had just occurred. Dozens of people lay scattered about, some killed on the moment of impact from the falling glass while others, bleeding profusely from their torn and ragged wounds, groveled on the floor as they slowly died.

John reached into his waist band, pulled out his handgun, and cocked the hammer.

The hall began to fill with the smell of death as more and more people bled out and died.

Scanning the horrifying scene for any sign of her,

John caught a glimpse of her through the tangle of chaos. Standing at the entrance, she gave him a small nod and then slipped away.

Careful not to lethally cut himself on the littered multitude of broken stained glass, he slowly crawled out from beneath the table and stood up.

Unexpectedly catching him by surprise, a woman, screaming in pain with half her face gone, ran up to him and grabbed him by his sport coat.

John tried to take a step back but her frantic grip held him securely in her hands.

"My God, help me! Help me!" she yelled at him as her one remaining eye stared at him with crazed intensity.

John raised his hands to push her away but stopped at the sight of several large pieces of glass protruding from her ample breasts and chest.

Astonished at her wounds, he looked her over and saw that her ivory dress had gone dark red from her open wounds.

Then, as quickly as she had ran up to him, she let him go and dashed away continuing to scream for help.

Under the cloud of chaos and confusion, John slipped out a side door and sped off in his car, missing the approaching police cruisers by mere seconds.

A half hour later.

John entered his darkened hotel room, blood streaked sports coat bundled under his arms with the handgun tucked inside it, and let the door closed behind him.

He let his ruined jacket and gun fall from his arm onto the carpeted floor with a heavy thud.

He leaned up against the door and closed his eyes as exhaustion suddenly over took him like a warm blanket thrown over his shoulders.

Feeling like he might fall asleep holding up the door, John opened his eyes and flipped the main overhead light on.

He walked over to the tiny closet, opened it, grabbed the entirety of his clothes hanging from the bar in one gigantic bear hug, and threw them on the bed.

Looking down at his clothes, he knew that he had to get away tonight. No matter just how fantastic her story might have been, one thing was certainly true, she was as unpredictable as she was violent.

'Distance and constant movement is my only way of staying alive for the time being until I figure out something else' he thought to himself.

He looked up and turned to fetch his duffle bags when suddenly his chest began to tug once again.

Frozen in mid-step, John cast a frightened look at the large bay window to his right and saw that the heavy curtains were open. He had forgotten to close them in his mad rush to get to the Pioneers' lodge.

Fearing that she might shoot him for real this time, John dropped to the floor and crawled, soldier style, away from the window, towards the bathroom.

Feeling the cold tile floor through his clothes, John raised himself to a sitting position up against the toilet and pondered what to do next.

Expecting to see the red dot at any second, his heart beat a mile a minute in his chest next to the constant tugging.

Suddenly, there was a knock at the door.

The tugging in his chest suddenly and unexpectedly ceased.

John stiffened.

The knock came again.

Avoiding the window as best he could, John slowly crawled to his bundled sports coat to retrieve his handgun.

Another knock and then a woman's voice bled through the door, "Mr. Poole?"

Gun in hand, John crawled back to the relative safety of the windowless bathroom and aimed the weapon at the door.

"Mr. Poole, it's the Front Desk," the woman's voice proclaimed from the other side.

Unsure of anything by that point, he cocked the hammer.

"Mr. Poole, are you there?" the woman asked and then knocked again.

Compelled to answer, he finally replied, "Yes?"

"Front Desk," said the woman's voice.

Unsure whether the tugging had stopped because she was at the other side of his door or she had left the area, John moved out from the bathroom and cautiously, stood up, and slowly walked to the door.

At the base of the door the shadows of feet could be seen.

He slipped his index finger into the trigger guard of the .380 and approached even closer.

Another knock.

John pressed his eye to the peep hole.

Seeing the small dot of light disappear from the peep hole, the woman on the other side squared herself to the door.

Slightly distorted by the lens, he saw a strawberry

blonde female in uniform standing by herself in the hallway in front of his door and recognized her as being one of the two girls who attended the front desk at night.

She blinked her brown eyes and gave a small smile at the eye observing her.

She shifted her weight as she continued to wait for the door to open.

Aware of the woman's shape shifting abilities, John pondered whether to start shooting through the thin hotel door but decided against it for fear of being wrong and killing the young employee so he called out, "Alright. One sec," then slipped the semiautomatic behind his left leg and opened the door.

The young woman, with a name badge that read Meg, looked up at him, smiled wider, and said, "A lady downstairs found your cellular phone," and then extended the very same cell phone that just been used to murder dozens of people.

Caught off guard by what she had just said and the terrible cellular phone staring back at him, John questioned, "I'm sorry... what?"

Still smiling bright and cheerful, the girl recounted, "A lady came in just a few minutes ago and handed this phone over to us... saying that you left it on the roof of your car."

Still holding the door open, John stared numbly at the small back mobile phone.

Giving the phone a little shake, the young woman said, "Here you go."

Continuing to stare at it as if it held an irreversible disease, John said, "That's not..."

The phone began to ring, cutting him off in midsentence.

Finding the timing humorous, Meg gave a small yelp and said through even white teeth, "Oh! You have a call," motioning again for him to take it from her.

Not knowing what else to do in front of the young employee, John took the ringing cell phone, gave her a quick thank you, and closed the door.

Rigid where he stood, John pressed the Send button and then put the phone to his ear.

"Hello, John," her casual tone of voice came through the phone's tiny ear piece, "Did you like the explosion? It took me two whole nights to wire it up… just for you."

Stunned at hearing her voice again, he made no reply.

"I guess… I always knew the answer would be 'no'," John listened to her speak, "But you can't blame a girl for trying… even one as old as I am."

Not knowing just how much more he could take, John's head swam in a whirlpool of fatigue, disgust, and bewilderment.

She took a deep breath, exhaled, and then solemnly said at the other end of the line, "There's this boredom with death that occurs when you've killed as long as I have." she paused and continued, "You see… after a while the never ending act of killing fades all the joy in your life away until you become nothing more than just a weapon."

He listened in silence.

"Which brings me to my reason for calling," she took a pause, "John… you are unique. You've survived twice… became infected whether by chance or fate I can't say… and you've even come after me," she took pause for effect and continued, "Plus, there's that feeling I get in my chest when we're close enough to each other... it's very dynamic."

John hadn't considered that she felt the tugging sensation as well.

She kept on, "Since you are not going to take advantage of my kind offer and hand yourself over to me... then I see no other option but to kill you before the night is over."

Suddenly angered, John exclaimed into the small phone, "Why don't you just leave me alone and go fu..."

"However!" she interrupted him, "However... because you are unique... you have brought a certain level of excitement to my life... which is something that hasn't happened in quite some time. I mean... once in a while... some people do intrigue me... here and there... but not often enough."

Frustrated, John rubbed his entire face with his free hand.

"So I propose a little game to keep the excitement going for a little while longer." she told him.

He removed his hand from his face.

"I'll let you guess... who I'm going to kill next," she told him.

John felt his insides go cold.

"Don't worry... it won't be that hard of a guess... you already know them," she said with a sudden wicked tone.

John blurted out into the phone, "What?"

"I said that I want you to guess who I'm going to kill next," she answered, "Your brother in Idaho or your parents in Illinois?"

CHAPTER 27

"I'm in some trouble."

John rolled to a stopped at the first security station he found, gave the horn a quick tap, and lowered the window.

From inside the tiny concrete hut, a uniformed guard, groggy eyed and sullen, raised himself from his desk chair and peered out to see who had come to disturb him.

With the cold crisp morning air filling the interior of the Honda, John looked at the dashboard's clock and saw that it read half past four in the morning.

Slowly and laboriously, the security guard made his way to him. He checked the time, mumbled a barrage of curse words underneath his breath, and adjusted his hat unenthusiastically on his head before finally stepping out of the little concrete hut.

Having just driven nonstop throughout the night to get to Boise, John was simply too tired to be hassled by a rent-a-cop.

Making a show of how cold it was by overdramatically rubbing his arms, the guard leaned forward and asked, "Help ya?"

Wanting to quickly get to his brother, John kept his demeanor cool, "My name is John Poole. I'm here to see my brother William Poole, he's a student here in the University," then passed his driver's license out the car window.

The guard took the license and flatly said, "No visitors allowed until daybreak."

Prepared for such a response, John replied with a hurtful lie, "There's been a family emergency. I need to see him."

With a visitors' pass tabbed to his shirt, John climbed the stairs to the second floor of the dormitory after speaking briefly to the dorm manager at the entrance of the building. When he reached a door marked B, he opened it and stepped into a long waxed floor corridor lined with identical doors and dozens of corkboards.

At the furthest end, standing at the threshold of his dorm room, dressed only in white boxers and flip flops on his feet, was his younger brother sleepily watching him approach.

John started down the long and brightly lit hallway towards his brother as the full weight of everything that had recently occurred to him and what he was about to ask of his family fell with pressing force onto his shoulders like sandbags.

He walked the full length of the corridor under his brother's suspicious stare and when he reached him, he spoke the first words to his younger brother in over two years, "Hey, Billy... how you been?"

His brother's reply was less than courteous, "Fuck, Johnny! What happened to your eyes?"

"My eyes?" John asked, caught off guard.

"Yeah, dude! They're all green and weird looking."

Feeling oddly foolish in forgetting about the new appearance of his eyes, John looked down at the floor, gathered himself, and said, "Long story. Look, we gotta talk."

"Yeah... ok. What's going on? The dorm manager said there was some kind of family emergency."

The innocent tone on his brother's voice pierced him deep in his heart. "Yeah... kind'a. Can I come inside... and talk to you?"

Billy returned, "What do you mean 'kind'a', Johnny? Are mom and dad ok?"

John held up his hands in a gesture for calm and answered, "Yeah, they're fine, but I need to talk to you. Can I come in?"

Billy gave a quick glance over his shoulder into his darkened dorm room and said, "No. You can't... I've four roommates. They'll be pissed off as all hell if they're totally woken up."

Focused on the matter at hand, John asked, "Ok, where then? It's important."

"Look... there's a common room down the hall. I'll meet you there, ok?" Billy answered.

"I've been driving all night, Billy. I really need to talk to you now," John told him.

"Yeah, ok, dude. Just go down there. I'll be there in a few," Billy said angrily, then gestured with both hands at his boxers, "I gotta put some clothes on... I'm not gonna walk around with my dork hanging out."

"Fine but hurry." John said as he turned away.

Minutes later, standing alone in the common room, John heard his brother's voice behind him, "Ok, Johnny... what the fuck is going on?"

He turned around and saw his brother, wearing a pair of Levis, t-shirt, and the same pair of flip flops walking up to him.

Not knowing how else to say it, John spoke directly, "Billy... I'm sorry but you need to leave with me tonight."

Shocked at what he had just heard, Billy responded, "What the fuck are you talking about?"

"I'm in some trouble," John answered then added, "And I need you to come with me right now."

"Dude, I'm not going anywhere. I'm in college for fuck's sake!" Billy exclaimed.

Feeling horrible at what he was asking of him, John said, "I know... and I'm sorry but you need to leave with me right now."

"Why?" Billy asked as confusion and anger continued to mount.

Knowing the truth was just too fantastic for anyone to believe, John settle on watering it down with a hastily prepared story, "I discovered something at work while doing an accounting audit."

Billy crossed his arms across his t-shirt, "Ok... and?"

Hating himself for lying, John continued, "I found something I shouldn't have, and now there are some people who are very upset."

"What people?"

"Dangerous people, Billy. Bad people, ok?" John speedily said, wanting to end the lying as fast as possible.

With a sudden look of concern, Billy unfolded his arms and asked, "Like terrorist shit?"

"No, not like that... but dangerous... nonetheless," John answered.

"Are you saying that you got yourself mixed up with... the Mafia?" Billy asked.

Touching the scar on his forehead, John replied with a deflective answer, "Like I said... 'dangerous'."

Raising his arms up with a shrug of his shoulders, Billy said, "So what the fuck does that... have to do with me?"

Speaking the truth this time, John answered, "It seems they know everything about me, Billy."

"So?"

The corners of his mouth began to itch as John found himself growing suddenly angry, "Jesus Christ, Billy! They know everything about me so they know about you, plus about mom and dad!"

Stunned by his brother's words, Billy with a stern look in his eyes slowly said, "What... the... fuck... do you... mean... by that?"

"I mean that I need you to leave with me tonight, Billy. I'm sorry but that's just the way it's gotta be."

"I can't leave. I'm on a B+ scholarship. I have a study group tomorrow in the morning. I have this ball busting prick of a professor in Anatomy, who basis his finals on only his lectures. Not to mention the paper I have due by next Thursday," Billy said with mounting frustration at his older brother's outlandish demand.

John touched the right corner of his mouth with his tongue and felt a small tear, then he said, "Look, Billy... either you come with me right now... or by God,... I'll drag you off of this campus by your hair... your choice, bro."

Billy said nothing.

Silently waiting for a decision on how his brother

wanted to leave the campus grounds, John stood motionless.

Finally Billy said, "Since you took off to L.A. in order to become some big time swinging dick corporate asshole, you haven't spoken to me in over two years, you know that?"

John looked down, ashamed at the truth his brother's words carried.

"And now you show up... out of the blue... telling me that I need to drop everything I have here and drive away with you cause you got involved in some shit?"

"That's right, Billy," John simply answered.

Billy stared into his brother's large green eyes.

"So what's it gonna be? Are you going to ready a bag and come willingly... or am I going to drag you outta here?" John flatly asked.

Billy looked at his older brother as if for the first time in his life. "You've never spoken to me like this before, Johnny. Never."

Knowing there was nothing else to say, John simply stared at his brother, waiting for Billy to still make his choice.

After what felt like an eternity, Billy sighed and said, "Give me ten minutes to pack some stuff."

CHAPTER 28

"Scorpio"

Later that day, John told his brother who sat on the passenger seat, "That's it, I'm done. I can't drive anymore," as they drove into Cheyenne, Wyoming.

Still dressed in his t-shirt and jeans, Billy looked at the dashboard clock, which read 2:30 in the afternoon. "Well, this is the biggest city in all of Wyoming so I'm sure we'll find someplace to crash."

Taking the most immediate exit off the east bound Interstate 80, John said to his brother, "Keep your eyes open and find us a place... I can barely keep mine open."

Shifting himself into an upright position in his seat, Billy craned his neck to stare out the passenger window and replied, "Fine."

Feeling the fatigue pressing heavily on his eyes, John drove into the heart of the city.

Minutes later, Billy said, "Over there." pointing to his right with a jerk of his thumb, "That looks like a good place."

John dipped his head under the Honda's rearview

mirror and saw a large six story red brick building with a hunter green awning over the front entrance with the word Hotel printed across the front.

After checking in, they entered their hotel room, a perfectly preserved show piece of Victorian era mid-west American refinement.

John crossed the richly decorated room and dropped his bags, one with his clothes and liquid assets and the other with his guns, at the foot of the bed.

Closing the door behind him, Billy said, "I'd like to call mom and dad."

Dropping to a sitting position on the side of the plush bed, John replied, "What are you going to tell them?"

Seating himself across his brother on the next bed, Billy answered venomously, still angered at being pulled out of school, "Well... I could always start with the fact that you yanked me out of college cus you fucked up in L.A.... and now we're on our way back to Chicago cus their lives might be in danger."

John, catching the dripping sarcasm, looked up with his large green emerald eyes at his younger brother and said, "What good is that going to do, Billy?"

Leaning forward a bit, Billy replied, "For starters... It'll make you look like the complete shit that you are."

With his feet, John slipped off his shoes, swung his legs onto the crimson red comforter and said as he closed his eyes, "You're right, Billy, I am a complete shit for getting you involved... so call them if you want," then fell asleep.

John opened his eyes, saw the room covered in darkness, and realized he had sleep through the entire day.

To his left, light from the bathroom spilled out from under its open door.

Unsure if he was alone, he called out to his brother.

Billy's voice answered back, "What?" and stepped out of the brass and wood trimmed bathroom, and flicked on the room's main light.

Rising to his elbows, John replied, "Just wanted to see if you were here."

Dressed in a white Oxford, jeans and dressed shoes, Billy asked with the same level of sarcasm as before, "What you think? That I was going to run away?"

Understanding how upset his brother was, John ignored the tone. "No. Just wanted to know if you were here, is all."

"Well I'm here," Billy countered, as he fiddled with the collar of the shirt, and then added wickedly, "Hey, hope you don't mind if I borrowed this shirt from you?" and puffed the front of the shirt with his fingers.

John looked at his younger brother, wearing the only white shirt he had taken with him from his condo and realized how little Billy looked like him or their father. Carrying down the majority of their mother's genes, Billy stood lank and gaunt with narrow features outlining his face and bone structure.

Feeling suddenly exposed under his older brother's stare with those new strange green eyes of his, Billy exclaimed, "What?"

John snapped free from his train of thought and replied, "No, nothing. Yeah, go ahead... wear it."

With a quick nod, Billy stepped back into the bathroom

John swung himself back to a sitting position at the

edge of the bed. "Where are you going?"

From the bathroom, Billy answered with a raised voice, "Downstairs. There's a bar and lounge. I could use a couple of beers right now."

Knowing he couldn't argue with such logic, John said, "Fine... but just do me a favor and stay in the hotel, don't go out."

Still answering from within the bathroom, Billy said, "Ok, fine."

John swung himself back onto the bed and put his hands under his head. He still felt tired; the long drive had wiped him out completely.

The light in the bathroom clicked off and Billy stepped out.

John looked over at him. "Did you call mom and dad?"

Putting his wallet in his back pocket, Billy simply replied, "No," then added, "I'll let you drop the good news on them in person when we get there."

With few words at his disposal at what his younger brother had just said, John only told him, "Ok... thanks," then turned his head back, closed his eyes.

Billy went to the door opened it, hit the light switch, and stepped out, leaving his brother alone in the dark.

With the aid of his eye's new ability to see in the dark, John watched the hotel room door slowly close behind his brother.

Purposely requesting the top floor when they had checked in order to avoid any more red dots, John gazed at the Cheyenne nightscape from out the window and thought again about the only plan he felt was available to him; take his brother and parents to some faraway place, where exactly he didn't know yet, wait for the sensation in his chest to reoccur, use it to locate her, then kill her.

"Or she kills me," he whispered the words to himself in the dark as sleep softly crept over his body once again.

Billy pushed the button marked L on the elevator panel, and the wood and mirrored elevator began its descent to the bottom floor.

Waiting to reach his destination, he looked at himself in the mirrored wall and gave himself a quick smile. As angry as he was at his older brother for pulling him out of school in the middle of the night, he had to admit; he enjoyed going to new places.

'Besides' he thought to himself, 'whatever credits I come up short... I can always make them over the summer.'

A tiny bell dinged above him.

The elevator doors slid open.

He stepped out in the hotel's yellow marbled lobby and turned left towards the bar and lounge, passing a closed gift shop on the way.

Hotel guests walked to and fro, lost in their own cares and worries.

He came to a stop in front of a pair of small shoulder high double swinging wooden doors, reminiscent of a western saloon.

The name of the bar, Cody's Place, shone brightly in red neon writing above him.

Billy stepped through the tiny doors with a determined smile to enjoy himself and forget the dilemma he had recently been thrust into.

Dimly lit by only glowing beer signs that were hung on every wall, the saloon had been furnished with small pub tables and chairs made of dark wood and varnished to a gloss. The bar itself, decorated with a large mirror behind the bartender and a green and white veined Guatemalan marble counter top, lined the entire length of the left side of the place.

Billy crossed the empty pub tables and chairs, noting what a slow night the bar was having.

The music interesting enough for a bar was a steady stream of classical music.

He sat himself at the bar in front of the draft dispenser and took a deep breath with a small smile. He liked the place.

The bartender, a middle aged looking local, stopped in front of him, and requested, "Your I.D., please, sir."

Billy fished out this Illinois driver's license and handed it over.

The bartender took it, felt it in his creased hands, held it up in the dim light and read its information.

Waiting, as the barkeep inspected his driver's license like a surgeon reading an x-ray, Billy noticed a woman walk into the dark and quiet bar. Using the bar's expansive mirror in front of him, he watched her walk past him and then take a seat just two stools down.

Breaking his sudden concentration on the only other customer in the entire bar, the bartender asked him, "What's your sign?"

Having been asked the same control question several times before, Billy answered with a single word, "Scorpio."

The bartender looked at the birth date one last time, handed the driver's license back, and asked, "What'll be?"

Billy took his license back and replied, "The local stuff", pointing to the large red handle in front of him, "On draft."

With a nod, the bartender went to work.

Waiting again, Billy gave the woman, sitting just off to his right, a quick glance from the mirror and found her staring at him. Feeling slightly caught, he dropped his eyes.

The bartender placed a frosted frothing mug of beer in front of him, "Here you go," then turned and walked to the woman who sat waiting patiently with a smile.

Playing as cool as he could, Billy took a long sip of the ice cold beer and stole another quick glance at her from the mirror. He found her attractive.

Placing his hands on the cool clean marble, the bartender generously asked the woman, he had never seen before, "And what can I get ya, this evening, Miss?"

Suddenly, to his surprise, Billy heard her ask him, "What are you drinking? It looks good."

In the darkness of their hotel room, John stirred in his sleep. The tugging sensation in his chest had started once again.

With the mug still in his hand, Billy turned to his right and gave her a good look; she wore a grey woman's business suit and her pleasant oval face with deep black eyes and rich red lips were framed by a bob of autumn brown hair.

Realizing he was staring without answering, Billy rushed, "Huh... I asked for a local brew... on draft."

She turned to the bartender. "I'll have one of

those."

"Coming right up," he replied with a quick nod of his head.

Then to Billy's amazement, he watched her stand from her stool, walk over to him, and sit beside him.

With a red lipstick smile, she asked him, "Mind... if I sit next to you?"

"Huh... no. Yeah, sure," Billy answered with the only words his brain could formulate at the moment.

A frosting mug of beer appeared in front of her.

She turned to the bartender and thanked him sweetly.

With a smile of his own, the bartender nodded and took his place at the furthest end of the bar, away from them both.

"What's your name?" she asked.

"William," Billy answered with the sudden desire to appear and sound older than he was in front of the business clad woman sitting next to him.

"William," she repeated then added, "Mine`s Abigail."

Billy caught the smell of fresh mint on her breath.

Still asleep, John's hands went to the center of his chest as the tugging sensation continued.

Billy set his mug of beer down on the marble counter top. "Nice to meet you... Abigail."

She repeated his words, "Nice to meet you... William."

Taking in her pleasing appearance and not knowing what else to say, Billy asked, "So... you from around here?" then cringed at the sound of the question slash pick up line.

Acting as if nothing awkward had been said, she replied, "I'm originally from back East... I'm here just passing through."

Accustomed mainly to drunken college girls, Billy racked his brain to keep the conversation going, "So... are you here for business or pleasure?"

She smiled again and answered, "Pleasure."

Stalling for time as he formulated another question, he took a long draft of his beer and watched her from the mirror take a drink of hers.

She set the mug down, dabbed her painted lips with a napkin, and asked, "What about you? What brings you to Cheyenne?"

Seeing no reason to lie, he turned to her again, and told her part of the truth, "I'm traveling with my brother."

She smiled again but said nothing.

Billy raised his mug to his lips again but stopped when she asked, "Where are you two heading?"

Billy set the mug back down and replied, "Illinois."

"Joliet is a great city," she said the word through her sweet smiling mouth.

Billy knitted his eyebrows at the way she had called out his hometown, "Yeah, it's great... it's a good town."

"I haven't been there in years," she told him.

Pushing aside the odd feeling that had suddenly crept over him, Billy asked, "Oh, yeah. How long ago?"

She raised her chin slightly up and cast her big black eyes upwards towards the ceiling in a gesture of trying to recall a distant memory.

Billy's eyes traveled down her jaw line to the smooth soft flesh of her neck and over a pair of delicate collarbones before plunging deep into her rich supple cleavage.

She lowered her head to look at him and said, "Longer then I care to remember."

Billy blinked his eyes at her answer.

Then, with a casual manner she added, "But I might just go there... you never know," then drained her beer as she gave him a piercing stare.

John's eyes snapped open and a rush of air filled his lungs.

The smile on Billy's face slipped away at the sudden dark tone in her voice.

Continuing to stare at him, she set the empty mug down on the counter and asked as a wide wicked grin suddenly spread across her face, "Tell me... Billy... how upset... do you think your study group was... when you didn't show up this morning?"

Using his eyes unnatural ability of see in the dark once again, John looked around the room as he called out in alarm, "Billy!"

Billy felt his organs turn ice cold.

She continued, "I'm pretty sure they all thought you were nothing more than a fuck'n asshole when they found out you just up and left in the middle of night."

With fear swelling up in his eyes, like hot tears, Billy stared at her, wordlessly.

"But don't worry about them," she told him through an ever widening venomous smile, "And don't worry about yourself or your brother... cus I'm going to see to it that both of you-"

Billy jerked to a stand and sent the stool toppling over onto the floor.

"Plus your parents are dealt with," she finished her sentence without missing a beat.

Realizing that Billy hadn't yet returned, John sprang from the bed and went to the duffle bag which kept his cache of weapons.

He dove his hand into his bag and rummaged around until he found the first handgun that fell into his hand, the Israeli 1911.

He pulled it out, pressed checked it, and made for the door.

Staring at the woman's sinister looking smile, Billy back pedaled to the entrance.

With a mischievous tone, she said out loud as he disappeared out the double swinging doors, "Don't worry, Billy... I'll get the tab."

Watching his only other customer rush out the bar, the bartender approached her, and asked, "What was all that about?"

She turned to him and said, "Remember your first beer?"

Catching her humor, he laughed out loud.

Smiling, she put her manicured index fingers in her eyes.

Watching her fiddle with her eyes, the scent of mint registered in his nose.

Slowly, she lowered her fingertips from her face with a black colored contact on each one.

The bartender looked directly at her large glossy emerald colored eyes.

With his chest still tugging, John stopped in front of the elevator and looked up at the numbered panel above the sliding doors.

The number 5 was lit.

He clasped the grip of the .45, hidden under his dress shirt.

The number 5 winked out and then the number 6 lit up. Two floors to go.

With his free hand, John wiped away the sweat from his brow with his shirt sleeve.

The number 7 lit up. One more floor.

John stared squarely in front of him.

The elevator dinged, the ornate wooden doors slid open, and the tugging at his chest suddenly stopped.

Billy, ashen faced, emerged from the elevator.

Knowing firsthand at her ability to shapeshift, John commanded, "Tell me your birth date."

Startled, Billy called out, "Holy shit, dude!"

Frightened and still groggy with sleep, John pressed, "Tell me!"

Flabbergasted, Billy exclaimed, "Are you fuck'n kidding me?"

John slipped the .45 caliber handgun from under his shirt and growled, "Your birth date...now!"

Realizing that his brother was armed, Billy raised his hands above his head and cried out, "Fuck you, Johnny! Fuck you... you fuck'n asshole," then added, "It's April tenth... you piece of shit."

Satisfied, John hid the handgun back under his shirt.

Billy lowered his hands as he spat the words, "Fuck you... Johnny."

Noting that something else was bothering his younger brother besides having a weapon pulled in front of him, John asked, "What happened?"

Billy darted past him towards the room and blurted

out, "Nothing happened."

The elevator doors closed.

Following him into their hotel room, John protested, "Bullshit, Billy! What happened! Tell me!"

Without breaking stride, Billy entered the room and yelled over his shoulder, "I said 'nothing'!" then added as he grabbed his own duffle bag, "I just want to go... right now!"

Hell bent on knowing what had happened downstairs, John grabbed his brother's arm, "God damn it, Billy! What the fuck happened!"

Scared and angry, Billy spun around with blinding speed and sunk his fist deep into John's gut.

John fell to his knees and doubled over.

Billy roared down at the top of his head, "I want to go now, God damn it! Now!"

Gathering his breath and fighting back the sudden urge to tear open his brother's throat, John slowly stood up and slumped on the bed.

Towering, Billy methodically said, "We... are... leaving... right now. I want to go see... mom and dad."

John took one final deep breath, realized that the sensation in his chest had stopped, and thought to himself, 'She's gone. She scared him shitless but she didn't kill him.'

Standing defiantly, Billy balled up his fists and waited for a response from his older brother.

John looked up, saw the fright that Billy was so valiantly trying to hide, and said, "Ok. Let's go see mom and dad."

A week later, the smell of decay would lead to the discovery of the bartender's disemboweled body inside his apartment.

CHAPTER 29

"Such a pretty name."

Without a further word between them, they had packed, checked out, and set out towards their home state.

They had agreed not to take the next flight out of Cheyenne to Chicago because of the cache of weapons, liquid money, and gold coins John had in the trunk. Instead they drove nonstop through Nebraska, each taking a turn behind the wheel, crossing into Iowa with the morning sun.

Taking his turn behind the wheel, John took his eyes from the road and looked at his brother, slumbering uncomfortably in the passenger seat. John knew whatever had occurred at the hotel's lounge had frighten him bad enough to put him in a lethargic state; barely a word had been spoken between them since Cheyenne.

He cast his green eyes back onto the road, looked out into the distance, and realized he had turned his brother's life upside down and in a short while from now he would do the same to his unsuspecting parents.

Then, before he could acknowledge what he was doing, John slowed and pulled to a stop along the roadside. The weight on his shoulders about everything that had happened was literally pressing him into the ground.

Feeling the change in the momentum of the vehicle, Billy stirred awake and looked about. "Wha... what's going on? Where are we?"

John rolled the gear shift into Park, gripped the leather steering wheel with both hands as he stared blankly out the windshield. "I want to talk to you."

Clicking his dry mouth, Billy followed, "Yeah, ok but keep driving."

John lowered his head and said, "In a minute... but right now I have to tell you something."

Sensing conflict in his brother's voice, Billy shifted his weight in the passenger seat. "Yeah... alright, bro. What is it?"

With his hands still on the steering wheel, John turned to Billy. "I just want to say that I'm sorry for everything that's happened-"

"Ok, but-," Billy cut him off.

John sidestepped the interruption and continued, "...but I'm even sorrier for not being completely honest with you from the very beginning."

Billy knitted his eyebrows. "What are you talking about, bro?"

"I've lied to you, Billy. About what happened to me in L.A.... about why I yanked you out of school... about why we're driving back home," John said, turning his gaze away.

"You lied?" Billy questioned with a flat tone.

"And it almost got you killed in Cheyenne," John said with a distant tone.

Billy knitted his eyebrows once again and asked, "What are you talking about?"

John turned his head once more to look at his brother in the face and replied, "Her."

The word had an instant effect. Billy tore his eyes away from his brother's and looked out the passenger window.

John pressed, "I know you saw her. I know it."

Billy said nothing.

John touched his scar and confessed, "She's the reason we're sitting in this car right now."

Billy sighed through his nostrils.

John continued, "There wasn't any fraudulent account at the firm and the Mafia isn't after me."

Billy turned and looked at him once more.

"She is," John simply added.

"She." Billy repeated the word.

"That's right, Billy. She. The woman you saw last night and are too afraid to admit that you did. She is the one after me. She threatened to hurt you, mom, and dad."

Billy looked away again.

John asked, "What did she look like?"

Without looking back, Billy took full minute before he answered, "Real pretty. She made me... feel like a nervous twelve year old boy...trying...to get his first kiss," and then chuckled with scorn.

John knew the feeling, remembering the parking structure.

"Who is she?" Billy asked.

John answered truthfully, "Honestly... I truly don't know."

Billy stared back at him.

"All I do know is that she's probably the most violent person I've ever come across," John said.

"What do you mean by that, Johnny?" Billy questioned.

"I watched this woman murder over one hundred people last week right in front of me."

"What the fuck are you talking about?" Billy returned, his voice laced with concern.

John continued, "It's true, man. In L.A., right in front of me, she set a bunch of homeless people on fire, then in Oregon, the night I came to get you, I watched her drop an entire stained glass ceiling down on a room full of people. She used something called C4 to do it."

"Jesus... Johnny," Billy said quietly as he ingested what he had just heard.

"She used a cell phone to ignite it... and then gave it to me as some sort of morbid memento," John concluded.

After a minute of heavy silence inside the car, Billy looked up and asked, "Why you? I mean... when did you first cross paths?"

John had been waiting for that question. "You know that vacation I took to the mountains a couple of years back?"

"Yeah... mom mentioned it," Billy quickly answered, eager to hear what his brother had to say.

"Well, she attacked me in the cabin on the very first day and nearly killed me," John told him, omitting the creature for the time being.

"Mom told me about that, she said that you told her you had been in a car accident or something," Billy commented.

"Yeah, I figured, at the time, no one would ever

believe me," John told him then pointed at the scar on his forehead, and said, "But it's true."

"So what does she want with you now? And us?" Billy asked.

"She views me as some sort of game to pass the time, nothing more really. She's completely insane."

"No shit," Billy returned.

John took a deep breath, let it out, and said, "And there's one other thing."

Sensing the sudden intensity in his brother's voice, Billy gave him a stern look and inquired, "What?"

"She attacked me a second time in L.A.," John focused on the right words to use, "She gave me some sort of infection... that changed my eye color to this," and then pointed with two fingers at his eyes.

"What?" Billy exclaimed. "That's impossible, Johnny. How?"

"I wish I knew... but here they are," John answered and pointed to his eyes again.

Billy shook his head again, overwhelmed by the entire conversation.

John decided to say nothing further.

Finally after a brief while, Billy asked, "So what now?"

Pondering just how asinine his 'great' plan was going to sound, he answered his brother's question anyway, "I take you, mom and dad some place far and safe... then wait to get a sense of where she's at-"

"Then what?" Billy cut him off again.

John looked at him square in the face with his large green emerald eyes and finished, "Then I kill her for sure this time or die trying."

Catching it, Billy asked, "What do you mean 'this time'?"

"What do you think I was doing at the homeless shelter the night she burned it down?" John answered, "I had gone there to put an end to her and get my life back."

With a sneer, Billy said, "You've always like guns, Johnny, but that doesn't make you a killer of killers. You're a God damn accountant for Christ's sake."

Recalling its face while pressed against the air conditioning unit, John nodded in agreement and said, "Well... it looks like that's... what I have to be now."

"Jesus, Johnny," Billy said in a low voice as he shook his head again.

Together, for a time, they sat in silence.

After a while, John looked at his watch. "It's almost noon. Why don't you give them a call? Don't tell her we're coming. Just see how they're doing."

Without saying a word, Billy nodded as he fished out his cell phone from his jeans pocket.

John watched his younger brother press the quick dial button on his tiny phone.

After a few seconds, Billy said loudly into the phone, "Hello, mom! Yeah, it's Billy. How are you? And dad? Cool. I'm good. School? It's going ok. Some classes are easier than others but that's just the way it is. So everything is ok, over there? Just asking. Ok, that's good to hear. What? Oh, I don't know, we just had spring break so maybe over the Christmas holiday. Yeah, I know... I miss you too. What? No, I'm fine, I just wanted to call and say hi and see how you and dad were doing. Yeah, I'll call this weekend and talk to dad. Ok, I'll talk to you later. Love ya, too. Bye."

Billy slowly shut the cell phone closed.

Looking intently at him, John asked, "Well?"

Billy gave him a small smile and replied, "Yeah,

everything seems cool. She's fine, dad's fine."

"Good," John stated, relieved at the good news, "That's good to hear."

Billy shifted back on his seat and said, "Lets get there. I'm dying to see how you're going to explain yourself to mom and dad."

John and Billy's mother, Cynthia, set the cordless phone back down into its cradle, picked up her tea cup by its tiny ear, and turned back towards the living room.

Balancing the delicate cup between thumb and index finger, she stopped at the edge of the Persian rug that marked the beginning of the living room and said, "That was my son William that just called. He's attending college in Boise."

"How nice," the woman who was sitting on the living room's plush suede sofa with a tea cup of her own, chimed.

Cynthia took a seat on the loveseat at the opposite side of the coffee table and asked as she stared transfixed on what she considered to be the most beautiful pair of eyes she'd ever seen, "I'm sorry... what's your name again, sweetheart?"

The woman raised the tea cup up to her mouth, looked across the bellowing steam with her large green emerald eyes and answered, "Abigail."

Ever the hostess, John and Billy's mom remarked with a smile, "Such a pretty name."

"Yes," the woman agreed, smiling behind her tea cup. "I'm beginning to like the sound of it all over again."

CHAPTER 30

"How the hell do you know that."

By the time they reached their childhood neighborhood it was well past nightfall of the following day. Tired and road weary, they drove past many of the landmarks of their upbringing in silence.

Billy steered the car into the residential section of Joliet and said, "It's well after eleven. Knowing mom and dad, they're probably already in bed."

In the passenger seat, John rubbed his face vigorously, "Whether they are or not, they're coming with us tonight."

"You got your work cut out for you. They're gonna be pissed as all hell... especially dad, " said Billy.

"Agreed. Nonetheless... they're coming," John said as he turned to look at his tired looking brother.

"And if they don't believe you and or refuse to come along... then what?" Billy asked.

"Then you help me drag them out of that fuck'n house and put them in the trunk of this car," John declared with a stern flat tone to his voice.

"Jesus, Johnny," Billy exclaimed with an exhausted tone.

John looked out the passenger side window and watched the stream of familiar houses sail past him. A stab of envy pierced his heart for not being in one of them sleeping peacefully.

Billy turned onto their block and asked, "So how..."

The tugging sensation struck his chest.

"Shut up!" John barked.

Taken back by the sudden objection, Billy returned, "Excuse me?"

"I said 'shut up'," John answered as he thought to himself, 'How can this be?'

Realizing that something was amiss, Billy asked, "What... what's going on?"

Focused at the sudden and completely unexpected sensation, John commanded, "Slow the car down. "Now!"

Billy complied, without question.

The sensation continued.

"She's here," he whispered as he reached under the passenger seat and produced the .45 caliber semiautomatic.

Billy looked at the large caliber handgun in his brother's hand and felt his insides go ice cold, "What?... She's here?" adding, "And how the hell do you even know that?"

All too accustomed by now to the sensation, John checked the rounds in the gun and replied, "She's somewhere close. Trust me... I just know."

Flabbergasted, Billy asked, "How could she have gotten ahead of us?"

Wondering that himself, John thought it over then answered with the most logical conclusion he could gather, "She took a plane out of Cheyanne."

"Fuck!" Billy exclaimed loudly, "She got ahead of us."

"Cut the lights, put it in neutral, and coast to a stop in front of the house," John instructed.

Catching the ice lacing his brother's voice, Billy did what he was told.

The car rolled to a quiet stop in front of the house they had spent the majority of their lives in. A two story dark wood and red brick single family dweller, the epitome of classic Americana living.

Billy put the car in Park. "What now, Johnny?"

John took a moment to figure out and then asked, "You have the house keys? I left mine when a left my condo."

Billy touched his right front pocket and said, "Yeah. I got them right here. I always carry them, even in school... force of habit, I guess."

"Good. Give them to me," John commanded with his hand extended out.

Billy fished for them.

Eager to get to their parents, John shook his hand. "Come on, God damn it."

The feeling in his chest kept tugging.

Billy drew them out and dropped them in his brother's hand.

John, staring at their darkened and quiet house, told him, "Ok. You come with me. I don't want to leave you alone.

His younger brother listened silently.

John continued, "We go in, get mom and dad, get the hell out, and then drive away as fast as possible," then turned and asked, "Do you understand?"

Billy looked at him and spoke, "Yeah, I

understand."

John cocked the hammer on the single action handgun. "Stay behind me and do exactly as I say," then opened the passenger door and stepped out into the night.

As his brother cut the engine and got out, John looked around the tranquil neighborhood block. Not a single person was outside.

Coming around the front of the car, wide eyed with fear, Billy gave himself a steadying breath.

"Stay behind me," John repeated one last time.

Billy nodded that he understood.

Together, they crossed the distance between the car and the house as quickly and quietly as possible.

When they reached the front door, the tugging in John's chest suddenly stopped which he knew, by now, meant that she was very close.

With the green luminous glow from his eyes helping him see, John quickly found the correct key on the key ring, slipped it into the front door's keyhole, and turned it.

The door from generations of use opened with noiseless ease.

Warm pungent air rushed out of the house.

John's heart sank at the smell coming from inside the house.

Billy, standing on the steps, watched in silence.

John turned to his brother and whispered out loud, "Stay close, Billy."

Billy nodded his head.

With his brother right behind him, John stepped into their quiet and lightless house.

Inside, John scanned the dark living room. The green glow of his eyes reveled nothing out of the ordinary.

Then from behind him, he heard his brother exhale sharply and whisper, "What's that smell?"

Instead of a reply, John said in a whisper, over his shoulder, "Come on... and stay close," then walked through the living room, across the Persian rug, which their father had bought on a business trip to New York for their mother's thirty-ninth birthday.

Gun at the ready, he reached the dining room and what he saw, glowing in the soft green light of his eyes, caused his knees to buckle almost completely beneath him.

Through the near-darkness, Billy watched his brother steady himself against the dining room's archway with his shoulder and whispered, "What is it?"

Oblivious to his brother's question, John continued to numbly stare into the dining room,

Sensing something terrible by his brother's sudden change in demeanor, Billy raised his voice from a whisper and asked again, "What is it?"

John could feel his mind and body slowly shutting down as he continued to stare vacantly at the scene in front of him.

Frightened by his brother's silence and sudden zombie-like state, Billy raised his voice and demanded through the darkness, "God damn it, Johnny! What's wrong?"

John simply heard nothing.

Unable to take it any longer, Billy pushed him hard to the side and stepped into the dining room.

John keeled over and fell to the floor beside the cedar lined wine fridge.

Billy stared into the darkened dining room and saw nothing but featureless shapes lost amid the darkness.

Crumpled on the floor, John blinked and shook his head as he fought to regain his senses.

Simply unable to see much of anything, Billy reached out and placed his left hand on the light switch.

In a green colored hue, John saw his brother go for the light switch in slow motion as his mind crawled to register what was about to happen.

Billy's index finger hit the light switch with a knowing swipe.

The chandelier directly above the dining room table flooded everything around it with light.

Billy's eyelids peeled back in horror.

Sitting at either end of the large oak dining room table were the decapitated bodies of their mother and father, a knife and fork in each of their hands, with a dinner plate, placed neatly in front of them, containing their severed heads resting on their amputated bare feet.

Billy bellowed out a heart shattering scream.

Shaken alert by his brother's scream, John scrabbled to his feet and clamped his free hand around his brother's mouth.

Still staring at the ghastly spectacle that had been laid out for them, Billy continued to scream through his brother's hand.

In need to get his brother under control, John shoved him out of the dining room and pressed him against the wall.

Stricken by the macabre image, Billy bucked and thrashed under his brother's surprising strength.

Suddenly, the wood creaked above them, and Billy instantly went silent and still.

With his hand still over his brother's mouth, John slowly raised his eyes and strained to hear anything further from the upstairs bedrooms.

Billy followed his brother's eyes upward as he gently removed John's hand from over his mouth.

John looked into his brother's eyes and whispered, "It's her."

Billy growled into his brother's face, "Then go kill her! Kill her. Go kill her, Johnny!"

Looking at his brother faced twisted in agony and rage, John suddenly wanted to do just that more than anything else in the entire world.

Again, Billy urged, "Go! Kill her! Please, Johnny!"

The weight of the .45 in his hand felt massive and comforting as he turned and looked at the stairs.

"Go! Now! Kill her!" Billy continued to yell.

John turned and looked into his brother's pain stricken face and, to his own disbelief at his own words, said, "No."

Aghast at what he had just heard, Billy argued as he tried to dislodge himself away from his brother, "No?... Why?"

John replied with the honest truth, "Because, I have to keep you alive."

"Fuck me! Our parents are dead! You have to kill her!" Billy commanded.

John forced himself to think about his only remaining family member, "You're right, Billy... I do have to... but not tonight... because right now I have to get you out of here."

"She killed mom and dad!" Billy yelled.

John grabbed a fist full of Billy's t-shirt, "There's nothing I can do about that now... but I can still do something about you," and then began to pull him towards the front door.

Billy continued to protest as he struggled against

his brother staggering strength, "If she's up there, go kill her, Johnny!"

Done talking and eager to get away before they were discovered at their parents' murder scene, John hauled his brother out the front door, "Keep quiet and get in the fuck'n car."

Still struggling to get free, Billy exclaimed, "She has to die. You have to get her for this."

Suddenly overwhelmingly exhausted, John let go of his brother and calmly told him, "I can't let her kill you... you're the last member of my family. I have to keep you alive."

Breathing hard, Billy only stared.

"I know she's up there... I do. Don't ask me how I know that ... I just do. Billy, please... I can't risk you getting killed too. If I go up there and she kills me... then there'll be nothing to stop her from getting to you."

Billy looked down and closed his eyes.

"Please, Billy... we have to go now. With all this noise who knows if the police haven't been called yet. We could spend years explaining this behind a cell," John implored.

Without uttering another word, Billy rubbed his face, nodded, and went to the car.

John gave his childhood home one last look then dashed off behind his brother.

CHAPTER 31

"Werwolves."

Watching from the window of John's old bedroom on the second floor, she saw them get into the car and race away into the night.

She licked the dried blood encrusted on her hands and smiled at the enjoyment she was having at his expense.

Listening to the smooth lonesome sound of his car fading into the distance, she closed her eyes and remembered...

A large paneled truck came to a stop in the middle of the dark country road three-fourths of a mile downhill.

With the moon far from being full above her, she used the ability of her green eyes to see in the gloom of the night and counted the number of men who emerged from the bed and cabin of the truck.

"Just six," she whispered to herself as she waited

for the rag-tag of men to join her.

They reached the top of the hill and a young Squad Leader of the Hitler Youth addressed her, "Hail Hitler. Good evening, Truppführer Müller."

Holding the sling of her MP44 machine gun with her left hand, she gave the Nazi salute with her right and returned the greeting in perfect German, "Hail Hitler. Good evening, Scharführer Fischer."

The other five men, all of them wearing mismatched uniforms mixed with civilian clothing, unslung their rifles and scanned the hill top nervously.

She looked at them and asked, "Why only five men plus yourself, Scharführer Fischer? I believe, I requested double that."

Despite the imminent collapse of the Third Reich, Otto Fischer, disciplined and loyal, answered with full military esteem, "Correct, Truppführer Müller, you did. However, with regret, I must inform you that tonight's mission has been compromised."

Tall and striking in her pressed and polished grey Nazi uniform, she asked, "How so... Scharführer Fischer?"

Unable to hide his contempt, he narrowed his piercing blue eyes and replied, "A traitor, Truppführer Müller. It seems that it only took a portion of butter and some jam from the Soviets to buy the bastard off."

She listened without saying a word.

"We were attacked the second we left the warehouse. The six of us... are all that remain of your command, Truppführer."

It made no difference; the way of life she had enjoyed in fascist Germany (the killing, the sex, and the parties) for over a decade was all but over.

She gave the young man and the five others a small

smile in the dim moonlight and told them, "Worry not! Tonight's mission will be a success."

At the sound of her words, Fischer filled with pride and smiled under his cap.

Looking at him, she gave her first order of the evening, "Assemble the men in front of me, Scharführer Fischer... I'd like to formally address them before we begin."

With a click of his heels and a stiffening of his back, he acknowledged her command with full military vigor, "Yes, Truppführer Müller," then turned to the men, who had fanned out about the hillside and hurled out his order, "Werwolves! Front and center!"

The men, all veterans and devout believers of Nazi Germany's lunatic dream of world conquest, gathered around in a half circle in front of the towering green eyed blonde.

She looked at Fischer and the five tired and bedraggled men and said, "Werwolves of the Third Reich... tonight, we continue to uphold the ideals set forth by our Führer, Adolph Hitler."

They swelled with pride immediately.

She continued, "As Werwolves, no matter what happens in Berlin, we will continue to fight on, whether in the Black Forest of the Fatherland, the sewers of Paris, or the alleyways of Moscow and New York."

Her status in the Nazi party was legendary, cemented by her beauty and validated by her taste for violence.

Considered a virtual Valkyrie from Wagner's famed opera by many, a single tear streamed down Otto Fischer's left cheek as his eyes dined on her beauty while his ears feasted on her words.

"On orders from the German High Command, we

have been instructed to leave nothing for the Soviets or to the Americans," she told them as she gestured with her free hand over her shoulder, "Behind me, down in the valley, is one of the four last functioning electric plants," she paused for dramatic effect and concluded, "It is to be destroyed by us tonight."

Comforted with a mission to fulfill, the men in front of her stiffened with resolve.

She roared into the night, rousing them into patriotic vigor, "For our Fuhrer and for Germany's future!"

Fischer and the five other men cried out in unison, "Yes, Truppführer Müller!"

Smiling at them, she unslung her rifle and addressed Fischer, "Scharführer... I hand these men over to you. I wish you success in tonight's mission."

Suddenly confused, Fischer asked, "Are you not coming with us, Truppführer Müller?"

"No," she replied as she removed her cap, "I'm going to stay behind."

"But... why?" Fischer asked with a pleading tone.

She unfastened the bun on the back of her head and answered as her long blonde hair fell about her slender shoulders, "Because, you were followed, Scharführer Fischer, and they're almost here."

Flabbergasted, his mouth fell opened. He turned to look down the hillside.

"Trust me, Scharführer Fischer... the Soviets will be upon us in a matter of minutes."

Looking back at her, he told her, "I'll send the men ahead... and I'll stay here with you."

"You are a Werwolf of the Hitler Youth, Scharführer Fischer and your orders have been given. Now go and fulfill them to the best of your ability for the Fatherland, for our Führer, and for the future," she told him with a stern tone as she continued to undress.

Hearing her words play upon his Socialist pride, Fischer stiffened his back, clicked his heels again, and said, "Of course, Truppführer Müller," then turned to the five other men and cried out, "Werwolves!"

Eager to begin, they fell into a combat stance in front of him.

Fischer raised his rifle high above his head and yelled, "Forward! For our Fuhrer and for our Germany!"

All five including Fischer rushed towards the power plant in the valley below.

As Fischer ran past her, she reached out and grabbed him by the arm, stopping him in his tracks.

Under the dim moonlight, he looked at her, his eyes alive with youth and vitality.

She gave him a small smile and said, "Good luck."

He returned her smile and said, "Hail Hitler... Else Müller."

"Hail Hitler, Otto Fischer," she replied and released him.

Without a backwards glance, he raced away.

She hadn't lied; the Soviets were in fact coming, off in the distance, she had seen a group of Stalingrad hardened soldiers coming up the road on a flatbed truck.

Carefully she set her machine gun on the soft dew moistened grass and finished undressing until she stood naked in her bare feet under the looming moonlight.

Using her eye's enhanced ability to see in the dark, she watched the Soviet soldiers pull to a stop next to the paneled truck that Fischer and the others had arrived in earlier.

Selecting only the essentials for battle, she

strapped the combat harness of her uniform onto her naked flesh and fastened her only bandolier of magazines across her chest between her bare breasts. She picked up the assault rifle, chambered a round, and then turned into the creature one last time for Nazi Germany.

With its long clawed hand, it grabbed a potato-masher German grenade from its web gear harness, pulled the fuse on the handle, and hurled it at the two trucks parked side by side below in the distance.

With incredible accuracy, the grenade turned end over end as it sailed across the night sky, bounced twice along the narrow dirt road and rolled to a stop under the flatbed.

Waiting for the explosion, the creature gasped with excitement; the killing was about to begin.

The parked trucks lifted into the air in a massive fireball when the grenade exploded, rupturing their gas tank and simultaneously igniting the combustible fluid stored inside.

Seven Soviets instantly met their end in a curtain of gasoline soaked fire and flying jagged pieces of metal.

Using the sudden confusion created by the unexpected explosion, the creature put the German made machine gun to its shoulder and fired an entire magazine into the remaining Soviets below, mowing down two more in the lethal volley of bullets.

The creature pressed the magazine release button on the side of its weapon, grabbed a fresh magazine from the bandolier across its white furred chest, reloaded and then began running down the hillside towards the battle hardened enemy below in a zig zagging pattern as it fired at them with deadly accuracy.

Quickly regathering their wits from the sudden and

expected attack, the Soviet soldiers hastily formed a firing line and returned fire, using the muzzle flash of their unseen adversary's weapon as their only point of reference.

With only their shoulders and helmeted heads exposed from their firing position along the shoulder of the dirt road, the creature killed three more in quick succession with three well placed bursts of machine gun fire as it bobbed and weaved through the onslaught of suppressive fire coming towards it.

Eager to stop the Werwolves from carrying out their objective, a young and battle hardened Soviet lieutenant stepped around from behind the burning remnants of the two trucks and shouted to his men, in Russian, "Keep your eyes open for those Nazi swines… and prepare yourselves to take this hill!"

Suddenly, something dense touched the toe of his boot.

He looked down to see what it was, and the image of his mother tending her rose garden flashed before his eyes.

The creature's last grenade exploded and wet mangled chunks of the twenty year old lieutenant's body showered the remaining soldiers.

Now leaderless, the remaining Soviets soldiers began to shoot wildly into the darkness in front of them.

Running at full speed, the creature emptied the last of its magazines, killing two more, and then let the emptied assault rifle fall from its hands.

Fifty meters from the burning trucks and the last six remaining Soviets, the creature made a hard left and sprinted headlong to the roadside at their right side.

With their night vision hampered by the

smoldering trucks, the Soviets failed to see the creature dash away from their field of fire.

Breathing heavily through its large gaping mouth, the creature drew a pistol from its holster and unsheathed a Hitler Youth dagger from its scabbard.

Firing sporadically into the nothingness of the dark night, they never saw the diabolical smiling creature come towards them on their right side until it was too late.

Now positioned to kill them all in a single file line from their right side, the creature raced up to the first one and drove the ceremonial blade into his neck, severing the carotid artery.

Feeling the lethal stab to his neck, he dropped his rifle and grabbed at the wound in a futile attempt to stem the dark rich blood from gushing out.

Catching unexpected movement to their right, the five remaining leaderless men turned to see what was happening and saw the creature rushing towards them.

Using the effect its appearance had on people when they first saw it, the creature plunged the bloodied dagger into the midsection of the staring soldier who was next in line, puncturing his diaphragm and piercing his heart while simultaneously gunning down the next three with the handgun in its left hand.

The last remaining soldier instinctively raised his rifle to fire.

Seeing the last one about to shoot, the creature threw the dead body still imbedded in its dagger at him.

The corpse soared through the air, its lifeless limbs flayed about in the night sky.

A split second before he pulled the trigger, the full weight of his dead Comrade's body struck him in the chest and knocked him to the ground.

The creature raced forwards, eager to close the distance before the soldier could dislodge himself from under the dead body on top of him.

Struggling to free himself, the young farmhand turned soldier watched in horror as the white monster ran up to him and emptied the pistol into his face thus ending the fight.

The victor, the creature slowly turned back into human form as it watched the disfigured soldier struggle for one final breath of air then die.

Feeling the cool of the night on her face and the radiant heat from the burning trucks against her back, she holstered the pistol and sheathed the dagger both of which would sell for a small fortune on the black market forty years later.

Content with the evening's kill count, she turned on the balls of her blackened dirty feet towards the hilltop and slowly made her way back up.

At the top, she stopped next to her crumpled uniform and boots that had been shined to a parade gloss earlier in the day.

Suddenly, an explosion rolled up to her from the valley below.

Redressing, she smiled and said out loud, "Werw-"

A large pickup truck with a rumbling engine belonging to a pool maintenance company passed in front of the house, pulling her out of her memory.

CHAPTER 32

"She'd find us."

In the early morning hours of the following day, after driving nonstop from Illinois to Minnesota, they had pulled off the road and checked themselves into a hunting and fishing lodge.

Now, with the morning sun peeking through dense clouds high overhead, John stood at the shore of the lake and looked at the span of vast still water spread out before him while his brother slept in their cabin.

The image of his parent's gruesome and humiliating death continued to sear inside his head.

He bent down and picked up the flattest rock he could find, stood, and skipped it across the crystalline sheet of calm water.

The rock bounced three times along the smooth wet surface before disappearing into the dark water.

Motionlessly and lost in the turmoil of his thoughts, he watched the water rebound from the disturbance and return to its mirrored finish.

He closed his green emerald eyes and touched the scar on his forehead as he tried to push back the vivid recollection of his parent's decapitated heads sitting on top of their severed bare feet.

Suddenly, he felt someone behind him. He turned around slowly, composing himself.

Walking towards him, dressed in jeans, a t-shirt, and flip flops, was his brother Billy, ashen faced and gaunt looking.

John silently watched him approach and realized that his brother suddenly looked ten years older. His youthful vigor had all but drained away over the course of a couple of days.

Sunken eyed and haggard, Billy slowly made his way to the edge of the lake.

John greeted him on eggshells, "Hey."

"Hey," Billy answered back in almost a whisper then added, "I was wondering where you were."

John gave the quiet lake a quick glance. "I wanted to let you sleep a bit more so I came out here."

Billy looked down at his sandaled feet. "I didn't sleep too well."

Hearing his brother's sorrowful words, John felt his heart roll over in his chest.

They stared at each other for a few minutes in serene quietness.

Finally, John, feeling the weight of his brother's grief, along with his own, blurted out, "Billy... I'm... sorry."

Billy crossed his arms and looked out across the still lake.

John decided to say nothing else.

A few minutes later, Billy turned back and told him,

"Don't be."

John was struck by what he had just heard and asked, "What?"

Looking squarely into his face, Billy repeated himself, "Don't be," and then added, "It wasn't your fault."

Staring at his brother with his large green eyes, John could find nothing to say in response.

"I mean it, Johnny... it wasn't your fault," Billy said.

Suddenly without notice, hot tears spilled out of John's eyes.

He clamped his hands over his wet face and sobbed.

"It wasn't your fault," Billy calmly repeated the words.

With his hands still covering his face, John nodded his head slowly and said, "Yes, it was."

Billy took a step closer and touched his brother's arm. "I know you, Johnny... and I know that you'd never willingly involve yourself with anyone like that fuck'n whore."

John stooped forward as the tears and sobs poured out of him.

Billy ran his hand up from his brother's arm to his shoulder blade, and said, "You were always the good son to mom and dad. You never did anything wrong... ever. When you got into guns in Junior high and joined the school's gun club... dad worried about that for a bit... but after a while he saw that nothing bad was going to come from it."

John pulled his face away from his hands and looked up at the ashen face staring down at him.

Billy continued, "Growing up, I never heard you once say anything bad about anyone. All you ever did was follow the course... high school, college, then work. I've always looked up to you, Johnny."

Rubbing his hands over his hot wet face, John slowly stood upright.

"I guess if anyone should be sorry it's me... for not telling you that sooner," Billy confessed.

John tried to say something in return but the words bottlenecked in his throat.

Billy finished, "So don't blame yourself, Johnny. You did nothing wrong to make that woman do what she did. You never had it coming just as mom and dad didn't deserve to die how they did."

John reached up and took his brother's hand in his hand and whispered the words, "Thank you, Billy."

Billy took John's other hand into his own. "It's ok."

They let go of each other and, together, they turned and looked at the peaceful lake before them.

Slowly, rich golden morning light spread across the water's surface, eternal and oblivious.

After a while, Billy asked, breaking the silence between them both, "So what now?"

Dragonflies buzzed along the shoreline.

With a long exhale, John turned and replied, "Nothing's changed. We continue going north until we're surrounded by desolation."

Billy listened intently.

He continued, "I leave you in the deepest darkest corner I can find where she can't possibly find you and then I find her... and kill her... ending all this fuck'n madness once and for all."

Billy looked into his brother's large glossy green eyes and said, "This is my fight now... as well as yours."

Not expecting to hear that, John asked, "What do you mean?"

"I mean, she killed our parents, Johnny, not just yours... but mine as well," Billy answered, "I want to help you find her."

Hearing his brother say those words, John closed his emerald eyes and said as he slowly reopened them, "A few days ago... you were a college student... and now you want to be a killer?"

"Yes... because now... our parents are in pieces on our dining room table," Billy replied with a touch of venom in his voice.

In response, John commented, "She told me herself that she's been at it for a long time. Killing is all she does. You wouldn't stand a chance against her."

"And you? What chance do you have?" Billy inquired with a flat tone.

John gave a small chuckle under his breath and answered, "Truthfully, not much of one. I escaped the first two times by pure luck and the third cus she let me live."

"Then why go after her if you know that you can't possibly win?" Billy asked.

John looked down at the sodden ground, thought about it for a bit, and then answered as he looked up at his brother's face, "It's the only plan I have... and I don't know what else to do to protect you."

Billy took a step toward. "We could... just keep... going... together."

John gave the idea a quick smile, let it melt off his face and said, "She'd find us."

Billy thought back to the night at the bar in Cheyenne and knew his brother was right.

John told him, "No, it's better this way. If I kill her then ok... and if she kills me then... perhaps that'll satisfy her enough to let you live."

Billy ingested the words, slowly shook his head, and said, "That's a big 'if' and a really big fuck'n 'perhaps', Johnny."

John nodded his head.

Seeing the situation as hopeless as it was, Billy looked away and stared at the calm body of water again.

John looked at his younger brother and sighed through his nose.

A few minutes later, Billy turned and said, "We could always go to the police. Throw ourselves at their mercy... hope that they believe us."

John took a deep breath, let it out long and slow.

Sensing something, Billy asked, "What is it?"

John knew the time had come to tell him everything.

CHAPTER 33

"This'll do just fine."

With the feel of plush moist earth underneath her bare feet and serene sound of nature all around her, she slowly and deliberately made her way through the thick forested hillside as she looked for the best vantage point available to her.

Savoring the task that lay ahead, she stopped next to a tall pine tree and placed the leather and aluminum case which held her collapsible sniper rifle down on the dark rich dirt.

A lonesome hawk lazily circled high above the treetops.

Surveying the beautiful view spread out in front of her, she smiled then sat down against the tree trunk and said out loud, "This'll do just fine."

CHAPTER 34

"Time is a curse and at times even a prison."

Billy drove through the darkened Minnesota countryside in silence. The outlandish and horrific tale he had been told by his brother earlier in the day still continued to numb his brain like ice.

Sitting at an angle in the passenger seat, John observed his brother with concern.

The night coated farmlands offered little in the way of view or distraction, giving the interior of the car an intense feeling.

Finally, hours after leaving the lodge, Billy finally spoke, "I still can't believe it."

Standing in front of the lake that morning, John had held nothing back and had told his brother every bizarre and fantastic detail about her, the creature, and what he was slowly becoming, and then, to bring the point home, had slashed his palm open down to the bone and tendon in front of him with a pocket knife and had forced him to watch the wound heal right before his eyes.

"I still can't," Billy repeated as he darted his eyes to the dashboard silhouetted form of his older brother sitting next to him, "Yet... there you sit with your hand completely healed after gutting it to the fucking bone."

John said nothing but only listened.

Billy lowered his voice, "So fucking crazy."

John huffed softly in agreement.

"Tell me... was that how you were able to know she was in the house... by that sensation you told me about?" Billy asked.

Knowing that the question was Billy's first step at accepting the harsh reality of their current situation, John said with a frank and open tone, "Yeah... the sensation told me she was somewhere nearby when we arrived at our neighborhood," then added, "Also, when we're totally close to one another the sensation sort of neutralizes itself. I don't know why it does that... it just does."

"Will you be able to feel her better... as time goes on?" Billy asked.

"Yeah, I think so," John answered, "I mean... I think that every day my connection with her grows a little bit stronger as the thing inside me grows. I also think how strong the sensation is, depends a lot on her..."

Billy darted his eyes quickly to John then back to the road ahead. "Meaning?"

"Back in L.A., the very first time I caught the feeling, she was in the process of blowing up a homeless shelter filled with people."

Billy inhaled and exhaled in quick succession.

He continued, "That was the strongest it has ever

been... as opposed to the other times."

Billy glanced over at him with knitted eyebrows.

John shifted his weight in the passenger seat and explained, "What I mean... is that... when she's committing some sort of act of violence the sensation is totally stronger then when she's not."

Billy gripped the steering wheel hard with both hands, "And when that thing inside you is done growing... what then?"

"When it does... then I think our connection will be complete... so no matter where we're at... we'll both know where the other is... at all times."

"So, that's how you plan on finding her... just wait for that thing to completely take over you and then use the sensation to locate her?"

John nodded slowly in the dim light. "I simply don't know how else to do it."

Billy mulled over his next question for a few minutes then asked, "If you do manage to kill her, do you think... what you have inside you... will go away?"

John huffed again and answered, "Well, it seems to work in the movies well enough but frankly... I don't think so. I mean... she bit me. You don't get rid of rabies by shooting the dog that gave it to you. As much as I would love... for that to happen... I don't see it playing out like that."

Billy steered the car into another wide curve.

"My main concern is getting to her before she gets to you, Billy," John reiterated the main part of his plan.

Billy eased out of the curve. "What about mom and dad, Johnny?"

Instantly, John knew what his brother was getting at.

"Sooner or later, their bodies will be found... then

what?" Billy inquired.

"Then... sooner or later, I'll be blamed," John answered.

Billy glanced over at him, "And you're ok with that?"

"I'm not... but what else could the police possibly conclude?" John replied matter of fact.

"How do you figure?" again Billy inquired.

"Well, this is the way I see it... once they find the bodies... they'll try and contact both you and me. They'll come to find out that I inexplicably quit my job, emptied out my savings, 401k, and abandoned my condo, then hauled you out of college in the middle of the night," John answered.

Billy let out a sigh as he stared forward.

"Plus, with all the cameras located in every tollbooth, gas station, hotel, and street corner, they're going have no problem tracking the path of this car directly to the front door of our house."

"You don't sound so concerned about being accused of our parent's murder," Billy stated.

"Remember... I saw her change her appearance right in front of me minutes before she brought an entire stained glass ceiling down on dozens of people. So... if they want to blame me... rather then you... that's ok by me... cus once this thing takes over they're never gonna find me," John commented.

Billy stirred uncomfortably under his brother's cold matter of fact responses and asked, "So what's to become of you while you wait to kill her?"

"Once you're tucked safely way, I'll just keep moving until the change is complete and I find her."

"And afterwards... I mean... if you actually succeed in killing her?" Billy asked.

John looked down at his recently healed hand, thought about the two men in the alley he had almost beaten to death, and answered without looking up, "Become just like her."

Billy sighed at his older brother's words and decided not to say anything else.

Sensing the end of their conversation, John looked forward and watched the headlights of his car tear into the darkened landscape in front of them and wondered if he actually even stood a chance against her or if all his plans were nothing more than fanciful thinking.

Billy kept the car at a steady speed as he continued through the Minnesota countryside towards the Canadian border.

John caught sight of a light up ahead in the distance, bright in its yellowish glow, and quickly realized it was night lamps on a bridge, illuminating its skeletal frame.

Billy continued to drive in silence towards it.

John shifted his weight once again in the passenger seat and narrowed his eyes as he studied the lighted structure that lay up ahead.

Billy suddenly asked as they approached the bridge, "What do you think our chances are of getting into Canada without any problems?"

With his eyes on the bridge, John was about to reply suddenly the tugging in his chest erupted with such maddening force that his mouth clamp shut with a snap.

Billy darted his eyes to his right and called out his brother's name in concern, "Johnny?"

Feeling as though his sternum was going to shatter, John opened to mouth to speak, "Billy, st-"

The sensation had never been to strong.

Now worried and scared at the abrupt change in John's demeanor, Billy asked as the car continued to speed towards the bridge, "Johnny... what is it?"

John mustered up his strength, choked down the overwhelming sensation, and blared out, "Stop the car!"

Confused, Billy turned his head forward but saw only the lighted bridge up ahead and nothing else.

John grabbed Billy's right arm at the bicep and screamed, "Stop the car, Goddamn it!"

The car rolled onto the tarmac of the bridge.

The sensation ceased, the windshield shattered, and Billy's entire left side of his head exploded in a kaleidoscope of meat, skull, brains, and blood.

John hollered in terror as pieces of his younger brother's head splashed across his own face.

The car veered out of control to the right and hit the guardrail with a deafening crunch.

Billy limp foot slipped off the gas pedal.

The damaged car careened violently to the other side.

John braced himself for the second coming impact.

The car smashed into the opposite guardrail and then rolled to a stop.

Unhurt, John opened the passenger side door and tumbled out.

He landed on the bridge's cold tarmac, gathered himself to up onto his knees, reached under the passenger seat, and produced the revolver.

Complete silence and calm return as if nothing had just happened.

Hunkered firmly against the opened passenger door, John focused on his breathing to steady himself as he readied himself for whatever was to come.

Heavy silence resonated all around him.

John slowly turned his head and looked inside the car.

Covered in his own gore and staring blankly into nothingness with his only remaining eye, Billy lay dead in the driver's seat with one hand still on the steering wheel.

John looked away and gritted his teeth as he fought back the urge to rush out from behind his cover and fire blindly into the night.

Then, off to his right, a cartoonish jingle reached his ear.

He turned towards the playful melody, saw a bluish flashing light coming from the banister of the bridge, and realized what it was; a cellular phone.

Looking at it, John's heart sank as he realized who was at the other end of the line.

The small mobile device continued to ring.

He lowered the hammer of the revolver, stood up from behind the protection of the passenger door, and calmly walked, exposed and unprotected, to the ringing mobile phone.

Up on the hilltop, she watched him go to the phone that she had placed on the banister earlier in the day.

He picked it up, pressed the talk button, and, before he could say a single word, she spoke, "You're getting expensive. That's the second phone I leave with you."

The sound of her nonchalant demeanor sent him into a rage, "I'm going to fuck'n kill you! You fuck'n BITCH!"

"That would be called 'purpose', an aspect of life you will come to treasure in the years to come... that is…if you live that long," she casually countered his threat.

John bit down and hissed through clenched teeth, "Did you hear me? I'm going to kill you!"

"Don't be so mad. After all, I did tell you that I was going to kill your family," she informed him, "So it couldn't have come as too much of a surprise."

John gripped the phone tighter as he struggled to keep his composure.

She continued, "In a hundred years from now as you find little solace in anything you do or in anyone you murder, you'll look back at this period of your life and smile fondly," she continued, "Look at it this way… you now have something to work towards that has touched you in a personal level."

"Like killing you," John interjected.

"Providing that you can find me or I don't kill you first."

Simmering into a steady burning anger, John said into the small phone, "Why don't we just get it over with right now… face to face."

Bypassing his words, she told him, "I watched Lindbergh land in Paris… so trust me when I tell you that I've been at this a long time and that 'purpose' is a treasure above all treasures."

"I will find you. Trust me… I will," John told her.

She said, "You have nothing but time to do so," then her voice took on a dark tone as she added, "Time is a curse and at times even a prison."

John stared at the river flowing underneath him.

"I'm done with you… for the time being. However, I'm positive… we'll meet again someday," she told him, "And on that day… we shall see who lives and who dies."

John closed his eyes. "I'll be there."
"See you around," she told him and hung up.

The Boredom with Death

John Belica

BOOK THREE

John Belica

CHAPTER 35

"A whole lot more it would seem."

Three days after his brother's murder, John, carrying all his remaining personal possessions in a single duffle bag, stood in the middle of the largest cemetery in St. Paul, Minnesota.

He had come here to find a new life, tucked away amongst the endless silent rows of etched marble.

Walking from one tombstone to the next, he carefully read the names and dates of each of the dead in order to find exactly what he was looking for.

The noon day sun warmed the nape of his neck.

He removed his ball cap, ran his forearm across his forehead as he glanced up at the sun above him, and wondered just how much more his life could spiral out of control.

"A whole lot more it would seem," he said out loud then topped the cap back onto his head and continued down the row of tombstones.

Hours later as he walked out of the cemetery with what he had come to find, Joliet police, responding to a call from a worried neighbor, entered his childhood home and found the decaying mutilated corpses of his parents.

CHAPTER 36

While her laptop accessed the free internet of the coffee shop, she gazed lazily out the window and watched Cleveland's busy traffic stroll past her.

The day was fresh and the sky was clear.

The fond recollection of her bullet shattering the windshield and hitting its mark with deadly accuracy unexpectedly darted into her mind, causing her to smile dreamily at the memory. Even days later, the killing at the bridge continued to provide her with a warm sense of satisfaction. It had been one hell of a shot.

With all her goals she had set for herself successfully completed, her thoughts turned to the serenity and desolation of the forest.

She figured a couple of years in the forest, living solely as the creature, would grant her a much needed rest from all the commotion, noise, and pollution of the cities.

Plus, a few years left alone would give him ample time to fully evolve into a truly worthy opponent, she thought to herself.

The homepage finished loading.

She shifted her weight on the leather club chair and faced the portable computer.

Her large emerald greens eyes glanced over the day's news and stopped on an article about Mexican drug lords.

She clicked on the headline of the article with an impeccably manicured hand and read its contents.

When she finished, she slowly closed the laptop.

Her plans had just changed and unbeknownst to her so had her fate.

CHAPTER 37

"Hey... this is what 'the beginning' looks like.

John stood, unshaven, at the entry counter of the Liberty Mission homeless shelter and watched the admission attendant begin to fill out his application.

Her tone of voice carried both patience and detachment as she asked him, "What's your name?"

He shifted the weight of the duffle bag on his shoulder and answered, "Douglas Michael Watts." The same name etched on a tombstone at the St Paul cemetery.

"Where are you from... originally?" she asked without looking up.

"From right here, St. Paul, Minnesota," he replied.

"How old are you?" she continued.

John gave the dead infant's age, who had lived just a few weeks, "Thirty."

The ample woman jotted down what he had told her, and said, gesturing with her hand, "I'll need to see your ID."

John reached into his pocket and produced the deceased baby's birth certificate.

She saw the elaborately decorated document and finally looked up at him.

Her eyes met his large glossy green eyes.

"This is all I have," he said as he watched her indifferent expression begin soften.

Staring into his big bright emerald eyes, she heard his words come to her soft and pleasant.

With a sudden agreeable tone, she told him, "I'm sorry... but I need to see some sort of picture ID, sweetie."

Noticing the considerable change in her demeanor since looking into his abnormally radiant eyes, John remembered how he had felt in the parking structure and realized that his new eyes were the cause to her sudden change in demeanor so he kept them trained on hers and said, "It's all that I have."

Feeling a rush of sympathy for the young tired looking man in front of her, she politely asked, "What happen to your ID?"

Feeding off the moment, John replied timidly, "Well... to tell you the truth, I honestly can't remember... I think that either I lost it somewhere or... I sold it for... for liquor."

She felt her heart break even though she had heard the same sort of story many times before and said while her eyes stayed on his, "Well, don't you worry. You came to the right place."

John pulled his hand away from the birth certificate. "Thank you. I need the help."

Sensing that the stranger with the piercing green eyes standing on the other side of the counter was completely trustworthy for some reason, she looked down at the half filled application, slid it aside, and said as she looked back up at him, "You must be tired. Tell you what... I'll fill this out later for you."

He gave her a small sweet smile, "Thank you."

She gave him a broad toothy smile in return and said, "Don't worry about it, that's what we're here for. The important thing is that you get the help you need to take back control of your life."

Sick with himself for having to lie; John simply nodded at the smiling woman.

With a satisfied feeling of doing the right thing, she pushed away from the counter, pressed an intercom button, and said into the aging paging system, "Rodger... could you come to the front?"

A garbled voice replied, "Sure, right away."

She turned back and informed, "You'll love it here. It's what you been looking for."

John gave her another smile, "I believe you."

A few minutes later, walking ahead of him, a portly African American, who had introduced himself simply as Rodger, spoke over his shoulder, "Liberty Mission was founded under the same principles as Alcoholics Anonymous. Which basically means that from this moment on the consumption of any type of liquor is completely prohibited and daily AA meetings are required during your stay."

John kept pace as he listened.

"Since most fail one or both of these requirements within the first few days; the shelter is never really filled to capacity, " he gave a smile and added, "So stretch out... we have the room."

John returned the smile with a nod.

Rodger continued towards the men's quarter as he

continued to speak, "Now, you're more than welcome to leave the facility during day but you must be back inside by ten o'clock… and you must be willing to submit to a breathalyzer test when you return." he gave another smile and said, "Rules of the house… no exceptions."

John smiled again, "No problem."

The heavy set man rounded a corner and continued speaking, "Good… hate having to see people go cus of that."

Walking in a steady pace, John looked around. The building was clean but heavily well used.

Rodger continued with his synopsis, "The AA meetings are given three times a day; nine am to eleven am, two to four, and six to eight. You pick which one works best for you."

John gave a nod of understanding.

Stopping at a set of double doors, Rodger turned and looked at him. "Well… here we are… your new home for the next ninety days, providing that you follow the few rules that we have."

John looked through the square wired glass portholes, saw the large room, the size of a gymnasium, patterned off with cubicles, and said, "Thank you for the opportunity. I can't wait to start those meetings."

The short stubby man smiled and replied, "That's what I like to hear," then pushed opened the left double door and walked them in.

The smell of soap and floor wax greeted John the second he stepped in. The few men that were inside gave him a quick look. A few of them smiled his way.

Standing just inside the threshold, Rodger commented, "The women's quarter is located upstairs which is of course off limits. However, relationships are not prohibited."

John simply nodded again to the words being said to him.

"Now, I'm not saying we're a single's scene or anything like that... all I am saying is that we don't say no to people coming together in that sort of way. It seems that for some going through the program with someone at their side is the key to their success," Rodger started walking forward and added, "We just had our eighth wedding last month... hell of a nice couple."

Weddings and happy couples was the last things on John's mind at the moment so he said nothing in reply.

Unabated, Rodger continued, "Now, if you do complete the ninety day program, you have the option to be transferred to the half-way house of the mission where you'll be allowed to use that address as a place of residence and take one of the many available jobs offered there."

Listening as they walked, John casually ran his eyes about the huge room and took note of the calm and sedate atmosphere.

At the far end, Rodger stopped them in front of a chest high brick walled cubicle and proclaimed, "Well, here you are... your own private villa."

John felt a heaviness drop onto his chest as he looked at the heartbreakingly humble space which consisted of nothing more than a cot, a footlocker, and a single drawer nightstand.

Rodger, accustomed to seeing the mixture of emotions on the faces of all new residents, gently touched his shoulder and told him in a fatherly tone, "Hey... this is what 'the beginning' looks like. Be strong, get clean, and become that great person you know that you are."

Feeling the touch of the man's hand, John pulled himself back into character. "This 'beginning' will do just fine. Thank you."

Smiling at the newcomer's positive words, Rodger dropped his hand. "Every man deserves a second chance... so you're welcome," then added, "Tell ya what... why don't you get yourself squared away and then I'll take ya to the cafeteria. There was plenty of hot dogs and tapioca pudding left over from lunch. I'll whip us up a snack since dinner isn't for another four hours."

John let the strap of the duffle bag fall from his shoulder to the crook of his arm, and said, "Ok, sure. That sounds good. Thank you."

"Cool. I'll be back in a few minutes to come get ya," Rodger responded with one final smile and walked away.

John slid the duffle bag off his forearm onto the floor (he had stowed his cache of weapons in a locker at a bus terminal earlier that morning), sat down on the cot, and quietly observed his new surroundings that were for now his new home.

CHAPTER 38

"Oh, fudge!"

From the driver's seat of her car, Wendy Beltran eyed the donut shop in front of her.

Having struggled with her weight most of her life, Wendy had come to the harrowing and startling realization years ago that she would always be overweight and there was nothing she could take, deny herself, or join to change that.

The manager of the shop took note of the late hour, looked out the window, saw his most frequent and faithful nightly customer in the parking lot, and signaled by tapping on his wrist watch with his forefinger that it was almost closing time.

Catching his gesture, Wendy glanced at the LCD clock of her car and saw it was 9:56, four minutes before the store was scheduled to close.

With haste, she quickly stepped out of her car and rushed inside.

Having come to know each other well enough over

the years, the manager greeted her with a friendly tone, "Hey, Wendy. For a second there... I thought you weren't coming in tonight."

Playfully, like a cowboy from an old Western, she walked her large figure up to the glass display case and said in her best cowboy impersonation, "Well, you know me, Frank... and you know my fix. So, how could you think such a thing?"

Enjoying her sudden company, he held up his open palms in mock surrender. "Hey, just wondering!" then asked, "So, what will it be?"

Mischievously, she bit her lower lip, looked down at the assortment of fried pastries, and studied each distinct row with an expert's eye.

Watching the heavyset woman make her nightly selection, Frank silently felt a tang of pity for her. Tucked underneath the soft excess of her white flesh, he knew, lurked a good looking woman.

With a plump manicured finger, Wendy pointed at the collection of apple fritters and said, "Let me have one of those," then ran her finger over the side and down the front of the glass and added, "And two of the jelly filled."

"I just made the buttermilk bars a little while ago. Care for one?" Frank asked.

She placed her hands flat on the display glass, gave her large painted lips a slight twist and replied, "Mmmm... ok...but just one."

Frank warmly smiled at her and said, "Sure. Coming right up," then started in on her order.

Watching him fill the paper bag with her selections for the evening, she knew how Frank as well as most people felt about her; the happy fat girl resigned to life of excess weight. No matter how much she put on playful smiles and ignored their side long stares, it bothered her as much as it had always had. However, she knew, just like so many like her, that it was her burden to shoulder and hers alone.

Frank set the tongs down on the glass counter and folded the filled paper bag shut, "Ok, kiddo, there ya are."

Wendy reached out and took the bag from his outstretched hand. "Thanks a bunch."

Frank replied, "Sure, anytime," then asked, "Want me to ring you up… or do you want me to tab ya?"

She gave him a smile and answered, "Tab me, Frank. Please. I'm all out of cash."

He smiled and replied, "Sure, no prob."

"Thanks again," she told him as she turned with a whip of her shoulder length chestnut hair and walked out with her nightly snack tucked under her fleshy arm.

Walking to her car, she went for her car keys in the pocket of her cardigan and realized they weren't there.

"Oh, fudge!" she cried out loud as she quickened her pace towards her car.

When she reached it, she tried the driver's door handle and found it unlock.

With a sigh of relief, she realized, in her haste to make it into the donut shop before it closed, she had left the vehicle unlocked and in all likelihood with the keys in the steering column ignition as well.

She opened the driver's side door wide to make room for her ample figure and climbed in.

Once inside, Wendy felt for her keys just behind the steering wheel and exclaimed, "Thank God!" when her soft fingers touched the keys exactly where she had left them.

She closed the door, placed the bag of fried goods

John Belica

on the passenger seat, and drove away into the night
back towards her apartment.

Merged into traffic and looking for a good country
music song to keep her company, she fiddled for a radio
station.

Finally, after a few trial and errors, one of her
favorites erupted over the sound system.

Content with the song, she removed her hand from
the dial and let the familiar lyrics and melody play their
heartwarming message.

Driving and singing along down the highway, she
glanced, almost subconsciously like all well-conditioned
drivers, into the rearview mirror, and saw the greenest
eyes she had ever seen staring back at her.

CHAPTER 39

"By walking around with those big beautiful green eyes of yours."

"I guess when I finally realized that my drinking had become my 'drinking problem' was when I found myself drinking a room temperature beer at ten forty-five in the morning at the bathroom of my work," John said to the room full of recovering alcoholics, who stared at him with knowing eyes and slow nods.

After a week of life in the shelter, he had stepped into his role of a homeless troubled drinker with the speed of a quick study.

He went on, "Until that moment, I had been telling myself that beers during lunch, during dinner, while watching TV, and just before going to bed were just my way of relieving the stress that I faced at work."

.   .   .

His parents' brutal death and demeaning crime

scene had made the national news. His old face; round, clean cut, and brown eyed, along with his dead brother's had been televised under the banner of "Persons of Interest". Undoubtedly, there were no leads as to their whereabouts.

.　　.　　.

The collection of downtrodden men and women looked at his new face, angular, stubbled, and green eyed as they listened to his invented story, "Looking back now... what made that one clear decisive moment in the bathroom take so long was how much I had lied to myself about how bad it had all become."

A fellow AA alumnus grunted his first-hand understanding at what he was listening to.

"Yet... even encased within the smell of piss and shit and warm beer inside that bathroom, I totally didn't come to fully understand just how much I had plummeted until... I found out that the bathroom wasn't my work's bathroom... but a public one in some fuck'n park that I had stumbled into during a three day binge, two weeks after I had been fired."

Listening to his newest member share his story, Rodger placed his hand on John's shoulder in a gesture of comfort.

Slightly ashamed at lying to everyone around him, yet impressed at his success thus far, John kept on and finished his tale, "So it was at that moment... that very moment... that I let the can of beer fall from my hand and I walked out of that public restroom and the shit that had become my life."

Knowing the exact moment as to when to relieve a fellow member from his burden of sharing, Rodger said with a kind smile, "Thank you, Doug," and then started a round of applause for the group to follow suit.

Clapping, one by one, the members of the two to four pm AA meeting took their turn to congratulate the man they had come to know simply as "Doug", "Thank you, Doug," "Thanks, Doug," "Thank you for sharing, Doug," "Doug, thank you," and so on.

John smiled in response to the admiration and swallowed down the swelling guilt lodged in his throat.

Rodger let the applause die down on its own then said to the group of ten, "Alright. Once again, Doug, thank you for sharing your story with all of us for the first time," then adding further, "Now, as with all new members sharing for the first time, donuts and coffee have been provided to us from the shelter director. So... let's all take a break and enjoy the coffee while it's still hot and the donuts while they're still there."

A rumble of approval rolled across the rag-tag collection of former alcoholics as they stood up from their seats and made their way towards the back table at the other end of the room.

John got up from the center chair and slowly made his way there with Rodger at his side who said, "I'm glad you came to us, Doug. Every new chance to help someone recover is a very special thing to all of us here at the shelter."

Being truth, John replied, "You know... I can tell. This place genuinely seems to care about every one here."

Unexpectedly, Rodger stopped, turned, and looked at John directly, "You said that... as if you were merely an observer... not as a fellow recovering addict."

Caught by the man's razor sharp deduction, John returned, "I've never really been a part of anything in my entire life... Rodger... so please just bear with me as I learn to do so for the first time."

Hearing his words and looking into his green eyes, Rodger's wide fatherly smile returned. "Of course... of course," then added thus dropping the subject altogether, "Lets gets some coffee, ok?"

John gave a smile and nod, "Sounds good."

Together, they reached the crowded table and found most of the donuts were already gone.

Roger gave a sigh. He could have killed for a jelly filled.

Two members standing by the window saw Rodger and called out his name beckoning him to come over.

"Get yourself some coffee, Doug. I'll be right back," Rodger told him then waved at the two people at the far left of the large room and went to them.

John gave a nod, took a cup from the tray, and poured himself the hot brew from the urn.

The afternoon sun bled through the cast iron bars and spread warm yellow light into the interior of the meeting room.

Suddenly, to his right, a woman's voice spoke to him, "Hey there, green eyes!"

John turned towards the unexpected voice.

Standing in front of him was one of the four female members of his two to four pm group. Her name he couldn't recall.

Smiling, she continued speaking to him, "You're quite the talk of the town around here."

John held the hot cup in both hands and asked, "How so?"

"By walking around with those big beautiful green eyes of yours," she answered with a toss of her soft curled hair.

John smiled as he realized that she was flirting with him. It had been a long time since such a thing had happened to him that he had almost forgotten what it sounded like. He decided to play along, "Maybe I'll double my efforts and see what happens."

"Or maybe you can have a real cup of coffee at a real coffeehouse with me sometime... and see what happens," she told him with a frank manner.

Caught off guard by her upfront aggressiveness, he dropped his eyes, like a school boy, and said, "Sure... ok."

Getting the desired effect she had been looking for, she extended her hand out to him and introduced herself, "Before you go all watery on me... the name's Rachael by the way."

John pulled himself together and took her hand as he gave her a real good look for the first time. Slightly plus sized, she wore her clothes loose and comfortable while the spirals of her naturally curly amber hair fell free about her shoulders. Her face, pretty in a Gaelic sort of way, carried an air of experience and hope.

He smiled as their hands touched.

She released her hold on his hand first and said, "The story that you shared was very touching. I hope that you do well here."

John lifted the cup of coffee closer to his lips and said, "I plan to."

"Good. I'd like that," she told him as she touched his arm.

With his large emerald colored eyes, he looked at her and absently touched the scar on his forehead.

She watched him touch the scar, gave him another smile and commented, "You know... most people wind up here looking to get clean and to start again...

because either they're running away from something or something ran away from them... but you... you're different."

John pulled his hand away from his forehead.

She gave him one last smile and concluded, "I think you're looking for something... or something is looking for you."

CHAPTER 40

"Certain things are better left unheard."

Sitting with her hands clasped lightly together on the skirt of her grey business suit, she watched the woman on the other side of the desk run through the resume of her last fake identity.

After about a minute, the woman, whose name read Paula Lynn on the name plate at the front of her desk, set the single sheet of paper down on the blotter and said, "Well, Ms. Harris..."

"Please, call me Dina," she delicately interjected with a lipstick smile under her stunning large green eyes.

Paula looked at the pleasant face of the woman in front of her and replied with a smile of her own, "Yes, of course... Dina."

Dina Harris, as the records, fabricated by Glen weeks before she murdered him, indicated her to be, gave a slow feline blink of her emerald eyes and a slight nod.

"Well... Dina," Paula Lynn, Lead Recruiting Officer of Human Resources for the entire city of Cleveland, Ohio, continued, "From what I see here on your resume... you seem to be very well qualified."

"Not too well qualified... I hope," Dina joked in an ever so casual manner as she focused her stare directly into the eyes of her interviewer.

Looking straight into what she suddenly figured were the most amazing pair of eyes she had ever seen, Paula replied, after a quick laugh of her own, "No, not at all. You're actually exactly what we've been looking for since-" she broke off mid-sentence and looked away.

Playing her part perfectly, Dina leaned forward and asked, "What's the matter? What's wrong?"

Fighting back tears, Paula answered, "I'm sorry... but it is just... that I... I mean we... all of us here are still coping with the loss of our last director."

Dina gave a heart rendering look of utter concern and inquired, "Tell me what happened? Talking about it always helps."

Paula looked into the eyes of the woman sitting on the other side of her desk, felt a wave of trust suddenly wash over her for some reason, and said, "Two weeks ago... our director was murdered."

Dina leaned back into her chair, "My God. I had no idea. I'm so sorry," then added, "How?"

"From what we've been able to gather, from what little we've been told, it seems that she went out during the night to fetch something to eat and-" Paula stopped again, unable to continue.

Fighting back the urge to laugh in the woman's face, transform into the creature right in front of her, and then rip her face to pieces, Dina knuckled down and stayed in character, "Let it out. You'll feel better. Trust me."

Paula looked back into the large green soulful eyes that were staring at her and continued, "We were all questioned. Once we were all cleared, one nice policeman was kind enough to tell us what little they knew. It seems that Wendy, our last director, was assaulted at some point while she went out for a snack during the night."

Hot tears spilled out form the woman's eyes.

Doing what she could from showing the pleasure of hearing the effects of her efforts, Dina gently pressed, "It's ok... go on."

"They, the police, I mean, believe someone worked their way into her car, took her to a secluded place, and then... killed her."

Dina stared and listened.

"Some kids, taking a short cut to school, found her body still in her car under an overpass not far from where she lived."

Holding back a smile, she asked, "Did they tell you how she was..."

"Killed? No," Paula said, "Since it is an ongoing investigation or so they tell us, they haven't said how. And quite frankly I really don't want to know. I don't think I could handle it."

'I severed her right breast down to the ribcage then cut open her throat as she screamed' she wanted to tell her but instead told the crying woman, "Certain things are better left unheard."

Paula looked down at her desk, let the bulging tears spill out, and replied with a whimper, "Yes... I guess, you're right."

Dina reached out, grabbed a tissue from the dispenser on the desk, and handed it to the woman,

"I'm here for you... Paula."

Paula took the tissue, looked up at the woman's face and replied, "Thank you."

Dina leaned back into her chair and patiently waited for the woman to compose herself.

After a few minutes, Paula exhaled a deep breath and said, "Well, perhaps you'd like to hear a little bit about our pool?"

With a soft friendly smile, Dina answered, "I'd like that."

"Well, we have one of the very few privately owned facilities on city land," Paula told her, "In fact our pool was here before the city of Cleveland constructed the public park around it. The pool is Olympic grade for both diving and swimming. The retractable roof which was installed just a little over two years ago has made our pool the only full size indoor outdoor swimming pool that operates year round within a three states area."

Dina gave an impressed expression, "Wow, sounds very impressive."

"It is... we're very proud to have such a wonderful facility," Paula returned.

Dina gave another warm smile.

Paula ran the palm of her hand over the resume sitting on her blotter and said with a sudden touch of unease, "If I can be perfectly honest... it has been only two weeks since Wendy was killed... and we've just getting around in finding a replacement for her position... so before I can make a decision on who we'll choose... I have to review and interview many more applicants."

Waiting for such a moment to arrive, Dina leaned forward, smiled seductively, and let the emerald green irises of her eyes revolve around her onyx black pupils.

As if falling into a bath of warm water, Paula felt her body fill with calming soothing warmth as her own eyes locked onto the large green eyes just in front of her.

Slowly, with her eyes locked into the woman's brown eyes, she said in a gentle yet commanding voice, "I'm the one you want. You will give me the job."

Staring, Paula said nothing.

The minutes ticked away as a deafening silence fell upon the small office as they stared into the other's eyes.

Finally, the woman that everyone would come to know as Dina, Director of The Thomas A. Lean Olympic Swimming Facility for The City of Cleveland, brought her spinning irises to a halt.

A sliver of saliva held at the corner of Paula's mouth as she continued to stare absentmindedly at the woman in front of her.

Knowing the power of her eye's ability to seduce all too well, she stood up and went for the door, knowing the job was hers.

With the connection severed, Paula blinked her eyes and shook her head.

Her fingertips touch the brass doorknob.

"Stop," Paula called out.

Smiling, she turned around.

Still seated at her desk, Paula dabbed a spot of wetness at the corner of her mouth with her right middle finger and asked, "What are your plans... when you start?"

"The kind that people will talk about... forever," she answered.

CHAPTER 41

"Sooner would be better."

Standing in his bare feet and dressed only in a pair of boxers, John stood in front of the mirror of the men's room hours after everyone had gone to sleep.

With his hands poised on the cool ceramic sink, he stared into the mirror with his large unnaturally green emerald eyes.

He had seen her change her appearance right before his eyes during their encounter at the Tea and Sympathy gala which meant sooner or later he would be able to do the same as well.

Narrowing his eyes in concentration, he leaned closer into the mirror in another attempt to shift his appearance in any way and whispered to himself, "In my current state of affairs... sooner would be better."

Though the murder of his parents and the disappearance of both his brother and he were no longer being broadcast on an hourly basis, they were nonetheless still being profiled regularly on TV and the internet. How long his loosely fabricated identity would hold before he was discovered was perhaps only a matter of time.

He pushed away from the mirror, whispering, "Nothing."

The ability to shift his appearance just like she could, it seemed, still needed more time to develop within him.

John leaned forward into the mirror once again and whispered at his reflection, "Sooner would definitely be better though"

CHAPTER 42

"You have more to offer than that."

"Now, don't get me wrong or anything, I love my kids, ok. It's just that what she keeps asking for is just too much for me to pay. I mean, I got bills of my own, ya know? Shit. Hell, I believe that I'm a good father and all. I'm following the rules the court imposed on me," Daniel Wharton Williams, a large heavy-set black man, said in the crowded pub as he gripped his drink of cognac and lime on the rocks like a life preserver.

Looking directly at him with her bright green eyes, she said in a soothing manner, "I understand. People just don't get... how hard it is to do the right thing."

He gripped the glass even harder and exclaimed, "Damn right! I'm doing the right thing. Paying and paying and paying and paying but does anyone ever see that? Fuck no! They only look when I am late with a payment or when I miss one."

With an Oscar worthy look of sympathy on her face, she nodded her head in acknowledgement.

The large slow brute, with who she had asked to share a table, continued talking, "Shit, I'm all alone in this. I know for a fact she's fucking some other dude. Look, don't get me wrong, I don't give a flying fuck who she's fucking... all I'm saying is just don't let my kids see that shit. Show some respect. And if he's staying the whole night then why not ask him for a little help with the goddamn diapers. I mean, I'm all alone on this."

It had taken her over a week to find the person with access to what she needed to fulfill her newest plan of mass murder.

"Life is all about money," he kept on, "If I were to make more at the plant then they take more... and if I make the same or less then they're all over my shit for paying so little. I mean, shit, I'm damned if I do and really damned if I don't."

She gave him a warm smile. "Daniel, I think you're right. It just isn't fair the way people are treating you."

He looked across the pub table at her, took in her beauty, and questioned, "Really? You think so?"

She reached out, across the wooden circular table, touched his large hand, and answered, "I know so. I also know that you're a good man put in an almost impossible situation which you simply can't win."

Looking directly into, what he considered, the most beautiful pair of eyes he had ever seen, Daniel told her, "I am a good man and a good father who... you're right... is in an almost impossible spot to be in."

What she needed from him required more convincing than the power of her eyes could give her so she listened intently and pretended to care.

"I really don't know what the hell to do. I know that I need a better paying job, but, at the same time, I'm only three years away from my pension at the plant," he said to the woman he had just met then drained the last of his drink with a quick toss.

Taking the empty glass from his hand, she asked, "Would you like another? My treat."

He looked her over with the eyes of good fortune and answered, "Yeah, ok, sure."

Using the same appearance she used during the interview to land the job at the swimming pool, she turned around, caught the waitress' eye, and signaled for another round to be brought over to them.

While they waited for their drinks to arrive, he slithered his gaze over her face and body. "Damn girl, you sure are beautiful. What the hell are you doing here listening to my ass go on and on about my goddamn problems."

With another warm seductive smile, she answered, "Don't know. I guess... I like goddamn problems."

He looked down at his hands and said, "Well, then... you picked the right table to sit at tonight cus that's all I have to offer... goddamn problems."

She reached out and took his hand again and told him, "You have more to offer than that."

Feeling the soft tender flesh of her hand, the rush of an erection flowed into his penis.

The waitress arrived with their drinks, sat them on the table, and left without saying a word, wondering why any woman would give such a wreck of a man a single second of her time.

She let go of his clammy roughened hand and took her drink, a Sidecar.

Taking his, he told her, "I tell ya, sitting here with you, all these people must be just fuck'n green with envy."

"Why?" she said, playing her part, "I'm no one

special."

He stopped the course of the glass going to his lips and said, "I don't know about that but you're really beautiful."

Pretending to be shy, she playfully covered her face. "Well thank you. You're not so bad yourself."

Not being complimented for just about anything, much less his looks, for as long as he could remember, Daniel, with a genuine tone of surprise, exclaimed happily, "Who me? Shit, lady, you must be blind to say such a thing."

She gave a shrug, smiled, and took a drink.

He drank from his glass, sat it on the thick paper coaster, and commented, "Man, if you had met me twelve years ago before that bitch came into my life... I would have shown you a real fine time," he swirled the ice cubes in the small puddle of liquor at the bottom of his glass, "But now I just don't have the money."

Seizing the golden moment that she had been waiting for, she asked, "Would you like to?"

He looked up at her, "Like to...what?"

"Have the money," she answered with a smile.

CHAPTER 43

"It's just the beginning that I always keep to myself."

Standing in line inside the coffeehouse located three blocks from the shelter, John turned his head and looked at Rachael who sat at the far side of the crowded room and wondered again if accepting her invitation for a cup of coffee had really been the best of ideas. However, her company and the friendship they had struck up over the course of their daily AA meetings helped him forget, if only for just the briefest of moments, the recent events in his life and his uncertain future looming in the near distance.

He looked at her closer. Sitting on a tattered sofa, which seemed to be the standard choice of furnishings in most coffeehouses, Rachael stared out the window with a quiet smile. Wearing her trademark purple sandals made from some sort of supposedly indestructible plastic and loose linen dress, she carried an air of tranquility won by defeat.

A man wearing a dull grey suit tapped his shoulder

and gestured with his chin towards the cashier.

John turned to the front and saw the line had moved forward, he was next.

Pre-assigned music played softly from the overhead sound system.

He ambled up the counter, which was cluttered with a multitude of packaged snacks and fusion Jazz CDs, and placed their drink order, paying with a twenty he had snatched from his duffle bag.

The two coffees he ordered went into the barista`s queue.

Waiting, John took a moment and looked around the small and cozy coffeehouse. People milled about or sat around small wooden tables enjoying the day seemingly oblivious to nothing more than their conversations and steaming cups.

Watching them, a touch of sadness struck his heart as he recalled the life he left behind and his family that no longer were.

A young female barista of about nineteen called out his name. Douglas.

John turned towards the sound of the dead infant's name.

Smiling professionally, the girl extended two decorated white paper cups to him.

With a smile and a nod, he took them from her and grabbed a serving tray on his left.

Rachael turned away from the window and saw John walking to her with two coffee cups and condiments on a stylish wooden tray.

Weaving through customers, he smiled warmly at her when their eyes met.

She smiled softly back and shifted her weight away from the window.

John sat the tray on the small chess table, cleared off all the playing pieces, in front of her and took a seat at her right side.

Ready to make the most of her coffee, she let the purple sandals slip from her feet and tucked her red painted toes underneath her on the sofa.

Succulent clouds of velvet and toffee notes rolled out from the two steaming cups of coffee.

Watching him set the small table, she couldn't help but wonder how completely odd and at times how unfair life was. A different time and a different place perhaps they could have been doing the exact same thing just not as recovering alcoholics living in a shelter.

John passed her cup and then took his own before settling into the narrow deck chair.

Rachael picked up her cup, brought it slowly to her lips, and took a sip of the hot black liquid.

The rich and robust Guatemalan blend instantly filled her with a sense of well-being and relaxation.

Watching her, John drank from his, careful not to burn himself.

She exhaled contently and set the cup down on her lap.

John smiled and commented, "Wow. I've never seen anyone enjoy a cup of coffee quite like that."

Shifting her bare feet underneath the folds of her sea foam linen dress, she replied, "Well, that's been my problem... I enjoy everything like that... even the not so good things."

He caught her meaning, thought about changing the subject, decided not to, and he asked, "Is that what brought you to the shelter... enjoying everything like that?"

She took another sip, pulled the paper cup away

from her lips, and answered, "Yes."

He gave a simple nod and waited to see if she would elaborate.

She wrapped her large lovely hands around the warmth of the cup, looked into his eyes, and said, "When I met my husband... well, my x-husband now, I felt that my entire life had found a linear sense of existence. He was everything to me... everything. I lived with the sole purpose of living for him."

John listened without movement, without sound.

"As he studied to become a commercial pilot, the world seemed to contain only the two us. He left in the morning, returned for lunch to the little apartment we rented above a video store, went back, then promptly at six he would return and eat the dinner I had prepared him. Later, we would talk about his day. I'd help him study and then we'd make love the entire night."

Another sip and she continued, "It went like that for years. My love for him only grew and grew to the point that, at times, I felt I could actually feel his heart beat miles away. Living above that video store was the happiest time of my life."

John continued to look into his her eyes as he listened.

"When he finally graduated he took the best offer from the many that were already waiting for him... trans-Atlantic flights. With a staggering salary, benefits, and an almost magical prestige, he became in reality what I had always knew he was... a man touched by God Himself."

She had never mentioned this part of her life in any of their AA meetings.

"Suddenly," she went on, "I found myself alone for the first time in years but not just alone... alone without him. His flights took him away from me for weeks at a time. I felt like I was being buried alive in an empty hole. Even the glorious house he purchased for me… for the family he said we were going to create, didn't offer anything but a deeper hole."

She lifted the cup back up to her mouth, stopped, and went on, "You see… he was all I wanted, all that I cared for… all that I loved. So… without him at my side, I wanted nothing, cared for nothing, loved nothing."

She gave a small sigh and pressed on, "Then 'it' stepped into my life and gave me what he couldn't… the promise, the bond to never ever leave my side. To always be there for me whenever I needed it, regardless of the time… day or night. Drinking."

John gave a nod, pretending to understanding.

"It filled the hole, completely, quickly, effortlessly. And with that hole filled, it and I began to build our lives together… without him. In a rapid span of time, he went from being my 'everything' to a 'someone' trying to take away my 'only thing', and, by God, I wasn't going to allow anyone to do that."

"He tried everything to pull me away from it, everything. He quit his job at the airline and bought a sandwich franchise so he could be with me… but by the time that happened all he was doing was being in the way."

She looked at him again and finished, "When it all came to an end, he found himself bankrupt and once again behind the controls of a jumbo jet over the Atlantic and I found myself laughing at anyone's stupid jokes at whatever bar I hadn't been thrown out of before so long as I could manage a free drink out of it."

With another sigh, she gave her Coda, "I even slept with a man for money once."

He only looked at her, knowing it was best to say nothing.

Together, they sat in silence as time moved slowly between them.

After a while, Rachael broke the heavy silence, "Quite a story, huh, Green eyes?"

Looking down at his cup of cold coffee, John smiled at the sound of the nick name she had given him and replied as he looked back up at her, "Yes... quite a story."

She sat her own cup of cold coffee on the chess table. "The rest you know from the AA meetings. It's just the beginning that I always keep to myself."

"Why? Why don't you share that part with the rest of the group?" he asked candidly.

"I don't rightly know... to be honest. I guess keeping that part private is my way of coping," she answered.

John sighed and asked, "Then why tell it to me? Why share something that's so private for you... with me?"

She leaned forward a bit and answered, "It's your eyes. I look at them and I feel like I could tell you anything. Those big beautiful green eyes... make me... trust you."

CHAPTER 44

"That was the last of them."

Tired after another long day at the pool's administrative office, she slowly made her way with her black leather pumps in her hand down the weathered carpet of the hallway to the apartment she was able to rent using her fake identity.

Though her plan was coming along at the pace she wanted, the grueling schedule in making it all come together was exhausting and long.

She reached the door to her small sparsely furnished one bedroom apartment, slid the key into the doorknob, turned it, and opened the flimsy door.

Darkness and the warm smell of confined air were the only things to greet her as she walked in and closed the door softly behind her.

Inside, she let her shoes and key ring fall from her hands onto the wooden floor.

With the greenish night vision that her eyes provided, she walked between the leather sofa and coffee table to the ottoman at the far side of the living room.

She dropped her tired body into it with a sigh of relief.

Feeling the soft supple leather conform to the figure of the body, she closed her eyes and listened to the bustle of traffic outside as people made their way to their homes and families.

She inhaled the warm air trapped in the apartment.

Slowly the cool wooden floor beneath her hot feet and the comforting caress of the leather cushioning of the ottoman allowed her body to relax and her mind to wander.

Softly she exhaled the warm mint scented breath from her lungs and saw...

The small apartment's door slowly opened.

Dressed in a khaki twill hunting dress with a pair of chestnut brown riding boots, she sat on a moth eaten fabric and wooden chair in the darkness of the dingy Brazilian apartment with a silenced semi-automatic handgun in her hand as she watched the silhouette of a portlier and older Otto Fischer appear within the doorframe.

Unaware of her presence in the unlit stifling hovel, Otto closed the door behind him and then went for the table lamp on the end table.

She cocked the small gun's hammer and spoke in German, "Leave the light off, Otto."

At the sudden sound of the unsuspecting voice in his native tongue, he stiffened and slowly pulled his hand away from the dangling chain under the lampshade.

With her eye's ability to see in near total darkness,

she looked him over. Dressed in pants from one suit and the jacket of another, Otto Fischer, the once crowning example of the proud and deadly Hitler Youth, carried the years of hard living like an unwanted badge of dishonor. His golden blonde hair of years ago now hung in weightless wisps about his balding head and his white creamy skin of his Aryan heritage now bore the leathery tan given to him by the harsh South American sun.

As his eyes adjusted to the low light in the apartment, Otto straightened and spoke in German at the faint slender figure sitting in the dark in front of him, "It has been a long time… Else Muller."

She smiled. "That it has… Otto Fischer."

Hearing his real name for the first time in over thirty years, he felt a wave of mixed emotions sweep through him.

Enjoying the sweet moment of the impending kill, she asked, "How have you been, Otto?"

"Tired," he answered with the simple truth.

"It has been a long road to this moment… has it not?" she asked as she slowly pointed the gun barrel at him.

"Was it Klaus Breker that turned me in? To save his life?" he answered with a question of his own.

"Yes… it was he… that turned you in," she replied, "And it didn't save his life."

"I see," he slowly shook his head.

"If it's any consolation… it took four of his molars, two fingers, and one eyeball for him to finally give you up," she told him as the memory of the torture she had inflicted on the elderly man flickered and dance in her mind's eye in vivid detail.

Otto confessed, "I should have never started that

correspondence with him... but one gets so lonely... for even just a few words from anyone familiar."

"Take comfort, my dear Otto... your friend's screams lasted only as long as were necessary," she informed him, smiling in the dark.

He looked about the cramped and rundown apartment for the final time. "So who are you working for now? Mossad?"

"Yes... Mossad," she answered.

"You know... the funny thing is... I never even saw a Jew during the war... much less even hurt one," he told her, "But I guess that doesn't matter... does it?"

"No... it doesn't, Otto," she replied.

"So, now you're killing for the Israelis. Killing the very Germans who once stood beside you... in defense of the Fatherland. Is that it?" Otto asked her bitterly.

"No... not Germans... Nazis," she proclaimed.

"So am I to die by your hand... tonight, Else Muller?" he asked with a proud tone.

"It is all that I have to give you, old friend," she answered.

She aimed the weapon directly at his belly.

"Just one last thing, Else Muller.", he quickly said, "That night when we attacked the power plant... I turned back and ran back up the hill to help you... and I saw... I saw you tur-"

She pulled the trigger.

The gun clicked, the silencer puffed, and a hollow point bullet struck Otto just above the naval.

Otto Fischer dropped to his knees in front of her, covering the bleeding hole in his belly with both hands.

Taking her time to lengthen the taste of the kill, she casually stood up, walked up to him, and leveled the tip of the silencer to his left eye.

Bleeding and going into shock, he looked up at her and said, "I saw you-"

She pulled the trigger a second time and sent a bullet through his left eye and into his brain.

Otto crumpled at her feet and died.

She slowly lowered the weapon.

The smell of gunpowder and blood mixed in the heavy air.

She took a step back away from the body and then said out loud, this time in Hebrew, "Done."

From the darkness of the apartment, three Mossad agents stepped out.

Aviv, the leader of the small band of assassins, congratulated her, "Good work, Else."

With the greenish night vision of her eyes, she stared down at the murdered body and said, "That was the last of them."

Aviv gave a regrettable sigh and replied, "Not quite," then fired.

With the slightest of sounds, the silenced bullet from his gun struck her in the back.

She gasped at the sudden burst of pain and toppled onto Otto's dead body.

From Aviv's left, Yinon, the second in command, spoke as he slowly approached, "Even though you had been fucking her half across South America, Aviv... you just did the right thing... she was a Nazi and a Werwolf."

Aviv looked down at the darkened female figure and let out a long slow breath from his nose, remembering the nights of passion and rapture they had shared together, interlaced in each other's arms.

At his right, he heard Lior, the youngest of the group and a veteran of the Six Days War, "It was what Central Command wanted, Aviv. You had no choice."

Without taking his eyes off her, Aviv erupted, "I know what Central wanted! I certainly don't need either of you to remind me!"

Both Yinon and Lior exchanged concerned glances in the dim light.

Aviv continued to stare down at the woman he had just shot. Though she had been a Nazi and at one point a concentration camp director, he had, in some way, fallen in love with her over the course of their mission.

Feeling the weight of the double murder, Yinon broke the uncomfortable silence, "Aviv, we must leave. It is unwise to stay here any longer."

Aviv swallowed hard then gave a slow nod of understanding.

Lior spoke next, "Remember the 'gesture', Aviv."

Yinon added, "Yes... the 'gesture'... Aviv... don't forget the gesture."

Feeling suddenly annoyed at the very sound of their voices, Aviv snapped at them for the second time, "I haven't forgotten the fuck'n 'gesture'... alright! No matter how much I fucked her."

Hearing the edge to his voice, both men on either side of him said nothing further.

Aviv focused his mind back to the unfinished mission at hand and approached her body.

Yinon watched in silence as the man he had come to value as a brother prepared to fire into the dead woman's face.

Aviv clasped his hand on her shoulder and turned the still warm body of the woman whose name he had whispered into her ear over the course of a year and a half.

With a light fragile ease that made his heart sink, he rolled her over onto her back.

Intrigued by what he had heard the old man say, Lior suddenly asked, "What did Fischer mean when he said 'I saw you'?"

Aviv raised his handgun up to her face as he prepared to administer the symbolic act of shooting their Nazi targets in the left eye for "having witnessed" the atrocities committed to so many Jews in Europe during the war.

Aviv placed the tip of the silencer against her left eye.

Suddenly overcome with a feeling of foreboding, Lior asked again, "What did he mean by that?"

Aviv looked into her delicate face and remember their final night in Sao Paulo where their bodies had intertwined into one on the roof of their motel.

"Aviv... wait! What he did he mean-," Lior cried out.

A silenced gunshot clicked.

Aviv fell backwards with a bullet hole under his chin.

Raising herself up with one hand and pointing the gun at them, her mouth tore at the sides all the way to her ears.

Startled into action from something so unexpected, Yinon and Lior simultaneously raised their weapons and fired into the semi-darkness.

One round caught her in the right breast. Skin, fat, blood, and gland matter from her destroyed breast exploded inside her dress.

Pushing back the staggering pain, she fired her last four bullets in quick secession at them both.

Three bullets hit Yinon in the chest and the forth caved in Lior's face.

With everyone dead except herself and clouds of

gunpowder smoke drifting inside the small apartment, she let the empty handgun slip out of her grip and land with a dull thud onto the old and stained rug.

Struggling against the overwhelming pain of her gunshot wounds, she pushed herself up to a standing position, crying out in pain as her vision swam towards the blackness of unconscious.

Aviv's bullet, still lodged inside her, was scrapping against her organs and the tattered remains of her breast were rubbing underneath the coarse fabric of her dress.

Feeling as if she were about to lose her bodily functions and shit herself from the pain, she bit down against it and started across the small living room towards the bathroom.

Doing her best not to trip over any of the dead bodies, she carefully maneuvered her feet around them.

Suddenly, to her horror, the last of her strength gave out and she collapsed back down onto the sofa she had been waiting in for Otto to arrive.

With her dress stained dark with thick blood, she realized that unless she got a hold of herself and allowed the abnormally rapid healing factor that she possessed to take over she would almost certainly die within the next few minutes so she relaxed her breathing, focused on a fixed point on the front door of the apartment and...

She picked up her cellular phone from off the end table next to the ottoman and pressed the green Send button with her thumb.

The phone dialed the last number that had been called.

CHAPTER 45

"I simply live to kill."

After an utterly relaxing night time shower, John laid on his cot reading a paperback Western, which he had checked out from the shelter's small library earlier in the day, as he waited for the lights to go out promptly at ten o'clock.

Suddenly, coming from within his footlocker a muffled vibrating sound reached his ear.

John lowered the book and listened carefully.

The vibrating sound continued.

He set the book aside, swung his feet onto the cold concrete floor and looked at the small wooden crate at the foot of his cot.

The sound kept on.

John went to the footlocker and opened it.

The vibrating sound increased in volume.

With a small sigh, he reached in and pulled out the same cellular phone that had been left for him on the bridge on the night of his brother's murder. Though he had destroyed the one given to him at the hotel, he had held onto this one, bought a charger for it, and kept it at the ready in case she called as it seemed she was doing now.

He pressed the green Send button and spoke into it with a flat emotionless tone, "What do you want?"

Her voice, tired sounding yet laced with a mischievous quality, reached his ear, "So you kept the phone. How sweet of you."

"What do you want?" John asked again, absently touching the scar on his forehead.

"Just felt like calling. We haven't spoken in a while. In fact, the last time we did... was right after I blew your brother's face off."

The image of his younger brother's death flashed across his mind and John snarled through his teeth, "If you've called just to get a rise out of me for your own amusement... you can forget it."

"I didn't call for that... even though, I must admit, you have brought me a great deal of enjoyment," she told him, "In fact, more than I've had in many years to be honest."

"Then why did you call?" John asked as he walked to the men's room for more privacy.

"To tell you... that... I know where you are," she answered his question in her usual casual manner.

He stopped dead in his tracks.

The icy cold tiled floor of the bathroom under his bare feet barely registered.

Finally, after what felt like an eternity, John asked her, "And where is that?"

"You're in a homeless shelter in St. Paul, Minnesota," she answered.

Bewilderment impacted into him like a freight train

hitting the side of a building.

"Are you still there, John?" she asked as if speaking to an old friend.

"Yeah, I'm still here," he replied, "What makes you think that I'm in some homeless shelter?"

"Oh, it's pretty easy to figure out. You see, John... after I shot your brother, I watched you push your car into the river with his body in it... and I saw you walk back the way you came."

John listened intently.

"Associated with the murders of your entire family... your only alternative, apart from turning yourself in and quite possibly spending the rest of your life telling an outlandish tale about monsters and shapeshifters from behind bars, was to hide in plain sight in a major city," she took a long breath, let it out, and continued, "And since you were walking, the closet major city is St. Paul... and the only place to stay without arousing too much suspicion is in one of its many homeless shelters... without using your real name or your credit cards, which... by the way...is how I was able to track you most of the time."

Numb at how seemingly smart she was, John closed his eyes and said nothing.

"Now, for maximum anonymity, you probably chose one of the three largest shelters that city has to offer; New Horizon, Liberty Mission, or True Beginnings. And since True Beginnings is primarily for recovering drug addicts via Medicare and New Horizon mainly shelters blacks... I guessing it's Liberty Mission."

Finding his voice, John opened his eyes and said, "Not bad. So why don't you call the police and have me arrested for your murders since they believe...I'm the one responsible?" then added, "Or better still... why not just come over here and kill me?"

"If you recall... I once gave you the chance to hand yourself over to me... so that I could... kill you quickly... but you refused," she simply stated, "So now... I want what you want."

"And what might that be?" he asked.

"For you to live," she answered matter-of-factly.

"What for?" he wondered into the phone as he walked to a sink.

She answered, "So that I may have a truly worthy opponent."

"And when that happens... what then?" John asked then added, "Are you going to kill me too with a bullet fired at long distance?"

"No... of course not," she replied, "We'll have ourselves a good old fashioned showdown. A 'last person standing' kinda thing."

Feeling a sudden dose of bitter anger grow inside him, he growled into the small phone, "My parents and my brother didn't have to die for that to happen. You didn't have to kill them."

"You're right, I didn't have to... but I did and they are. It wasn't personal... it just... turned out that way," she told him, "And if by chance... you're the one who gets to live... then one day you'll know... just how impersonal killing will become."

John closed his eyes at the insane conversation he was having with his family's killer.

"Still there, John?" she asked.

"Yeah... I'm still here," he replied and said, "Tell you what... why don't you go out and bite a whole bunch of people and infect them... that should give you all the worthy opponents you can handle... and keep you entertained".

"Don't you think... I've thought about that a thousand times as I've watched the world spin on its axis decade after decade... as I've stared at the days and nights blend into an endless stream of light and dark?" she returned.

"Why haven't you then?" he questioned.

She remained silent over the phone.

He insisted, "Well... why haven't you?"

"Because of it... the thing inside me and now inside you, doesn't let me," she finally answered.

John felt himself go slightly numb at the answer.

She added, "I simply live to kill. There has been no other purpose to my life since I was bitten other than to kill person after person... one at a time or in large numbers. It doesn't want to create an army of monsters or to conquer the world... it just wants to see death... hands on."

He kept the phone to his ear and stared into the mirror directly into his own eyes.

"You see, John... you're a fluke... an oddity," she told him, "You've survived two attempts on your life, you've become infected, and you've even come after me. However, after it's all been said and done... in the end... there can only be one of us... the creature within will not allow another."

"Believe me, bitch... it's going to be me," he told her.

"Since what's inside me is now inside you... that's exactly what I expected to hear you say," she confessed.

"You want me to finish becoming that thing... fine... but when I'm done I'm going to find you... and then I'm going to kill you," he told her.

She slowly clicked her tongue and said, "Take all the time you need, John, as you'll learn soon enough...

time is now meaningless."

John rubbed his face, exasperated.

With a smile on her end, she told him, "Anyways, I'm currently busy planning the deaths of another couple of hundred people... so I can wait."

"Just know... that the next time we meet... I'm not going to be the same person you so easily beat on that Los Angeles rooftop," he warned her.

"And then we'll see... on that day... if you're truly worthy of being the only one," she said into the phone and hung up.

CHAPTER 46

"Death is life. Kill to live."

Wearing only a pair of shoes, slacks and t-shirt, John dashed out of the shelter's double doors and ran at full sprint down the street into the night as her mischievous voice and mocking tone continued to resonate inside his head.

With an indescribable swelling anger at the woman who had completely shattered his entire life and murdered his parents and brother, he blindly ran past bystanders on the sidewalk.

Focused on the mounting surge of acidic rage boiling within him for her rather than anything else, John cut right across double lines of traffic without even a side long glance.

The sound of screeching tires and startled honks were only an echo to his ears as he bolted down a long and darkened alley, its length cluttered with garbage bins and strewn trash.

Alone and cradled by massive buildings on either

side with a crescent moon looming overhead, he raced with an unbelievable level of speed, impossible for any normal human, down the wet and foul smelling narrow alleyway.

'How sweet of you,' her words suddenly boomed in his head.

He poured on the speed in an effort to outrun her voice.

Slowly the memory of the two innocent men he had severely assaulted in Los Angeles came to mind. Their cries of pain and the look of stunned agony on their faces bellowed out of the darkness of his mind.

Running ever faster, he pushed them back as best he could and caught sight of a fire escape ladder extended halfway down the side of the building on his left.

With the gathered momentum of his run, he leaped onto a covered garbage bin then launched himself an incredible twenty feet into the air and slammed into the ladder, catching it with a desperate embrace.

Winded, he scrambled up it, reached the first wrought iron deck, and then ascended the tethered steps, two at a time, until he made it to the rooftop, ten stories up.

'...blew your brother's face off,' her voice echoed once again inside his head.

John raced across the rooftop at a blindly speed to the other side, bobbing and weaving around air conditioning units, exhaust pipes, and skylights.

Without slowing or thinking, he leaped into the air, traversed the street below, and hit the roof of the neighboring building in a rolling tangle of limbs.

'I must admit our paths having crossed,' her voice

said loud and menacing in his brain.

Recovering quickly from his leap, John scrambled to his feet and headed to the other end of the building.

While picking up speed, he looked at his left hand, which had suddenly began to throb, and saw that his pinky finger was grotesquely bent back under the second knuckle, clearly broken.

With his right hand, he grabbed it and pulled it straight. The shattered ends of the mangled bone grinded together back into place, and a burst of scalding pain erupted up the length of his arm.

'Are you still there, John?' her voice reached him over the pain.

He reached the edge of the building at break neck speed and jumped.

Sailing in the air, between buildings, over double lanes of traffic far below, he stretched out in order to produce less drag.

At the apex of his leap, time seemed to literally suspend itself, turning the few seconds caught in midair into an eternity.

Then, an instant later, the concrete rooftop came rushing at him.

John tucked and rolled and came up running in one fluid motion.

'I simply live to kill,' she said in a casual tone in his head.

Feeling neither fatigue nor any kind of pain from his broken finger, John bore down and continued to the other side of the building he was on.

Halfway across, he saw what lay ahead; another double wide street, a vacant lot, where a textile mill had once stood, and finally the next building, a total distance of over one hundred yards.

'You're a fluke... an oddity,' her words sang out within him.

Running at his absolute top speed, John decided he was going to jump the span whether he lived or died as a result. It seemed pointless to him to do anything else, after all, the life that now lay in store for him seemed as bleak and desolate as anything he could have possibly imagined.

Then, with just two more yards to go, he heard a strange and ghastly voice speak to him from somewhere deep within himself, "Death is life. Kill to live."

Running faster than he could ever have thought possible, he roared into the night at her, "I'm going to find you!"

The edge of the building was upon him and the time to jump had come.

CHAPTER 47

"Dina... what is it?"

The morning after calling him, she sat behind her desk and fiercely typed away at the computer keyboard.

Unexpectedly, the soft telltale knock of her assistant was at the door.

Torn from her concentration, she mustered the most pleasant voice she could manage, "Yes, sweetie... what is it?"

"Sorry to interrupt, Dina, but there's a delivery man here to see you about some kind of farming equipment," her assistant, Kimmy said while peeking her head through the office door.

With the quietest of sighs, she looked up from the computer screen that she was using to completely pillage the pool's substantially large financial coffer, which had been left behind by the founder in order to provide a clean and safe swimming facility for the citizens of Cleveland.

In her youthful voice, Kimmy added, "He's right out

front. It's big... the piece of equipment he brought."

Realizing just what the young girl was talking about, she gave a slow wide smile. A most important piece to her murderous plan had arrived.

Her assistant stirred uneasily at the unexpected smile and said, "He's... waiting for you in the reception area."

She looked back down at the computer screen one last time, there was still time to shift the entire sum to her oldest existing offshore account before everyone was dead, and inquired, "Did you say 'farming equipment'?"

"Yeah... that's what it looks like," Kimmy replied.

Pushing the chair back with her rump, she stood up and told her assistant, "Well, we don't get much of that sort of thing in Cleveland very often, do we?" then added, "Let's go see."

Walking together down the hall towards the front reception area, she asked the young woman, "How's our web page coming along?"

"I was told this morning that it will be up and running as scheduled," Kimmy answered.

She turned her head slightly and asked, "What about the event? When will it be displayed on the site?"

Kimmy answered, "Tonight. I plan to upload it myself at home... so it'll be ready for you to look over tomorrow morning."

She nodded in approval and gave a large green eyes a slow blink.

They rounded a corner and kept on walking.

"Any word from the printing company?" she inquired, "We need those advertisement posters out and about across the city... as soon as possible."

"No word as of yet but I'll check for emails when I get back to my desk," Kimmy said to her.

"Please. I want everyone to know about our Polar Winter Night," she said with a sidelong glance.

With a nod, the youthful blonde reassured her boss. "I'll see to it... I promise."

Smiling and with a motherly tone, she told Kimmy, "Thank you, sweetie."

Always eager to please the woman she had quickly grown to like rather quickly, Kimmy blushed and smiled in return.

Together, they rounded the last corner, stepped through a pair of double doors, and entered the ample reception area where they found a man, stocky and in his forties, wearing a blue and orange piped uniform, earnestly looking over the assortment of historical photos, framed and mounted on the west wall, of the facility's history through the years.

At the sound of their entrance, he turned towards them and was about to speak when his eyes fell upon the older woman's large glossy emerald ones.

Noticing the reaction to her eyes, her first thought was to make him tonight's kill.

Kimmy spoke first, "Uh, Dina, this is the gentleman... I was telling you about."

Hearing the young woman's voice, the delivery man pulled his eyes away from what he considered the most unbelievable pair of eyes he had ever seen, glanced once at Kimmy, then back again at the woman who looked to be in charge and asked, "Ms. Dina Harris?"

Always in character, she answered, "Yes... I'm Dina Harris."

Gripping his clipboard with both hands, he

introduced himself, "I'm Ted with U.S. Machinery and Supplies," then adding, "I have here a delivery for a piece of equipment."

She gave him a small subtle smile and asked, "Is it out front?"

Ted, who would be reported missing by coworkers three days later and whose body would never be found, replied, "Yes." then asked, "Would you like to see it before signing, Ma'am?"

Still smiling, she answered, "Please," then motioned with an exquisitely manicured hand for him to lead the way.

Together, the three of them walked out into the bright radiance of the rich morning sun.

Off in the distance, at the east side of the park, two sororities battled it out in a fierce game of softball while children squeaked and laughed joyfully on the jungle gym.

When they reached the piece of equipment, which looked to Kimmy as a grotesque mechanical rendition of an elephant, Ted spoke first, "As you can see Ms. Harris, though ordered on very short notice, we found exactly what you asked for."

Shielding her green emerald colored eyes from the sun's glare, she looked up at the industrial looking apparatus and felt the corners of her mouth begin to itch. Everything was coming together so well.

Kimmy turned towards her boss and asked, "Dina... what is it?"

Without taking her eyes off the machine that was going to spell an agonizing doom to countless of children and parents, she steadied her breathing and answered the question, "It's a snow blower, Kimmy."

Ted gave the industrial machine a quick glance,

looked at the woman's face and her big green beautiful eyes, and added with a certain level of pride, "The best in the market. It can blow a ton of snow faster than any other machine of its kind."

Kimmy looked back at the snow blower again with an inquisitive look.

Without taking her glossy green eyes off the piece of equipment in front of her, she took the clipboard off the man's hands, scrawled her fabricated signature across the bottom of the delivery invoice, and handed it back.

Still looking at her, he asked, "Where would you like my men to put it?"

Slowly, she looked at him and answered, "Next to the swimming pool... of course."

CHAPTER 48

"Well it seems like death and violence is all that's going on."

In the end, John had not jumped but instead had slid at the very last moment into the building's concrete guardrail with a deafening crunch, like a baseball player scoring home from third, and had stayed there the rest of the night, under the stars.

Then with the sun of the new day casting its glorious light across the skyline of the city, he had returned to the shelter, only to find Rodger waiting for him at the front of the double doors, breathalyzer in hand.

Rodger, visually upset over the unexpected commotion and disappearance, had demanded that John blow into the Law Enforcement grade breathalyzer and hand over the cellular phone in order to reenter the shelter.

John had complied with both requests without question or argument.

Now, two days later, and more determined than ever to find her, John sat in front of a computer in the media room of the shelter as he scanned the internet on an aging computer monitor for anything that might have anything to do with her.

Focusing his initial search within his immediate vicinity, he searched for any recent murders, disappearances, and unexplained deaths within a three state radius and then slowly work his way outward. It was a daunting task with very little hope of tracking her down. However, it was all he could think of at the moment to do.

She had mentioned that she was currently planning another mass murder which he knew she was capable of doing.

Committing mass murder took time, and, most of all, it took resources which he figured might leave a mark somewhere large enough for him to spot on the internet.

He found a story about a bible salesman who had been found dead in a seedy motel room while wearing a pair of his eldest daughter's panties.

He leaned in to read it in detail when, suddenly, Rachael's warm scent reached him.

John took his hand off the mouse, turned in his seat, and watched her enter the computer room and come to him.

Cup of coffee in hand and dressed in her trademark linen dress and sandals, she crossed the distance between them and said, "Those beautiful green eyes are going to fall out of your head if you sit in front of that monitor much longer."

John took the coffee from her supple white hand.

"Don't worry. The green reflects the glare."

She laughed then placed a hand on his shoulder.

Her touch had a comforting and relaxing feel that he openly accepted.

She leaned slightly forward and asked, "So what's got you all interested so suddenly with the internet?"

Though her question carried a polite and casual tone, John knew it was really baited. From what he could gather, Rodger had assigned her to keep an eye on him since the other night.

"I don't know really," he answered, "I guess... I just like to pass the time by seeing what's going on."

She straightened up, wrinkled her nose at the sorted details of the dead bible salesman, and said, "Well it seems like death and violence is all that's going on."

John told her, "You're right about that."

Her hand slowly slid off his shoulder. "Well, hope you find something interesting."

John looked back at the computer monitor and replied, "I hope so too."

CHAPTER 49

"There can never be an 'over' when there wasn't even a beginning."

With Daniel's large roughened hand resting heavily on her left bare breast and his seed still hot inside her, she lay on his dingy bed and listened to his rhythmic breathing.

After so many years of being alive, the joy of sex had disappeared long ago, leaving behind a necessary and at times a required means to an end.

Looking up at the ceiling, she went over the few remaining steps that she still had to do before her deadly plan came together. Though most were already done, the last unfinished ones required the greatest amount of care.

He slipped his hand off her chest and then rolled over to his right with grunt.

Taking advantage of the recess from his attention, she quietly swung her bare feet onto the floor, instantly felt the grit of the dirty carpet under the soles of her feet, and stood up.

Sensing the shift in weight on the battered mattress, Daniel asked without turning towards her, "Do you get anything out of sleeping with me or is it just part of the business transaction?"

She walked across the disheveled tiny apartment, stopped at the small round dinette table, and said out loud, "I wouldn't necessarily call it 'sleeping with'... it's more like 'fucking' if you ask me."

He blinked at her harsh words.

She looked over at him and added, "And just in case you're wondering... sex with you wasn't part of the deal... I just threw that in myself."

Still with his back to her, Daniel asked, "Why?"

"Like I told you before...'I guess I like God damn problems.", she replied as she reached for a cigarette from the pack on the table.

He rolled over and faced her. His eyes fell upon her naked form and her large glossy green eyes staring back at him in the dim light.

She lit the cigarette in her mouth with a match.

"And when this is over?" he asked, "Does it mean... that we're over?"

Enjoying his sudden case of vulnerability, she hurtfully replied, "There can never be an 'over' when there wasn't even a beginning."

He dropped his eyes and questioned with a boyish manner, "So once you get what you want... I probably won't see you again... am I right?"

Keeping him guessing and unsteady with the lure of money and plenty of sex until she had what she needed from him, she replied, "Relax, my love... the organization I work for will always need something from your plant which means I'm not going anywhere anytime soon," and then took a deep drag from the cigarette between her manicured fingers.

Daniel looked up at her with raised eyebrows. "Really? I mean... I damn sure need that money but... damn, you sure are the most beautiful woman I've ever been with."

She exhaled a long trail of smoke from the stale cigarette and said, "With such romantic words as those... how can a girl resist," and then smiled wickedly through the cloud of smoke.

He smiled back at her and chuckled, "Girl, you crazy."

With an arch to her eyebrow, she crushed her cigarette in a nearby ashtray, turned, and walked to where her clothes lay crumpled across the back of a chair.

Daniel silently watched her nude body sway about the apartment.

She picked up the black leather attaché case next to the battered old chair and carried it over to the bed.

Daniel swung his large unkempt feet onto the floor and sat up, eager to see the contents within the case.

Tucking her left bare foot under her, she sat down next to him, briefcase in hand.

Since meeting her, he felt his life had taken a turn for the better. As far back as he could remember just about every single person had always told him that he would never amount to anything other than the shit kicking nigger he was destined to always be. Yet, sitting next to him was the most beautiful white woman he had ever talked to, much less slept with.

She gently set the black case next to him. "Open it. It's what we promised you."

He looked down at the black leather briefcase.

Smiling, she encouraged him on, "Go ahead... open it. It won`t bite."

With a nod, Daniel placed both thumbs on the catch levers, gave a steadying breath, and then flipped the catches open.

With mounting cold excitement, she watched as he sealed his fate and, if all went according to her plans, the fates of over two hundred additional people, most of them, with any luck, children.

He slowly opened the case and saw neat rows of banded hundred dollar bills splayed out in front of him from within its interior.

"Ten thousand," she said out loud.

Staring at the money, which seemed to stare back at him, Daniel slowly nodded at her voice.

"You'll receive the rest after I pick up the product and its potency has been confirmed by our technicians," she told him with the same business manner to her voice whenever she mentioned the fictitious organization she supposedly represented.

Daniel slowly closed the case, looked up at her, and said, "Don't worry about the potency of that stuff. It's definitely what your people want... and more."

She gave him another smile. "Oh, we're not worried... cus if you deliver less than what you promised or skip out on us... the breakfast you buy with that money..." she pointed at the black case, "will still be hot in your belly when we kill you."

Listening to her speak so candidly about the violence that awaited him should he fail, Daniel felt the crawling fingers of dread slowly move up his back.

Knowing just how much to toy with him, she let the threat sink into his guts a few seconds longer, then softly smiled, and said, "But, of course, nothing like that is going to happen, love. I feel it in my heart," she cupped her left bare breast, "that this transaction is going to play itself out beautifully."

Still holding the briefcase in both hands, Daniel could find nothing to say.

She leaned forward, placed her hands on his cheeks, and asked, "Will it be ready tomorrow night... as you promised?"

Filling his nostrils with her intoxicating aroma of freshly cut mint that seemed to naturally come off her body, he looked up at her face and answered, "Yes."

She went down to her knees between his legs, ran her hands down the length of his body until they stopped at his groin, and quietly whispered, "Good. Tomorrow night we shall have what we want," then placed the tip of his penis to her lower lip and whispered, "But tonight... you can have... what you want."

CHAPTER 50

"Where are you hiding in plain sight?"

As she readied herself for work in Daniel's small and dingy bathroom, John stepped, barefoot, onto the shelter's rooftop.

The new day's sunlight, bright and without much heat, greeted him as he walked to the center of the roof.

Willing to try any and all avenues available to him in order to find her, John extended his arms outward, like a crucifix, closed his eyes, and slowly began to turn around like a radar dish with the hope that the sensation he felt when he was closed to her might perhaps increase in potency as the creature continued to evolve within him.

Something in her voice or perhaps the quality of the connection between their cellular phones had given him the impression that she was probably, at most, only a state or two away.

Feeling the cool morning breeze glide from the

front of his face to his left ear as he continued to slowly turn in a circle, he whispered out loud, "Where are you hiding in plain sight?"

Sometime later, with the heat of the noon day sun beating upon his head, John lowered his arms in defeat. It seemed that the ability to sense her at any greater distance than what he already could wasn't developing at all or not fast enough to be of any use to him from where he was right now.

Sweating, he placed his hands on his knees, took a deep breath, and whispered, "Where are you?"

CHAPTER 51

"You'll just have to believe me and take it on faith."

Sitting in the darkened cab of a moving truck that she had rented earlier in the day, she stared, using her night vision, at the rear gate of the chemical factory where Daniel worked for.

The late hour and the ruined streetlamps that she had shot out with her sound suppressed 9mm handgun earlier in the week offered all the cover she needed from anyone who might accidentally pass by and observe the final transaction to her deadly plan.

Dressed for the occasion, black upon black and a shoulder holster, she shifted her weight inside the industrial one-size-fits-all interior of the rental and waited for Daniel's lumbering form to show itself.

Finally, after an hour of waiting, Daniel, steering a small forklift with a palette of steel drums, emerged from the rear gate of the chemical plant, stopped at the edge of the alley, and looked around for any sign of where she might be.

Watching him through her big shiny emerald eyes, she slid her right thumb onto the keys of her cellular phone and pressed.

The light from the screen of the cellular filled the cabin of the truck with a faint eerie bluish glow.

Some fifty yards away, Daniel caught sight of her signal and waved.

She placed the phone face down on the passenger seat, turned the ignition, slipped the transmission into gear, and then drove slowly forward.

The evening's new moon cast a vague glow across the city's industrial center.

As she steered the rental into a three point turn, Daniel positioned himself perfectly behind it and raised the palette to a height above the running boards of the truck.

Slowly but surely, she backed up until she reached Daniel and the forklift.

When she was just a few feet away, Daniel waved for her to cut the engine.

She turned the motor of the truck off, opened the driver's side door, and stepped out into the night air and casually walked, with a large folded envelope in her hand, to the rear where Daniel was waiting.

Watching her approach, he smiled at the shape of her figure dressed all in black.

She stepped between the truck and his forklift, in order to open the rear of the truck. She turned the locking hook over, slid the door up its entire length, and said as she moved aside, using a vulgar innuendo that she knew he would find endearing, "Stick it in."

He smiled at her sweet sounding voice talking dirty as he eased the small forklift's burden carefully and easily into the rear of the truck.

She waited for him to back away and then slid the rolling door all the way down.

Daniel cut the electric engine of the forklift.

She swung the locking hook over, sealing the metal drums safely inside and bringing to a conclusion weeks of scheming and conniving.

Daniel removed his large bulk from out of the small cab and walked over to her, smiling at a job well done.

She waited for him to reach her and asked, pretending to care, "Are you sure it was safe for you to do this?"

He stuffed his hands into the front pockets of his jeans, looked over his shoulder toward the rear gate of the plant, and replied, "Yeah, don't worry 'bout nothing, hon. Since the owner's son took over, this place is more fucked up than a one legged man in an ass kicking contest."

She couldn't help but genuinely smile at his answer.

"Hell. In fact..." he continued, "the way things are going... I'll be lucky to see my pension. The owner's son is more concerned about the cocaine in his nose and pussy around his dick than looking out for the well-being of the plant. He's cut back so much staff that the entire place is running on a skeleton crew, day and night."

Continuing to play her roll, she asked with convincing concern, "So no one saw you. We don't need you getting caught and I don't want you getting into trouble."

He smiled at the luscious white woman standing in front of him. "Na. There's only a handful of us left on the night shift and half of them are taking their third lunch break. Like I said, this place is so fucked up now since the owner retired I could empty out half the plant through that gate..." he gestured with his thumb, "and no one would notice."

"Good," she said with a smile and then added as she handed the envelope out to him, "I got them to advance you another five thousand against the final installment."

Daniel took the packaged money from her outstretched hand, jammed it into his waistband, and told her, "Thanks, babe. That was awesome of you."

She looked up at him and waited for the question that was sure to come.

He looked into her beautiful green eyes and asked it, "When am I going to see you again?"

She stepped closer to him and replied, "Soon."

Like a child, he whined the word, "Soon? When the hell is that gonna be?"

Unable to use her eye's seductive power in the dimly lit alley, she stepped even closer, touched his large ample chest, and answered, "Just as soon as I get this stuff to those waiting to analyze its strength and I'm given the rest of your money."

Feeling her soft warm touch through his clothes, Daniel dropped down a notch, and asked, "How do I know that you'll actually come back?"

She smiled at him and replied, "You don't. You'll just have to believe me and take it on faith."

He looked down at her beautiful face and said nothing as the first stirrings of love for her, not just lust, turned in his guts.

Having seen that very same look so many times before on so many faces of so many men and women, she hit her queue perfectly, "Look... I have to get these drums checked out otherwise... I can't go and collect the rest of your money."

He gave her a sullen nod.

She reached into the front pocket of her black jeans, pulled out the wedding ring that had belonged to John's mother, and said, "Just so that you know that I'm coming back to you, I want you to hold onto his. It was my mother's."

He followed her left hand with his eyes and watched her dropped a diamond solitaire ring set in yellow gold into the palm of his hand.

With the delicate weight of the ring resting in his hand, Daniel opened his mouth to speak but stopped when her fingertips touched his mouth to hush him.

"When I get back, I'll have your money, you'll give me back my mother's ring, and then... we can go on a proper vacation... together," she told him as her delicate fingers slowly slid off his unshaven face.

Daniel found himself unable to add anything further so he curled his fingers around the dead woman's ring and watched her turn and walk back to the driver's side door of the moving truck.

She opened the door and hoisted herself in.

Suddenly, Daniel called out to her.

Hiding her annoyance, she leaned her head out the window.

He ran up to her. "Listen, you be real careful around that shit."

She cocked her head slightly to the side, pretending not to know the exact lethality of the contents within the drums.

With the ring still clutched in his hand, he continued, "I mean it. Be real fucking careful. That's industrial grade caustic soda."

Listening to him, she suppressed the desire to

smile.

He went on, "We make it in limited quantities since the product is so Goddamn dangerous."

"We know that already. That's why we contacted you," she told him.

"Yeah... I figured that out... but I'm telling you because I don't want you to get hurt by that stuff," he informed her.

His pathetic show of concern for her made her want to laugh in his face.

Daniel continued, "It's ten times more corrosive then commercial grade caustic soda. I mean, when that shit comes in contact with water not only will it melt the meat clean off the bone but then it'll melt the bone down to a chunky soup as well."

"Just like the narcos in Mexico, I read about on the internet, use it," she told him.

Daniel knitted his eyebrows at her comment. "Yeah... kind of... like that."

She gave him one final smile and drove away.

In the morning, she would place a call to the FBI.

CHAPTER 52

"Yes... you are absolutely going to die tonight."

Four days later, she steered her sedan to a stop in front of Daniel's large dilapidated apartment building, flicked off the headlights, and cut the engine.

Using the ability of her eyes to see in near total darkness, she reached for her cellular phone, pressed the number 2 button, and the small black mobile phone speed dialed the number that had been assigned to that particular button.

On the other end, a phone began to ring.

Suddenly, Daniel's haggard angry voice boomed, "Hello?!"

With the zest of an enjoyable evening that lay ahead, she calmly and collectively spoke into her phone's tiny mouthpiece, "Hello, Daniel."

Instantly Daniel's voice exploded with rage, "Bitch! Where the fuck have you been, bitch? Do you know what's happened?"

"I can only imagine...," she began to say but was

abruptly cut off.

"Imagine? Imagine?! Bitch... this ain't no fairytale book! Imagine has nothing to do with what's happened."

Smiling at the fear and anger in his voice, she coolly told him, "I'm here. I'm right outside. I've come to see you."

"Outside?" he yelped, "You're outside?" then yelled, "Bitch, what the fuck are you doing right outside my apartment... at this hour? Don't you know they could be watching me right this fuck'n second?"

She swallowed back the urge to laugh out loud. "I've come to make it all better."

Unable to climb down from his perch of bottled up fear and fury, Daniel yelled again, "Make it better? Hell, bitch... you and who-ever-the-fuck people you work for didn't make it better for me... ya'll fuck'n made it worse."

She pushed herself deeper into the car's leather seat, gave a sigh, and asked with a tone of finality, "May I come up?"

Silence came from him.

"Well... Daniel... may I come up?" she asked again.

He swallowed hard and answered, "Come up," then slammed the phone's receiver down into its cradle.

A few minutes later, she turned the doorknob, found the front door unlocked, and stepped into his apartment.

The strong musky smell of trash and human fear instantly engulfed her uncanny sense receptors.

She slowly closed the door behind her with her backside and looked around the dimly lit and dirty apartment with her night vision.

Slumped in a dining room chair, Daniel stared at the outline of her figure.

"So what exactly happened?" she asked smiling in the darkness.

Without standing up, he replied in a slow controlled angered voice, "Bitch, you know what happened."

Since she had been the one to make the call the following morning after receiving the deadly caustic soda, she knew very well what had happened. Nevertheless, she wanted to delight herself in hearing it come from him. "Just tell me," she pressed.

"Home Land Security arrived two days after I gave you those drums of soda." Daniel informed her, "Those fuckers knew exactly what to look for, what to ask, and who to ask."

Ever in playing her roll, she acted concerned, "The soda... and you."

Daniel ran his large dirty fingernails through his disheveled afro and said, "Ya got that fuck'n right."

She walked to the edge of the dining room and stared down at him.

"I cooked the inventory books good enough for the owner's idiot son not to notice but those fuck'n guys from Home Land are going to see right through them," he told her like a sinner in a confessional, "It's only a matter of time before they figure out that it was me that altered those records, stole the soda, and sold it to you and your people. And if it turns out that you guys are in any way affiliated with some terrorist organization then I'm looking at about twenty years in concrete box."

Still standing, she told him, "We're not going to let

that happen. That's why I came here tonight. We take care of our own."

He looked up at her and questioned, "Is that what I am now... one of you?"

"Yes," she simply answered.

He gave a huff and commented, "I used to be an American. A piece of shit based upon everyone's opinion but an American nonetheless... now... I don't even know what am going to be... I since I don't really even know who you people are."

Bathing in his misery, she kept the role playing going, "We are people who take care of each other."

He stared at her a moment longer and then looked down at the sticky table top.

"How much of the money have you spent?" she asked him.

Without looking up, he answered, "I still got pretty much most of it."

"Ok. How much is that?" she questioned.

"Oh, just about all of it," he replied and then added, "Except for what I paid my uncle... for this!"

With a sudden burst of speed she hadn't expected to come from someone with his size and bulk, he blew off the dining room chair and put the barrel of a .44 Magnum revolver to her forehead.

With the cold steel of the handgun pressed firmly to the front of her head, extraordinary healing ability or not, she knew that the damage caused by just one pull of the trigger from a gun like that at such a close range would kill her.

Looking down the length of the impossibly huge handgun, she saw that the hammer was cocked back, making the weapon incredibly dangerous in his hands.

Daniel neither spoke or moved but held the gun

firmly against her forehead and stared at her from behind its fixed sights.

Taking stock of her situation, she knew the apartment was too dark for her eyes' seductive power to be of any use and, with only a fraction of pressure needed to drop the hammer and send her brains splattering all over the place, attempting to disarm him was simply out of the question.

Finally he spoke, "So… tell me again, bitch… how are you… and your people… going to take care of me?"

She saw her chance to save herself and took it. "I've come to take you with me. Faraway."

The cold barrel stayed where it was as he said, "With the amount of trouble I'm in… it's gonna to have to be pretty God damn… 'faraway'."

From behind the large firearm pressed to her head, she asked, "How about Russia? Is that God damn 'faraway' enough for you?"

Daniel blinked at her words.

Watching his feeble brain work the idea, she remained quiet and motionless.

After mulling it over, he asked, "With you? To Russia?"

Knowing that her words had penetrated, she smiled and answered, "Yes… with me… all the way there."

Finally, after what felt like a thousand years to her, he lowered the gun away from her head.

She gave a quiet sigh of relief.

"Russia," Daniel repeated then added as he gently uncocked the hammer, "' All the way there'… with you."

She gave another quiet sigh and nodded. "Take only the money. Don't bother to pack… you're not going to need it where you're going."

Hours later, in one of the many harbors that lined the coast of Lake Erie, she steered her sedan to a stop in the darkest parking space she could find.

After being driven the entire distance from his apartment to the harbor, Daniel turned to her from the passenger seat and asked, "What are we doing here?"

With her hands still on the leather steering wheel, she looked at him and answered, "This is the way out. It starts here."

Daniel looked at the desolate moon lit marina filled with both sail and power boats splayed out in front of him and shook his head slowly as he commented, "This is not how I wanted it to go."

Fighting back the urge to scream in laughter into his face then rip him apart, she said, "I know, Daniel. Don't you worry none... before you know it... you'll be in a whole different place."

He looked back at her and asked, "What about my kids, my two girls? Whatever piece of shit I may be... they're still going to wonder what the fuck happened to me... to their dad."

"Your two little girls will be taken care, I promise," she told him with a comforting touch on his left leg."

Sick with the realization of how much he truly loved his daughters and how much his life had come crashing to a halt over the course of the last couple of weeks, Daniel forced his mind forward. "Ok... so tell me... how's all this supposed to go down?"

"I have a boat here that we are going to take all the way up to Canada..."

"Why a boat? Why not just drive there?" he interrupted with a whine.

Playing her roll perfectly, she answered, "Trust

me... when it comes to getting out of the U.S.... a boat gliding silently up into Canada is entirely more discrete."

He turned away from her and looked out the windshield.

She continued, "Once we're in Canada, using a car that will be provided for us, we'll drive west all the way to Alaska, then board a seaplane, which will be fueled and waiting for us at an unspecified locale, and fly, under the cover of night, into Russia."

Daniel listened in silence.

Making up her fantastic tale as she went along, she continued, "When we're in Russia, you'll receive a new identity. With it, we'll be able to take a train which will carry us all the way into the heart of Moscow."

"Moscow!" he exclaimed then asked, "And what the hell am I supposed to do in Moscow? Hell, I don't even speak Moscow... or Russian... or whatever the hell they speak over there."

"We've already arranged a job for you there. We think you'll like it," she answered.

"A job? What kind of job?" Daniel inquired.

"Ever wanted to be a bartender?" she answered with a question.

"No. I mean, I guess not. Hell, woman, I don't know," he told her.

She smiled devilishly at him and said, "Well, you're going to be one. You're going to tend bar in one of our underage brothels."

"Say what?" he said with raised eyebrows.

"I figured that would catch your interest. That's why I personally chose it for you," she said.

Daniel blinked in rapid secession as his mind went into overdrive.

Knowing how sexual vulgarity always swayed him,

she told him, "Trust me, in about two weeks you're going to be up to your neck in fifteen year old Croatian pussy."

He raised his eyebrows again and a faint trace of a smile emerged on his lips, sealing his fate.

Later. Under the faint silver light of the moon, she steered the Lolita, a thirty foot sailboat that she had just recently relieved from a just recently murdered elderly couple out of the harbor into the languishing open waters of Lake Erie.

Sitting to her right, Daniel watched the moonlit docks slowly disappear into the distance and the life he had known and hated along with it.

Within a half hours' time, the Lolita was surrounded by water all around her as her course was set due north.

Daniel looked up at the bare metal pole at the center of the regal sailboat. "Aren't you going to use the sails?"

With the rushing wind bellowing her hair in waves about her head, she replied, "No. I'm not that good... especially by myself."

He narrowed his eyes. "But you know how to drive this thing. Right?"

She smiled at him and said, "First, you don't drive a boat, you steer or sail one. Secondly, sailing a thirty-two footer at night is not part of my job description. And thirdly..." she smiled even wider, "...yes, I can drive a boat."

Daniel turned, looked over the length of the bow, saw nothing but moonlight speckled water and blackness, and said with a heavy sigh, "Ok."

Late into the night, the Lolita plowed northward over the moonlight tipped black water as Daniel and the woman who had given him a reason to live and to live without reason traveled over the sleek darkness in silence.

Finally after some time, she spoke out loud over the steady beat of the engine and the slapping water against her hull, "Daniel, go up front to where those chains are and see if the crack I repaired hasn't come open again."

He craned his neck to see what she meant, saw the chains, and asked with a measure of unease, "At the front of the boat?"

She looked directly at him. "Yes. There. It's important."

With a grunt, he lifted his heavy bulk from the bench and hefted himself onto the small walkway along the starboard side. Slow and fearful of slipping and falling into the water below, he made his way towards the bow of the boat.

Smiling, at the steering wheel, she watched him intently.

When he reached the chains, resting beside four large padlocks, he looked about, and saw nothing that looked like a crack in the boat's exterior.

He opened his mouth to call out to her but stopped when he heard the sailboat's engine slow to a halt and the sound of running feet coming towards him.

Suddenly, before he could even turn around to see what was happening behind him, he felt a devastating pain flare across his lower back and fell face first onto the cold metal chains.

Struggling to catch his breath that simply didn't

seem to want to return to his lungs, Daniel twisted his face to his right to see what had just happened, and, to his shock, he saw her standing over him with a wicked smile on her face.

Stunned and in inexplicable pain, Daniel caught sight of her right arm and saw that it was covered in dazzling white fur and her hand had knurled into a knuckled claw.

Confused and frightened by what he was looking at, Daniel fumbled under the immense pain coming from his bruised kidneys and tried to get up.

She took a step forward and punched him hard across the right side of his face with her clawed hand.

With a loud grunt, Daniel came down onto the deck face first once again and vomited.

She straddled his body, avoiding the hot congealing puke that surrounded his face, produced a syringe from her back pocket, and flicked the cap into the night with her left thumb.

Half unconscious from the pain, Daniel rasped for air around his vomit.

Without care or tact, she drove the syringe needle hard between his shoulder blades and then pressed down on the plastic plunger.

Instantly, Daniel felt his entire body paralyze under the prick of the needle in his back. The pain remained but his body no longer responded.

Finally she spoke to him, "Nothing like a good arm bar to the kidneys to start the night's festivities," then flexed her fur covered arm in front of his face.

Unable to move at all, Daniel simply stared into his vomit on the deck as he heard her speak to him.

"How's the jaw? I felt it break when I hit you," she casually asked him.

Terrified beyond belief and completely paralyzed, Daniel moved his eyes as far right as they would go to look at her.

With the aid of the silver moonlight and the night vision of her eyes, she took stock at the man lying in a stinking heap beneath her and said, "I'm sure you're wondering two primary things right now," she took a dramatic pause for effect and continued, "First, why can't I move and the second… am I going to die tonight?"

He stared at her, listening.

Slowly her arm began to retract back into human shape as she told him, "Allow me to answer the latter first. Yes… you are absolutely going to die tonight."

Somewhere deep within his paralyzed body, Daniel whimpered like a child.

With her right hand back to a normal woman's, she said to him, "And as to the first… the reason you can't move is courtesy of a certain recently sanctioned terror cell. The serum I injected you with is a very effective form of Succinylcholine. Though you can't move… as you already know… you're still going to be able to feel… everything… that I do to your body."

She bent down and sat on his large rump. "Daniel, do you know how long I've wanted to kill you?" she gave his backside a slap, "Since the moment I first met you. You truly are a worthless piece of shit. After centuries of murdering innocent people… I honestly do believe that killing you will be a contribution to the world."

"Watching you," she told him, "fall in love with me. Listening to your pitiful stories about your life. Feeling your breath on me when you fucked me," she patted his head like a dog, "It was all worth it… for what I'm about to do you and... what I'm going to do... to about two hundred people this coming Saturday."

His eyes bulged at the sound of her words.

She leaned in close enough to smell his vomit. "Would you like to guess what I'm gonna do?" she asked with a mocking tone, "Come on... guess."

His terror stricken eyes burned holes into hers.

She sat back up, flipped her hair over her right shoulder and said, "Ok. I'll tell you. I'm going to take that wonderfully potent caustic soda that you stole from your employer, load it into a snow blower, and spray it into a Olympic size swimming pool filled with people."

Daniel hollered in rage silently within himself.

She smiled and continued, "The screams that I'll hear as they melt right in front of me... will be... glorious."

Paralyzed and helpless, Daniel watched her close her eyes, lift her head up to the sky, and lose herself in the festered thoughts of her mind.

She slowly opened her eyes and looked back down at him. "Oh... by the way... I sent a personal invitation to your ex-wife. She confirmed with my assistant this morning that she and your two little girls are definitely going to attend."

Daniel's eyes rolled violently in their sockets as the first strands of his sanity began to snap inside him.

Watching her words take the desired effect on him, she laughed out loud into the night.

Hearing her startling demonic laughter and losing his mind with fear and dread for his two young daughters, Daniel struggled with every fiber of his being to move but his body had simply become nothing more than a cocoon of dead meat.

She stood up, stepped to his left and faced him. "Once I'm done killing them and everyone else who comes, I'm going to pay an old friend a visit," she smiled at the thought and continued, "I was going to wait until he became something far better... but I've decided that it'll be more fun to surprise him."

The lake water gently lapped and licked at the boat's hull.

She bent down and rolled him over onto his back.

Screaming and pleading silently, Daniel's eyes quivered in fear inside their sockets.

"Now... enough about everyone else. Your main concern, really at this point, should be about you," she told him as she began to wrap the chains around his body.

"You're going to die a drowning death," she explained as she rolled him back onto his belly and continued to fasten the heavy iron links. "By the time pieces of your bloated body rise to the surface, I'll be long gone and killing somewhere else."

Manhandling him, she rolled his large frame once again onto his back.

Daniel cast his eyes downward and watched her snap the four large padlocks closed onto the interwoven chains around his paralyzed body.

Finished, she stood up and took a step back. "Would you like to see something?" she asked, "Would you like to see what you were really fucking?"

She gave him a soft smile and then began to undress in front of him.

Daniel watched silently as she removed her clothing and shoes until she was completely naked.

The cold breeze coming off the lake chilled her skin.

Her nipples hardened under the licking wind.

Standing in her bare feet next to Daniel's cold vomit, she took in the sharp brisk air into her lungs, held it, and exhaled it long and slow.

Daniel looked up at her, defeated.

She gave him one final look, smiled, and turned into the creature right in front of him.

Trapped inside his body, Daniel screamed in harrowing terror.

Completely transformed, the creature calmly looked down at him with its immensely large green eyes.

Unable to turn away, Daniel's eyes bulged in horror.

With a casual ease, the creature took hold of the heavy links of chain and lifted Daniel's large and dense bulk high over its head.

Suspended in mid-air, Daniel realized, as his heart sank at the memories of his sad and wasted life, that he was truly about to die a humiliating and lonely death.

The creature dropped him into the dark black water without fanfare.

Daniel hit the water with a thunderous splash.

As the cold black water slowly took him under, Daniel and the creature stared at each other until he disappeared into the dark depths below.

Later, naked and in human form once again, she steered the gliding thirty-footer back towards the harbor while the moon waned overhead in the predawn hours of the new day.

With Daniel finally out of the way as planned, she smiled and went over the rest of the arrangements still needed in order to carry out her murderous scheme.

In the distance, the harbor crested the horizon, its night lights still lit against the grey-bluish sky of the coming day.

Staring at the beautiful scenery spread out across the bow of the sailboat, she recalled another time when...

Seamus Cass, an ASU (active service unit) Lieutenant of the Irish Republican Army, breathed a sigh of relief as he caught sight of the looming docks in the distance.

The overnight journey from Kilkeel, Northern Ireland's southernmost port town, to Malahide, just north of Dublin, had been the tensest assignment given to him by the Quartermaster to date. The cargo which he carried was considered by some as the deadliest and the most closely held secret of the IRA.

Knowing he needed to have what sat at the bowels of the boat on dry land before sun up, Cass eased open the throttled a bit more.

The nondescript tug boat continued to close the distance as the dawn of the new day inched upward, threatening to spoil the Quartermaster's carefully laid plans.

Feeling the dark seawater slapping against the hull, Seamus thought once again at the tremendous cost the IRA had paid in bribes, distractions, and "accidental" deaths for the safe passage and the unrestricted delivery of his cargo. So much was riding on the successful completion of the mission ahead that if anything went wrong it would be his head on a plate.

Behind him, his armed entourage, ski masked and carrying Japanese automatic long rifles, entered the captain's bridge and began their initial preparations for docking at the prearranged slip.

Cass glanced at them as they went about their duties and recalled the Quartermaster's exact words to him, just before shoving off into the night, "Deliver... the Angel of Death and see to it that our mission is completed fully and successfully."

With the harbor only one hundred yards away, he let go of the wheel for the first time in hours, turned, and said to the small strawberry blonde girl of about thirteen that had been sitting behind him for the past few hours, "Tell the Angel... that we're almost there... and to please ready herself."

Dressed in a white communion dress and black saddle shoes, the young girl gave the captain a small delicate smile, stood, and, without uttering a single word, took the wooden stairs down into the dark confines of the tug boat's belly.

Aided only by a single light bulb hanging overhead from an electrical wire, the girl made her way towards the stern of the boat.

Men, armed and cold staring, stepped aside as she walked past them. Her post within the IRA was well known and fearfully respected.

She reached the Captain's stateroom and knocked on the heavy wooden door.

From inside, she heard, "Come in."

The girl turned the knob, felt the latch give, pushed the door slowly inward, and stepped inside.

Sitting on a wicker chair with a shell shaped backrest and dressed in jeans and a cream colored boiled lamb's wool pullover, the woman, who had come to be known as the Angel of Death within the socialist army, turned her large green emerald eyes towards the small girl and asked in a heavy Northern Irish accent, "Is it time, Mary?"

The girl, whose full name was Mary Irene Gorten, an orphan since the death of her parents at the hands of the Ulster Volunteers gave a small curtsy and answered with the same robust accent, "Yes, Miss Angel. I was told by Mr. Cass to let you know that we're just about there."

"Thank you, Mary, my sweet," she said as she stood up then extended her hand out towards the small girl and added, "Will you sit with me until we dock?"

Mary stepped into the stateroom and closed the door behind her.

When they finally arrived, Cass's men, under the growing light of the new day, fanned out about the small marina and set about their duties to ensure a safe transition from ship to vehicle for the woman assassin, whose reputation as a seductress and killer had become so renowned that no man was allowed to converse with her or, much less, be left alone in her company. It was said amongst the tales of liquor infused nights that the Angel of Death personally escorted you to your death as you smiled like a love-stricken fool all the way there.

Under the direct supervision by Cass and with the persistent fear of British commandos lurking at every shadow with orders, both professional and personal, to eliminate her and avenge the many deaths of military personal and civilians alike, she was taken off the tugboat and into a paneled van in one swift stroke.

Inside, she and her child aide found themselves being swiftly driven by a female driver out of the marina and into the North West countryside of Dublin.

Craning her delicate young neck in order to peer out the front windshield, Mary asked, "Where are we going to, Miss Angel?"

Kate McKie, as she had originally been known as when she had volunteered into the IRA seven years ago, slowly closed her large glossy emerald eyes, nestled herself as best she could in the uncomfortable rear seat, and replied, "You know that we're never told such things... for fear of divulging the information under the torment and agony of torture."

Accustomed to man's grotesque violent nature, Mary gave a small nod of understanding then turned back to look out the windshield once again.

Relaxing as best she could, she let out a long soothing breath and told her aide, "Wake me up when we get there... wherever... there may be."

Mary watched her fall asleep amongst the crate and barrels and thanked the Holy Virgin, her patron saint, for the hundredth time for the glorious blessing of having been chosen to serve such a beautiful and important woman.

A few hours later, Mary reached out with her small delicate hand and lightly touched her mistress' arm.

Instantly, her large green eyes flew open.

Taken by surprise by the sudden staring eyes, Mary jerked her hand away and cautiously said, "We're here... Miss Angel."

Staring at the young girl, she slowly smiled, "Thank you, Mary," then lifted herself just enough from her sleeping position to peer out the windshield.

Under the late morning sun, she saw a large old farm house, meticulously kept and cared for, complete with a red barn and water well fitted with a hand crank at the left of the property. A classic IRA safe house, ordinary enough not to draw attention yet big enough to house the men and supplies needed to carry out a successful mission.

The caravan of vehicles entered the large farm and rolled to a stop at the front door of the main house.

Both Mary and she waited patiently to be let out from the cramped van.

The female driver, known only as Darling Emily, opened her door and stepped out in the fresh morning country air, made her way to the sliding door of the van, and slid the door open its entire length.

She and the girl stepped out and looked at the farm that would be their home for an undetermined amount of time as they stretched their legs.

Darling Emily looked around the confines of the vehicle, found the suitcases, collected them, and took them to the farm house as she had been instructed to do so. Her freckled face glowed under the morning sun and the strain of the suitcases.

"It looks lovely," Mary commented.

Taking in every aspect of her new surroundings; the sounds that filtered into her acute hearing, the smells which slipped and slid about her nose, and the hundreds of different vibrant colors that filled her green eyes, she couldn't help but agree with the child standing beside her.

The wind whipped the trees and their leaves rustled with a tranquil calming sound.

She turned and saw Cass and his men, now dressed as farm hands, go about their duties of securing the area with military precision, and then said in a casual tone, "Loveliness hides death best."

Aware of her mistress' reputation as a black widow, Mary took the woman, who would later kill her seven years later while she showered, by the hand and motioned towards the house and away from the men, "Let's go inside."

She looked down at the child, nodded, and, together, they walked into the large eggshell white colored house.

Going about their duties about the property, male volunteers stole quick glances at the beautiful woman with the amazing green eyes.

Later that evening as she stared out the window of the second story bedroom at the landscape covered in the darkness of the night, she wondered how long they would keep her here until they called upon her to kill whoever they felt needed to be killed to further their political and religious agenda.

The IRA provided her with an abundant and elaborate amount of kills for her to satisfy the creature that lived within her. However, there were times, like this one was shaping itself out to be, that the killing was delayed due to external factors. Though they called it a war, The Troubles, it seemed to her, was nothing more than an endless tide of bickering and petty squabbles over real estate and the infinite question of whose God was holier.

She turned her gaze from the window to the girl who sat cross legged on the floor, reading an outdated issue of some entertainment magazine.

From outside, a rustling wind made the leaves whisper in the night air.

She turned away from Mary and looked back out the window. With her night vision ability, she picked out three volunteers standing close to each other beside the barn smoking cigarettes.

Suddenly, a knock was at the door.

Mary's head perked up at the sound.

Another knock.

Mary leaped to her feet and went to answer it, her dress fluttering about her thin bare legs.

She turned from the window and crossed her arms under her breasts.

Aware that the person on the other side could be a man, Mary asked who it was before opening the door.

Still by the window, she heard a woman's voice respond to the child's inquiry and realized it was Darling Emily, the driver of the van.

Mary cracked opened the heavy wooden door and spoke to the woman on the other side.

Watching them speak to each other, she reflected how much she enjoyed the label of black widow given to her by the IRA, cultivated in part by her actions and in part by Catholic superstitions. It gave her all the solitude she needed against the confined environment of the guerrilla army.

Mary soundlessly closed the bedroom door, turned, and said, "Miss Angel. The Quartermaster has arrived and he wants to say a few words to the volunteers. He has requested for you to listen in."

She thought it over for a bit and then said as she turned back once more to the window, "Very well. Inform them that I'll be attending tonight's gathering."

"Yes, Miss Angel," the young girl replied then opened the door and left to relay the message.

On behalf of the Quartermaster, who had come to personally oversee a successful outcome to the intended operation, the living room of the farm house had been hastily converted into a makeshift gathering hall by its owner, a sympathetic widower to the IRA's vision of a truly free Ireland.

Beside the stairwell, Seamus Cass and a few of his men quietly talked amongst themselves as they waited for the assembly to begin.

The farm owner's eldest daughter passed hot coffee and biscuits to the gathering crowd.

Dressed in denim, black pumps, and a navy cardigan over a white t-shirt, she stood with Mary at her side in the darkened hallway just at the threshold of the living room.

With the smell of hot fresh coffee lingering in the air and the comforting warmth of body heat, the tone of the room took on a relaxed subdued hue.

Twenty minutes later, a large man in his late forties with rosy cheeks and tasseled brown hair stepped into the room and faced the crowd. The movement of his gestures and the firm stare from his eyes made his authority obvious.

The numerous conversations ceased almost instantly and everyone turned to look at him.

Standing behind a makeshift podium set up in front of the living room's large bay window, he spoke to those in attendance in the same heavy Irish accent as everyone else, "For those of you who don't know me, my name is Quartermaster Liam Rander. For those of you who do… then you know that I'm a man short on words and large in action."

Cass and the rest of the men stared soundlessly.

"My whole purpose in being here is to see… if need be… the death of many people," he looked around the living room at the faces staring at him then continued, "Your purpose in being here is to see… if need be… that those people die."

Her large green eyes took in the man.

"Our fellow brother-in-arms Robert Strand sits in that British hell called Mace prison, slowly starving to death in a valiant effort to win the honor of being recognized as a political prisoner."

"The Royals sitting comfortably in Buckingham palace have ignored all requests by many organizations on behalf of Robert's family to grant his petition," he rested his hands on the wooden podium and continued, "All of which have either been rejected or dismissed with nothing more than a wave of a bejeweled hand."

"If Robert Strand dies as a result of his hunger strike which I've been told, by our inside sources, won't be much longer... so too will all of those associated with his capture and conviction."

He pushed off the podium. "Most importantly, the coward and traitor Owen Shea who not only saw to it that Robert Strand be captured but has also been involved in the capture and murder of three other beloved IRA volunteers."

"Now...in order to succeed, should we be called upon to carry out the eliminations of our purposed targets... we have been substantially outfitted both financially and supply wise," he quickly glanced her way and added, "As well as being afforded the proper personal."

She gave him a slow nod in recognition

He returned the nod and concluded, "That is all I have to say... for now."

Seamus Cass stood up from his chair, rounded the podium, and took the Quartermaster's hand in his. "Thank you for your words of encouragement and your own personal attention in what lies ahead, Quartermaster."

The large man who towered over Cass by close to

four inches, returned the handshake and replied, "Your ASU is considered one of the best in all of Ireland, my friend. I only hope that Robert Strand is given what he is so desperately fighting for with his life."

Cass let go of the Quartermaster's hand then touched him on the shoulder as he stepped away from the podium and left the room without a further word.

Alone and standing in front of everyone, Cass spoke out loud, "Before we adjourn for the evening, let us pray for Robert Strand, his family, our families, and our immortal beloved IRA."

In unison, the entire room stood and lowered their heads.

Cass gave the woman and girl a glance as he closed his eyes and lowered his head. "Dear Lord, we pray to You this night... Wednesday, August the twelfth of the year 1981... to thank You for Your grace that You've seen fit to bestow upon us, Your soldiers of the church. We pray for Robert Strand... that his hunger pains end soon and that his family can soon rest knowing that his suffering has ended. We pray for our families that they may find comfort in knowing that we fight in Your name, in the name of the Holy Catholic church, and for a free Ireland," then took a deep breath and continued, "Please repeat after me."

Cass and everyone prayed as one, "Our Father, who art in heaven, hallowed be Thy name; Thy kingdom come; Thy will be done on Earth as is in Heaven. Give us this day our daily bread... and forgive us our trespasses, as we forgive those who trespass against us... and lead us not into temptation but deliver us from evil," he took a long breath and continued on with everyone following suit, "Hail Mary, full of grace... the Lord is with thee... blessed art thou amongst women, and blessed is the fruit of thy womb, Jesus. Holy Mary, mother of God, pray for us sinners, now and at the hour of our death. Glory be to the Father, and to the Son, and to the Holy Spirit. As it was then, is now, and ever shall be, world without end. Amen."

The room fell silent.

Seamus Cass opened his eyes, looked at the hallway entrance, and found it empty.

Together, she and the girl walked calmly away from the warm interior of the farm house and into the cool crisp night air and its darkness. With everyone inside, the entire property was at their disposal.

Listening to prayers sickened her to the core, they remained her of the hell that ultimately awaited her in the afterlife should she one day die for all the murdering, raping, burning, and torturing she had done side by side with the creature that lived within her.

Walking in silence, they took in the sounds of the living dark as the night hummed with life all around them.

They reached the furthest edge of the property of the farm and stopped.

A vast forest stood in front of them.

Staring at the mesh of lush green foliage, she stepped out of the black pumps.

The cold wet earth felt like an electric shock on the soles of her bare feet.

She bent down, picked her shoes, and handed them to the girl.

With shoes in hand, Mary looked down at her mistress's naked feet nestled deep in the moist ground and commented, "You might get sick standing in the cold like that, Miss Angel."

Without looking at the small girl, she told her, "I don't get sick," then added, "I can't get sick."

Mary looked up and observed how her large green glossy eyes seemed to ingest the forest in front of them.

Without uttering another word, the Angel of Death, as she would always be referred to during this chapter of her life, walked towards the ominous dark forest in front of her.

Staying where she was, Mary asked, "Would you like to be alone, Miss Angel?"

She stopped, thought about the creature within her, and answered the girl, "I'm never alone," then continued walking into the rich lush forest growth until it swallowed her whole.

With the noon sun high overhead, in the master bedroom, she moved the Chantilly lace curtain slightly to the left with her index finger and looked out the window at the farm spread.

Still waiting for Robert Strand to either die or be granted what he sought, the atmosphere about the farm had taken on a relaxed and tranquil feel for everyone, except for her. With the creature's need for constant fresh kills, waiting to be called to action had gone from aggravating to maddening.

The curtain slipped from her finger.

She knew that if she had to wait much longer to kill someone then everyone on the property was in jeopardy as well as her established position within the outlaw organization.

Needing to quell the bloodlust boiling inside her guts, she turned towards the interior of the bedroom and stepped to the foot of the wrought iron bed frame where Mary lay fast asleep in the fetal position on top of a hand quilted comforter.

The afternoon sun bled into the bedroom with a yellowish warm glow.

Staring at the small girl, she took in her slight delicate figure and smooth supple white skin

The girl's chest rose and fell rhythmically with each sleeping breath.

She griped the bed frame with both hands as visions of tearing the slumbering child apart with her bare hands flashed across her mind. She desperately needed a kill.

Mary stirred on the soft warm bedding.

In an effort to calm the murderous thoughts against the sleeping child, she slowly took in deep calming breaths as the corners of her mouth began to itch.

Feeling the sensation of someone staring at her, Mary opened her eyes and saw the IRA's master killer, looking intently at her. "Miss Angel... is everything alright?"

She answered the girl matter-of-factly, "No, Mary. Everything... is not."

Suddenly very afraid for her own safety, the young girl sat up and slid her knobby knees to her chest.

They stared at each other in silence for a long while until she told the girl, "Mary, my sweet... please... tell the Quartermaster and Lt. Cass... that I request... company."

With only a nod to acknowledge what her mistress had just said, the girl climbed off the bed, stepped into her shoes and left the room as calmly yet as quickly as possible.

Suddenly all alone, she let go of the bed frame, looked at the palms, and saw the coral design of the wrought iron had embedded itself deep into the flesh of her hands.

Walking down the hallway, Mary felt the sweat underneath her dress turn clammy and cold against her chest. She had seen her mistress once before behave as she was doing now and knew she had been lucky to walk out of that bedroom alive.

She scampered down the single flight of steps, rounded the banister, and made her way, past a couple volunteers dressed as farmers, towards the kitchen.

Three men and one woman sat in the living room, cleaning automatic weapons.

Mary entered the warm scented kitchen and spotted the property owner's daughter tending to the stove.

Coached in all manners and etiquette before becoming one of Northern Ireland's youngest volunteers, Mary approached the tired looking woman, gave a subtle curtsy, and said, "Good evening, Miss Hanlon."

Focused on the numerous pots and pan on the overworked stove, the woman, who would later run away to Spain with her young lover the following spring, looked over at the small girl and instantly stiffened. Knowing full well who the elfin looking child represented, she replied with a cautious and polite tone, "Yes, Mary. What can I do for you?"

Accustomed to being treated with a level of anxiety and curtness from those around her, Mary kept the exchange short, "Where may I find the Quartermaster or Lt. Cass?"

With a sense of relief in not being asked to wait upon the strange woman upstairs, she gave the caldron of stew a quick stir and answered, "You can find them both in the study," then pointed with the broth covered wooden spoon to a small hallway to her left.

Mary turned towards the direction of the spoon and said, "Thank you, Miss Hanlon," then curtsied once again and left the kitchen.

"My pleasure... my dear," the woman replied with a nervous smile and then returned to her stirring as she watched the young eerily mannered child leave the kitchen.

With the authority to access whatever or whoever was needed for the good of The Angel of Death, Mary knocked on the door of the study and entered.

Sitting across from each other, Lt. Seamus Cass and Quartermaster Liam Rander looked up from the cluttered table filled with maps, ledgers, and field reports.

Mary gave them a full deep curtsy, complete with a delicate lift of her dress and a slow bow of her head, and said, "Quartermaster Rander... Lt. Cass... good evening."

Aware of the power the child in front of them held as an extension of the woman assassin, Rander cleared his throat and returned, "What may... we do for you... young Mary Gorten?"

Mary came out of her curtsy, straightened to a standing position in front of them, and replied, "Miss Angel requests... company."

Robert Hall, ex-military, ex-husband, and ex-involved father of three, slowly made his way up the four steps to the front door of his two story apartment as he regularly did every Thursday night.

With his head swimming in robust stout, he dumbly slumped against the door when he reached it.

431

He fumbled for his keys, drew them out from his coat pocket, and, after a few failed attempts, slid the correct one into the lock and opened the door.

Warm air stored away inside the apartment greeted him like a comforting hug. Robert smiled at the sensation.

He closed the door behind him, dropped both his coat and keys on the floor, and then carried himself up the single flight of steps that lead to the bedroom he had once shared with his wife and had since shared with numerous prostitutes.

Once upstairs, in almost total darkness, Robert used his intimate knowledge of his home to round the banister and head towards the bedroom at the far end of the hall.

He pushed open the bedroom door, ran his hand on the rose petal wallpapered wall towards the light switch but stopped just short of the switch.

There was an unfamiliar smell lurking about.

Feeling suddenly incredibly sober, he drew in the air around him through his nostrils as his eyes desperately worked against the darkness.

The interior of the small room loomed dark and silent.

He moved his hand towards the light switch and then, a split second before flicking on the lights, he balled his hand into a tight fist and shot it into the darkness.

Robert heard the soft thud of his fist land squarely against the face of whoever had been waiting for him in the dark and felt that person's nose break on his knuckles.

With the lights still out, he spun on his heels and drove the same fist deep in the abdomen of a second person.

Gurgling blood through his shattered nose, Aedan White fell to the wood flooring while Garret Murray, gasping for breath, collapsed onto the metal framed bed in a heap.

Knowing that the element of surprise was no longer on his side, Robert went for the light switch, eager to see who had broken into his home and even more eager to get to his service weapon in the top drawer of his nightstand.

He flicked on the light to the bedroom and caught a glimpse of a rifle butt a split second before it came crashing down between his eyes, knocking him instantly unconscious and crumpling him to the floor.

Seamus Cass lowered the Japanese assault rifle to his side, looked down at the two men who had come with him and asked them as they struggled to their feet, "Are you two turkeys going to live… or what?"

Standing on unsteady legs, White gingerly touched his nose, winced in pain, and said, "Old fucker smelled us."

With a smile, Cass looked down at the retired British paratrooper and said, "Company awaits… Staff Sergeant Hall."

The following night, under a full moon, she stood next to the young girl, facing the forest once again.

The evening air wisped and flicked around them.

She heard footsteps off in the distance coming their way and instantly knew who they belonged to from the walking pattern.

Breaking with protocol, not to directly speak to her, in order to insure a proper evening, Seamus Cass addressed the imposing woman in front of him with an impersonal and professional tone, "Good evening, Miss Angel."

She addressed him in the same tone without turning around, "Good evening, Lt. Cass."

Hearing her voice for the first time ever, he felt a chill flutter over his entire body as he looked to the right of the woman and saw the child liaison, dressed in her trademark white dress and black saddle shoes

Mary turned to him, curtsied, and greeted the IRA operative, "Good evening, Lt. Cass."

"Good evening, young Mary," he returned, gathering himself.

"What have you brought... me?" The Angel of Death asked.

Listening to her, Cass began to wonder if he had made a terrible mistake by coming himself to speak with her.

Noticing how comfortable he had suddenly become, Mary stepped away from the woman's side and approached him. "Miss Angel asked a question... Lt. Cass."

He looked down at the girl, realized the sooner he said what he had come to say then the sooner he could get away from them both, and replied, "His name is Rob..."

"I don't need his name!" she snapped viciously. The need for a kill had all but eaten away at her patience.

Stunned by the sudden burst of fury from the IRA's legendary assassin, Cass blinked, swallowed, and started over again, "He's ex-military. Former British paratrooper to be exact. At one point, he even tried out for the SAS."

She said nothing, only listened.

Cass went on, "He's still got plenty of fight left in him. He took out two of my men with just his bare hands. One's suffered what appears to be a bruised liver while the other got his nose broken in three places."

She continued to listen.

"The best part to him is he's still relatively young enough to pose a genuine challenge for you... yet old enough not to be missed very much," he told her.

She asked, breaking her silence, "How did you find someone so... well qualified... so quickly?"

"He's been on the IRA's target list for some time," he confessed, "So... when you requested to have someone brought to you... we picked him out as the best candidate from that list."

Cass continued, "He's a tough old bastard, I tell you. He'll give you what you're looking for."

"Where is he now?" she asked.

"We chained him up to a tree in the centermost part of the forest and left him with a hacksaw for the chain around his ankle and a loaded revolver six paces away."

He was about to add something further but was cut off by the young girl suddenly dismissing him, "Miss Angel thanks you, Lt. Cass."

He looked down at the child. "Thank you, young Mary," then he added, "Is there anything else... you'd like to know before you begin?"

Slowly, she finally turned and faced him.

With the aid of the bright silver moonlight, he looked into her eyes and saw the most beautiful pair of greens eyes he had ever seen. A sudden and inexplicable desire to touch her swelled within him.

Though her eyes were lush and succulent, her

voice, when she spoke to him face to face, was cold and sharp like the blade of a knife, "Clear you men. Take them inside and keep them there until I'm done," she took a long pause for effect, "If anyone is caught outside after I begin... I will not be held responsible for what happens to that person or persons."

Cass simply nodded in response.

Eager to maintain her position amongst the army of guerrilla fighters for as long as possible, she asked, "Have I made myself perfectly understood, Lt. Cass?"

He slowly answered, "Yes... Miss Angel."

She turned casually back around and bid him a good night, "Then good evening, Lt. Cass."

"Good... evening... Miss Angel," he returned.

"Good evening... Lt. Cass," Mary bid him farewell with another curtsy.

Cass acknowledged the child liaison, "Good evening to you, young Mary," then added over the girl's head, "Good luck tonight, Miss Angel. May he serve you well."

Staring into the forest in front of her and savoring the kill that lay ahead, she gave no reply.

Without anything else to do or say, he turned around and walked away, realizing now why such strict orders, when it came to interacting with her, existed and how appropriate the many titles that she had earned over the years were; The Angel of Death, The Killer of Killers, and The Black Widow of Belfast.

A short time later, the final volunteer entered the crowded house and the door closed behind him.

Mary turned and said, "Everyone is inside, Miss Angel."

"Very good... now come over here and help me

with my clothes," she told the young girl.

Having been with her once before in what she was about to do, Mary helped her undress until she stood naked in her bare feet in front of the forest's thick foliage.

"Thank you, Mary. Now, please go inside with the others," she spoke to her for the last time that evening.

With her arms full of clothes, Mary watched her silently step into the thick green growth and disappear from sight.

The feel of the overgrowth of the forest licking at her naked skin and the wet earth at her bare soles felt exhilarating as she walked deeper and deeper into the forest.

When the thick canopy of the trees blocked the silver moonlight overhead, she used her eye's night vision to maneuver easily around the foliage with ease.

With each passing minute, her body shed a bit of the tension of not having killed in days and the lust for violence slowly surged within her.

Then off in the distance, she heard the sound, no louder than a whisper, of metal systematically tearing into metal.

She stopped in her tracks, closed her large glossy green eyes in concentration and listened to the faint sound. It was neither frantic nor hurried in any way but even and methodical.

She smiled. The target, it seemed, was calm and focused on getting free with the hacksaw, a clear sign that he had indeed been an excellent choice.

She took a few more steps silently forward.

The sawing continued.

Carefully, she made her way closer and closer to

where the sound was loudest.

The sawing continued.

Finally, through the thick vegetation, she saw him.

Attached to a chain at the ankle to a tree, Robert Hall was steadfastly focused at working through the metal links with the hacksaw he had been given.

His vulnerability and his sheer desire to survive made her nipples harden and her large green eyes dilate.

Either unknowing or uncaring that he was now being watched by the person who had come to murder him, Hall sawed away in even rhythmic pace without stopping.

Watching him desperately trying to free himself, she felt the creature inside her awaken. First a slight warmth at the base of her spine then a slow even bloom throughout her entire naked body.

The chain snapped in two.

The corners of her mouth ripped to her ears.

They bolted into action at the same instant; he dove for the revolver off to his right and she leaped, turning into the creature in midair, into the small clearing.

Hall tucked and rolled in order to keep his forward momentum going, came out of it on his knees, and grabbed the weapon.

The creature landed in a squat, six feet from its intended victim, bared its shark like teeth through its gaping mouth, and let out a loud blood curdling growl.

Robert Hall swung the gun in the direction of the demonic sound, caught sight of the long limbed white furred monster, and screamed out in terror as he fired.

With incredible speed, the creature sprang forward and raced across the short distance between them.

The bullet tore across the night just over the creature's pointy ears.

Scared like no other time in his life, he watched in a sort of slow motion the thing close the gap between them.

It reached him in less than a second, and, in one fluid motion, swept its dagger sharp clawed hand across his right leg.

Fabric, skin, and muscle tore open to the bone in a red gush of blood.

Hall raised his head up into the dark sky above him and hollered out in agony.

Without slowing or stopping, the creature continued past him and bound into the thick foliage at the other end of the small clearing.

Fighting back the urge to vomit from the searing pain at his leg, Hall turned around as fast as he could and fired into the forest, wasting a bullet.

The creature, tucked safely among the thick foliage, licked its bloody claws in delight at the sudden and intense dose of violence.

With the weapon pointed out in front of him, he scanned about to locate the thing that had attacked him while the pain and shock from the devastating wound darkened and tunneled his vision around the edges.

Sheltered by the forest growth, it watched him bravely and pointlessly keep the revolver out and up.

Finally, he staggered on up to his feet as he struggled, from the blood loss, to keep the weapon up and level. Humiliated and alone, he screamed out with the last of his strength, "Where the fuck are you!"

Knowing that he didn't have very much time left before succumbing to the grave injury on his leg, it slowly began to circle the circumference of the clearing in order to pounce with maximum efficiency.

Mortally wounded and only minutes away from dying from the lack of blood, Hall, suddenly too tired to yell again, whispered, "Where the fuck... are... you," as his eyes grew laden and the gun too heavy to point.

Slowly and in complete silence, the demonic creature stood up directly behind him.

The smell of mint gently touched Hall's dwindling senses a second before the creature drove its railroad spike shaped fingers deep into the man's ribcage, puncturing his liver and right lung instantly.

Too weak to scream and too overcome by shock, Robert Hall's mouth gaped opened in a silent scream of pain.

The revolver with four unused rounds still in its cylinder slipped from his hand and fell uselessly onto the carpet of blood soaked grass.

It lifted him up off his feet by his ribs then flung him into the dark.

Hall soared through the air in a graceless tangle of limbs and ribbons of rich crimson blood and then hit the tree which he had been chained to earlier face first, shattering his facial skull like an egg shell and rocketing his teeth down his throat as his left eye ejected out its socket.

The creature watched with satisfaction as its victim crumpled in a heap at the base of the tree.

Severely injured and in shock, he watched, with his one good eye, as the white clad demonic figure casually walk up to him and knell down next to him.

An instant before dying, Robert Hall, ex-military, ex-husband, and ex-involved father of three, gave the faintest of smiles as a one final image flashed across his mind; a red ball slowly rolling along a desolate road.

The creature fell on him and dismembered him with its bare clawed hands.

The following day as the sun waned slowly downward in the late afternoon, she languished on the quilted bed in the bedroom with the girl nestled tightly against her. With the creature satisfied, the hunger to kill had been replaced with a sense of peace and calm.

Slowly, enjoying the sheer pleasure of the soothing moment, she opened her eyes, and looked about the bedroom. The sunlight, amber rich in color, rested lazily across her bare feet while the lace window dressings waved slowly against the gentle breeze.

From the open window, the placid sound of people going about their duties around the farm drifted casually in; giving the serene afternoon a peaceful comforting feel.

Gently, she inhaled the delicate smell of the child tucked neatly under her arm, sighed, and closed her eyes again.

Drifting in and out of sleep, Mary shrugged closer against the woman's gentle caress, enjoying the soporific day after such a terrible night.

The girl's gentle body heat and the cool draft from the open window blended into a comforting slumber inducing mixture.

Together, they fell into sleep while the shadows lengthened across the faded pink carpet as the sun continued its downward path towards sunset.

Somewhere deep in the slumbering pit of her mind, she felt a sudden change in her surroundings and opened her eyes.

The bedroom glowed in the soft light of her night

vision.

Realizing it was night time, she glanced at the nightstand clock. It read half past eight in the evening.

She turned her head to the left and looked at Mary still nestled peacefully in her arms, sleeping.

Not wanting to disturb the sleeping girl, she slowly and carefully slid her arm out from under her and climbed out of bed.

Dressed only in a pair of jeans, a loose fitting t-shirt, and no bra, she walked barefoot across the thin carpet to the open window.

She placed her hands on the sill, looked about the farm grounds below, but saw no one.

Under the bare soles of her feet, she felt the distant rumble of commotion coming from the ground floor.

Quickly, she turned around and dashed back to the bed.

Still using only her night vision to see, she sat next to the girl and gently shook her awake.

Mary blinked in the darkness and asked, a bit startled, "Miss Angel... is everything alright?"

She moved her hand from the girl's slight shoulder and delicately combed a lock of fine strawberry blonde hair away from the child's forehead (a gesture she would repeat once more years later on a late autumn Sunday afternoon right before killing her) and said, "He's dead."

Before Mary could ask who had died, she was pulled from off the bed, and led, by the hand, out the bedroom door and down the stairs to the living room.

Half way down the stairs, they ran into the farmer's daughter. "I was just coming to get you."

With a passing nod, she continued down the

remaining stairs with the girl in tow and stopped at the entrance of the living room.

Packed with every IRA volunteer Cass had brought with him, the living room hummed with life.

Watching from just inside the hallway, she saw the Quartermaster take his place at the makeshift podium once again.

He raised one large hand for silence, waited a brief moment, lowered it, and spoke to the crowd, "My dear fellow volunteers... I have gathered all of you tonight to inform you that our brother in arms... our symbol of unwavering commitment to a free Northern Ireland... has died," he took a deep breath, lowered his head, and said, "Robert Strand starved to death just a few hours ago in Mace prison.

She smiled at his words. The blood was about to flow deep.

The Quartermaster slowly raised his head, looked directly at her, and gave her a small nod as if he had read her mind from across the room.

The corners of her mouth split at their web as her smiled widened with the excitement at what lay ahead.

"And now...my dear..." she whispered to the girl, "the real killing... begins."

Helen Strong, dressed in her maid's uniform, fluttered about her small kitchen, coffee cup in hand. Always running late for work, she tidied up whatever mess she might have made during breakfast as she tried to eat it, consisting of nothing more than buttered toast with jam and coffee.

Black bobbed, elfin face, and slim figured, Helen looked younger than her thirty two years.

With no man of which to speak of, her aging

mother was all she had in the way of constant company.

She placed the tepid mug on the counter next to the sink and ran a damp cloth over the crumbs of her toast, knowing full well that her mother would still find speckles and comment on them later during dinner.

Finished cleaning, she threw the wash cloth on top of the faucet, jammed the last of the toast into her mouth, took hold of her mug, and set about to find her worn black leather loafers.

In her nylon feet, she ran from the kitchen to the tiny room that served as a living room. With one eye on the clock, she looked about for her shoes as best as she could without spilling her coffee all over herself.

Then, just as she was beginning to believe that she would have to go to work in her bare feet, she caught sight of the scuffed tip of her right shoe poking out from underneath the drape of their battered sofa. "Thank you, Jesus!" she exclaimed then gave her coffee one final draught and stepped into her shoes.

The old and familiar sweat softened leather greeted her toes like a lover after a long absence.

Shoed, she skipped back to the kitchen sink, rinsed the mug, set it on the drying rack, and turned around to begin the surmounting task of finding her purse and keys.

The doorbell rang.

Helen turned on her heels towards the door.

The doorbell rang again.

She wondered who could possibly be at her door so early in the morning.

Again, the doorbell rang.

Perhaps, she figured, it was someone from church for her mother. She stepped across the small living room, undid the dead bolts, turned the knob, and opened the wooden door.

Her first thought was that someone, as a joke, had left a full sized mirror on the front step but then, after a moment, she realized that it wasn't a mirror she was looking at but an actual woman, identical in appearance to her in every way possible, maid's uniform and all.

Together, they silently stared at each other without moving.

Utterly confounded by the whole thing, Helen gave a nervous laugh and was about to speak when, all of a sudden, the woman's large and dazzling green eyes begin to spin at the irises around the pupils.

Staring in absolute wonder into the churning green color, she felt her body become light as a feather and a warm gush of moisture froth between her legs.

Then without warning, Helen's doppelganger struck her in the throat.

Crumpling to her knees, she grabbed her damaged throat, struggling for air.

The lookalike took a step over the threshold, placed both hands on either side of Helen's head and then rammed her left knee into her face, shooting her nasal septum upwards into her brain, killing her instantly.

Staring down absently at the dead woman's body with her large green eyes, she slowly closed the door behind her with her left foot.

From the rear bedroom, an old woman's voice drifted out, "Helen, darling... is everything all right, dear?"

She stepped over the dead body and went into the kitchen.

"Helen, dear, are you alright?" the elderly mother of seven children and grandmother of five called out to her murdered daughter.

Smiling, she carefully selected the largest knife available from the kitchen cabinet and then walked into the bedroom.

A few minutes later, while inspecting her maid's uniform for any visual signs of blood, she stepped out of the bedroom and went into the small living room.

She slipped her hand into the front pocket of her uniform and pulled out a small plastic case which contained one set of brown colored glass contact lens. Still years away from general availability, the tinted lens had cost the IRA a hefty sum to procure.

Delicately, she placed each one over her green eyes. Their thickness and weight made her blink in discomfort until she grew accustomed to their uneasy sensation.

Next, she scanned around for the dead woman's purse and keys and found them just to the right of the sofa on the floor.

She slipped the keys into the same front pocket as the contact case, looped the tooled leather hand bag over her left forearm and left the apartment.

A brisk walk later, she entered the service entrance of the Four Leaf Hotel fifteen minutes after 9 am.

The clerk at the door gave her a look over a raised eyebrow, glanced at the clock on the wall, and then back to her. "A fine day to be late, Helen." he commented.

Aware that the glass tinted contacts in her eyes wouldn't pass close scrutiny, she gave him a slide long nod as she walked past him.

She walked down the west hall, took a left, just as

she'd been coached, and entered the female locker room.

Devoid of anyone else, the large changing area echoed her footsteps with an ominous sound.

Knowing full well that she was behind schedule, she quickly located the dead woman's locker, marked by her first and last name, sat down in front of it on the wooden bench that ran along the entire length of the aisle of lockers, and waited for the IRA collaborator to make contact with her.

A few minutes later, Grace Malone, the slightly overweight forty-eight year old headmistress to The Four Leaf, stepped into the empty locker room and called out in a hushed tone, "Helen, dear... are you ready?"

Without turning, she answered with only a nod.

Baffled by the excessive amount that she had been paid by the IRA (a visa to the U.S. and twenty thousand dollars in cash) just to make sure that Helen, a simple and hardworking maid, delivered breakfast to the Northern Irish traitor on the fourteenth floor, Grace gulped down through the tightness of her throat and asked again, "Are you ready, my dear?"

She nodded again and replied, "I just need a minute."

Chalking it up to nerves, Grace gave a motherly smile and told her, "I'll be at the kitchen, love," then turned and walked away.

The second her collaborator had cleared the room, she sprang from the bench, ran headlong down the aisle, past the showers, and through a door at the far end marked Electrical Room Level-Sub.

She swept her eyes around the small wire cluttered

room until she found a small upside down three leaf clover drawn in black marker on the wall, next to a circuit breaker box, and went to it.

Standing in front of the tiny drawing, she shape shifted her right hand up to her elbow, balled it up into a tight fist, and punched a hole into the wall with full force.

The dry wall caved in around her disfigured fur covered clawed hand.

She closed her eyes in concentration and searched around the cavity until her railroad spiked fingers came upon the bundle that had been left for her months ago by clandestine IRA masons.

Careful not to drop with she had in her hand, she pulled out a small wooden box wrapped in oilcloth from within the wall, hunkered down, and placed it on her lap.

As her right hand slowly returned to human form, she undid the yellowish cloth from around the box and opened it.

Inside, against soft supple purple velvet, she found a 9mm semiautomatic handgun and a folding knife, both still in perfect condition.

Quickly, she inspected the handgun, found it with one round in the chamber and full magazine, then slipped it and the knife into the front pockets of her uniform.

She stood up, returned both the oilcloth and box back inside the hole, stepped out of the small electrical room, and closed the door behind her.

Knowing that time was at an essence, she quickly exited the empty locker room, and, drawing from memory from the mission briefing the night before, made her way towards the kitchen area.

Wondering why the woman she thought to be Helen was taking so long, Grace Malone stood just at the entrance of the large industrial kitchen of the hotel while the finishing touches on Owen Walsh's breakfast were being done.

Hovering amongst the kitchen employees was a chef from a British commando garrison who insured that nothing foreign or poisonous was administered in the IRA traitor's meals. Like a rabbi overseeing strict kosher practices, he silently scrutinized every single step of every single meal that was prepared for the most notorious guest at The Four Leaf.

Finished, a rosy cheeked kitchen aid with plump hands slid the breakfast of hotcakes, eggs, and links towards the garrison chef.

With nothing more than a nod, he gave his approval of the entrée and then backed out of the way.

Grace stepped into the spotless white tiled kitchen and readied the trey; Morning paper in the slot along the side, condiments at the upper left, flatware on either side of the plate, water, juice, and coffee at the upper right, and a clean linen cloth draped across the entire arrangement.

With Helen nowhere in sight to take the trey up to the 14th floor and without any other course of action, Grace gathered the breakfast trey in her hands and decided to do it herself.

As everyone in the kitchen area went about their duties, Grace exhaled a centering breath, mustered up her courage, and turned around only to find Helen's mirror image standing in front of her, hands extended to receive the trey of food.

Startled by the young maid's sudden appearance,

Grace gave a nervous smile and said, "Oh... Helen, my love...there ya are," aware that the military chef was still only a few feet away, she quickly composed herself, "Now, be a dear and take this up to 1409."

From behind her false contacts, she looked at the head mistress as she took the trey. "Yes, Miss Grace," then turned and walked out.

Grace Malone watched the person who she thought was Helen leave the kitchen area, and later, while boarding the trans-Atlantic airplane, she'd wonder how the diminutive maid, who had once squealed in terror over a spider, could have killed so many men so quickly.

Walking down the service hallway towards the elevators, she balanced the trey in one hand and with the other slipped both the knife and handgun under the linen cloth.

She removed the brown contacts from her eyes, exposing their lush emerald color, and dropped the tiny colored glass disks into a pocket.

When she reached the elevators, she stopped in front of a young British soldier assigned to guard the elevator at the service level.

Having met already the real Helen Strong, who along with her mother would be found days later from the smell of decay, he greeted her with a casual nod.

Eager to get the killing underway, she quickly locked her eyes to his and sent the lush green irises spinning.

Instantly mesmerized by their power, the young soldier swooned.

With their eyes locked on to one another, she quietly told him, "There is nothing here for you to check."

Motionless, he listened to the woman's beautiful voice.

She continued, "You will let me enter the elevator."

He made no reply.

"When I start going up, you will radio in and simply report that breakfast is being sent."

Staring ever deeper into the spinning green of her irises, he simply nodded in understanding.

She smiled at him and added the finishing touch, "When I come down, you can take me into the broom closet and fuck me as long and as hard as you want."

His penis went rock hard as he finally found his voice, "O...o...ok."

Still holding him with the power of her eyes, she commanded, "Let me in."

Without taking his eyes away from hers, he extended his left hand out and with his middle finger pressed the elevator button.

The double metal doors dinged and opened.

She gave a slow blink and turned her head, breaking the connection she had on him and stepped into the mirrored cubicle.

Looking at her with a boyish grin, the young soldier, who would later be court martialed and imprisoned for three years for dereliction of duty, pressed the special button specifically installed to take the elevator car directly up to the 14th floor without any stops along the way.

The double doors slid closed and the elevator lifted upward.

Inside the cramped elevator, she placed the trey on the floor and disrobed.

The lighted numbers above the elevator doors

climbed as she went upward and upward.

The numbers climbed.

Bare foot and completely naked, she took the handgun and blade from under the linen cloth and went over her mission one last time: Former IRA volunteer and considered by many as the single biggest threat to the paramilitary organization, Owen Walsh, who had been seduced by the lure of money and the feminine wiles of a British counteragent, now sat in the master suite on the 14th floor as he waited to testify on yet another captured volunteer. Instrumental in the arrest and conviction of Robert Strand and three others, he had been targeted for assassination since May the previous year. Her objective was simple; eliminate Owen Walsh while two IRA hit-squads sanctioned their own targets at the very same time; the lead prosecutor at Strand's trial and a Mace prison guard who had reportedly abused him as he had slowly starved to death.

The main obstacle to her mission was, by and large, the design of the hotel itself. Shaped like a shoebox on its side, the elevator stood at one end and the master suite at the other with guest rooms down the left side, bay windows on the right, and heavily armed soldiers down the entire length of the narrow hallway.

The elevator dinged to a stop on the 14th floor.

She closed her eyes and let the monster within her take over.

The double doors slid open.

Standing at attention, seven British soldiers, four along the left side and three along the right, assigned to protect the United Kingdom's most coveted witness against the IRA, turned their heads toward the open elevator doors, expecting to see a maid with a breakfast trey but what they saw was something else entirely.

Staring back at them with brilliant large green eyes was a long limbed monster, clad in dazzling white fur and a gaping mouth filled with razor sharp shark like teeth.

Dumbfounded by such an unexpected and shocking sight, they simply stared back in awe.

Using their reaction of its appearance to its advantage, the creature simultaneously pressed the Hold button on the console of the elevator with the hand holding the knife and fired with its left.

The two farthest soldiers on the left side instantly fell, mortally wound.

At the sound of the 9mm's discharge, the remaining five sprang into action and went for their rifles slung over their shoulders.

With a burst of startling speed, the creature leaped out of the mirrored elevator, landed in front of the nearest soldier, Pvt. Upton, on the right, and then drove the blade deep into the young man's neck, instantly silencing him before he could utter a sound.

Down to four, the remaining soldiers placed their weapons up against their shoulders and took aim at the monster that was killing them off one by one with lightning speed.

Acting on instinct and momentum, the creature turned the dead body still in its hands towards the leveled rifle barrels.

The soldiers fired in unison.

The bulletproofed vest and dead body absorbed the rifle rounds.

Behind the bloodied and battered corpse it held like a shield, the creature fired twice at the soldier to its immediate left.

The first round missed but the second struck the young corporal to the face, killing him instantly.

Watching everyone being killed all around him, Sgt. Reedus, who was the oldest and the highest ranking, yelled at the rest of his men, "Keep at it… tear into this thing!" as he continued to fire his weapon.

The creature pulled the trigger again, a bullet from its handgun streak across the hallway, and struck the last soldier on the left between doors 1404 and 1405, dropping him to the carpeted floor, weapon still in hand and a bullet hole to his forehead.

The Sergeant and his Lance Corporal, the last two, fired until their magazines ran empty then lowered their rifles in order to reload them.

Making full use of the small window offered to it by the mechanics of reloading an assault rifle, it rushed at them head on while using the bullet riddled body as a battering ram.

Seeing the hideous monster coming at them like a runaway freight train, Lance Cpl. Wetherell cried out in despair as he desperately tried to hastily reload his weapon.

The creature with its emerald green eyes blazing from the excitement of killing barreled into the Sergeant first, knocking him to the floor.

Undaunted and set on staying alive, Reedus continued to reload, eager to send whatever it was back to wherever it had come from.

The creature dropped the bloodied body of Pvt. Upton on top of him and then gripped the knife blade down.

Pinned under the corpse's dense weight, Sgt. Reedus struggled in vain to free himself in order to fire.

Fast and sure, the creature buried the blood

stained knife through his left eye and deep into his brain, sending the Sargent into a series of convulsing spasms before dying.

With a fresh magazine finally inserted into his rifle, Lance Cpl. Wetherell, the last of them, chambered a round and raised the weapon to fire at the creature at point blank range.

Ever quicker and deadlier from generations and generations of killing, the creature raised its weapon first and pulled the trigger, striking him in the throat.

Mortally wound and drowning his own blood, Wetherell crumpled onto the floor and died.

With everyone in the corridor dead, the creature let the 9mm fall from its clawed hand and stood, leaving the knife imbedded in the dead man's eye socket.

It walked to the first soldier it had shot, knelled down, and relieved him of his .45 caliber semiautomatic still holstered at his hip.

The creature pressed checked the firearm then stood up.

A repellent odor of blood and spent gunpowder hung heavy throughout the bullet riddled hallway.

Focused on ending the task at hand, the creature went to the front door of the master suite and kicked it open.

The wooden frame splintered at the lock and the door swung inward, slamming against the inside wall with a loud rattling bang.

The creature stepped into the room with the dead soldier's handgun out and up.

The smell of talc and tobacco instantly basted its nostrils while its large pointed ears took in the eerie silence as it slowly crept inward.

It passed the bathroom and walk-in closet on

either side of the suite's hallway and entered the main room.

Standing straight as an arrow against the wall at the right side of the ample living room, Owen Walsh, clad in a nipple pink bathrobe and holding an assault rifle, stared in horror at the large lanky white furred monster.

The creature caught sight of the man it had been assigned to kill, aimed, and fired a heavy slug into the center of his chest.

Walsh's image shattered into a thousand pieces and shards from the full length mirror hit the floor in a sparkle of dazzling dancing light.

Before Owen Walsh had become a traitor to the IRA, he had been one of its most renowned volunteers in both tactics and fortitude.

Realizing it had just been tricked, the creature dove headlong and out of the way from the deadly path of flying 5x56 rounds that were sure to be coming its way at any second.

From the left side of the living room, Walsh brought the American made machine gun up to his shoulder and fired at the creature.

Missing their mark by only a fraction of a centimeter, the rifle shots slammed into the wall and dresser. Glass and wood exploded into thousands of pieces all around the creature.

Calm and collected, Owen Walsh paced his shots in a steady volley as he tracked the creature throughout the living room.

Still holding onto the handgun, the creature twisted and turned in a valiant effort to keep from being hit by the onslaught of oncoming machine gun fire.

Round after round, Walsh kept the pressure on, hell bent on living to see another day.

Knowing that sooner rather than later, it would be struck down, the creature tucked, rolled, and leaped into the air in a last ditch effort to come out the victor.

Watching the creature soaring in midair towards him, Walsh carefully sighted in and pulled the trigger.

The rifle clicked empty and Owen Walsh opened his mouth to scream out in defiance.

In midair, the creature aimed and pulled the trigger.

The .45 caliber bullet struck Walsh at the hairline and exited out the back, taking half of his brains with it.

She landed on her hands and feet, naked and sweating as Walsh, staring absently into nothingness, fell back dead between the wet bar and dinette set.

She stood, looked around the bullet riddled suite, and said out loud, "Gonna have to try that mirror trick one day," then padded around the shattered glass and walked out the master suite, leaving the .45 caliber handgun next to Owen Walsh's dead body to further add to the confusion as to the events of the day.

In the hallway, she made her way past the dead bodies, stepped into the elevator where she redressed, grabbed the breakfast tray, then walked back to the hallway and sat down on the carpeted floor.

A minute later, her acute hearing picked up the sound of over a dozen booted pairs of feet running up the stairwell to the 14th floor, no doubt SAS commandos this time around.

She put her back against the papered wall, drew her knees up to her chest, and slipped into character as the simple and dimwitted Helen Strong, the hapless maid who had just had the misfortune of being in the wrong place at the wrong time.

Waiting for the stairwell door to be kicked opened at any second, she looked out the bay window and caught sight of the hotel's famed view. The entire city, a lush mixture of brick structures and rich green trees, spread across the horizon while off in the far distance...

The marina grew closer and closer into view as she steered the Lolita in the morning light.

Smiling at the pleasant memory of her days with the IRA, she said out loud, "Still have to try that mirror trick."

Daniel's waterlogged and bloated body would float to the surface six days later.

After examining the remains, the cause of death would be determined to be suicide due to financial problems and an active investigation by Homeland Security over the suspected thief and sale of a hazardous and potentially lethal material to an unknown subject or terror cell.

CHAPTER 53

"With death... I guess."

As the late afternoon waned slowly below the city skyline, John stared at the computer monitor, exhaled, and placed his hand on the computer mouse. After weeks of searching for anything, however small, that might indicate where she could possibly be, he had turned up absolutely nothing.

With a sense of hopelessness, he clicked a Lansing news web page closed and opened one for Cleveland.

John sighed and leaned forward and began to read news articles about that city.

After some time, he came across one that caught his eye. It detailed the ongoing investigation by Homeland Security into a number of missing drums containing military-grade caustic soda, labeled XF-II, from a Cleveland chemical plant and the sudden disappearance of the investigation's prime person-of-interest, Daniel Wharton Williams. The anonymous caller who had tipped off federal agents had not been identified or found as of yet. One source speaking under anonymity had said all they knew so far about the mysterious caller was it had been a woman.

When he finished reading the article, he pushed back on the desk chair once again and thought about what he had just read. Something about it for some odd reason had spiked his interested.

He leaned forward into the computer again then referenced caustic soda into the internet.

Within a few seconds the computer monitor displayed countless search icons.

John scrolled around a bit until he found exactly what he wanted; an article having to do with caustic soda XF-II. He double clicked on an English translated news article from Acapulco, Mexico and read it under his breath.

The article referenced XF-II, a corrosive chemical agent when combined with water had the ability to completely dissolve any organic matter. Used primarily by the region's leading drug cartel as their favorite choice of disposal of ransomed abductees, migrant travelers, and for the torturous death of informants and deserters.

He finished with the article and looked up over the top of the computer monitor, and caught sight of Rachael walking down the hall towards the kitchen area.

Holding a pie tin with one hand, she smiled and waved at him with the other as she passed in front of the shelter's computer room.

He smiled back and gave his chin a thrust at her as she rounded the corner and disappeared then turned his attention back to the internet once more.

He clicked back to the Cleveland news site and

slowly scrolled through its archived articles until he came across a particular one about the gruesome and senseless murder of Wendy Beltran, a fellow native of Cleveland, whose torn and mangled body had been found inside her car under a desolate overpass by a pair of school children taking a short cut home.

Intrigued, John read on.

A fellow native of Cleveland, Wendy Beltran had worked as the director of The Thomas A. Lean Olympic Swimming Facility for The City of Cleveland for over five years and according to the victim's family she had been well-liked by everyone. No leads into the motive or variable suspects had been comprised by investigators as of yet.

Half-heartedly, John noticed a link to the swimming facility and clicked on it; a fate changing decision.

The official website of the swimming pool appeared on the computer monitor.

Using the mouse, John moved about the webpage, reading the history of the facility, a list of local and national celebrities who had visited the pool, and then finally the calendar of upcoming events proudly showcasing the pool's first annual Polar Winter Night extravaganza, complete with snow blower and artificial snow.

He ran the cursor to the pictorial section of the site and clicked on it.

Archived pictures and film reels of the pool throughout the years appeared in rows of minimized thumbnails.

At the top, he saw a file labeled Staff and clicked it open.

Dozens of pictures of employees from decades past to the present appeared on the screen.

He glanced through photo after photo of happy smiling young people in either business attire or swimwear until he reached one labeled Wendy Beltran. The image, taken the previous year during a Christmas party, showed a heavyset woman, holding a pastry in her right hand while smiling happily into the camera.

John looked at the picture closely and felt a touch of pity for her.

He scrolled down to the final picture and felt his heart roll in his throat when he saw it.

The photo, taken by cellular phone, showed a woman with large dazzling emerald green eyes holding a flyer for the Polar Winter Night event in her hands and flanked by half a dozen employees.

John dropped his hand from the mouse as he stared numbly into the photo.

He had found her.

At lights-out, John bedded down for the last time in the large dorm.

At half past eleven, he rose from bed, dressed, gathered his tote bag which contained every scrap of personal possession to his name from the footlocker and quietly walked out of the dorm with the use of the night vision from his eyes.

With nothing more than a squeak from his rubber soled leather shoes, John carefully made his way out the shelter.

He rounded the last corner and saw the front entrance wide open.

Inhaling the smell of the night's air from cool breeze coming in through the opened doors, John quickened his pace.

Suddenly from out of the shadows, a voiced called

out to him, "John."

He stopped in mid-stride and scanned the area out in front of him.

Again, the deep gentle voice called his name, "John."

It was on the second time that he realized that it was his real name being called out and not the name of the dead infant he had been using.

From a fold of shadows, Rodger stepped out.

John stared at him, ready for whatever came next.

Rodger took another step towards him and extended his right hand out. The cellular phone he had confiscated from him was in it.

"I thought you'd like your phone back," Rodger told him.

John gave no response.

Still holding the phone outward, Rodger said, "The agreement was that you could have it back when you left."

John blinked his large green emerald eyes.

"And since it's quite apparent that you are leaving," he took another step forward, "Here you are... John."

John gave the small black phone in the man's hand a quick look and asked, "How long have you known... who I really am?"

Rodger lowered his hand to his side, "For a while now. It really wasn't that hard to figure out... at least for me."

John listened in silence.

"Changed your appearance by losing weight, growing a beard, and changing your eye color... I assume with contacts. However, you can't change bone structure and expressions."

"And you never turned me in."

"I never saw the need," said the black man.

"You know... what I'm accused of... don't you?" John inquired.

"Yes," Rodger calmly answered.

"Then?" John pressed.

With a sigh, Rodger took a side step to his right, leaned against the wall, and replied, "You see, John... criminals have been part of my life... my whole life. My father was criminal who pimped and loan sharked. He was murdered by a criminal. After my father was no longer around... my mother became a whore first then a drug addict later... and then finally a victim to a criminal who bashed her brains out with a cement block over a sex for drugs deal gone wrong.

Motionless, John listened.

"By the time I turned thirteen, I too became a criminal, first with a street gang and then on my own... robbing, burglarizing, pillaging. At nineteen, I was sentenced to fifteen years in prison... which I wholeheartedly deserved. My very first night into my sentence I was raped by a criminal. During the next fifteen years, I slept and ate amongst criminals. And... on my very last night in prison... I murdered the criminal who had raped me fifteen years before," Rodger sighed again and continued, "And ever since then I have spent every waking day trying to make criminals, drunks, addicts, and the rest of society's discards into better people... here at this shelter."

John swallowed a click in his throat.

Rodger raised an eye brow, gave his lips a slight twist, and concluded, "All of which means... John... that I know a criminal... when I see one," he looked directly into John's large green eyes, felt a chord of fatherly affection for the young man standing in front of him, and said, "And you... are no criminal, John."

John lowered his eyes at the sound of the last sentence.

Rodger stared back.

After a bit, John looked up and said, "Thank you."

Rodger gave a nod and a small smile, and casually tagged a question, "You're going after the person who did it... aren't you?"

John felt his intestines go cold.

"Aren't you?" Rodger repeated.

John could only muster up a single word, "Yes."

"Who is it? The person who did it." Rodger asked.

John let out a sigh and then replied, "I truly have no idea. All I know of her is what she's capable of. She had already killed my mother and father by the time my brother and I arrived... hacked into pieces and displayed for us to find. Later she would blow my brother's face off right in front of me as we drove to get away from her."

"And now... you've found her and your off to kill her," Rodger said.

"Yes," John answered.

"Which explains all those hours on the computer," Rodger commented.

"Yes," John answered again.

"Why?" Rodger finally asked, "Why did she do those things to your family?"

John huffed and replied, "Cause... she was bored."

"Bored!" Rodger spoke up.

"Yes. Bored," John repeated in a flat tone.

"With what...for God's sake?" Rodger inquired.

"With death... I guess," John said.

"I... don't... understand," Rodger said matter-of-factly.

John cleared his throat and said, "It's all she does... kill. She lives only to kill."

Rodger rubbed his face and exclaimed, "Man, that's crazy."

"She is... totally... fuck'n crazy," John told him, "And ... I'm going to kill her."

Knowing that every person's destiny was their own, Rodger extended the cellular phone once again and said, "Here's your phone, John. I hope you win."

John took it, pocketed it, and said, "Thank you, Rodger. Thank you for taking me in, for believing in me, and, most of all, thank you... for letting me go."

With his right hand now empty, he gestured with it towards the door, "Good luck, John."

John gave a nod and a small smile, and then exited the building he had come to call home.

As he walked down the steps, from behind him, he heard Rodger speak to him one last time, "If Rachael asks what happened to you... what should I tell her?"

At the sidewalk, he turned and replied, "Tell her the truth. That I simply walked away."

Rodger walked to the edge of the steps. "She really liked you, you know. She'll miss you."

John gave another smile and said, "I really liked her as well... and I'm going to miss her."

"Will we ever see you again?" Rodger asked.

The smile on John's face slowly disappeared as he replied, "If you're lucky... you never will".

CHAPTER 54

"Am I... worthy now?"

To Whom It May Concern:

This is Dina Harris, Director of the Thomas A. Lean Olympic Swimming Facility, writing to you. I am the person solely responsible for murdering those people with the chemical agent Caustic Soda XF-II the previous night. As to why; the reasons are my own, and yours to figure out with whatever time it takes you to do so.

Obviously, by the time you read this letter, I shall not be present to be questioned, prosecuted, or sentenced for my crime. However, if you are willing to invest the time and effort in finding me, you may start by decrypting the following message. It will provide you with what I plan to do next.

Xr ywh xkh brvot'w qyaohdv dvpdphqxw djdlqwx lxwhoi wr xkdx L pdf bdon wlth ef wlth blxk pf adsxrv dw L bdw svrplwht wr zhvf orqj djr.

I wish you the best of luck. God's speed.

Best regards,
Dina Melissa Harris, M.A.
Director / Thomas A. Lean Olympic
Swimming Facility

She removed her manicured fingertips from the keyboard, leaned back into the leather desk chair, and looked over the note she planned to leave behind.

The silence of the emptied facility hung heavy in the air.

She rubbed her large green eyes, puffed her cheeks and exhaled hard. She was tired, and there were still plenty left to do before her plan of mass murder could begin.

Within the darkened office, using only the glow of the screen and her night vision, she looked at the clock on the far wall of her office. It read half past two in the morning.

She took her eyes off the clock and looked once more at the computer screen. The note glowed peacefully in front of her.

She spoke out loud to the creature inside her, "To walk side by side... when we are the only two left... on the planet."

She hit the print icon and pushed away from the desk with the balls of her bare feet.

The plastic chair mat felt cool and comforting under her feet as she stood up.

She stepped off the mat and made her way to the laser printer.

The note was already waiting for her in the catch trey of the printer when she reached it.

Under the eerie greenish glow of her eyes, she

reached out and took the single sheet of paper from underneath the printer, held it up, and began to read it out loud.

Suddenly, the middle of her chest started to tug.

The sensation catching her off guard, the note slipped from her fingertips and softly landed between her bare feet.

Knowing full well the sensation meant that he was close, she dove for her desk, landing on her knees between the chair and workstation.

Astonished as to how he had been able to locate her, she yanked opened the upper left drawer, hauled out her 9mm semiautomatic, and racked a round into the chamber.

Gun at the ready, she huddled deeper behind the heavy wooden piece of office furniture and braced herself.

The minutes ticked away with deafening silence.

After a short while, as the sensation in her chest continued, she raised her head and scanned her immediate area with her night vision but saw nothing out of the ordinary.

She stood up and her acute hearing picked up a rumbling sound coming her way.

She craned her head sideways in order to hear it better as the unknown sound grew louder and closer.

Unable to make out what it was, she raised the 9mm towards it and braced herself.

A second later the rumbling sound reached its apex, and the entire complex shook and shuddered with a deafening boom.

She went down to one knee and curled up behind her weapon, ready for whatever came next.

However, nothing else followed, and the silence of

the empty facility returned once again.

Slowly, gun in hand, she stood up again, stepped around her desk, and walked out of her office.

Judging by the sensation in her chest, she knew he had been behind whatever had crashed into the facility.

Guided by the greenish glow of her eyes and still in her bare feet, she walked down the darkened corridor towards the storage room at the back left of the facility where she had stored the drums of XF-II.

She reached the door marked ´Storage´, drew a ring of keys from her skirt pocket, unlocked it, and pushed it open.

Inside, she was shocked to find a garbage truck thrust inside and her drums of military grade caustic soda thrown about all over the place.

She scanned the mess and saw that one barrel had actually ruptured under the heavy impact and its corrosive crystalline granules lay scattered all over the concrete floor.

She slowly closed the door, leaned against the wall, and closed her eyes with a long exhaled breath. With a garbage truck imbedded into the side of the building and the drums filled with a deadly substance strewn all over the storage room; her plans for tomorrow were undoubtedly over.

She ran her hand over her face in defeat. Either by sheer luck or careful planning, he had scored a devastating blow against her.

A ringing phone reached her ears.

She opened her eyes and focused on the sound.

The ringing was coming from the storage room.

She opened the door once again, listened, and located where it was coming from.

Skipping over the soda, she rounded the crushed

front end of the garbage truck, wrenched opened the door, and peered inside.

Wedged between the dirty and matted cloth seats of the truck's cabin, a cellular phone rang and danced with light.

She took one look at it and laughed out loud. It was the one she had left on the bridge.

She reached in, grabbed it, and answered it.

His voice fell into her ear, "I just thought you'd like your phone back."

Smiling as she pictured just how much he was probably relishing the moment, she said to him, "I planned on getting it back at some point."

"Saw you on the internet. Good photo," he told her.

With a huff and a shake of her head, she replied, "Thank you. Should have covered my eyes with contacts."

"I guess you should have," he said.

"Tell me, John... what do I owe the pleasure of your phone call tonight?" she asked.

"I just wanted to ask you one question," he said to her.

"And what question might that be?" she inquired.

"Am I... worthy now?" he asked.

In the distance, police sirens whaled their approach and the end to her murderous plan.

She smiled and answered, "Yes."

CHAPTER 55

"You... will kill... forever."

Under a near moonless late night, with the use of his eyes' night vision, John walked through a deserted dilapidated smelting factory an hour after speaking with her.

Stealing the garbage truck had been easy enough. He had slipped into the passenger seat, shoved the barrel of his .45 under the driver's jawbone, and then had politely asked him to exit the vehicle before driving away with it into the night.

Shirtless and dressed in nothing but a pair of grey gabardine slacks and rubber soled dress shoes, John made his way through the abandon plant, carrying his handguns tucked in his waistband and their magazines in his pockets.

At the park, he had wedged a crowbar, he had

found in a tool box, between the front seat and the gas pedal, jammed the small black cellular phone between the soiled cushions of the seats, and then had sent the garbage truck on a one way course towards the west wall of the swimming facility.

With the night air licking at his bare chest, John took hold of the .380 in his left hand and .45 in his right as he continued deeper and deeper into the heart of the abandoned factory.

From his vantage point, just behind the bleachers of the park's baseball diamond, he had felt the thunderous boom of the garbage truck burying itself into the wall.

Walking at a steady pace through the green colored darkness, John followed the sensation in his chest to where she was waiting for him.

He had dialed the number of the cellular phone he had left inside the truck from a pay phone as police sirens wailed in the distance.

John descended a flight of rusted and pitted metal stairs and plunged deeper still into the vacant and dilapidated factory.

After getting the directions to the smelting plant from her, twenty miles South of the city, he had watched her skitter out a side door, dive into a sedan, then quickly drive away a fraction of a second before a horde of police cruisers arrived at the scene.

Climbing down a rusty ladder and walking passed a broken down water purifier, the tugging in his chest heightened. She was just up ahead.

He had driven out of the city towards the factory in a late model German import after stealing its keys from a valet caddy of a fancy and overcrowded restaurant.

Guns at the ready, John walked towards the rear of the smelting plant and her.

He had steered past the broken chain link fence and the abandoned guard shack and had parked next to the sedan he had seen her drive away in.

John stepped onto the loading dock of the factory and saw her.

Smiling and still looking like the Dina Harris he had seen on the internet, she stood on the other side of the loading dock, bare foot and completely naked with a handgun in one hand and two extra magazines in the other.

She gave him a simple nod when she saw him emerge from the darkness into her green colored field of vision.

Looking at her across the span of the dock, John realized that this was just the third time he had seen her in human form.

She looked up at the waning night, which had gone from black to a velvety navy blue, and called out to him, "The coming new day will be glorious... for only one of us," and then turned into the creature right in front of his eyes.

Watching her transform into the very thing that he

was undoubtedly going to become, he knew the time had finally arrived for one or both of them to die.

Together, they raised their weapons at each other and fired.

A round from the creature's 9mm missed his abdomen by an inch and bullets from his .45 and .380 struck the thick concrete wall on either side of the monster's head.

With a surge of adrenaline, the creature dashed to its left and sped down the length of the walkway of the loading dock.

Focused like no other time in his life, John went after the creature with an equal burst of speed.

Running down parallel walkways with only a parking slot for eighteen wheelers to separate them, they fired at each other in a continuous volley of bullets.

Round after round, they missed each other by mere fractions.

They reached their own set of stairs at the same time and ran down them towards the parking slot as they fired the last of the bullets in their guns.

At the base of the stairs, they stopped and stared at one another, panting.

In unison, they quickly reloaded their emptied firearms. John knowingly worked his fingers over the .380 and the .45, while the creature coolly manipulated the mechanisms of the 9mm.

They hit the slide releases of their weapons at the same time and rushed towards each other, firing at almost point blank range.

John felt a bullet tear into his side and glance of a rib. Staggering slightly, he kept on running and shooting at the creature.

In the middle of the slot, they collided into each other with bruising force.

The impact sent the .380 flying out of John`s hand.

While gripping its last magazine with its long thumb against its palm, the creature extended its clawed fingers and slashed out in an arching sweep, tearing open John's entire right cheek down to the skull.

Growling in pain, he felt his vision darkened for the briefest of seconds as shock from the trauma to his face tried to overtake him.

Taking advantage of the injury, the creature took a step back, leveled the 9mm, and fired.

With a speed now equal to the creature's own, John darted out of the bullet's deadly trajectory a mere millisecond before the creature pulled the trigger and then buried his right foot deep into the creature's stomach.

Taking the full force of the front kick in its midsection, the creature doubled over and hollered more out of surprise than in pain.

Flowing with the momentum of the fight, John fired the .45 and the creature's left triceps exploded in a shower of blood, meat, and white fur, sending the magazine flying from its clawed hand.

Knowing it had just been severely wounded and that one more slug from the large caliber handgun would prove fatal, the creature somersaulted into the air and landed in a crouch twenty feet away.

Feeling his new healing ability begin to work on his face and gunshot wound to his ribs, John pressed the magazine release button, dug into his pants pocket, brought out the final magazine for the Israeli made handgun, and reloaded.

Off in the distance, the creature leaped high into

the air.

John watched the creature soar into the night sky above him and leaped after it.

Streaking towards each other in the predawn night, they fired bullet after bullet at one another.

At the apex of their jump, they slammed into each other once again and then plummeted down towards the ground below.

Clinging onto each other, they clawed, punched, and fired at each other the entire way down.

At the very last second before they hit the ground, John dug his fingers into the ragged gaping hole at the creature's arm and turned the white furred and bleeding monster under him.

They hit the tarmac with a bone crunching impact.

Like medicine balls, they bounced off each other, landing about a yard apart from one another.

The creature with its pelvis broken in three places and a punctured lung painfully rolled onto its back as dark rich blood oozed from his gaping mouth.

Shivering in pain from a broken leg, shattered ankle, and broken collar bone, John searched with outstretched hands for the .45 that had slipped from his grasp on impact.

The creature, struggling against the shock from its injuries, slowly rose onto its right elbow and aimed the 9mm at him.

Simply unable to locate the .45, John turned his head and saw the barrel of the creature's gun bearing down on him.

The creature gave a blood stained smile and pulled the trigger.

The 9mm merely clicked. Its firing mechanism had broken in the fall.

John felt an icy splash of relief wash over him.

Weaponless and gravely injured, the creature dropped the ruined handgun, rolled over back onto its belly, and began to crawl away in an attempt to buy some time for its healing ability to take effect.

Determined like no other time in his life, John reached out with his right hand, yelled out against the pain in his shoulder, and grabbed its ankle.

The creature's large green eyes peeled back in terror at the feel of the vice-like grip at its limb.

John tightened his hold as the creature desperately tried to free itself to no avail.

Securely latched onto the creature's limb and in nauseating pain, John suddenly remembered the .38 Special at the small of his back.

Clawing, the creature continued to try to get away.

With his free hand, he reached for the five shot revolver, nestled between his slacks and his lumber spine.

Simply too weakened and wounded to get away, the creature stopped moving and looked back.

Slowly and methodically, John drew the weapon and aimed it directly at the monster's gaping face.

Looking down the barrel of the revolver, the creature suddenly knew that the time to die had finally arrived after so many centuries of killing and let out a sigh.

With one hand still on the creature's ankle and the other holding the gun squarely at the creature's face, John closed his eyes and lowered his head as a sudden and unexpected feeling slid over him.

The creature which had lived inside an innocent girl's body for centuries, smiled and spoke one last time, "You... will kill... forever."

John slowly raised his head and, through a mouth torn from ear to ear in a hideous gaping grimace, said to it, "And you… shall be… my first," then pulled the trigger.

John Belica

CIPHER

D	-- -- -- -- -- -- -- --	A
E	-- -- -- -- -- -- -- --	B
A	-- -- -- -- -- -- -- --	C
T	-- -- -- -- -- -- -- --	D
H	-- -- -- -- -- -- -- --	E
I	-- -- -- -- -- -- -- --	F
J	-- -- -- -- -- -- -- --	G
K	-- -- -- -- -- -- -- --	H
L	-- -- -- -- -- -- -- --	I
M	-- -- -- -- -- -- -- --	J
N	-- -- -- -- -- -- -- --	K
O	-- -- -- -- -- -- -- --	L
P	-- -- -- -- -- -- -- --	M
Q	-- -- -- -- -- -- -- --	N
R	-- -- -- -- -- -- -- --	O
S	-- -- -- -- -- -- -- --	P
U	-- -- -- -- -- -- -- --	Q
V	-- -- -- -- -- -- -- --	R
W	-- -- -- -- -- -- -- --	S
X	-- -- -- -- -- -- -- --	T
Y	-- -- -- -- -- -- -- --	U
Z	-- -- -- -- -- -- -- --	V
B	-- -- -- -- -- -- -- --	W
C	-- -- -- -- -- -- -- --	X
F	-- -- -- -- -- -- -- --	Y
G	-- -- -- -- -- -- -- --	Z

John Belica

DELETED SCENES

John Belica

DELETED SCENE 1

Miles away, John pulled over, opened the driver's door, and vomited out the contents of his belly, hot, acidic, and foamy.

Crashing from the adrenaline high, his body shook and shuttered as the insanity of what he had just done a few minutes ago was now beginning to hit him; he had assaulted two complete strangers, probably almost killing one of them.

Gathering himself as best he could, he wiped his mouth with his shirt sleeve, leaned back inside his car, and closed the door.

Sitting in the darkness of the interior of his car, John closed his eyes and took deep breaths in an attempt to steady himself.

"That was so crazy," he whispered to himself and ran the back of his hand across his damp brow.

A few minutes later, he opened his eyes and found a lump of sadness caught in his throat. The thing now living inside him had made him do it.

He flipped the sun visor down and looked at

himself in the small mirror. His new green dazzling eyes, framed within the visor, stared back at him with their haunting intensity.

Disgusted, he slapped the visor shut, closed his eyes once again, and rubbed the scar on his forehead.

Slowly his thoughts turned to her. Twice she had meant to kill him and twice he had survived only to be infected on the second encounter with something that tonight had taken over his body and had seduced him into hurting complete strangers.

"I never asked for any of this," he whispered to himself again as he put the car into gear, opened his eyes, and drove into the night.

Later.

Blue and red lights bounced off the rearview mirror and into John's eyes.

John narrowed his eyes and saw in the reflection of the rearview mirror that a police unit was behind him and it wanted him to pull over.

Its siren blared once and its spotlight, bright and harsh, filled the inside of his car.

John rolled to a stop on the side of the road. Gravel crunched and groaned under his right tires.

The squad car stopped just behind him.

As he put the transmission in park, John noticed to his far left more police cars and more lights, all clustered around a mass of activity.

After waiting a few minutes cocooned within the white glare of the spotlight of the squad car, the butt end of a flashlight tapped on his driver's side window.

John lowered the powered window and looked straight into a beam of light.

A male voice, stern and commanding, behind the

blinding light asked, "Sir, may I ask what are you doing here?"

John suddenly realized that he didn't know where 'here' actually was.

"Sir?" the faceless police officer said as his flashlight swept round the interior of car.

Trying to understand why he had driven to wherever-here-was instead of going back to his motel room, John forgot to answer.

Not receiving an answer to his question, the LAPD officer trained his flashlight once again on John's face, took a step back, and said, "Sir, I'm going to need you to step out of your car."

Suddenly completely absorbed in knowing why he hadn't driven to his motel room as he thought he had been doing, John turned away from the police officer's bright piercing light and looked once again at the commotion just up ahead; lights and lots of people in uniform were swarming around a parked German import that sat facing the L.A. skyline.

Without warning, the driver's side door was yanked open, and the officer's voice rained down on him, authoritative and threatening, "Sir! Out of the car...NOW!"

At the sound of the man's booming voice, John shook himself free from his train of thought and turned back to the captive shining light.

"Sir, out of the car now," the faceless voice repeated.

Doing as he was told, John undid his seatbelt and stepped out of his car.

From under the glare of the flashlight, a hand shot out and seized him by the right shoulder, spun him around and pressed him against the rear driver's side window.

The cold black metal of the flashlight's tubular body came to rest just under John's left ear as the officer's right hand glided up and down his body in search of a weapon.

After the pat down, John was roughly spun around again then shoved back against his car.

With his hands held up instinctually, John saw the police officer for the first time as the flashlight was lower away from his face. Standing in front of him was someone out of a law enforcement recruitment poster; young, fit, and very sharp looking in his pressed dark blue uniform.

The police officer spoke again, "Sir... for the final time... what are you doing here?"

Though, he truly didn't know why he was here or what had possessed him to come here, John understood that he had to answer the question somehow so he chose what he thought was best; a half truth, "I'm an accountant. It's tax season... and... I couldn't sleep. So... I decided... to go for a drive."

Taking his answer at only face value, the officer demanded, "Your driver's license, Sir."

John slowly reached for his wallet in his rear pocket, fetched out his license from out of the leather tri-fold, and then handed it over.

Handling the license, the young officer said, "Don't move," then touched the small radio handset clipped on his left shoulder.

While waiting for the officer to finish whatever he was doing, John noticed another police officer, a short square built Hispanic female, standing just off to his left and guarding him with her eyes.

After a minute of listening to what sounded to John

like nothing but gibberish from the little radio on the man's shoulder, the officer said, "Echo Park is a long way away from your address of residence, Sir."

John continued with the lie he had started, "Tax season is very stressful. I couldn't sleep."

The young officer motioned for his female partner to step forward.

John watch them mumble a few words to each other then saw them part.

"Sir," the male officer said to him, "I need you to step over here with me while my partner inspects your vehicle."

Suddenly feeling very unsure about the situation he was in, John did as he was told and walked over to the police car.

Keeping his distance just beyond arms reach, the police officer matter-of-factly instructed, "Rest your backside against the hood and place your hands, palms down, at your sides."

Sitting against the grill of the police unit, John watched the female cop rummage through is car, obviously looking for anything that could be turned against him.

The young officer stepped directly in front of him, obscuring his line of sight, and asked, dripping with suspicion, "So, you couldn't sleep. So you just decided to drive in the middle of the night to Echo Park from Inglewood... is that right?"

John glanced over the officer's right shoulder, saw yellow tape being applied around the white German import, and answered, "Correct, sir. I didn't know this was Echo Park. I was just driving around... trying to unwind."

"So you just happened to show up here... right

now... tonight?" the police officer asked. The name badge on his chest read Ponce.

"That's right, officer. I just couldn't sleep," he replied then asked, "What's going on over there?"

Without breaking eye contact, Ponce, answered with fresh stern, "That over there... is none of your concern, Sir."

John looked over the officer's shoulder once again and realized with a numbing chill that it was a murder scene.

The short female cop approached both of them and uttered a single word to her partner, "Clear."

Officer Ponce nodded to her then said as he handed the driver's license back, "Sir, you're free to go. However, I want you to drive away from here immediately. If... for any reason... you were to return... you'll be arrested on the spot. Do you understand, Sir?"

John took his license back then answered in a grave voice, "I understand, officer."

Officer Ponce stepped back, gestured with his hand for John to step back into his car, and gave a parting word, "Like I said... don't come back. We have a crime scene here."

John thinned his lips and nodded his acknowledgement as he walked to his car.

Without anything further to say, Ponce sternly watched him slip behind the steering wheel and shut the door.

Sitting quietly inside his car, John looked at the crime scene and surmised that she was responsible for what had happened inside that other car and somehow the thing inside him had got him to drive here. As odd as that sounded, somehow it felt like the truth.

Stunned numb by the events of the entire evening,

John ran his hands through his hair, touched his scar, turned the ignition, and drove away.

An hour later, the bloodied body of Matthew Hill would be removed from the German import and placed inside a body bag for transfer to the coroner's office. His family and fiancée would be informed in the morning about his gruesome murder.

DELETED SCENE 2

A purple bullet proof limousine came to a stop in front of two other cars parked on the ice.

The night was bitterly cold and the light from the full moon above gave the thick crust of ice of the frozen lake a crystalline and barren appearance.

Doc, his street name given to him for the two years he had spent in medical school before dropping out, stepped out from the warmth of the vehicle on the left, in order to greet the people inside the limousine, wrapping his purple scarf tightly around his neck as his tasseled burgundy shoes crunched against the ice underfoot.

Slowly the others, all members of the Shorefront crew, exited their vehicles and faced the limousine.

Pulling his purple fedora down around his ears, Toes exclaimed into the night, "Jesus fuck! It sure is frick'n cold out here!"

"If ya want to be a criminal... ya gotta freeze your ass off occasionally, Toes," Two Tone told him over his shoulder, "If you want to spend every night curled up

with ya old lady then go be a second grade teacher...
and see how much that pays ya."

Poodle, a street name that aptly described his thick
tight curly hair, joined in, "Ya better watch out, Toes. Ya
don't want ya other nines toes to freeze and break off,"
and then clapped his hands, clad in purple mittens,
around his arms.

Laughter erupted all around from the eight smartly
dressed young men.

Being good at taking it as he was at giving it, Toes
shot back, "Hey, Poodle. Let's see if snowflakes bead
up on ya hair just like water does when ya moms gives
ya ya weekly bath."

Another round of laughter as Poodle and Toes
playfully threw punches at each other.

Suddenly, the driver's door of the limousine
opened, instantly cutting off the banter and laughter,
and a man dressed in a double breasted purple suit and
black camel hair topcoat stepped out into the cold night
air.

Doc, the de facto Sargent of the crew, took a step
closer and greeted him, "How ya doing, Sponge."

Sponge, a man known for his fierce loyalty within
the ranks of Chicago's Jewish mafia and his brutal
interrogations, hence the street name 'Sponge', walked
up to Doc and replied, "Not too bad, Doc... except for
this damn cold."

"Tell me 'bout it," Doc returned the gesture of
mutual discomfort.

Glancing around their surroundings, Sponge
commented as he looked down at his feet, "Ya sure
we're not going to fall through this ice and turn into
popsicles?"

Doc reassured him, "Don't go worrying yaself into a

batter... all these lakes this time of 'ear are frozen over pretty solid."

Sponge tapped his left foot against the ice and shook his head slowly, not feeling very convinced.

"Plus..." Doc added, "Since we're in the middle of the lake... there isn't a soul around for miles to interfere with tonight's transaction... which is why I set up the meet here... for the seclusion."

With a sigh, Sponge nodded, then looked up and said, "Ok, Doc. You're the college kid... I trust ya."

Eager to head up his own crew someday soon, Doc gave a smile, "Thanks, Sponge. That means a lot."

Shifting his topcoat higher onto his shoulders, Sponge said, "Alright then... let me talk to the boys."

"You got it," Doc said then turned on his heels and walked back to the other seven men, "Ok... yous mugs! Look alive. Sponge has something to say."

On stiffening legs because of the strangling cold, Two Tone, Toes, Poodle, Squirrel, Salty, Pasta, and Frankie lumbered to the front of the two parked cars.

Still uncomfortable to be walking on top of a frozen lake, no matter what Doc had to say about it, Sponge slowly made his way to them, stopped, and said, "Listen up, Shorefronts! I know it's late... I know it is cold as your uncle's oven... but we have a job to do... and we're gotta do it. Get me?"

Words of affirmation bubbled out from everyone, "We're with ya, Sponge." "We'll get it done, don't ya worry." "Count on us, Sponge." "Sponge for president."

Raising his hand, Sponge said out loud, "Ok, ok. I hears ya," then lowered it and continued, "As I speak... we have a truck coming down from Canada... filled to the brim with bottles of their least favorite hooch."

A rush of razor cold air ran up The Squirrel's leg,

numbing his right butt cheek and making him bite down on his lower lip with his pronounced overbite.

"Now to make things easier on all of us... those boys are going to simply hand over the truck to us, in good faith that we're going to return it to them on the next deal, so we don't have to do any unloading and loading in this God damn cold."

Francis "Frankie" Albert Weinstein whispered to Pasta, the only half Italian half Jew in the crew, "Remind me to send them a nice fruit basket for Boxing day, will ya."

Sponge continued, "Now... I don't have to tell ya apes how important this transaction is... do I? But just so you know... Johny the Flea told me that all of these bottles have had a deposit put on them alreadys. Two Bar Mitzvahs, three graduation parties, five weddings, two funerals, and three mayors are waiting for this stuff... so I expect no fuck ups tonight... just smooth sailing."

Then before anyone could say anything, he added, "And just to make sure that all does go smooth..." he paused for effect, "The Old Man himself asked me to bring along someone to make sure it does."

"Who?" Salty was the first to ask.

Relishing the effect that would come from what he was about to say, Sponge held his tongue for a moment and then answered, "The Dame."

On cue, a flutter of comments erupted, "The Dame... did ya hear that?" "Holy Christ... The Dame!" "I heard she killed a guy once with a corkscrew." "I took an elevator once with her... smelled like mint... and what a looker." "The Dame... here... tonight... with us... wait till the guys in the neighborhood hear 'bout this!"

Sponge held up both hands and said, "Alright...

alright Shorefronts... pipe down."

His crew quieted down and turned to look at him.

He lowered his hands and told them, "She wants to say a few words to you all." then walked to the limousine and opened the rear passenger door.

The young men stared at the limousine.

With a delicate ease, she stepped out of the vehicle and faced the crew of young Jewish mobsters. Dressed in a purple evening gown with a plunging neckline and draped in a silver fox fur coat, she looked at them with her emerald green eyes and exhaled a plume of mint scented warm breath into the freezing night air.

Closing the passenger door behind her, Sponge said over her left shoulder, "They're ready for you."

With nothing more than a nod, she stepped away from the limousine and went to them.

Watching her walk on the ice in her patent leather black high heels, Sponge felt a wave of attraction engulf him; she was beautiful as she was deadly, steadily becoming a living legend within the five major crime syndicates that controlled and ran Chicago.

She stopped in front of them, took a deep breath of the ice cold air, and said, "All of you know who I am so, if it's all right with you, I'll just skip the introductions and get right to the point."

Salty looked at her face, which was framed within a mass of loose blonde curls, and felt a surge of pride suddenly swell within him at being so close to the woman who people said had single-handedly taken out the Irish's entire Southside chapter.

"What I want you to know is... that this is more than just about booze and having a good time getting liquored up at some wedding or graduation party. This is about respect... gentlemen."

Sponge nodded in agreement behind her.

She continued, "Complete your task tonight and you will earn the respect that comes from having done what had needed to be done."

Listening to her, Pasta decided that he would rather die than fail in front of her.

With a meticulously manicured hand, she gestured to their cars and said, "Return to your vehicles and keep warm... it won't be much longer," then turned on the ice and walked back to Sponge and the limousine.

When she reached the long purple vehicle, he opened the rear passenger door for her and she stepped back inside.

Inside, she watched him opened the driver's side door, seat himself, and then close it against the harsh cold.

Nestled in her fur coat, she looked out the window and remembered her days as a child when she would plunge into the soft powdery snow outside her family's cabin.

Looking at her in the rearview mirror, Sponge said, "Well... I guess all we do now is wait for them to show."

She turned away from the window, looked directly into his eyes in the rearview mirror, and said to him, "Waiting is an exercise in futility... depending on who you ask."

Not knowing how to respond to such a strange comment, Sponge looked away from the rearview mirror and wondered how he would ever get away with his life if this were to fail in front of her.

A half hour later, two lights, off in the distance, came into view.

Seeing them first with her eye's night vision, she said, "Look alive, Sponge. They're here."

Shifting his weight in the leather bench seat, he strained his eyes to see but saw nothing other than ice and a moonlit barren landscape.

"They're masking their headlights with something to make them dimmer... but trust me... they're here... one sedan and a truck," she told him.

A minute later, Sponge saw the dimmed out lights himself and exclaimed, "Hey... I see them! On the left," then switched on the headlights of the limousine, signaling both the approaching vehicles and his crew to ready themselves.

Not waiting for her door to be opened this time, she swung open the rear passenger door and stepped out once more into the cold frozen night.

Eager to see a successful transaction between his crew and the Canadians, Sponge stepped out of the limousine himself with a leather duffle bag in hand and went to join the others who were already out of their cars.

Asked to act as syndicate liaison on tonight's transaction and then to submit her findings on Sponge's ability to conduct syndicate business on his own, she stood behind the opened passenger door and watched.

A midsized delivery truck and black sedan stopped about fifty yards away.

Walking briskly to his men, Sponge caught whiffs of their excitement filled chatter, "Here we goes." "I wanna make this clean, fast, and easy... but most of all fast... I'm freezing my fuck'n balls off standing out heres." "Can't wait to get back to town and crack open one of those bottles... for quality control... don't ya know."

Wrapping his topcoat tightly against him, Sponge came to a stop among them and said in a commanding voice, "Ok... listen up, Shorefronts. Keep your mouths shut, your eyes peeled, and this trigger fingers ready. If this goes south on us... I want you to spray them down with enough hot lead to be able to roast marshmallows over their bodies."

Knowing when to goof off and knowing when to keep quiet, Doc and the others nodded their understanding at what they were being told.

"Good. Now when the transaction is done... I want Doc and Pasta to drive the truck... while the rest of us keep it covered until we get off this ice cube," Sponge told them then added, "Any questions?"

There were none.

"Good," he commented, touched the tip of his numb nose, and said, "Doc... you come with me... all of yous stay by your cars and keep your eyes open for anything screwy."

Doing as they were told, Pasta, Squirrel, Two Tone, Salty, Frankie, and Poodle returned to their respective vehicles.

Standing at the trunk of the first car, Frankie called over to Salty, "Hey... Salt. I bet all this waiting around in this cold kinda makes you think about Havana and all those warm beaches and warm... guys."

Everyone listening erupted in a bout of laughter.

"Hey... do me a favor," Salty replied, "Try not to remind me. I didn't know she was a damn crossdresser."

Joining in, Two Tone said, "A crossdresser makes her a he, Salt."

Smiling and laughing with the rest of them about the evening that earned him his street name, Salty said in his defense, "I was drunk... and she looked ok to me."

Squirrel jumped into the friendly ribbing, "He... Salt... he."

Salty turned to him and said, "She looked like a she."

"He... you salty dog," Two Tone remarked over the laughter.

Listening to them laugh as he made his way to the truck with Doc at his side, Sponge relaxed a bit; if they were laughing then it meant they weren't shooting and that of course was always good news.

With only a bit more to go, Doc turned his head slightly to his left and said, "Ya still feel good about this, Sponge? That's a lot of money you got there in that duffle bag."

Cocking his head to the right, Sponge replied, "Don't go worrying about me. Prohibition isn't about to end anytime soon. Everybody just wants to do business... make some money... get drunk... or both."

Unable to argue against such logic, Doc nodded, "Amen to that brother."

When they finally reached the delivery truck, a voice from behind the headlights covered in cloth spoke to them, "Evening gentlemen. Stop right there... please."

Sponge and Doc stopped walking.

Slowly two men emerged from behind the headlights.

Studying them, Doc's hand moved ever so slightly to the .45 semiautomatic under his coat.

The man on the driver's side spoke again, "It's too cold to make this last any longer than it has to... so let's begin shall we?"

Eager to be off the ice, Sponge replied, "Agreed.

Let's get this done."

The one on the passenger side walked forward, extended his hand, and said, "The name's Paul."

Sponge took his hand, "My name is Ervin Benowitz... but everyone calls me Sponge."

Under the dim light from the headlights and the glow of the moon, Sponge could see that the man in front of him was the spitting image of a farmer; tall, well fed, muscular, and wearing overalls.

The Canadian of Irish descent let go of Sponge's hand and commented, "You fellas sure have some colorful names."

Sponge narrowed his eyes and asked, "Which one... Sponge or Benowitz?"

"Ervin," the man replied.

Catching the man's sense of humor, Sponge laughed out loud and said, "Tell that to my aunt Veronica... she suggested it to my mother."

With the ease of an old friend, the Canadian switched topics, and asked, "Did you bring the money?"

Gesturing to the duffle bag in his hand, Sponge said, "Right here."

The Canadian gave the leather bag a quick look then said, "As your associate and mine agreed on... you give us the money and we hand over the truck and the whiskey."

Noticing that his toes had already gone numb inside his kid skin ankle boots, Sponge nodded and said, "That's what I've been told too."

"Good," the Canadian commented then added, "My cousin, Dennis, will show whoever's going to drive the truck how to work the clutch... it sorta sticks on second."

Sponge gave his lieutenant a sidelong glance,

"Doc... the truck gets a bit tricky on second gear... go with cousin Dennis there and get yourself sorted out."

"I'm on it, Sponge," Doc replied and trotted towards the truck and its driver.

Turning his attention back to the man in overalls, he extended the duffle bag and said, "Count it."

With a smile, Paul told him, "Too cold. Best leave it to trust... that's the Canadian way."

Sponge handed over the cash filled duffle bag.

"But keep in mind... that if this bag is short by just one dollar or if we don't get our truck back... we, you, and your people are done doing business." Paul told him as he took possession of the money.

Respecting anyone who spoke his mind openly and directly, Sponge said in response, "Keep in mind... that if this shipment is short by just one bottle or someone goes blind from drinking it... you and your people are gonna find out how many sponges it will take to clean the blood of your families off the walls and ceiling. That's the Chicago way."

Nodding his understanding, the Canadian simply smiled back.

Still watching from the limousine as Sponge tended to the transaction at hand, she curled her toes inside her high heeled shoes, looked to her left, saw the wide open frozen scape, and considered simply walking into the darkness and living among the solitude of nature once more. However, the killing in Chicago at the moment was nothing short of open season on just about everyone who resided there, keeping the creature's thirst for murder quenched with fresh kills.

She turned her gaze back to Sponge and the others. In the greenish hue of her night vision, Doc emerged from the cabin of the truck.

"I'm good, Sponge. We can go whenever you're ready," Doc told his crew leader as he took his place beside him once more.

With a tone of finality, Sponge said to the Canadian, "Well then... I guess we're done here."

Lifting the duffle bag of money slightly in gesture, Paul remarked, "So we are." then added, "Enjoy the whiskey. We gave it a touch of maple... so over ice will do you just fine."

"Thanks. I'll try that," Sponge commented then watched both men turn and simply walkaway towards the sedan that had been waiting for them.

Doc turned to Sponge and said, "If prohibition ever ends... a lot people are gonna be outta a job without any marketable skills."

With a small chuckle, Sponge replied, "Including us," then slipped his hands into the pockets of his coat and added, "But not tonight. Get in the truck, Doc... we're leaving this ice box."

With nothing more than a nod, Doc pinched the brim of his fedora and ran to the truck.

Sponge turned on his heels and strode back to the others, "Pasta... remember you're going with Doc... get in that truck before we all die of the cold."

"Ya got it, Sponge!" Pasta replied as he jogged past him towards the truck.

"The rest of yous... get ready... we're leaving right now," Sponge, eager to bask in the light of a ultra-successful transaction in front of the syndicate's committee, added as he walked towards the limousine, "I want cars all around the truck until we reach the highway... and once we're there I want two at the front and two at the back until we make it to the city."

With words of acknowledgment, they climbed back

into their vehicles, "You got it, Boss!" "Righty-o Sponge!" "Coffee's on Sponge when we get back!"

When he reached the limousine, he took hold of the rear passenger door and said to her, "Please get back inside. We're done here. It was a total success."

Stepping back inside the large plush cabin, she said, "We're not back in Chicago... yet."

Knowing what she meant by that, he replied, "And we will be... soon enough," then shut her door, took his place behind the steering wheel, closed the driver's side door, and turned the ignition.

The large engine of the purple limousine roared into life.

With nothing more than a glance in the rearview mirror at the stunning woman behind him, he put the car into drive and sped off to join the others who were already making their way back towards the main road.

Driving cautiously over the ice, Sponge took his place at the rear of the truck.

Flanking the whiskey filled truck on its left was Salty behind the wheel with Two Tone in the back seat while on its right, Poodle kept up with Squirrel and Frankie.

Into the night and over the crunching ice, the convoy of Chicago's young and finest up-and-coming mobsters drove at an even steady pace towards the main highway that would lead them back home.

Inside the purple limousine, Sponge looked into the rearview mirror and said, "I plan to become Chicago's largest importer of hooch. I want to take me and my boys to the top of the dung heap."

Remembering Chicago as it had been one hundred years ago, filled with untouched hilltops and meadows, she looked up at him and simply replied, "I wouldn't necessarily call it a dung up... it's just a bit overcrowded... but I get what you mean."

Knitting his eyebrows for a split second at another odd comment, he continued, "I'd be totally stupid if I actually thought I could do it without some high level help."

"You're right...you would be... stupid," she replied again.

Hoping that he hadn't made a fatal mistake in talking to her, he pressed on, "I could use your help...your connections, your influence... to make what I want to happen."

Still looking at him, she said, "You know what they say about me... what I've done... what I can do."

Darting his eyes from the frozen landscape in front of him and the woman in the rearview mirror, he told her, "Yeah... I do."

"And even still... you want to continue having this conversation with me?" she inquired.

Knowing that fear was a sign of weakness in their line of business, he said to her "Yeah... I do."

Genuinely peaked now, she simply asked, "Why?"

"Cus... if what they say about you is true... then you're exactly what me and my boys need to be more than what we already are," he answered.

Pushing back herself back into her fur coat, she quickly whispered, "How interesting."

Sensing that he had struck something with his candor, he touched forward, "So... what do ya-"

Suddenly four pairs of headlights appeared just off to their left.

Knowing that any other vehicle in the middle of a frozen lake spelled nothing but trouble, Sponge hollered into the windshield, "God damn it... no!"

Sitting calmly against her fur coat, she watched him jerk the steering wheel of the limousine hard to the right and stomp down in the gas pedal.

The large engine of the luxury vehicle roared under the hood.

Gripping the steering wheel hard and hunching his shoulder forward, Sponge said without looking back at her, "Just hold on will ya! I can still fix this... and get all of us outta here alive."

Without saying a word, she uncrossed her legs and slipped her patent leather heels off her feet.

Roaring over the ice, Sponge steered the limousine between the truck and Poodle's car.

Sponge rolled the down his window and motioned for Pasta, sitting in the truck's passenger seat with a worried look on his face, to roll down his.

While holding onto his revolver in his left, Pasta cranked the passenger side window down, leaned out into the cold and yelled over the sound of engines, "Sponge... we got company!"

Sponge stuck his head out and yelled back, "No shit... ya retard!"

"Doc wants to know what to do!" Pasta yelled out.

"You tell that son of a bitch to keep driving no matter what happens! Keep driving!" Sponge gave them their orders.

With nothing more than a wave of his hand and a big nod that he understood, Pasta pulled himself back inside the warm cabin of the truck and rolled the window back up.

Driving the old truck as fast he dared, Doc asked, "What did he say?"

Answering, Pasta said as he gripped his revolver in both hands, "Sponge said to keep driving... no matter what."

"No matter what... got it," Doc whispered over gritted teeth.

The four unknown vehicles continued to close the distance.

Steering the limousine around Poodle's backend and to the right, Sponge came up on the passenger side and found Squirrel already leaning out waiting to hear what his captain had to say.

Driving as close as he dared to get to the vehicle on his left, Sponge yelled out, "Stay with the truck!"

"But... what about those bastards almost on top of us?" Squirrel hollered.

"I'm gunna take care of those sons of bitches. You protect the truck... got it?" Sponge hollered back.

With a wave of his hand, Squirrel replied loudly over the sound of the engines, "Ok Sponge... you're the boss," then slipped his torso back inside.

Sponge slowed for a second then swung the limo hard left towards Salty and Two Tone.

Catching a glimpse of the woman sitting behind him from the rearview mirror, Sponge said, "I'm not going to lose this night... not after all me and Doc have put into this deal."

Eager to see how it was going to play itself out, she looked into his eyes and said, "We're about to find out."

In the car to the left of the truck, Salty watched in the rearview mirror as Sponge steered the large limousine into position between them and the truck.

"Stay with the truck! Stay with the truck!" Sponge yelled over to the two of them.

Disciplined when they needed to be and rowdy when they could, Salty and Two Tone each gave big nods.

With his orders administered, Sponge turned his attention on the four approaching vehicles as he slowed, letting his men drive on ahead, and said to the woman behind him, "I don't know who the fuck they are... I'm not going to give those bastards not one bottle of my hooch. I don't care if they're the cops... the Germans, the WOPs, or those Irish cocksuckers... not one bottle."

The four unknown vehicles were almost on top of them.

Gripping the steering wheel hard, Sponge said to her, "This purple tank is a mean as they come... completely bullet proof... from head to toe... the windows, the door panels, the engine's firewall...even the tires... solid rubber... no tube," he took a deep breath, let it out, and said, "So hang tight... cus I'm going to ram those bastards into next Tuesday," then cranked the wheel hard to the left, hit the gas, and plunged headlong into the four headlights just in front of him.

Like a joust from the past, the limousine and the four unknown sedans race straight at each other.

Then, seconds before Sponge collided head on into them, three of the vehicles, with pinpoint precision, slipped behind the lead car in a near perfect tandem formation.

Caught by surprise at the sudden maneuver, Sponge cried out, "What the fuck!"

Like two trains passing each other in opposite directions, the limousine and the four cars crossed.

Realizing what was about to happen, she dropped to the flooring of the limousine and pressed herself as low as she could.

A heartbeat later, eight .45 caliber automatic

machineguns, two in each car, opened up with their drum magazines on the passing luxury vehicle.

A tidal wave of ball ammo tore into the left side of the limousine.

Ducking instinctively under the bulletproof window, Sponge stomped the gas pedal down to the flooring and yelled, "Jesus... fuck!" over the deafening sound of machine gun fire.

Unable to withstand the sheer number of automatic fire at such a close range, the limousine's bulletproof glass exploded.

Heavy loads of .45 caliber machinegun fire tore into the interior of the limousine.

Sponge's fedora was shot off his head and his left ear was ripped in shreds from his head.

Bleeding, in pain, and utterly beside himself, Sponge cranked the steering wheel hard to the right and sent the large sedan into an out-of-control spin, stalling the engine.

Leaving the battered and disabled limousine alone in the cold dark, the four cars continued towards the convoy.

Cupping the tangled remains of his ear, Sponge looked over the backrest and asked, "Are you ok? Were you hit?"

Calmly sitting back up, she replied, "I'm good... thank you."

Sponge distantly said, "Good... good. That's good to know," as he fought against the pain to his tattered ear.

Without looking back over her shoulder, she told him, "They're going after the truck."

Feeling the first wave of shock from the injury to the side of his head, Sponge quietly said, "The truck... I know… know… I."

She slipped out of her mink coat, the stunning cold coming from the shattered windows slithered across any exposed flesh, and said, "Why don't you turn this thing around… and get us back into the fight."

Dumbly staring at her, Sponge heard her words with his only remaining ear but couldn't find the means to gather with they truly meant as the pain from his injury slowly began to take full effect.

Struggling out of the tailored purple evening gown, she said to him, "One step at a time… try the engine."

Holding his mangled ear, Sponge nodded, faced forward, slowly took hold of the ignition key and turned it.

The heavy engine sputtered and went still.

Seated in the backseat now in nothing but her black bra, panties, and garters, she calmly told him, "Try again," as she gently set the purple dress on top of her fox fur coat.

Closing his eyes in concentration, Sponge turned the key over again.

The engine struggled once then roared into life.

With a smile, Sponge let go of the ignition key and slumped back into the seat, suddenly feeling very sleepy.

Unfastening her black silk stockings from her garters then sliding them off her legs and feet, she raised her voice, "Keep awake, Sponge… we're not done yet, Sponge!"

Slowly he opened his eyes, looked into the rearview mirror, and said as he fought back against the pain and shock, "You know… they're going to change my nickname after this," and then pointed at his ruined ear.

In her bare feet and nearly naked, she told him, "Turn this heap around and get us back into the fight."

The four unknown vehicles bore down on the small convoy.

Salty, still driving on the left side of the truck, watched as the four sets of headlights grew closer and closer, "Holy fuck, Two... they're almost on top of us."

In the back seat, Two Tone slid over to the left side, rolled down the window, and said out loud, "Let them come... I'm ready for them," then removed two .45 semiautomatic handguns from his waist, one in a dazzling nickel finish and the other in a matte black, thus his nickname; Two-Tone.

Salty eased away from the truck. "I'll get you close... then unload on those bastards."

Filling with adrenaline, Two Tone stuck both handguns out the window, smiled, and said, "Just like taking candy from-"

He would never finish his last sentence.

At that instant, the four cars turned to the left at the same time, bringing their right sides to bear, and all eight automatic machineguns opened fire on the two young Jewish mobsters.

The sedan's non-bullet proofed metal siding rippled like water under the tremendous onslaught of automatic fire and both Salty and Two Tone literally exploded inside the cabin.

A second later, the heavy loads of ball ammo found their way into the engine block and the car with its two dead passengers erupted into a ball of fire.

Driving as fast as he dared over the ice with his headlights turned off, Sponge yelled, "Holy fuck! They just took out Salty and Two Tone! Those filthy bastards!"

As the burning wreck slowly careened out of the way, the four vehicles turned their attention to the car on the right side of the whiskey filled truck. With fluid ease, they banked and swerved around the rear of the truck and then descended upon Poodle, Frankie, and Squirrel.

Still keeping pace with the truck, Poodle exclaimed, "Fuck! We're next!"

Eager not to die, Frankie took hold of the same type of machine gun that had just killed his two best friends and said, "No... they're next!" then shattered the back window with the barrel of the weapon and fired.

Bullets from Frankie's weapon ripped into the windshield of the lead car, killing the passenger instantly.

Instinctively, the drivers of the four approaching vehicles began to bob and weave in order to make themselves less available targets.

Laughing and firing, Frankie said out loud, "Ha! Look'um move like panties drying in the wind," as the back passenger from the damaged lead car leaned out the right window and fired.

Still laughing, Frankie caught a bullet to the shoulder and three to the face.

Squirrel, sitting in the front passenger seat, saw Frankie get killed and ducked down a split second before a hail of bullets shattered Poodle's head into a bloody mass of skull and brains.

Armed with nothing but a nickel plated five shot .38 Special, Squirrel, now alone in a driverless car, watched the four cars, two on the left and two on the right, bore down on him.

He closed his eyes and braced himself to die.

All four cars zoomed past without firing a single shot.

Slowly Squirrel opened his eyes, saw that he was still alive, and said, "Count them lucky stars, Squirrel me boy."

A second later, the two grenades that had been thrown into the car from the shattered back window exploded.

The fiery detonation lifted the car into the air and cracked the ice beneath it.

"Holy fuck'n shit!" Sponge screamed at the cold night blistered into a ball of immense light and heat.

The burning and twisted wreck of a car came down hard onto the broken ice and plummeted into the dark freezing water, taking its three dead and mangled occupants down into the murky depths below.

The remains of the car would be found sixty-eight years later by a cable history channel.

Within the cabin of the truck, Doc said out loud, "I think it's just us two now, Pasta."

With worry clearly showing on his face, Pasta said to him, "I don't know if we're gunna make it, Doc. Whoever those boys are... they're pretty good at what they're doing."

Continuing to drive, Doc said, "Well... I'm not stopping for nothing til we make it back to Chicago"

With a sigh, Pasta told him, "Ok... Doc... I'm with ya."

Glancing at the side mirrors, Doc said, "Good... cus here they come."

Roaring towards the action and fighting through the pain of his injury, Sponge said to the woman behind him, "They're going after the truck now! What can I do... it's basically four against one now."

Over his right shoulder, her manicured hand appeared at his shoulder as she said, "Hand me your gun."

Caught off guard, Sponge exclaimed, "What? My gun. Why?"

Wagging her fingers slightly, she answered, "Because... I'm going to make those odds... zero... to one."

Suddenly remembering exactly who she was and what her reputation was back in Chicago, Sponge pulled out an Army issue .45 with ivory grips and two spare magazines from his waistband and put it in her hand.

Leaning back, she inserted the extra magazines into her bra, one over each breast, pulled out a .45 of her own from out of her purse, and said, "Now get us as close as you can," then shattered the bulletproofed right passenger window with her elbow.

Continuing to glance at his side mirrors, Doc yelled, "They're going to encircle us! Get them off our ass... will ya!"

Armed with a ten shot .380 and a .45, Pasta said his last words, "You got it!" then rolled down the rickety passenger side window, leaned out to shoot, and then died in a hail of bullets a second later, splattering the interior of the cabin of the truck with blood.

In horror, Doc watched Pasta's lifeless body slip out

the window into the cold darkness, and yelled out to no one but himself, "Pasta... ya dumb shit... ya got yourself killed!"

Suddenly one vehicle appeared at the driver's side while two came around the front of the truck and the fourth crept up on the right.

With little recourse, Doc kept his foot on the gas pedal, gripped the large steering wheel tight, and ducked down as best he could.

Still unsure what they were possibly going to do against four heavily armed cars, Sponge asked over his shoulder, "What... what do you want me to do?" as he crept up behind the vehicle at the truck's left.

She climbed onto the backseat, turned towards the broken window, hunkered down on her bare heels, and then said, "Get up along their left side... and when the shooting starts... stay as close as you can without getting yourself killed."

Not knowing what else to do but follow her instructions, Sponge gripped the steering wheel of the limousine tight and hit the gas.

Cloaked in darkness with its headlights still turned off, the large purple limousine sped around the left side of the car, catching the unknown occupants inside off guard.

She raised both .45s and fired into the back passenger window, killing the gunman in the back seat instantly, and then leaped out of the limousine and into the other vehicle.

Sponge's mouth fell open when he saw her, from the rearview mirror, fly out the window and land inside the other car. Astonished at what he had just seen, he took his foot off the gas pedal and trailed back as he had been told to do so.

Inside the other car, she landed on the dead body in the back seat, leveled both handguns, and shot the driver once in the back of the head and the front passenger in the face as he twisted around to fire at her.

With the driver now dead, the car instantly began to slow and weave on the frozen lake top.

Driving just behind her, Sponge leaned over the steering wheel and mouthed, "Wha... the... hell?" as he watched gunfire flash in the interior of the car in front of him.

Also noticing the gunfire within the vehicle, the car at the front left of the truck veered off to investigate.

With her night vision, she watched the car in front of the truck making its way towards her. Not wasting any valuable time, she climbed out of the car through the broken window and onto the roof as it slowly rolled to a stop.

On the freezing roof, she rolled onto her back, ejected the magazines from her guns and inserted the two from her bra as the driverless vehicle rolled to a stop.

The other car pulled alongside the one she was on, and a man sitting in the backseat, wearing a pinstripe suit, rolled down his window and leaned out to peering into the stopped car.

With over a century of experience in killing, she marked her moment and sat up.

Catching her movement in the corner of his eye,

the man in the backseat looked up and saw a half-naked woman pointing a gun at him a second before dying.

She pulled the trigger.

His forehead caved in and the back of his head exploded.

She stood up onto the balls of her bare feet and leaped onto the hood of the other car, and then emptied both magazines into the driver and passenger.

Dropping both spent handguns, she motioned to Sponge to come to her then reached into the vehicle, cutting her abdomen on the shattered windshield in the process, and hauled out the dead passenger's machinegun.

Sponge drove up to her, stopped, and then cranked down the passenger side window.

With the ease of an acrobat, she slid off the hood, took hold of the limousine's passenger door frame, and placed her freezing bare feet on the limousine's right running board.

Holding the machinegun in her right hand and holding onto the door frame with her left, she yelled into the cabin over the steady hum of the running engine, "Only two left. They don't want to damage the whiskey... which will work to our advantage."

Sponge looked out the windshield; saw the truck and the two other cars continuing onward.

"We need to take out the one on the right next," she told him.

Hurt and still bleeding, Sponge simply nodded, his mind racing to make sense of everything that was happening all around him.

"Now!" she commanded.

Hearing her rise her voice, he blinked twice,

gathered himself, and said out loud, "Yes... yes... ok... you got it," then hit the gas.

Snatching only glimpses of what was occurring behind him from the driver's side mirror, Doc, alone and determined to make it back onto the highway, said a silent prayer and pressed on.

Coming up fast on the third car, she leaned her head into the limousine's cabin, "I need you to get up alongside its right side... and when I tell you to... I want you crank the steering wheel hard... hitting their right rear tire with the left side of your bumper. We have the heavier car... we'll get the better of them."

Concentrating on his driving, Sponge glanced over at her and confirmed, "Yeah... ok... right rear tire... got it!"

She straightened, looked the car just ahead of them, and said, "Good. Get ready... and wait for my signal."

Finally noticing the large limousine was right behind them, the left rear passenger window of the vehicle with the unknown killers began to lower.

"Now! Sponge, now!" she cried out.

Doing as he had been instructed, Sponge floored the gas pedal, jogged the purple limousine to the right of the car in front, turned the steering wheel with all his might, and hit the other car's right rear tire just has she had wanted, unseating it from the traction of its tires and sending it into and uncontrolled spin on the icy surface.

As they passed by the spinning car, she leveled the machinegun, one handed, pulled the trigger, and killed all three men inside with a barrage of automatic fire.

Sponge let out a thunderous battle cry as he watched her spectacular ability to kill.

Eager to end this, she poked her head back in and said, "One left… get me to it." as she let the emptied machinegun fall from her hand.

With adrenaline surging through his veins, Sponge yelled, "Fuck yes! You got it!"

Realizing they were now the only ones left, the final car cut and ran. It pulled hard to the right and accelerated dangerously over the ice.

Now with the upper hand, Sponge went after them with resounding vigor, forgetting about the searing pain from his ruined ear.

Still standing on the running board and hanging onto the door frame, she studied the fleeing car as freezing wind tore at her bare flesh.

"Get me as close as you can," she yelled into the car over the sound of the limousine's roaring engine.

Focus on his driving, Sponge simply replied, "Ok," without taking his eyes off the escaping vehicle.

Suddenly from the car in front of them, the rear and front passenger windows rolled down.

With the use of her eye's night vision, she saw what was about to happen, "Get ready… they're about to open fire."

Still without the use of the headlights of the limousine's, Sponge narrowed his eyes for a better look.

Two machinegun barrels emerged from the open windows.

Without a second to lose, she yelled, "Bank left... now!"

Sponge cranked the steering wheel hard to the left as both machineguns erupted in automatic gunfire, missing their mark.

"Get me closer or else we're both dead. They won't miss a second time," she told him.

Realizing that she was right, Sponge floored the gas pedal while thinking that he would rather die than let them get away after killing almost his entire crew.

Harnessing the power of the limousine's larger engine over the car they were chasing down, he closed the distance to mere feet within seconds.

The rear window broke into pieces in the lead car as the back passenger prepared to fire at them at almost point blank distance.

Making full use of the limousine's momentum, she ran up on its hood and launched herself into the air.

In awe, Sponge watched her arch in the air and land on the roof of the other car.

A second later, the gunman in the back passenger seat opened fire, peppering the battered but still bullet proof limousine with automatic fire.

In an act of self-preservation, Sponge cranked the steering wheel again to the left and sent the large luxury sedan spinning into the night.

On the roof of the car, she pressed herself against

the freezing metal in order not to slide off as her left arm changed into a clawed furred covered muscular limb.

From inside, the muffled voices of the last three surviving men reached her acute hearing; the worried and frightened tone in their voices was evident.

With her arm fully converted to that of the creature's, she slid over to the driver's side, craned her left arm back and then drove it through the driver's side window.

Hollers of surprise erupted within the car, apparently they hadn't realized from the machinegun fire that someone had landed on the roof.

She took hold of the driver's face, tearing into the flesh, muscle, and skull, and tore him out of the car, breaking his legs and separating his spine in the process, and flung him into the night.

Startled by the sudden act of unnerving violence, the last two opened fire up at the lined ceiling of the driverless car.

Bullet holes pockmarked the roof next to her as they haphazardly sprayed the area above them with automatic fire.

Eager to get off the roof before she was shot, she hoisted herself into the interior of the slowing car through the driver's side window, bare feet first.

She landed on her hunkers behind the steering wheel, looked at the two men who were desperately trying to reload their weapons, and then tore them to pieces with her bare hands.

Off in the distance, Sponge watched the car slowly come to a stop a few meters from the shore and the highway.

Not knowing what else to do, he cautiously drove to the car and stopped just behind it.

He switched on the headlights, illuminating the car in front of him, and then realized that he had handed his handgun to her just early; leaving him completely weaponless.

In the driver side mirror, he caught sight of Doc pulling up in the truck behind him and getting out, and decided to do the same.

Out of the limousine, the icy chill instantly found any bare flesh to freeze.

Hitching his coat high around his neck, Sponge asked Doc, "You good?"

Rubbing his arms against the cold, Doc replied, "Yeah... I'm good... but I lost Pasta... went right out the window after being shot to bits."

Sponge sighed at the news and said, "Well... I'll just forget to mention that part when I tell his mother that he's dead."

With a sigh himself, Doc lowered his head and nodded.

Suddenly, the perpetrators' driver's side car door opened.

Both Sponge and Doc turned and saw her step out into the cold night.

Standing on the icy top of the lake in her bare feet with blood splattered across her bare flesh and her left arm back to human form, she gave them a simple nod.

Looking at her, Sponge told Doc, "Do me a favor... get her shoes and coat for me will ya."

Staring at the incredible sight she projected, Doc replied, "Yeah... ok, Sponge... you got it," then walked to the limousine.

Feeling the intense cold on the soles of her hot

feet, she slowly trekked across the icy surface to where Sponge stood and stopped a few feet in front of him.

Still staring at her, he asked, "Are you ok?"

"It isn't my blood," she said to him.

At his right, Doc appeared with the patent leather heels and the fur coat, "I got her stuff," then walked over to her, set the shoes in front of her feet, and extended the lush coat out to her.

Without a word, she stepped into her heels and slipped into the warm luxurious coat.

Doc rejoined Sponge who said, "That was... by God... the most amazing fucking thing I have ever seen."

Casually she slipped her left hand into the left pocket of the fur coat and said, "And the last," then drew out a .25 caliber semiautomatic that she always kept in her fur coat and shot them both.

Sponge took a mercury tipped bullet to the throat and fell to his knees.

Doc, before he could even register what was happening, was shot twice in the forehead. He fell back on his ass, shuddered, and died sitting up.

Crunching snow and ice under her high heels, she walked over to Sponge, knelled down next to him, and said, "I don't want you to go without knowing."

Holding his throat with both hands, Sponge turned his eyes to her as he frothed blood from his mouth and from the hole in his neck.

With a devious smile, she confessed, "I placed a call to New York... anonymously of course... and saw to it that all those men that I killed tonight were sent here to intercept your deal."

Struggling harder for air with every passing second, Sponge tried to speak.

"Don't bother... I know what you want to say...

'why'," she leaned a bit closer and continued, "I...
guess... you could say that... I just wanted to destroy
your plans... and kill a lot of people."

Feeling his life slipping away, Sponge fell to his
side, vomited blood and the contents of his stomach,
and died.

She gave a small sigh, stood up, walked over to the
truck, and got in.

Inside the blood stained cabin, she closed the
driver's side door, cranked the engine to life, and drove
towards the road.

Prohibition would end just two years later and she
would move on to something else.

The Boredom with Death